Loving Lizzie March

© Sally Flegg

Susannah Hardy is a freelance writer whose work has appeared in countless print and online publications such as *The Sydney Morning Herald*, *Domain*, *Country Home Ideas*, *Modern Home*, *Peppermint*, *Babyology* and *Practical Parenting*. Originally an actor, Susannah completed a Bachelor of Arts at the University of New South Wales before running away to study acting in Paris. Returning to Australia, her work has involved anything from film and television roles to being one of two singing and rollerblading Carmen Mirandas, *Tutti & Frutti* (she was Frutti), and creating sketch comedy for Foxtel.

These days, in between covering real estate, home interiors and parenting issues, Susannah enjoys writing women's contemporary fiction and creating stories about the more comic side of life and love. *Loving Lizzie March* is her first novel.

Susannah lives in Sydney's inner west with her husband, two daughters and a puppy. Find out more about Susannah on her website at www.susannahhardywriter.com

SUSANNAH HARDY

Loving Lizzie March

MACMILLAN
Pan Macmillan Australia

Pan Macmillan acknowledges the Traditional Custodians of country throughout Australia and their connections to lands, waters and communities. We pay our respect to Elders past and present and extend that respect to all Aboriginal and Torres Strait Islander peoples today. We honour more than sixty thousand years of storytelling, art and culture.

This is a work of fiction. Characters, institutions and organisations mentioned in this novel are either the product of the author's imagination or, if real, used fictitiously without any intent to describe actual conduct.

First published 2021 in Macmillan by Pan Macmillan Australia Pty Ltd
1 Market Street, Sydney, New South Wales, Australia, 2000

NATIONAL LIBRARY OF AUSTRALIA
A catalogue record for this book is available from the National Library of Australia

Typeset in 12.5/17.5 pt Adobe Garamond Pro by Post Pre-press Group
Printed by IVE

FSC www.fsc.org MIX Paper from responsible sources FSC® C018183

The paper in this book is FSC® certified. FSC® promotes environmentally responsible, socially beneficial and economically viable management of the world's forests.

For Andrew, my very own Mr Right.
Our girls, Maggie and Phoebe.
And Mum and Dad, my ever-supportive parents.

This book belongs to you all.

1

I know relationships can hurt but I didn't think I'd end up in hospital as a result. Total accident. No one's fault. I just happened to be passing by his home. Yes, I was a good forty-five minutes out of my way, it was getting late and I wasn't exactly invited, but somehow, before I knew it, I was standing outside his house! Complete coincidence.

Okay, maybe it wasn't a *complete* coincidence, but it certainly wasn't intentional. I was out for an evening stroll and takeaway latte to clear my head. But I couldn't stop thinking about him. So much so that my subconscious took over and led me straight to his front door. Understandable, really, when three weeks earlier you've had a one-night stand with someone who's possibly The One. And when you haven't heard from that someone since. Quite frankly, it would have been weird if I'd found myself anywhere else.

Seeing as I was there, I thought I'd take the matter into my own hands. I mean, why waste an opportunity? I knocked on the front door, but no one answered. Lights were on and his motorbike was out the front, so he couldn't have been far. Maybe asleep or in the shower? Perhaps lying under a piece of heavy furniture or unconscious after slipping on wet bathroom tiles . . . ? You never know, he might have needed help. The only conceivable thing to do was to hang around – just to make sure he was okay, I mean. But I didn't want the neighbours thinking I was some sort of crazed stalker, so I set up camp behind a bush to wait it out.

Eventually, a bit bored and desperate for a toilet – I knew the large-sized latte was a mistake – I decided it was time to take further action. By now, I was convinced that he was out cold on the floor, perhaps bleeding, with only moments to live. And maybe after I saved his life, bandaged his head wound and got him a couple of Panadol, he might let me use his bathroom? So, I crept out from behind the bush and slunk around the side of the house.

About halfway down there was a room with lights on. The shutters were closed but by my calculations it had to be the lounge. I may not have remembered a great deal about our night together but I did recall the layout of his home, which was actually quite spacious, with a lovely sense of flow. I stood on my tippy-toes, trying to squint between the bottom slats, and noticed that the window was unlocked. I only wanted to open it a little, so I could adjust the shutters and get a better view. Nothing illegal. Well, only a little bit illegal. But I couldn't get a grip on the window frame.

There simply had to be a way to see in. I scanned the pathway for something that might help, but all I could make out in the dark were a few rusty gardening tools, a broken chair and a pile of bricks. I was totally prepared to build a mini staircase with the bricks when I spied a wheelie bin, which seemed a far better option. I put my bag down on the broken chair, rolled the bin over to the window and climbed on top – not as easy as I had anticipated, but the potential love of my life was inside, quite possibly dying. Nothing was going to hold me back.

As I carefully stood upright on top of the wheelie bin, I felt strangely empowered. Like a goddess at the peak of a mountain with the world kneeling before me, awaiting my every command. I stretched my arms out wide, ready to take flight, superhuman strength soaring through every cell in my body – and it was intoxicating. Everything was as clear as a crystal glass and I felt amazing. I *was* amazing. Invincible. I could achieve anything and everything, and nothing stood in my way.

Except I couldn't open the window, as it was a bit stiff.

Plus, every time I moved with any force, the wheelie bin (true to its name) wheeled a little bit further away from the window. I made one last frantic attempt, this time with all the strength I could muster, and the window jolted open, pushing the wheelie bin in one direction and me in the other.

I plummeted towards the ground and all I could do was close my eyes and hope for the best. Everything seemed to happen in slow motion, but in reality it was probably only a second before I landed awkwardly, face first, on the sandstone path.

I lay motionless. My head hurt and my face felt warm and sticky. I sat up and touched my throbbing chin to find that it was cut and bleeding profusely. I slowly got to my feet, checking that my limbs were intact and still working, and felt a pang of guilt as I surveyed what now looked like a crime scene, with the wheelie bin upturned and rubbish spilling out. The window was wide open and splotches of blood stained the path. At least any burglars would be put off as it looked like the house had already been well and truly done over.

I grabbed my bag and staggered back to my bush, unsure what to do next. Maybe he wasn't lying injured on the bathroom floor? All the noise of the wheelie bin falling over would surely have prompted him to call out for help or to limp outside and investigate. I decided he must be out after all and had just left the lights on in a confusing (and environmentally insensitive) manner. I wobbled down the street in a daze. It was quite late now, and there was no one to help except a random dog walker, who quickly crossed the road as I approached. The fact that I was lurching from one side of the footpath to the other, with blood trickling down my chin, probably didn't help.

I'd had no intention of going to hospital, but the only taxi driver who would stop for me took one look at my dishevelled appearance and insisted on dropping me right at the sliding door of the Emergency Department. By the time I stumbled up to the reception desk I was feeling woozy. My skin was clammy and, suddenly, I found myself flat on my back on the blue lino. A nurse appeared and assured me everything would be fine while the other waiting patients stared at me crankily, knowing full well I'd pipped them at the post in the emergency status stakes.

Everything got a bit hazy at that point, but I do remember being helped onto a hospital bed and wheeled into an examination room. I also remember thinking that perhaps the situation I found myself in was a little extreme, even by my standards.

But when it comes to securing the heart of my future partner, there's nothing I won't do. At least I had put myself out there and gave it a go, right? And if that meant falling off a wheelie bin, splitting open my chin and fainting in the waiting room of the ED, then so be it.

*

'What happened? Are you okay?' Clem, my best friend in the world, is devastated to hear I've spent half the night in Emergency and, despite the early morning hour, has immediately raced to the hospital to be by my side.

'I'm fine, just a few scratches and bruises and three stitches on my chin,' I say, trying to make it sound like the most normal thing that could happen on a Friday night.

'What were you doing?' she asks.

There's absolutely no way I can tell Clem what I'd been doing.

'Lizzie, what were you doing?'

I say nothing, determined to be strong. The effort is killing me, but I don't need to hear the how-many-times-have-I-told-you-so speech right now, which is exactly what Clem will deliver. That, or the you-are-such-an-idiot one. Either way, I'm not in the mood.

'Lizzie!'

'Okay, okay. I was outside Jake's place.'

And there it is. Unfortunately, as hard as I try, I can never keep secrets from my best girlfriend, who reads me better than my mother.

'Lizzie, do I want to hear this?'

'It wasn't my fault!'

'It never is.'

She has a point, but this time it *really* wasn't my fault. It was somebody – well, some*thing* – else's fault, namely: a fabulous pair of ridiculously high green satin stilettos that I haven't even paid for yet. They're still on my credit card.

Right now, they're banished to the top of my cupboard, totally grounded until I don't know when, after disgracing themselves (and me) at a recent work function. The minute I fastened those dazzling gold buckles and stood up on those towering heels, I was filled, from the soles of my feet to the tips of my salon blow-dry, with an embarrassing amount of self-confidence that was nothing short of trouble. Even the last-season little black shirt dress I threw on for the night looked a million dollars. When I arrived at the venue, I found myself strutting from one end of the room to the other for no apparent reason, rubbing my (what felt like) sexy long legs suggestively against any person or inanimate object that crossed my path. I paraded around like a movie star at the hottest Academy Awards afterparty, throwing back tequila shots, working the room and striking up witty conversations filled with humorous anecdotes. It was like I'd unravelled the mystery of how to be fabulous and become the person I'd always dreamt of being: popular, successful, hilarious and dangerously attractive to every member of the opposite sex.

Don't get me wrong, it's not like I'm normally some wallflower who hides in the corner. I've been known to flirt a little at a work event. Actually, rather a lot. But on this occasion, I impressed even myself.

The night was winding up, but my shoes were not ready to go home and neither was I. A few of us went to a nearby bar for a drink. Well, a few drinks, to be honest. I was definitely the life of the party. I started dancing and there wasn't even a dance floor. Then one raunchy pash led to another and I found myself having a one-night stand with my work supervisor.

When I say work, I mean WineCall – the soulless, fluorescent-lit call centre where I sit for five hours a day, convincing people to buy wine. And when I say supervisor, I mean Jake Wheeler, the biggest heart-stopping hottie you've ever seen, with dark tousled hair, a motorbike and a body that simply should not be allowed out in public without some sort of warning label.

Jake started at WineCall six weeks ago and we instantly clicked. He asked me if I'd pick up an extra shift and I said, 'No problem.' Then he smiled and held my gaze for a second longer than what would be considered normal for a supervisor–sales representative relationship, so I knew it was definitely on. We were as good as an item. Which led to the work dinner three weeks ago, and our night of passion (at least I think there was a bit of passion; I don't remember much, if you want to know the truth). And I haven't heard from him since. Which is odd considering I put my number in his phone the next day, before he woke up.

I explain to Clem how last night I went for a walk and bizarrely found myself staring at his doorbell! I also explain how it would normally be a forty-five-minute walk according to my Google Maps research (in anticipation of having to regularly make the trip seeing as we're practically almost going out) but there I was in just twenty-three minutes! Clearly this is a sign it's meant to be. But Clem is not convinced.

'What happened, did he see you?' Clem fires questions as she always does, in her aggressive lawyer no-stone-left-unturned fashion. Usually, she has this annoying knack of wearing me down until the truth is revealed. It's no wonder she's so good at her job, and will probably be made partner soon. If I ever need a lawyer (and the way I'm going, I might), I would hire Clem in a heartbeat. But right now I don't want to give everything away. I have a sneaking suspicion Clem wouldn't approve of my lengthy surveillance – even if I only did it out of concern for Jake's welfare. And luckily there's no danger of doing so as the conversation is interrupted by the appearance of an attractive doctor with a lanky frame and chocolate-brown hair styled like a toothbrush.

'Lizzie March?' he asks with a smile that illuminates the hospital beige.

'Yes?'

'Hi, I'm Dr Mitch Peters. The doctor who did your stitches has finished her shift, so I'm going to check you out and hopefully let you go.'

'But you're so young!'

Did I say that out loud? Clem rolls her eyes, so I must have. He just seems so much younger than me. Still, I guess that's not hard these days. His eyes are incredibly blue. I wonder if he's wearing contacts?

'Sorry?' Dr Mitch (what was his surname?) looks up from his clipboard.

'That sounds fun,' I say, in an attempt to recover.

'Right,' he says slowly, as if he's reconsidering discharging me.

Clem clears her throat. 'I'll give you some space,' she half whispers. 'Meet you in the café.'

She runs out the door before I can even ask where the café is, leaving me with my new and rather cute doctor. Not my type, but I'm wondering if he's Clem's, judging by the flustered way she reacted.

'So, you were locked out of your house in the middle of the night?' he says, reading his notes.

I don't really want to discuss it, but there's something about those vibrant blue eyes that makes me want to share.

'Actually, it wasn't my house.'

'Oh?' He looks up, eyebrows raised.

'I mean, it was a friend's house, actually my boyfriend's. I was waiting for him.' There's no reason to be completely honest.

'Says here you fell off a low window ledge and onto a stone path,' he says, finger pointed at the clipboard.

'Yes, well, he wasn't home and I was trying to climb in the window.'

'Where is he now? Will he be picking you up?'

'He's at work. Just called to check up on me. He was so worried but he couldn't get away. Clem, who was just here, she's taking me home.'

He nodded. 'How are you feeling now?'

I close my eyes, take a deep breath and exhale. To be honest, I feel sore and uncomfortable. My head aches and my sleepless night is taking its toll. Why do I find myself in these situations? I don't even know for sure if Jake wants to go out with me, but here I am, in Emergency, as a result of trying to find out. I don't see other girls coming into Emergency with these kinds of injuries, so it must just be me.

I can't say this to Dr Mitch, so the lies keep tumbling out of my mouth. 'A little confused, to tell you the truth. I don't really know what's going on. I mean, he said he'd be home, but then I got there and not so much as a note to –'

Dr Mitch coughs gently. 'No, I mean, how are you feeling physically?'

'Oh, fine.' Dizzy, actually, but I keep that to myself. 'Can I go home?'

'Soon. There's just a couple of things to check,' he says, looking again at his notes.

I wait and then blurt out, 'Is everything okay?'

He nods. 'But you should be more careful in future.'

'It was just a cut on the chin,' I say, wondering why this doctor is looking so serious. 'And as far as Jake not telling me where he was, well, it's a new relationship. There're a few teething problems. You know, stuff to work through.'

'No, I mean . . . there's something else. We took a blood test because you fainted.'

'What? What's wrong?' My heart starts racing. 'Am I sick?' Please God, not something awful. I can't cope with a terminal disease this week. Just as my mind stumbles into a maze of dark corners, blue-eyed Dr Mitch answers all my questions with two swift words, throwing my life upside down.

'You're pregnant.'

'What?!'

'You didn't know?'

I shake my head, unable to speak. Pregnant?

'And I'm guessing the boyfriend whose house you were trying to break into is the father?'

I stare at the concerned doctor, trying to appear as if this is all very normal while my thoughts race so fast they could win gold for Australia. The room is spinning and I can't think straight. Pregnant? How is that possible? Well. I know how, but why and who are more appropriate questions. Now that I think about it, my period is late and I haven't even given it a thought. My mind flips back to that recent work function. Damn those green stilettos. I'm definitely taking them back to the shop.

It has to be Jake. I haven't slept with anyone else in ages. Actually in seven months, two weeks, three days and about an hour. Give or take. Jake broke the drought. With great force, it seems. And maybe the condom too? I can't remember many details of the night, but I do remember a condom was unwrapped and put exactly where it was supposed to go. But then again, Jake did go hunting in the bathroom cupboard for a while so maybe it was a bit old. Damn, why didn't I insist on checking the expiry date?

But surely it couldn't have happened then. Doesn't it take ages to get pregnant? Missy from work tried for eighteen months and she and her husband were both on some special diet of disgusting Chinese herbs. I have one careless moment and I'm up the duff, without so much as a cup of green tea.

I look at Dr Mitch, who is waiting patiently while my head sorts through the facts.

'How pregnant am I?'

'When was the date of your last period? We take it from then as that's really the only certainty.'

Looking at my life, I can't argue with that. And in fact, I definitely remember that day. Very clearly indeed. The day I got my last period coincided with what I refer to as the Street Date. Jake had only been working at WineCall for a week and I saw him in the street. I'd finished early (because I was feeling crampy) and he was on his way to the call centre, obviously doing a late shift. Our eyes met across the traffic and he waved at me. I waved back and gestured, 'Should I come over?' and he gestured back, 'No, in hurry to get to work, sorry, but let's have a drink soon.'

Okay, I'm not entirely sure about the 'have a drink soon' bit, but the whole encounter was as good as a first date. In fact, I consider it to be a Very Significant Moment in our relationship. It was definitely a turning point, because two weeks later was the work function where we –

'March twenty-fourth,' I say.

I must look as confused as I feel because Dr Mitch smiles and gets out some sort of wheel chart to explain how the dates work. I feel like I'm back in biology class.

'So that means you're five weeks pregnant. It's calculated from the first day of your last period,' he says. 'Does that make sense?'

What did he say? Five weeks! That sounds very pregnant to me. It doesn't make any sense, actually, but then, nothing does today.

'Well, that's great news!' I try to sound together and positive about the future.

'Obviously you weren't trying?'

'No, well, not really, but I'm sure Jake will be thrilled. He loves kids and it's always something we were going to consider down the track. It's just a bit earlier than expected.'

Does Jake like kids? I have no idea. I don't even know if he likes *me*. I try to focus on what the doctor is saying. Something about decisions and counselling. He gives me a pile of brochures and rings the antenatal clinic to book me in for a check-up in a couple of days. He has to do a bit of negotiating to fit me in, but he succeeds in talking them down.

'It's a bit soon to come in for a first appointment, but under the circumstances, it might be good to have a chat with one of the midwives,' he says.

I look at Dr Mitch, trying to appear completely at ease with my life and the odd direction it's taken. Usually I would have attempted to secure a first date by now. But asking out the doctor who tells me I'm pregnant when I'm in Emergency because of an accident I had while sort-of stalking the father of my unborn child? Well, that's just weird.

Then I notice that I don't even feel inclined to ask him out. Goodness, what's happening to me? I've only been pregnant five minutes and I'm a changed woman.

'I must love Jake.'

'Sorry?'

Right, so I said that one out loud too.

'I must tell Jake,' I say. 'I can't wait to see his face.'

Which is about the first truthful thing I've said to anyone all morning. Jake will definitely be surprised.

'Okay, if you're sure you feel all right, then you're good to go. I have to head off too. It's very busy today. The full moon. People do crazy things.' Dr Mitch makes a move towards the door.

'Yes, of course, you must be flat out. Thanks, Doctor.' I try my best to sound like the sort of person who would never do crazy things around a full moon, but it's probably too late for that.

Dr Mitch smiles his brilliant smile, wishes me luck and rushes off. I grab my bag and wander out, slightly dazed, in search of the café, Clem and maybe a whole new life.

2

Eventually, I find the hospital's café where Clem is waiting impatiently. Having finished her coffee, she's now coating her hands with sanitiser and rubbing them together. She's terrified of germs. According to her, a hospital is like a germ dance party where they all gather in hordes to celebrate their power over the human race.

'You've been ages.'

'I got lost,' I explain, not quite ready to share my news. Maybe a coffee first. Hang on, am I allowed coffee? 'And that doctor had to check me out. Took a while. You should have hung around, he seemed nice.'

Clem rolls her eyes. She's definitely over me today. I decide I'm desperate enough to risk it and order a much-needed flat white at the counter.

'I'm over you today,' she says grumpily as I sit back down.

'Sorry, but I did hurt myself. They don't call it the Emergency Department for nothing.'

Clem sighs. 'Sorry, you're right. Are you feeling okay?'

'A bit tired and –'

'It's just that you didn't come to hospital till late. What on earth were you doing outside Jake's house for so long anyway?' she demands, clearly not really sorry and not ready to let the whole thing go.

'I knocked but there was no answer, so I just thought I'd wait a while in case he came home.'

Clem is instantly suspicious. 'A while? How long were you there?'

'Um, only an hour or two. Or . . . three.' I look at the floor. Without even raising my head, I know Clem is giving me that look she uses for clients when they're not being entirely honest. A look I know very well.

'Okay, it was four hours,' I say. 'Five at the outside.'

Silence.

'So you were stalking him!'

'No! Not at all!' I say indignantly. 'I was just seeing if he was around to have a drink or a coffee or something.'

'Maybe he was inside and didn't want to answer the door,' says Clem. 'Maybe he knew you were there and was frightened by your obsessive behaviour. He wouldn't be the first guy to experience that!'

'I'm pretty sure he wasn't inside.'

I feel like, once again, I've said a little too much. Clem only needs a breadcrumb thrown her way and before you know it, she's found the whole loaf. She'll work out I'm pregnant any second now if I'm not careful, and I'm not quite ready to broadcast that news.

Clem leans forward and lowers her voice. 'Lizzie, what happened? You know there's not much I can do to get you out of a break and enter.'

'No, it was nothing like that! Well, only a little bit – but not exactly.'

Clem lets out a world-weary sigh. 'Go on.'

I retell my story, focusing more on Jake's excellent taste in plantation shutters (painted a stylish antique white) than on the bit about my attempt to open a window belonging to a guy I slept with once who hasn't rung me since. In fact, the way I tell it, the incident doesn't sound like anything out of the ordinary. Which it's not. Perfectly normal. Who wouldn't take an opportunity to say hi if they found themselves outside the house of the man of their dreams? My methods may have been a little unorthodox, but sometimes you have to do whatever it takes.

'Then I fell off a wheelie bin onto the path. Hardly surprising as it was quite cluttered around the side. I mean, it's a lovely house, he just really needs to do a bit of a clean-up.'

'Lizzie!'

'Okay, okay, the cut wouldn't stop bleeding and the taxi driver brought me to the hospital.' I pause. 'So what do you think?'

'Lizzie, I hardly know where to start –'

'No, I mean, why do you think he wasn't there?'

Clem gives me a reproachful look. 'He might have been there.'

'But he wasn't.'

'So?'

'Where was he?'

'I don't know. Why are you asking me? I think you might be focusing on the wrong –'

'Do you think he was with someone else?'

Clem makes an impatient noise. 'Urgh. Maybe.'

'Really?'

'Lizzie, I don't know – but was it worth all of this?'

I think about the Emergency ward where I spent the last couple of hours with a drug addict, a man with a gammy leg and an old woman who'd barely stirred. She might have passed away. I rub my aching head, which I bumped when I fainted, I feel the bandage on my stitched-up chin, I see the scratches on my knees and the concern in my best friend's eyes – and there's no doubt in my mind. It was worth every single minute.

If it meant the possibility of finding out what's going on with Jake, then I simply had no choice. And now I know I'm carrying Jake's baby, the stakes are even higher.

'It's just that there's always some drama with you,' says Clem, still not finished. 'Usually connected to some innocent guy you're hunting down.'

'That's not true. And Jake's not that innocent, let me tell you!' I put a hand on my stomach, but then quickly remove it in case it gives Clem the wrong idea. Or the right idea, as the case may be.

'Come on, Lizzie. Every time you get involved with a guy, there's some sort of mishap that ends in someone getting hurt or arrested. Usually you.'

I feel mildly offended but to be completely honest, I can't deny it. That last comment refers to a speed-dating night at a city pub that got a little out of hand. The police were even called. Clem always brings it up. It's like her go-to incident whenever we have a discussion like this one. I don't know why – it was a complete misunderstanding and I wasn't even arrested! But I can see there are similarities with what happened last night. I'm starting to realise that she might have a point.

'Okay,' I admit. 'There have been a couple of occasions where things have gone a little crazy. Once or twice . . . maybe three times.'

Clem eyeballs me.

'Okay. Four times, but that's it! And one of them was in a dodgem car so that doesn't count.'

'You rammed into the poor guy so hard he was thrown from his car, landing on his arm which he broke in three places. I don't think we'll ever be welcomed back to the Royal Easter Show,' says Clem. 'Not every guy is The One. And in the unlikely event any guy had the potential of being The One, you scare him off by doing insane things and causing him or others physical harm.'

Clem's words buzz around me like persistent mosquitoes. They seem a little harsh. Why can't anyone see that it's me who suffers when relationships don't work out? Sure, Dodgem Guy broke his arm, but I got a stiff neck. No one ever remembers that bit. I couldn't quite turn my head completely to the right for at least a week. But you don't hear me going on about it.

That's the difference between Clem and me. I'm the eternal optimist and she most definitely is not. She's been that voice in my head, dragging me back to reality, ever since we met at school on the first day of Year 7. She had thick dark brown pigtails and absolutely no friends and to my horror we were seated next to each other. Surprisingly, we developed a friendship that has remained strong ever since. Sometimes I wonder why. We even look odd together – Clem, who is quite short, her hair now cut neatly to her shoulders, and me, towering over her with my scruffy wild blonde mop. Chalk and cheese.

That first day out in the playground, I wanted to sit on the steps during lunch so I could tan my legs and Clem said quite firmly that suntans were aging, even life-threatening. It's no wonder she chose a career that deals in worst-case scenarios. She ended up being right, of course. And now I have unsightly freckles all over my legs. Maybe that's why we're friends. Clem benefits from my great sense of fun and fantastic people skills, while she helps me face the many challenges that life throws my way. Whatever it is, it works. And not a day goes by without a catch-up over a coffee or glass of wine or at least a chat over the phone. I don't know what I'd do without her. And in my present state, I need her more than ever.

Today, however, Clem is being particularly negative. And certainly not very understanding. *I'm* the one with a string of failed relationships. *I'm* the one who has just been through a major ordeal. *I'm* the one who has just found out she's pregnant. Not that Clem knows that yet.

'What's wrong with you, anyway?' I say. 'Did Mal forget to pick up his bath towel again?'

Clem and Mal have been going out for about a year, and things are pretty serious. They went to Thailand for a month last summer and when they got back, he moved into her apartment. It's all on. Clem thinks he's definitely The One for her.

'He moved out.'

'What?' I almost fall off my hospital café chair. Not hard considering it's made of flimsy plastic but I can't believe my ears. 'Moved out? What happened?'

'I'm not really sure. I thought everything was fine. He was a bit distant last week, and when I asked him what was wrong, he said the relationship was over.'

'Oh, Clem,' I sigh, reaching over to give her hand a little squeeze. 'I'm so sorry. Have you spoken to him since?'

'He rang to ask if he could pick up his stuff, a few clothes he'd left behind, some CDs and his surfboard, and when he left, he handed me my spare key and said, "Thanks, mate".'

'He didn't!'

'Yes, he did! Now he won't answer my calls or texts and I really need to talk.'

'About what?'

'I need to know what happened, and why it happened. I need closure.'

I sigh again. I've been dumped enough times to know there's nothing to say and you never get closure. It just hurts until it stops hurting anymore, which is usually when you have great sex with someone else. It doesn't even have to be great. Average would do the trick. I mean, sex is sex. Unless you get pregnant.

God! I can't tell Clem now. If anyone wants to be married with a baby, it's Clem. Having kids is part of her grand plan and she'd make a great mum. So much better than me. If she finds out I'm pregnant first, without even wanting to be, she'll be furious. And incredibly sad. Still, if Jake and I stay together and decide to have the baby, she'll have to accept it sooner or later. But I can't tell her now, I just can't. That news will have to wait.

'Forget about Mal, I never really liked him anyway,' I say loyally. And truthfully.

'Really? You never said that!'

'No, but do you remember he flirted a bit with my cousin Maria at my last birthday drinks?'

'That wasn't Mal's fault. Maria practically threw herself at him.'

My cousin Maria is the quietest, most conservative mouse you've ever seen. She's probably still a virgin, even though she's engaged to be married. She wouldn't pass Mal a bowl of chips, let alone make any other sort of pass. But I decide not to press the issue.

'Right, well, whatever. Anyway, if he's not The One, you're better off finding out now rather than further down the track when you have kids.'

Kids? Did I actually say that? I'm only five weeks pregnant and I'm already talking like a mother who says embarrassing things in front of her teenage daughter. I'm also craving pizza. But I always feel like pizza, so maybe I'm just hungry. My mind starts to wander through all my possible lunch options. I feel like a bit of a treat after my accident. Does Jake like pizza? I don't even know if my future partner likes the same food as me. Feeling guilty, I push those thoughts to one side and force my mind back to my friend's dilemma, which is so much clearer than mine.

'Sorry, what were you saying?'

'I was saying that I thought Mal and I wanted the same things.'

Just quietly, I don't think Mal ever wanted the same things as Clem, apart from having as much sex as possible, but now is not the time to say that. Clem looks so desperate. She doesn't need a lecture.

'I know you love him,' I say gently. 'But you can do so much better. What about the other day when we had brunch down at

Bondi and he reminded you that you owed him ten dollars. In front of me! And he insisted you give it to him, then and there, so he could pay for his breakfast. And even then, it wasn't enough! You had to pay extra to cover him.'

'He was a bit short that week,' says Clem defensively.

'And remember when he moved in, he tried to pay less on the electricity bill because he said he hardly ever used any appliances. Didn't you think that was strange?'

'Not really, it made total sense at the time,' snapped Clem. 'Look, I know Mal's not perfect but he made me happy. Besides, nobody is perfect – you of all people should know that.'

She had me there. Nobody's perfect. Particularly me, with my woeful inability to find the model boyfriend – before the 'having a baby' part. Who am I to judge?

'I'm sure he'll change his mind,' I say. 'I bet he's already at your front door, wanting to get back together.'

Although this seems highly unlikely to me, Clem sits to attention. 'Do you think so?'

'He'd be mad not to.' Which is the absolute truth. Strong, successful and gorgeous, Clem is such a catch. Wish I was a bit more like her.

'Then let's go. I'll drop you off first.' Clem gets up to pay for our coffees, faster than one of my first date moves. 'Come on, Lizzie. Hurry up! If Mal is at my front door, I don't want him to leave before I get there.'

My coffee hasn't even arrived so I ask if they can put it in a takeaway cup. It looks like it's going to be ages so I cancel it altogether and follow my deluded friend out the door. Still, as I say, who am I to judge?

Clem drives like a demon to Elizabeth Bay, stopping outside my apartment building only long enough for me to jump out. I almost do a commando roll onto the footpath.

'Speak later,' she calls as she zooms off, in pursuit of Mal and the improbable notion that he's sorry and still loves her.

He isn't sorry and he doesn't love her. Anyone can see that.

But I have my own problems to worry about right now. Jake, for one thing, and his baby, for another. Not to mention all the stuff that has to happen in between to try to marry these two issues. Pun absolutely intended.

3

After so little sleep, a jet-lagged haze kicks in and I only just make it to the sofa before my legs give way. The fact that I've just had some barely digested, life-changing news probably isn't helping.

Pregnant!

Like *really* pregnant.

Not just 'maybe' or 'I hope I'm not' or 'I really think I might be this time', but actually well and truly knocked up. A cut on the chin and a baby. It's been a big twenty-four hours.

And not only am I pregnant, as if that's not enough to deal with, but also I will eventually have a baby!

A real live baby.

Looking around my pint-sized apartment, the reality of the situation hits me harder than Jake's stone path. Where am I going to put a baby? Don't they need heaps of stuff? Like a cot. Where will

I put a cot? What about a highchair? And a pram? Oh my God, prams are enormous these days. How will I get it up two flights of stairs and in through my front door?

This is clearly a huge mistake. I'm not supposed to be having a baby. Something I probably should have considered more deeply when Jake was fishing around for that dodgy condom.

I can't quite get my breath as panic sweeps over me. I stagger to the kitchen table and grab my keys. I need to go back to hospital and have this sorted out immediately. What was I thinking? I should have told that nice Dr Mitch right there and then that this couldn't happen. There's no way I can do this. I've only been pregnant for about two seconds and I'm already riddled with doubt and anxiety. How could I possibly survive motherhood?

I open the front door, but stop just as suddenly. What about Jake? Surely he will be there to help me through this muddle? I take a deep breath and calmly close the front door. He will definitely be part of this picture. I'm sure of it.

Fortunately, the phone rings before I change my mind, but when I see it's my mother calling, it does little to ease the stress. That's all I need right now. I consider not picking up, but that will only cause her to worry, which will be infinitely worse in the long term.

'Mum.'

'Darling, how are you?'

'Fine.'

'What's wrong?'

'Nothing.'

'There's something wrong, I can hear it in your voice.'

I decide to come (partially) clean. She'll draw it out of me eventually so I may as well save time and spit it out in a casual, non-dramatic way.

'I had a little accident.'

'What?'

'It was stupid, I just fell over and cut my chin. Couple of stitches. There was a bit of bleeding so I got it checked out at the hospital. You know, tetanus shot and all that.'

This satisfies my mother who, after a little more assurance that I'm fine, swiftly turns the conversation to what she really wants to talk about. 'And how are you apart from that? What's going on? Have you seen that Jack boy from work again?'

My heart jumps a hurdle at the almost mention of his name.

'Jake, and no.' I brace myself for what's obviously going to be one of 'those chats', which may take some time and far more energy than I have right now. Nor do I want to discuss my relationship with Jake, which has suddenly become more complicated. 'I'm not sure what's going on with him.'

'Lizzie, you have to put yourself out there. Relationships are hard work. They don't just land on your front doorstep. I practically proposed to your father.'

Most conversations with my mother centre around the same subject: Mr Right. And how and when I'm going to meet him. As far as she's concerned, being thirty and single is a tragedy. She simply cannot understand why I haven't been snapped up. I usually invent stuff just to keep her happy. That's why I told her about Jake. As long as there's a slight possibility of a boyfriend, she stops hassling me for a couple of days. Well, maybe for one day. But I can't make it too much of a thing because then she wants to know when she can meet him, when we're moving in together and when we're setting the date.

'Mum! I *am* putting myself out there.' If only she knew how much.

'You just don't want to end up on your own, sweetheart. No one does.'

'I like being on my own.'

Okay, an absolute lie, otherwise I wouldn't have been in Emergency as a result of semi-stalking my latest love interest. Of course I don't want to be on my own, but I'm not going to admit that to Mum. There was a time back at university when I was never on my own. I was popular with the opposite sex and I dated whoever I wanted. None of my 'relationships' continued longer than a couple of months, but I was having fun with no one holding me down.

That was until I met Jean Paul. Beautiful, perfect, one-quarter French Jean Paul (JP for short), with his long hair and a face like an angel. He captured my heart and quickly became the centre of my world. We were inseparable for nearly a year until the day I saw him having coffee with another woman. And when I say 'having coffee', I mean locking tongues over a couple of cappuccinos. She was beautiful, with creamy skin and a chic Parisian bob. How could I compete?

All I could do was watch. Just for a moment. Then sneak away, my heart shattered. Naturally, we broke up the next day. But only because I brought it up. JP may well have kept two-timing us indefinitely. Apparently he and Parisian Bob had been 'friends' for a few months and the 'coffee' they shared wasn't the first.

I've never trusted anyone since. Is it any wonder, then, that I found myself indulging in a little bit of casual stalking? Hence my 'checking in' on Jake. Nothing creepy, just an attempt to find out what's really going on. I don't normally end up in hospital. That's a first, even for me.

'Rubbish. Of course you don't want to be alone! Everyone I know feels sorry for you . . . what's that?' Her voice becomes muffled as she turns away from the phone. 'I *am not* interfering!'

As usual, my mother and father start discussing my life while I can hear their every word.

I try to keep Mum on track. 'Who feels sorry for me?'

'Your father thinks I'm talking out of turn, but if I don't, then who will? Yes, she does . . . yes, she is . . . well, why don't you talk to her, since you know all about it?'

'Mum . . . hello?' Honestly, it's no wonder I'm never in a relationship if this is all I have to aspire to. 'Mum, who feels sorry for me?'

'The family, Aunty Jane and her girls. Maria just got engaged, you know.'

'Yes, to an absolute bore. I could be engaged too if I was happy to accept the dullest man in the world.'

Maria, my cousin who Clem accused of flirting with Mal, is marrying a guy who actually makes me yawn when he starts talking.

'Lizzie, don't say that, he's charming – and he's perfect for Maria. There's nothing wrong with a guy who's nice, kind and honest. You seem to only go out with boys who don't treat you very well. You deserve better.'

Clem, like Mum, thinks I go for the wrong guys, but they're both wrong. You're either attracted to someone or you're not.

It's just that I seem to be attracted to the ones who don't want long-term relationships. Except Jean Paul. He was totally into relationships, just with more than one person at the same time.

Clem also says I chase too much and that I should wait for a guy to come to me, which is completely ridiculous and incredibly old-fashioned. I would end up like a cheery old unmarried aunt character in Jane Austen's England if I simply waited for The One to knock on the door. Except even in Jane Austen novels he always *does* knock on the door. Stuck in the countryside, the nearby house has a new resident and what do you know? It's a devastatingly attractive wealthy single man and naturally he falls for the single girl.

If that were me, the neighbouring house would be bought by some stiff childless middle-aged couple who like to shoot birds and go to bed early.

Whenever I catch a plane, I always hope that a super-hot guy will be seated next to me. Never happens. Last year I went to Melbourne and sat beside two elderly women off to some patchworking festival. They were very sweet and chatty and shared some homemade biscuits, but they weren't quite what I was hoping for.

Then they started asking questions.

'Are you married?'

I didn't feel like getting into it, so I lied. 'No, but we've just got engaged.'

'How wonderful,' gushed one. 'Congratulations!'

Probably a good time to stop, but their joy was infectious. 'Yes, it's worked out really well. After the wedding, we're moving to Paris so I can pursue my career as a fashion designer.'

It went on and on. They loved it. And it felt great.

When the plane arrived and we stood up, I immediately clocked an exceptionally good-looking guy who'd been sitting behind me. (God knows how I had missed that at take-off!) He smiled. I smiled. He was gorgeous, so I chased him down to the baggage claim area and struck up a conversation.

'Hey, do you want to share a cab into town, maybe get a coffee?' I asked, feeling like I'd possibly met the love of my life.

'Probably not a good idea,' he said with a wistful look in his eye. 'Your fiancé might not approve.'

Luck has never been on my side.

'Maybe just try something different.' My mother jolts me back to my current dilemma. 'I really think you're attracting the wrong types. Everyone in my book club agrees.'

'What! You discuss my personal life at book club? I thought you were supposed to talk about books.'

'We do, but afterwards everyone talks about their families, particularly their grandchildren, so what am I supposed to do?'

'Maybe talk about the fact I'm a failed fashion designer. Or is my disastrous love-life more entertaining?'

'Sweetheart, it's just that we're all hoping you meet a gorgeous man soon. To be honest, they can't understand why you haven't already. They all think you're an absolute stunner, a terrific girl, such a great catch.'

'You could tell them I'm gay.'

'We did think you were for a while, but we all decided that even if you were gay, you'd probably have the same problems finding the right partner. Marcie's daughter is gay and she's been with a lovely woman for ten years. They're about to have their first baby.'

'I'm going, Mum.'

'Just one more thing –'

'Thanks for calling. Bye.' Hanging up is the only way to end a conversation with my mother. Especially when the subject turns to my lack of career and disastrous personal life, which it inevitably does, every time we talk. I know she wants me to be happy, but I'm trying my best. I even ended up in Emergency as a result of my dedication. Surely that counts for something?

I drag myself to the local shops and get the largest flat white possible (note to self, must google whether caffeine is allowed for pregnant people). I also consider buying a home pregnancy test from the chemist. Just to be sure. But then I figure a doctor is probably more reliable. Unless I'm not really pregnant and it's all just a cruel joke Emergency doctors play on unsuspecting stalkers. What if that Dr Mitch is having a laugh with his colleagues over bad hospital coffee right now, telling them how this girl really thinks she's pregnant? But who would go so far with a joke and risk losing their job and reputation? Even I can see I'm clutching at non-existent straws.

There's no doubt about it, I'm definitely pregnant.

I know I want Jake – but do I want his baby? What am I going to do with a baby? I can't possibly have it. But can I get rid of it?

Once again, panic rises from the pit of my stomach. I can't even begin to answer these questions because I have no idea. I always imagined I'd have a baby. But like this?

A quick glance through the hospital brochures when I get home tells me I have a little bit of time before I need to make any irreversible decisions. First, I'll see how things go with Jake. Yes, it was only a one-night stand, but relationships have started from less. Maybe the baby bit will speed things up and everything will work out? What I need to know now is whether or not Jake really is The One. And for that, I need an awesome and slightly devious plan.

Certainly the time frame is clear. In another eight months there'll be a baby. Good to have a deadline. First I have to make Jake fall in love with me, then I'll tell him we're having a baby and that will be that. Pretty straightforward, right? I'm definitely well on the way: there's little doubt of Jake's interest. He flirted with me outrageously prior to our one-night stand, then slept with me without too much persuasion (I think) and had a good time (I think). Plus, he has worked during every one of my shifts since. As a manager, he has access to everyone's schedules, so obviously he arranges his shifts accordingly.

Everything indicates a natural attraction and the more I learn of the real Jake, the more I can see how much we have in common and how ready he is for commitment. Not that we've actually talked much. I've just done my research. Something I'm good at.

I know where he does his grocery shopping. I just happen to see him at the local supermarket. And from what I observed, he doesn't just get sliced bread and boxes of cereal, rather things like capers and prosciutto. I also saw him pick up a jar of what looked to be preserved lemons. He's obviously into good food but has no one to cook for. Jake puts out this ultra-cool, man-about-town persona, but it's pretty clear to me he's screaming out for a relationship.

He goes to the gym. And so do I.

Well, I accidentally on purpose discovered that he goes to the gym right near work. I saw him go in there as I was heading home after a shift one day. Then I accidentally on purpose joined up for a three-year membership. Money well spent.

However, apart from what he buys at the supermarket and what sort of weights he lifts (impressive ones), there're a few gaps in my research. Like, who are Jake's friends? I've never seen him with any non-work people. Ex-girlfriends? How many and who are they? Is he financial? Can he support me, and our baby? It's all very well him falling in love with me, but can he provide for our little family-to-be?

I've seen his house and from what I can remember, the decor is quite stylish. I don't particularly like the exterior colour, but I can always have it repainted. It's not enormous but there's potential to extend, maybe go up a level, perhaps install a swimming pool.

I never usually consider these sorts of things when I date a guy. Clem is always looking at the finer details of a man's situation to see if he has long-term potential, and she's always berating me for not taking that stuff more seriously. Like the time I went out with a tightrope-walking trapeze artist. Clem didn't approve because he was in a high-risk profession. But he was only training so he never walked or swung on anything very high. Nothing was going to happen at those heights, he assured me. Maybe a grass stain on his baggy harlequin pants. Besides, he was particularly flexible in the bedroom. But Clem would not be convinced.

He wasn't The One as it turned out, and Clem was right about the risk factor. He ended up falling off the training tightrope (only half a metre off the ground) and breaking his collarbone. He gave up after that and now he works in banking, earning a fortune. Oh well . . . as I say, luck and me . . .

That's another big difference between Clem and me. She thinks things through carefully and I . . . well, I don't really think at all. If life were a wild, unpatrolled surf beach, I would run straight into the sea without a second thought. Whereas Clem would check the depth, rips and shark warnings, organise a lifeguard patrol and set up some flags to safely swim between, then weigh up the risk and make an informed decision about whether or not to hit the waves. I always felt she lacked a sense of adventure and excitement, but now I'm not so sure that's fair. Maybe Clem's right to be cautious. In all my adventurous unplanned risk-taking, nothing has ever worked out, exciting or otherwise.

However, all that's going to change. I will now plan my moves with the precision and foresight of a chess grandmaster. Only a little more quickly, as I won't be able to hide the baby for too much longer. Otherwise I'll look like a beached whale while I'm convincing Jake to marry me, which may prove a tad more challenging.

Clem is always telling me to play hard to get. She has a complicated dating system, an amalgamation of various self-help books with ludicrous names like *Make Him Think Marriage was His Idea* and *You've Got Him, Now Hold on to Him.* In Clem's opinion, if a guy asks you out, you have to say you're busy the first two times. The third time you can be available, but there should be no physical contact until after five successful dates.

That's as much as I can remember. Apart from being quite complicated, the one time I tried to follow her guidelines, I only remembered the 'no physical contact' bit when I was naked in my date's bed, and by that time it was too late. For me, it's quite simple. If I like someone, I go for it. And 'physical contact' plays an essential role.

But maybe Clem's right. Maybe now is the time to take a long, hard look at my dating techniques, which to be honest have not yet proved incredibly successful. I need to try something in between Clem's rigid hands-off system and my overly friendly approach.

I ponder this concept, fighting to keep my eyes open, when the answer suddenly pops into my head like the final piece of long-forgotten jigsaw puzzle.

I'll just play *a little bit* harder to get!

That's it! So subtle, so sneaky, Jake won't even see it coming. I'm amazed it's never occurred to me before. I'll still show interest and have sex with him. No need to go completely crazy. But I'll hold back *just a little bit.*

I'm thrilled with my idea. I've never had any sort of plan before so I'm already one step ahead. Now, all I have to do is be mysterious and aloof – and occasionally resist the advances of a devastatingly handsome man to whom I'm pregnant, as well as incredibly attracted and desperate to marry.

Piece of cake.

4

Morning sickness is a myth. Either that or I have special powers that render me immune. It's most definitely Monday morning yet I jump out of bed feeling fantastic and head to work with a spring in my step.

Just as I arrive at the café near the call centre, I remember that I still haven't determined whether or not caffeine is bad during pregnancy. Missy was talking about it in a lunch break recently, but at the time it didn't mean anything to me. Now I wish I'd taken notes.

The guy who always makes my coffee looks at me expectantly. I'm not sure if he's waiting for an explanation for the stitches on my chin or my coffee order. Either way, I don't know how to respond. At the last minute, I ask for a decaf and he seems surprised. Oh no, he's worked it out! Or am I imagining it?

'I'm on a bit of a health kick,' I say by way of explanation, but my coffee guy has already turned back to the pile of orders in front of him. Phew, that was close.

Cup in hand, I make my way to the building where WineCall is located and join the crowd gathered at the lift in the foyer. I quickly draft a story in my head to explain the state of my chin, should anyone ask. Something about walking into a ladder precariously sticking out the back of a ute. I haven't got all the details sorted but it will be enough to get through a lift conversation.

I can't believe I still work here after all these years. It was only ever meant to be an interim job. When I left school, I had no idea what I wanted to do. I loved designing and sewing my own clothes but never considered it a viable career. Well, my parents never considered it a viable career. So, like many hopeful creative types, I did a Bachelor of Arts. I had a great time, only just scraped through, but still wanted to design clothes. So, against my parents' advice, I went to TAFE to study fashion design with the hopes of wowing the crowds at Fashion Week and forging a career in Europe.

But after I graduated from TAFE, I couldn't find my groove. I always felt like I was a Butterick pattern trying to break into a haute couture fashion show. Nothing seemed to work, but I was sure I had something to offer. I designed my own label, selling pieces at the markets. Cute skirts, dresses, the sorts of clothes I thought would be popular. But that was the trouble, they were the kind of thing everyone was making and buying, and not unique or special in any way. I sold a handful of items over the period of one summer, but I'd spent an enormous amount on fabrics and other supplies. I'd rented a studio and put my name on a lease for a little shop. I'd focused on the big picture and, rather like the other night, I'd fallen flat on my face. I didn't make enough money to cover my costs. The debt was huge and I couldn't pay it off. So, I decided to get a job.

That proved even harder than creating the latest must-have styles.

I worked on reception at a big fashion house, but they were never going to let me do anything other than answer the phone and book couriers. And eventually they didn't even let me do that. Just because I once got the staff lunch order mixed up with a belt shipment, and fifteen sandwiches were delivered high priority while a dozen chunky industrial belts never turned up to a *Vogue* photo shoot. Innocent mistake, really. In fact, they should have thanked me because the belts were truly hideous.

So I left.

And when I say I left, it was a mutual decision between them and me.

To be perfectly honest, when I say 'mutual', they encouraged me to go and I was happy to oblige.

Oh look, I was fired.

Mind you, as with my visit to hospital, it wasn't my fault. After the belt incident, I accidentally slept with the work experience boy who turned out to be the boss's nephew. How was I to know? He seemed so much older than eighteen. And he certainly knew what he was doing.

After that, I couldn't get any sort of job in the fashion industry, nor could I see my kitchen table for the pile of overdue bills. After six months, my parents helped to pay off my debts but then I had to pay them back. Mum had a friend who had a friend who had a son working at a call centre, selling wine over the phone, making an absolute fortune, and they were recruiting. So I thought I'd give it a try.

Of course, I got the job. I mean, I was completely over-qualified. Wine plus talking on the phone – no one does either of those tasks as well as me, and certainly not at the same time.

Five years later, I'm still here. I don't earn a fortune, but I paid back Mum and Dad and can now cover my rent and bills. I also get to drink a lot of wine (well, you have to know what you're selling), and I've done my Bronze, Silver and Gold wine appreciation courses. It turned out that the friend of a friend's son was like some sort of freak super seller who went on to sell high-end real estate. I'll be moving on too when the right thing comes along. This is only an interim job. Did I say that already? It's just a longer interim than I expected.

The lift arrives and everyone files in. Just as the doors are closing, a black motorcycle boot jams them open. The dull grey of the lift transforms into brilliant colour and my stomach turns inside out.

Jake!

Ridiculously hot and dishevelled in dark jeans, a cowboy shirt, and with hair that looks like it just woke up. A motorcycle helmet in one hand and a black leather jacket in the other.

My God! I fight every impulse in my body that's providing rational explanations as to why I must immediately throw myself against that crumpled shirt and three-day growth. But I'm pretty sure throwing yourself at a guy is not allowed under Clem's play-super-hard-to-get rules. Even I can see it wouldn't fit into my new plan.

In the end I don't have to throw myself at him, because the lift is so crowded he's squashed into my shoulder, so I can't help but touch him. He smells divine, like a caramel milkshake. I feel pressure against my thigh as he leans towards me. Is he doing that on purpose? Or is it just normal crowded lift behaviour? Whatever it is, he's certainly making his presence felt and turning me on in the process. I look sideways at him, but like everyone else, he's gazing up at the numbers.

I tear my eyes away from Mr Too-good-looking-for-his-own-good and focus instead on a dirty mark on the lift wall. I must not initiate conversation, which could well result not only in physical contact but also in complete embarrassment for everyone in the cramped lift. I breathe slowly. In and out. This is going well. I'm so restrained, I hardly recognise myself. But unfortunately, I look up just as Jake is looking at me, and that's it. All intentions slip down the lift shaft and the floodgates are flung wide open.

'Hey, do you want a coffee?' I blurt out. 'I'm going to get one; it's no problem, my shout, what do you have?'

'Aren't you going up now? Morning brief's in five,' says Jake, in his best rockstar voice. 'And it looks like you've done one coffee today already.' I forgot about the takeaway coffee cup in my hand. Damn! Still, I keep going because that's what I do in situations like this.

'Yeah, I know,' I say, with a ridiculous giggle that even makes me cringe. 'But I'm desperate for another so I thought I'd dump my bag and quickly race down, get a coffee, maybe a muffin. I'm a bit hungry. Are you? Do you want a muffin? Maybe go halves?'

'No thanks.'

'Just coffee, then?'

'No thanks.'

Damn. Now I have to go back down and get another coffee, which I don't want, but he might think I'm a bit weird if I don't follow through. I'm glad I got a decaf after all. Surely two decafs are okay? I don't have to drink it anyway.

'I'll have a coffee,' says a voice from the back of the lift that belongs to an extremely annoying guy who always wants to chat to me during shifts. He's constantly sniffing, like he's got a cold. Excruciating when you're in the workstation next to him.

'Oh, okay, sure.' What else can I say? At least Jake is going to think I'm a generous person.

'I will too, decaf skim flat white,' says Missy, pushing her way to the front of the lift, as everyone readjusts to make way for her pregnant belly. Which has become so big. Wow! I stare at her tummy like I'm in a trance. I can't help it. Will mine really get that huge? 'Er, thanks, Lizzie, that's nice of you,' adds Missy, trying to interrupt my stomach stare, which is developing a slightly manic edge.

I force myself back to the moment and attempt a smile. I can't believe I now have to get a coffee for that pretentious do-gooder Missy with her perfect hair, perfect husband, all living in their fabulous terrace house in Paddington. How come she got the husband before the pregnant tummy? Without so much as a graze, let alone stitches on her chin. Life is so unfair.

'I'd love a coffee,' says a girl I don't even know. 'Soy decaf with a dash of vanilla.'

'Just a flat white for me,' says another voice, which belongs to someone who doesn't even work on our floor. 'But with almond milk and one sugar, please.'

I end up having to get six coffees and no one offers to pay, which means going across the road to the ATM because the café's EFTPOS machine is down and I don't have enough cash. Then they don't have any trays left so I have to carry them precariously all stacked up, one on top of the other, so naturally I get coffee down the front of my top. I'm also extremely late for the morning brief in the boardroom.

'Lizzie, do that on your own time, okay?' Steve, the call centre manager, is not impressed.

'I said she could go,' says Jake, quick as a flash. 'Sorry, but everyone needed a caffeine fix and I thought it better to have one person do a coffee run than the whole lot.'

'No worries.' Steve nods and goes back to the very boring morning brief, detailing what wines are on special today and how we need to sell more, whether people want them or not.

I can't believe it. Jake stood up for me. I mouth the words 'thank you' and he gives me a smile that sends shockwaves through every part of my body.

Everyone heads to their workstations to start the shift, but I can't concentrate with Jake standing up at the supervisors' podium, in the middle of the call centre. How can I be expected to sell anything under such conditions? We barely speak, but I'm aware of his constant gaze and it's sending me into a frenzy. He has been so cool and distant at work, but today, he can't keep his eyes off me. It can't be my outfit, what with the coffee stain down my front. Perhaps he's impressed by the selfless way I got coffees for half the building? Or he's wondering what I've done to my chin? Whatever is going on, the heat dial has definitely turned up.

Finally, ten minutes before the morning break, he comes over to check a problematic computer in the workstation next to mine. Our eyes lock. My heart bungee-jumps down to my ankles and bounces back up into my throat.

'Hey, gorgeous, how you going?' he says. 'I hope you're not going to distract me from my very serious work here.'

'Maybe.' I giggle nervously, unable to believe that Jake has actually struck up a conversation. That's more than he's ever said to me during a shift. Clearly my plan is working.

Jake leans in closer and lowers his voice. 'Actually, babe, you've been distracting me all day, so why stop now?'

I blush, unable to speak. He's so close to me, I can hardly breathe. As always, I'm totally blown away simply by the way his face is formed. It's the perfect combination of beauty and danger. I could stare at it for hours, like a precious piece of art, and normally I do, but right now, I have little time to waste. I get straight to the point.

'When do you finish tonight?'

'About six. Why? What have you got in mind?'

I take a deep breath. 'A few of us are going to the bar across the road for a drink if you want to come down.'

Actually no one has yet planned to go for a drink. I make a quick mental note to myself to suggest it during lunch.

'Yeah, maybe. Sounds good. See how I go,' he says, totally undressing me with his eyes. 'Will you be wearing that skirt?'

'Um, at least for some of the night,' I say, trying to sound as seductive as possible despite my heart pounding furiously. Jake leans over me, pretending to check out an order on my screen. I feel like I'm going to burst.

'So, it may come off at some point?' he asks in a low voice that sends a quiver through my entire body.

'It might.'

'In that case, I'll definitely try to make it.'

Jake slowly stands and heads away without another word.

I breathe out suddenly, my hands shaking. He said yes! Well, he said he would 'definitely try' but to me that was a very clear 'yes'. And he was flirting outrageously. Even with unsightly stitches on my chin. It won't be long now before he falls in love with me and wants to have a baby. Which is when I can tell him that we already have one on the way! What could go wrong?! Ha ha. Okay, plenty of things could go wrong. But seriously, playing a bit harder to get is working a treat and it's only been a few hours.

'By the way, were you around my house on Friday night?' Jake turns back, assuming a work-like voice, a little too loud for my liking. 'I thought I saw . . .'

Whoa. I quickly assume a look of (what I hope) is mildly concerned confusion. 'What? Me? No. Why would I be . . . ? No, no, I don't think so.'

'Oh, I was coming home and thought I saw someone out the front who looked a bit like you, walking the other way.'

So he hadn't been at home after all. But where had he been? And who with? Did he meet up with someone? Was it another woman? I didn't see him arrive, yet he saw me? WHAT IS GOING ON? So many questions that I can't really ask, not without sounding like a complete weirdo. Besides, that's what the old Lizzie would have done. Not the new, cool, hard-to-pin-down Lizzie.

'Wasn't me,' I say again, as casually as I can.

Jake walks towards the supervisors' podium. Clem would be so proud of me right now.

'So . . . where had you been anyway?' I ask before I can stop myself. Damn! Sorry, Clem.

Jake turns back. 'Just out.'

'Oh.' Stop right there, Lizzie, I tell myself sternly. 'Right, well, maybe see you tonight.'

I put my head down and pretend to take an incoming call so Jake thinks I don't care whether he comes tonight or not. And before he works out I'm just a little bit obsessed. He might take it the wrong way and think I'm completely unhinged. Time enough to learn that fact after I've pushed his baby out of my vagina. And by then it will be too late to get out of it.

5

My hands are bound behind my back and a harsh light is shining in my eyes. A distorted voice fires questions to which I don't know the answers. It sounds like Steve from work, but also a bit like Clem. I want to ask what's going on, but when I try to speak, no sound comes out. It's like I'm underwater, but it's as hot as a desert and the light is blinding. I can't breathe. I try to scream, but can't. No one can hear me. Help! Help! Anyone, help!

I sit up in bed, gasping. Where am I? What's going on?

Slowly, slowly, reality sinks in. Just a bad dream. Thank goodness. My breathing slows to a normal pace and I sink back under the covers, every muscle in my body aching with exhaustion. My eyes hurt and my head is pounding. What's going on? I can't be hungover as I didn't drink last night, unless you count all those mineral waters that I pretended were vodka, lime and sodas. The hot morning sun streams through the window, right onto my face, making me feel even worse. That's what is was. No wonder I thought I was being tortured.

Turning over, I try to settle in for a bit more of a snooze when, once again, I sit up, startled. Something's not right. The sun never shines through my bedroom window in the morning. It's a west-facing room. I look at the full-length drapes on either side of the window, wishing they were drawn. Not mine. Chic and elegant in a classic Victorian way. But far too heavy-looking for me. Where am I?

I scan my unfamiliar surroundings until my eyes fall on the lump next to me.

Jake. Looking like a Greek god.

Suddenly the night before comes tumbling back. Okay, so I didn't play that hard to get. In fact, I didn't play hard to get at all, but I have to say things are nonetheless looking quite positive. He stirs from his sleep.

'Hey, babe.'

I attempt a reply, but as he pulls himself out of bed and heads to the bathroom, words escape me. I don't think I've ever seen such a ridiculously well-put-together body in my entire life and I've seen a few variations on a theme. Obviously he spends more time at the gym than I realised. He has muscles I never knew existed on a human being. It's no wonder I have zero self-control whenever he's within a five-kilometre radius.

'This seems to keep happening, doesn't it?' he says, sauntering back into the bedroom with that bad-boy grin that makes me weak at the knees.

'I know, maybe we should just get married!' Oh my God, did I just say that?

'Yeah, right.' He laughs. 'Want a coffee?'

'Sure,' I say, sincerely hoping he didn't think that's what I'm really thinking – though in all fairness, it's exactly what I'm thinking.

He plants a quick kiss on my cheek and makes his way to the kitchen. I can hear him pottering around, clanking pots and chinking cups. I guess this is what our life will be like together. Me, lying in bed, while my handsome husband makes coffee. Then we'll have incredible morning sex and go out for brunch, look in a few bookshops, second-hand stores, buy some quirky retro lamp, maybe catch a movie. Later we'll meet friends for a drink then head off for a bite to eat in a cool hole-in-the-wall restaurant no one's ever heard of. Then we'll get a taxi home but we won't be able to wait. Consumed with desire, we'll just rip each other's clothes off right there in the back seat and . . . hang on, where's our baby? Damn, I completely forgot. Maybe our child will be so well behaved and adaptable that he/she will just go wherever we go and fit right in. Apart from the taxi scenario, that would be wrong. Maybe he/she is staying with my parents that night . . .

'Milk?' Jake's gravelly morning voice cuts right through my fantasy.

'Sorry?'

'You want milk?'

'Yeah, great.'

'I'm going to have a shower.' He walks off.

'No coffee for you?' I call after him.

'Nah, gotta get to work.'

'Oh. I'll come with you. Want to get some breakfast on the way?'

'Sorry, babe, no time.'

As he turns on the shower, the thought of Jake, wet and naked, is excruciating. I simply can't sit here while all that is going on only a few metres away. I follow him into the bathroom.

'Is there room for me?' I say at the bathroom door. 'I'll make it worth your while.' If he's going to rush off, I have to make sure he's thinking about me all day.

'Tempting, but I'm running late. Next time?'

He jumps out of the shower and into unironed clothes. How can he look so good after such a big night? It would take at least an hour and a half for me to look vaguely presentable and even then people would ask if I was coming down with something.

'Speak to you later?' I say hopefully.

'Sure.' He gives me a short but very sweet kiss on the lips. 'Pull the door behind you when you leave.'

I climb back into Jake's bed. He didn't ask me to go so he must not mind me staying in his house. It's like we're living together already. I'd love to snuggle in for more sleep but I'm pretty sure I've got something on. If only I had my diary at hand. It was fairly important, but for the life of me . . . Hang on! My check-up! At the hospital. That's right, I'm pregnant. I feel a bit guilty that it keeps slipping my mind. Probably because I've been too focused on securing a father for my unborn child. Still, I have made progress in that department. After last night I would even go so far as to say that the situation is well under control.

I'm home, changed and out the door in record time. I hardly ever use my car as it's so expensive to run and has a tendency to break down, but today I have no choice. At the hospital with a minute to spare, I can't find any street parking, so I swerve into the hospital car park and nearly faint at the cost. Next time, I'm catching the bus.

I take the lift up to reception and stop, transfixed. A pregnant woman is standing just in front of me, talking on her mobile. Is that what I'm going to look like? Another one ambles past. And another. In fact, everywhere I look I see women who look like they've just swallowed a basketball. Or a large beach ball, in some cases. One woman shuffles by with what has to be the biggest belly I've ever seen. She looks so uncomfortable she can hardly walk. And she's got different shoes on. Not surprising. The poor thing probably couldn't see past her unborn child to get dressed.

Everyone in the world is pregnant. Okay, everyone in this hospital foyer, but still, it's like an epidemic and I'm the latest victim. I feel like leaving right now and pretending it never happened. But that's obviously not going to work. I have no choice but to join the snail-like trail of mums-to-be.

'Hi there,' I say when I get to the head of the queue at the reception desk. My voice is oddly upbeat and unfamiliar. 'I'm having a baby.'

I don't mean to say it quite like that, but it falls out of my mouth before I can stop it. A middle-aged man with bleached white hair styled into a sort of a quiff looks up as if he hears this every day. Which he probably does. Isn't that why most people go to hospital? Apart from accidents that occur when trying to see through the window of the home of the father of their unborn child.

I haven't actually said those words out loud and they seem completely foreign. Oh my God, I really *will* become one of those whale-like women with different shoes and shuffling walks. A deafening voice screams in my head:

I'M HAVING A BABY!

Fresh waves of panic gush through me and I can't catch my breath. I need to escape, but I'm stuck in a line of happy smiley pregnant women. Can't move. Can't breathe. Can't do this!

'Are you okay?'

I try to focus my attention on Bleached Hair Man, despite being in the middle of some sort of mini anxiety attack.

'Sorry,' I whisper. 'What did you say?'

'I was asking if you're having a baby right now?'

'No, but soon . . . not sure when, I mean, I guess in about, what, eight months from now?'

Bleached Hair Man is not interested in when the baby is coming, as long as it isn't going to happen at his reception. I manage to explain that I have an appointment and he gives clear directions to the antenatal clinic. I thank him and try to walk away, but my legs aren't working very well. Maybe I should ask for a wheelchair. I don't think I can make it on my own.

Did I mention I'M HAVING A BABY?

Somehow I arrive at the antenatal desk. The receptionist gives me some forms to complete and tells me to wait until someone is ready to see me.

I fill out the forms and flick through all the well-thumbed, outdated magazines, and despite the fact that all the gossip is old and all the quizzes are completed, it does help me to calm down. And before I know it, an hour passes. Wow. Getting pregnant seems to be instantaneous but getting someone to discuss your pregnancy takes a lifetime!

'Elizabeth March.'

I jump to my feet at the sound of my full name, like I've been caught doing something naughty. Which I suppose I have.

'That's me. It's Lizzie actually.'

'Hi. I'm Sue,' says a woman who looks not much older than me with sandy-blonde hair scraped back into a ponytail and a comforting smile. 'I'm a midwife and I'll be looking after you today.'

She seems nice. I relax.

'Sorry you've been waiting so long. Busy day. If you could just give me those forms then go down to the door on the right and take a seat, I won't be long.'

I go and sit in Sue's room, where there's not much except a desk, two chairs, a hospital bed and lots of posters showing happy mums and babies. I don't feel like one of them. I shift my chair so I don't have to see their glowing smiles and loving expressions but they're everywhere. Panic rises again in my chest. I'm in the wrong place if that's how I should look. Maybe I should just go now . . .

'Right, Lizzie, how are you feeling?' Sue comes in, closing the door firmly behind her, and sits at the desk.

'Fine, thanks.' I try to calm my breathing.

'How many weeks are you? You haven't got that on your form.'

'Five, I think. I came into Emergency early on Saturday morning, after a little accident' – I point to the stitches on my chin – 'and the doctor told me I was pregnant, so if I hadn't tripped over, I still wouldn't know.'

'Right. Well, you must be in the system then.'

Sue turns to her computer and enters my name.

'Ah yes, it was Dr Peters you spoke with, wasn't it?'

'Yes, just in Emergency, all above board.' I laugh with an accidental snort. Why did I say that?

'Sorry?' Sue looks up from her screen.

'I mean, yes, he was the one who told me I was . . .' I start explaining, but Sue is not in the least bit interested in my conversation with Dr Mitch. She goes back to the computer.

'So the first day of your last period was March twenty-fourth?'

I nod, wondering what other personal information the doctor added to my file.

'Right, let me see.' Sue is now looking at that same round calendar that Dr Mitch showed me. It's like a magic wheel that reveals every intimate detail from my menstrual cycle to catastrophic one-night stands.

'That makes you now almost six weeks, so still early days. We don't usually see patients until at least eight weeks, but that's okay. Have you been to your GP?'

'No, I haven't done anything.' I feel like Sue is my new best friend, so I decide to be completely honest. 'I'm not sure how anything works from here.'

Sue nods. 'Normally, you might first visit your GP, who would organise blood tests and perhaps go through the different options for antenatal care. Are you planning on having a private obstetrician or public care?'

My blank look spurs Sue on to explain my antenatal options. Did I want my own obstetrician or to go through the public system? Did I want midwife care? My mind whirls. I didn't realise I had to make such important decisions today.

'Um, midwife care is what I imagined.' I pluck out an option while trying to sound informed and organised.

'If that's the case, it's time to get started,' says Sue, reaching for a pile of brochures and forms. 'You need to have blood tests done. I'll give you a form for that. Is this your first pregnancy?'

I nod.

'So, how are you feeling?'

'Still a bit shocked really,' I say, trying to stifle a yawn. 'And tired. Sorry, I had a late night last night.'

'Were you working?' asks Sue.

'Not exactly; well, I was definitely *with* work colleagues – we went out and one thing led to the other, you know how it is . . .'

Sue looks at me sternly, as if she knows exactly how it is.

'You might find you need to make a few changes to your lifestyle. Your body will be working very hard. Now, I'll just take your blood pressure and then weigh you.'

Weigh me! I only ever hop on the scales first thing in the morning, completely naked, and even then, I pick my days. I look at my shoes and jeans: they're going to add a bit on. I guess it doesn't really matter now. I'm only going to get heavier.

After confirming that my blood pressure is absolutely normal (good to know), that my weight is a little more than I thought it was (shoes and jeans) and my body mass index is acceptable (never really knew what that was anyway), we sit down with a list of questions that Sue is required to run through.

'What do you do for work?'

'I'm a clothes designer,' I say, trying to sound confident.

'That sounds exciting. Where are you doing that?'

'Er, I'm not at the moment. I'm working in a call centre, selling wine.'

'Right,' says Sue. 'So not physically taxing?'

I shake my head mournfully. It's not, unless you count a sexual encounter with a call centre supervisor followed by pregnancy. That's been exhausting.

'Do you do much exercise?'

'I've been going to the gym,' I say victoriously. I knew that membership would come in handy.

'What about your diet? Plenty of fresh vegetables, lean meat and whole grains?'

'Yep, for sure,' I say, regretting the tub of ice-cream I demolished for dinner last week because I couldn't be bothered cooking. 'I've also given up caffeine – I ordered a decaf coffee the other day.'

If Sue is impressed with my recent caffeine cut-back, she doesn't show it. Tough audience!

'What about alcohol?' she continues.

'Yes, well, that's what got me into trouble in the first place,' I say with a giggle.

As my joke collapses into awkward silence, I quickly explain that while I did consume a few alcoholic beverages before I knew about the baby, I've given it up now. But this doesn't seem to be the right answer either.

Sue the Reassuring Midwife is fast becoming Sue the School Prefect, trying to spoil my fun, rather than being the best friend in whom I can confide. So I don't tell her that last night, in an attempt to woo the father of my child, I stayed out way too late, (sipping mineral water, naturally) and then casually bedded said man, yet again. I think sorting out the father is the best thing I could do for the baby. Still, I'm not going to share that with Serious Sue.

'Yes, giving up alcohol completely would be best. We recommend zero alcohol during pregnancy.'

Sue's questions continue until my head feels like it's going to burst. Especially as my life doesn't offer easy answers to any of them. Is my partner supportive? Does he do drugs? Is he financially secure? Jake and I definitely have some talking to do.

'Go and have your blood tests and come back in about six weeks,' says Sue, finally giving up on her list of questions, probably disillusioned by my vague responses. 'You'll be twelve weeks pregnant by then so it'll be time to have your nuchal. There's a waiting list so you'll need to book in soon. I'd do it today. You also might want to book into prenatal classes for later on.'

Sue is now talking another language altogether. From the casual way she said 'nuchal', it seems it's something I should know about. She gives me a form for the blood tests and, sensing my confusion, hands me another mountainous pile of brochures and a pregnancy information book. As I flick through the pages, all I see are pictures of gorgeous model-like mums with beautiful, neat bellies and happy, contented faces. Will I ever look like that?

'This is a comprehensive guide for early pregnancy. It has all sorts of information about what's going on and what you have to do.'

'Right. Thanks,' I say, trying not to sound as overwhelmed as I feel. Surely it can't be that hard? It's not like I'm the first woman to go through this. But considering my unusual circumstances, I think I have good reason for feeling a little out of my depth.

'Remember to eat well, and get plenty of sleep,' continues Sue. 'And you might experience some morning sickness soon – there's a few tips in the book on how to deal with it.'

'I haven't had any yet,' I say proudly. 'Maybe I won't.'

Sue gives me her warm and comforting smile, but I swear, there's an evil twinkle in her eye.

'Yes, you never know. You just might be one of the lucky ones.'

I walk out of Sue's room, shell-shocked. I book in for the nuchal, despite not really knowing what it is. The woman at the desk gives me a date an eternity away, so I've plenty of time to research it. It's probably in the book Sue gave me. I put my hands on my still flat stomach. How can there be another human being growing inside me when I feel nothing at all? It can't be very big. Maybe the size of a peanut? A walnut? Maybe more of a brazil nut. They're quite big as far as nuts go. Not only do I have absolutely no idea about what's going on inside my body, I'm not sure what I'm supposed to be feeling emotionally. Should I feel a connection with the nut inside me? I love nuts as much as the next person, but when did I agree to grow my own? And how can something so small and nutritious possibly make me feel sick? It doesn't make sense. But in my life right now, nothing makes much sense at all.

6

I wake up the next day awash with nausea. Oh my God! Did someone press some sort of morning-sickness button when I wasn't looking? How do women do this? And why would they go through it a second time when they know exactly how vile they're going to feel? In fact, how in the hell have we managed to populate the earth? You'd think by now we'd have cottoned on to it and gone on strike!

I'm hungry yet the thought of food makes me want to throw up. It's so confusing and I can't even say, 'Why didn't anyone tell me about this?' because Sue the Midwife told me yesterday. And I didn't believe her.

I just want to curl up into a ball and die, but I have to go to work. I'm tempted to call in sick with my best croaky voice, but I know Jake will be there and I must see him.

My phone dings at me. Really loudly. Is it always that loud?

I feel like I'm hungover, which I'm definitely not. I look down to see a text from Clem.

Drink after work?

That's the last thing I want. Even the written word 'drink' makes me want to puke. Maybe I can have a mineral water like I did the other night, but even non-alcoholic bubbles are completely unappealing right now. And Clem will definitely think it's odd. But then she'll think it odd if I don't go as well. She probably wants to debrief about Mal. I text back.

Sure. 6.30 pm at the usual?

Her text comes back before I'm even out of bed.

Great, see u then x

She must be desperate to talk. I look at the clock. Better get up. Maybe I'll share my news with Clem tonight. I'm going to have to tell her at some point, even though it's going to be hard for her to hear. Not only is she desperate for a baby, her chance of having one anytime soon might have just walked out her door.

Still, look how quickly it happened for me. My situation should give her hope. Well, maybe not my exact situation; it's by no means a romance novel. But surely it's encouraging for the recently single girl to see how quickly the tables can turn? Single one minute, up the duff the next. It's nothing short of a miracle, right?

Somehow I don't think Clem will see it that way. Perhaps I won't tell her yet. Tonight will be all about Clem. I will simply listen and be the really great, sympathetic friend that I know I can be, and try not to let it show that secretly I'm relieved Mal may no longer be on the scene. He was never good enough for Clem. Still, it's always easier to see other people's mistakes. I've certainly made a few dodgy relationship choices of my own.

Like the Texter, so-called because quite literally all he did was text. We hardly ever talked face to face. Once he even texted me when we were having sex. I still don't know how he did it. He must have had magic fingers. If only he had put them to better use, the relationship might have gone somewhere. One day I went through his phone and discovered he was having a few other texty relationships. I texted all the girls and we got together for a drink. Had a great night and decided to cut all ties with the Texter. United and strong, we made a new gang called The Girls Are All Right. We were going to meet once a month to celebrate our female solidarity. Until two of the girls got together and the other one went back to the Texter. So the group disbanded. Just as I had the t-shirts printed.

Luckily Jake never really texts me, so there's little danger of falling into that trap. I put a protective hand on my tummy, which I swear is definitely a little rounder than it was yesterday. I'm not just looking for a boyfriend now; I'm looking for a life partner.

As the morning progresses, I start to feel less like I'm about to vomit on my shoes and more like a regular person who really should know how to practise safe sex. I arrive at work to find two items on my desk, both of which send my head into a spin. The first is the most enormous bunch of tulips wrapped in designer brown paper and string. I grab the card with trembling hands, hoping they're from Jake. Who else could they be from? Please be from Jake . . .

I love you, Mike xxx

Mike! Who's that? Have I been out with a Mike?

'Somebody sending you flowers, Lizzie?'

I look up from the mystery card to see Nathan, a work colleague, smiling at me.

'Looks like it,' I say with a confidence I don't feel.

'Who are they from?'

Nathan started working at the call centre at the same time as me. We did our basic training together. He's not really my type. Bit too clean-cut in a Tommy Hilfiger way, but cute nonetheless. Wants to be a filmmaker. Apparently, he's made one short film that was picked up by some overseas festival and won a couple of awards. Something very nearly happened between us at a work function. Well, I was drunk and tried to kiss him and he backed away.

Later, Missy told me that all the girls in the call centre are desperately in love with him, but to not bother because he's definitely gay. No wonder he freaked out when I cornered him. So now we're friends, which has worked out well. He's a nice guy with great dress sense and helpful relationship advice, but I'm certainly not going to let on that I have no idea who sent the flowers.

'Sorry, Lizzie, they're for me.'

I turn around to see Frankie, the coolest woman in the world. Of course! Frankie, mid-forties, has been married to Mike (happily) since forever, and they have three kids who are equally hip. They've done the whole marriage-mortgage-babies thing but made it look like it's the latest fashion. Mike works in TV; I think he's a producer, so they're always off to some glamorous event. Frankie has a way of wearing clothes that's quirky and original, like she has a personal stylist who specialises in alternative fashion. She's also an incredibly nice person. Yes, Frankie has it all, but you can't hate her because she is genuinely lovely. It's infuriating.

'So sorry, I left them there while I went to find a vase,' Frankie explains.

Nathan gives me a condescending look of sympathy as he walks away.

Damn.

'How come Mike's sending you flowers?' I ask. 'Is it your birthday?'

'No, he's just a romantic.' She smiles, with a faraway look in her eyes.

Their relationship amazes me. I want one like that.

'Is there someone on the scene who might be sending *you* flowers?' asks Frankie.

'Me? Oh no, nothing like that,' I say, looking straight towards the supervisors' podium where Jake has just arrived looking obscenely handsome.

'Are you sure?' Frankie follows my gaze.

Does she know? Is it obvious?

'No, as usual, there's no one in my life,' I say. 'You got the last good man.'

'I got him ages ago and trained him up. You don't want to leave it too late otherwise you're left with all the bad boys who don't want to commit.' Frankie looks towards the podium again. 'And you can do a lot better than that.'

Frankie doesn't say another word. She's definitely onto me but she doesn't know Jake like I do. As she gathers up the flowers and walks away, I focus my attention on the other item left at my workstation: a pretty pink envelope with a picture of a stork saying, 'See you soon' on the back. Panicked, I look around. Who sent this? Who knows?

I tear open the envelope and pull out a card in a flurry of sparkles. It's an invitation to Missy's baby shower. Of course, she's due any day. I'd completely forgotten.

'Hi, Lizzie, you got the invitation?' Missy appears out of nowhere. 'Can you come? It's next Saturday. I know it's short notice but I've been so busy preparing everything for the baby, I almost forgot to organise a shower.'

To be honest, it's the last thing I feel like doing. Particularly considering my current predicament. I've been trying to avoid the baby part of pregnancy, but I see that life isn't going to let me.

I also have a problem with the whole baby-shower concept. It seems like it's just a convenient way for soon-to-be mums to acquire all the pointless stuff they've been told to buy in order to give their baby the best possible start in life.

And the games! I don't like party games at the best of times but from what Clem has told me, baby-shower games are the worst. Pin the Umbilical Cord on the Baby (I don't even know where it actually goes), Predict the Baby's Birth Weight (no idea, how heavy is a baby?), Give the Best Baby Impersonation (just embarrassing) and Pass the Nappy (sure, Clem said it was a clean one and the prize at the end was a sterling silver bracelet, but it just sounds wrong).

'I think so,' I say, trying to give the impression of consulting an imaginary and extremely full diary. It might be good for me to go. Maybe I'll learn a thing or two about what lies ahead.

'Great!' Missy seems relieved. Maybe she's worried no one will come.

'Do you mind if I bring a girlfriend?' I ask, deciding I need Clem by my side. 'You met her once. Clem? She's just broken up with her boyfriend. She needs the distraction.'

Missy is delighted with the idea. 'Bring anyone. Should be loads of fun.'

I doubt that very much but refrain from saying it. Instead, I ask about what baby tasks she has yet to complete.

'I have to wash all the baby clothes. Pack my bags for the hospital. There are still a few things I need to get for the big day, like orange oil for my oil burner and bendy straws. I need to stock up on groceries, do some cooking for the freezer – there won't be much time once bub arrives. I have to do my daily relaxation exercises and visualisation to get ready for the birth. At least I finally decided on which nappy bag to get, but I haven't got any nappies. I need to buy nappies!'

'Right.' I tune out. Missy sounds a little manic and is not making sense. Bendy straws? Why? And what's so important about a nappy bag? Surely any bag can hold a few nappies.

'When are you due?' I ask, before Missy works herself into a state of anxiety and has the baby on the spot.

'Two weeks on Wednesday.'

'Nervous?'

'Not at all. I feel so ready, I'm just dying to meet this little one.' She gives her enormous tummy an affectionate pat. Despite her stressful list of jobs, she looks happy. She really is glowing like pregnant women are supposed to. That's how a mum-to-be should feel. Not unsure and anxious while she tries to find the right time to spill the beans to the soon-to-be father. That would never be on Missy's list of things to do.

It shouldn't be on anyone's. But here I am, doing everything the wrong way around. I wasn't longing for a child like Missy was. It just happened. And unfortunately, it happened before the relationship part. Now I'm pedalling at a furious rate to catch up and I don't know if I can. It certainly isn't what I envisaged. But maybe I, too, will miraculously transform into a Missy-style mum-to-be, preparing hospital bags and buying nappies. You never know, it could happen. And I just hope with all my heart that Jake is by my side when it does.

7

After what can only be described as a shocker of a day, during which I sold even less wine than my last shift and barely spoke to Jake, I make my way to a little bar not far from work where Clem and I meet for our catch-ups. Clem is there waiting, looking a little happier than last time we spoke. She has already ordered me a white wine, which I will have to pretend to drink.

'Hi,' she says brightly, while picking up on my negative vibes. 'What's wrong with you?'

'Jake ignored me all day at work and when he finally spoke to me, it was only to tell me that my sales had dropped.' I don't mean to start straight in on my problems but they just pop out. When I see Clem's face I immediately feel guilty.

'Can we not talk about your non-existent relationship for one single night?'

'Sorry, Clem,' I say, resolving to focus on the fact that Clem is the one who needs my support right now, not the other way around. 'But it's not exactly non-existent,' I can't help but add. 'The other night we met for a drink and went home together, so I think we can start calling it a relationship, don't you?'

'Hang on a minute! Did *he* ask *you* for a drink?' Clem's razor-sharp ears detect a hole in my story.

'No.' I hesitate, knowing exactly what's coming. 'I asked him.'

'Lizzie!'

'It was a group of people from work. We were having a drink after a shift and I asked him along.'

'So, it wasn't a date.'

'Not exactly.'

'Did you end up at his place or yours?'

'His. He invited me without prompting and was really sweet in the morning. Even made me a coffee,' I said smugly.

'Wow! Maybe you should have his baby!'

'What?' I almost fall off my stool before I detect her sarcasm.

'A coffee isn't much. Don't get excited about a coffee. He needs to do more than that.'

'Have you heard from Mal?' I ask, changing the subject to avoid a lecture on what constitutes acceptable post-sex behaviour. And the baby comment was a little too close to home.

'As a matter of fact, I have.'

'What happened?'

Apparently, last night at about eleven, Mal texted Clem saying how much he missed her and could he come over. Even I know a text like that, at that time, only leads to trouble. Not that I'm one to talk. I've sent one too many of those texts myself.

And I've responded inappropriately to more than I like to admit. Naturally, I assume that Clem said no.

'I said yes.' Clem smiles proudly.

I'm momentarily impressed. Clem never diverges from her set of rules. I think she even takes her rulebook to bed with her every night for a quick study to ensure she hasn't slipped up.

'That's unlike you. What's going on?'

'I think he's really missing me. And, Lizzie, the sex was *amazing*!'

Clem is always saying that her sex with Mal is 'amazing'. I wonder what they do that makes it so great? As she continues talking about their night in intimate detail, my mind wanders to the sex I've had with Jake. I was drunk the first time and preoccupied with being pregnant the second, so I have no idea if it was good, bad or indifferent, let alone amazing. I shove this thought into my brain's too-hard basket. Jake is the sexiest guy I've ever slept with so I'm sure the sex is totally great. I force my attention back to what Clem is saying.

'Anyway, I think he might want to get back together.'

'Did he say that?'

'No, but I know Mal. He wouldn't have come over if it hadn't meant something.'

According to Clem, they didn't need to talk, as they were obviously thinking exactly the same thing. I nod encouragingly, sincerely doubting that Mal was thinking any of the same things as Clem last night.

I desperately want to tell her again to forget about Mal. He's just not good enough for my amazing friend but she can't see it. And what about my news? I would love to talk it all through and

I feel bad for not telling her, but the timing is terrible. I know Clem would be happy for me, but I imagine there'd be nothing worse than seeing your friend in love (and pregnant) when your own relationship is so fragile.

'So, when are you seeing him again?' I ask.

'Not sure, we haven't made any definite arrangements. I don't want to rush him. He'll probably call later.'

'Sure. Sounds good.'

I don't think it sounds good at all. Mal probably has no intention of getting back with Clem. But who am I to give advice? At least the sex Clem had last night was 'amazing', so she's one step ahead of me there. And she's not up the duff. So two steps, in fact.

After finishing our drinks (and by 'finishing our drinks', I mean that Clem drank hers and the pot plant next to me drank mine while Clem was checking her phone), Clem and I go our separate ways home. As I walk, I decide to ask Jake on a proper date. Not a drunken hook-up, but dinner complete with conversation. I know his birthday is coming up, so that could provide the opportunity. Okay, I confess, I was going through his file, trying to absorb as much personal information as is legally permitted in the workplace, but all I learnt was the date of his birthday. Not all that useful, apart from revealing his star sign – Scorpio, which is a bit of a worry. Never had much luck with them. But that's about to change.

I check my watch. It's only a quarter to nine so I call his mobile. There's no answer and it goes to voicemail, so I leave a message asking him to give me a ring. Well, that's a start, anyway.

By the time I get home, I feel completely washed out. I can hardly keep my eyes open and I'm only six weeks pregnant.

How am I going to last nine months, let alone motherhood, if I can't even stay awake now? All I want to do is get into my comfy PJs, get under my doona and . . .

My phone dings at me. A text.

Hey babe wanna come over?

Jake! I look longingly at my cosy bed, but I know in two minutes, I'll be jumping into my car and driving to his house as fast as I can. I know me and it's inevitable. Still, as planned, I attempt to play a little bit hard to get. Something I'm having trouble doing in person, so I might have better luck via text.

Why?

That'll challenge him. My phone dings right back.

Think you know sexy lady.

I try again. *Do I?*

So does he. *Don't you?*

This is ridiculous. What exactly am I trying to achieve? I give in. *Pretty sure I do. See you soon.*

I throw on some clothes. Not too dressed up. I try to look casual but cool. How Frankie might look in this situation. Actually, Frankie is married so would never be in this situation. But if she were, she would look effortlessly stylish. All I can find in the mess on my floor are my trackie pants, gym top and trainers. But I do stumble upon my best sexy underwear in a drawer, sulking and unloved, so I pop that on too. Can't hurt.

I'm at Jake's place approximately fourteen minutes after his first text arrived. A record. I knock on the door and almost immediately Jake appears, looking delicious in nothing but a pair of boxer shorts. I want to jump on him immediately but I attempt a little restraint.

'Hey, gorgeous,' he says in his deep, husky voice that sends shivers right through me to my sneaker-clad toes.

'Hi,' I say casually, determined to maintain a little distance between us. 'How's it going?'

But Jake's not listening. He starts kissing me in the hallway and within seconds, my top is off. Fast work. He's not bothered about showing restraint. The sexy bra is tossed aside without so much as an appreciative comment. I guess it's what's inside that counts. And what's inside is exploding every time he touches it.

'How was work?' I persist with a little light conversation, but it's to no end. Who am I kidding? The desire to get as close as possible to Jake's magnificently defined chest is far greater than my need to hold back and chat.

Still kissing, we clamber to his bedroom, knocking over a lamp along the way. Somehow, I whack my elbow on a chest of drawers, which really hurts, but is a small sacrifice to make. My trackie pants are off and before I know what's what, I'm flat on my back on Jake's bed. Why bother slowing things down? He's so incredibly hot and such an awesome kisser. I don't want to go slow. I don't want to talk. I just want to feel those big muscly arms all over my body, which are prompting a tropical storm deep down where I didn't think a pregnant woman should be feeling anything at all. This is incredible! Now I know what Clem is talking about, this is AMAZ–

Then it's over. For him.

'Wow, babe, that was incredible.' Jake closes his eyes and lets out an almost immediate and very gentle snore.

Right. Well. Was that good? Of course it was. It was wild and crazy. He's probably tired. But unfortunately I'm wide awake.

Sex does that to me. Especially if I don't quite get to the finishing line. I rub my leg against his to see if he's up for a bit more action, but it doesn't seem that he is.

'Hey, Jake,' I whisper in my most sexy-sounding voice, which is obviously not that sexy as there's no response.

Damn! I didn't organise a date. That was the point of my phone call. But maybe we've already become that relaxed, laidback kind of couple that doesn't need to date? Some people just get into it, without all that running around, wondering what's going on, does he like me, will he ask me out? Dating is completely overrated, if you ask me. Except I can't ignore the niggling feeling that, with Jake, I'm still running around, wondering what's going on, if he likes me and if he'll ever ask me out. It's like I have all the stress of dating without any dates. Not so much as a box of takeaway noodles, let alone dinner in a nice restaurant.

Normally, I wouldn't mind a fast and furious casual encounter, apart from the bit where I banged my elbow and also pulled a calf muscle somewhere down the hall, but if I'm honest, it felt a little empty and unsatisfying. Not just physically but emotionally. I don't know what it is, but for the first time in my life, I'm starting to want something more. Maybe it's the thought of becoming a mother or the fact that I really like Jake, but this time I want a proper relationship. Something real, loving and long lasting. I've always wanted to fall in love, there's no doubt about that. And I've always put in considerable energy and effort to do so. But for what? I've never found anyone to share my life with, let alone a baby. I'm certainly attracted to Jake and feel like we really connect, but am I special to him? Or is there a list of girls like me who he calls up when he's feeling amorous? Maybe I'm not even on the top of the list. What if I'm halfway down and all the others before me were simply unavailable?

Flickers of doubt sneak into my brain, but I push them away and focus on the passion between us as we ripped each other's clothes off. Okay, the sex was fleeting, but it was fiery. He doesn't know about the baby so, as far as he's concerned, we're still in that crazy beginning phase which is all sex and fun. But I'm ready to fast-track to the next stage.

Lying in the darkness, trying to block out Jake's increasingly train-like snoring, I think about Clem's recent encounter with Mal. She would never normally do that and now I can see why. Mal doesn't want her back. She was simply available and familiar. As I have been with Jake. Well, not anymore. Absolutely no more sex until I get a date. Time is running out: I will have to tell him about the baby soon, and I need him to fall madly in love with me before that happens.

Eventually, I fall asleep, and when we wake up in the morning, we have sex again. Whoops! So much for my midnight resolution. I mentally adjust the start time on that to today. Jake seems to have benefitted from a good sleep because this session lasts considerably longer. In fact, he's so energetic, it's more like a cross-training session at the gym with a buzzer every two minutes to change exercise. At least I have a chance to fully appreciate his outrageously chiselled abdomen, among his many other mind-blowing features. All in all, a satisfying (if somewhat exhausting) experience.

Apart from feeling like I'm going to throw up over him at any minute. I'm totally over this morning sickness. It's not going to be a good look if I'm always running off to the bathroom to vomit. But then I guess most pregnant women aren't trying to seduce the father of their unborn child. They probably sleep in while their devoted husbands get up to prepare a nice cup of peppermint tea and a bite of Vegemite toast. Yes! That's exactly what I feel like! White toast with Vegemite and the crusts cut off.

'I need toast!' I blurt out.

'Um, don't think there's any bread. Coffee?'

That's the last thing I feel like.

'Have you got any herbal tea, maybe peppermint?' I never drink peppermint tea but suddenly the thought of it is comforting.

'Nah, sorry.'

'Never mind.' I try to lie still to ease my nauseous stomach. 'You working today?'

'Yep, better get ready. You?'

I nod. 'Not till two. Do you want to get some breakfast? I'm starving.' I'm not exactly what I would normally classify as starving, but I need something in my tummy before I puke all over Jake's soft and creamy cotton sheets.

'I start at eight, so better go straight there. Stay in bed if you want.'

He ambles off to the shower. I'm actually thrilled to be staying in Jake's bed once again. I belong here. Plus things seem better in my stomach if I don't move too much.

In no time at all, Jake is ready to leave, looking like he has just jumped off a shoot for a sexy men's aftershave, which is annoying because I won't be able to admire him from afar until I get to work.

'Stay as long as you like. Just pull the door –'

'– Behind me when I leave. Yeah, I know.' I can't believe I'm already finishing his sentences. We're like an old married couple. I pause and take a deep breath and ask what I came over to ask.

'Hey, isn't it your birthday soon? What day is it?' I know full well it's this Friday.

'This Friday, why?' He leans in and kisses me slowly on the lips. My stomach does a backflip and I don't think it's because there's a baby in there. I take a deep breath. Stay focused, Lizzie.

'Why don't I take you out to dinner?'

'Yeah, sure, why not?' he says distractedly. 'Man, you look hot in my bed. Gonna think about that all day.'

He gives me another quick pash and with that, unfortunately, he's out the door.

I did it. We're going on a date. Hooray. I want to do a mini victory dance, but I don't think my stomach is up for it. I snuggle back down under his doona, which smells divine, just like him.

It's all going to work out. I have a really good feeling about Jake. Not that my feelings are always reliable. But this is different. He's already attracted to me. Surely an intimate birthday dinner will clinch the deal. He'll be in love with me by the time our mains arrive. And hopefully he'll be more than ready for a baby by dessert. Okay, that's a bit far-fetched; even I know it's going to take a little longer than one dinner date. But it's a step in the right direction, isn't it? And I'm running out of time. So the faster I convince Jake that I'm the love of his life, the more chance I have of achieving the happy ending I really deserve.

8

I finally tear myself away from Jake's bed, go home and call Clem.

After I'd had a look around his room. And nearly pocketed a tub of hair product that smelled glorious like him. I just wanted to keep a little bit of Jake close to me all day. But then I thought that might be a bit weird, as he would definitely notice if his hair product was missing (he wears rather a lot) and having been the last one (surely?) in his flat, I didn't want to have to do any explaining. In the end, I thought I'd leave something behind instead, and decided on my undies. For two very good reasons:

1. He would find them and remember our night together, fondly, I'm hoping.
2. He would have to return them to me, so we would have to arrange another meeting. But since we've already arranged a meeting, it would give me an excuse to go back to his place and 'pick them up'.

Not nearly as weird as swiping his hair product. I'm making real progress in the laidback man-chasing department.

Clem's voice breaks me out of my reverie. 'I can't talk right now, Lizzie. What's up?'

I'm surprised I actually get to speak with Clem. During work hours, her mobile always goes through to her assistant who doesn't really like me. Her name is Zoe and she always finds an excuse to not put me through, such as Clem has 'just popped out of the office' or has 'gone into a meeting'. I know I call a lot, but there's no need to lie, or be so happy about it. She's like a protective mother who's worried her daughter is being led astray by a bad boy. Or a high-level security guard, watching over the *Mona Lisa* (Clem) for fear a random art thief (me) might happen by. Maybe she's jealous because I'm a better friend of Clem's than she is, and always will be. Whatever the reason, her behaviour is completely over the top. Once Clem and I were meeting for lunch and I rang to confirm the time and café.

'Clem's unavailable, Lizzie. Can I take a message?'

I asked if she could let Clem know to meet me at our usual café at twelve-thirty.

'Sure, no problem,' she said, sounding like it was the biggest problem she'd ever encountered.

Of course Clem never got the message and I was left waiting at the café. As she hadn't heard from me, Clem just thought lunch was off. I tried to tell her about Zoe's obsessive behaviour, how she was trying to come between us. Clem told me I was imagining it.

But I know the truth. And Zoe knows that I know.

Determined to get through today, I resorted to an accent, which was supposed to be Yorkshire until it morphed into some strain of cockney. Accents are not my strong suit but it did the trick and Zoe, unwittingly, put me straight through.

'I have a date with Jake. On his birthday.'

'Oh good,' says Clem distractedly. 'Did he ask you?'

'Well . . . yes, he did.'

'That's great.' Clem sounds mildly impressed. 'I have to go, but I'll call you when I've finished. I need more details.'

Clem hangs up before I can properly explain, not that there is anything to explain. I just told an out-and-out lie. Except Jake *did* ask me over last night, so that was really like a first date. Or second, if you count the Street Date. Surely I'm allowed to instigate another date by now? Especially as it's his birthday. Why should a guy do all the asking, anyway? Jake didn't have to say yes. He could have made up an excuse if he didn't want to go. But he said yes. Straightaway. He didn't even have to think about it. I believe my arguments would stand up in court, but I sigh inwardly, knowing it would take more than that to persuade the tough lawyer in Clem. I didn't want to get into that with her over the phone, so I lied. Sometimes, it's better that way.

I have only a few days to prepare and I don't think I can do it alone. Clem seems too busy, so I pick up the phone and call in the big guns.

'Hi, Mum.'

'Darling, what's wrong?'

'Nothing's wrong.' Mum thinks I only call when something's wrong, which is sort of true, but beside the point. 'I'm working this afternoon, but thought I might go shopping now for a new outfit. Do you feel like coming, maybe get a coffee?'

'Love to!'

'Okay, do you want to meet at Westfield at ten? Maybe at that café you love so much, down near the food court?'

'Yes, great idea. They give a discount for seniors.'

'I know. Ten per cent. So worth it!'

'It is! I also like their coffee, and do you know –'

'See you then, Mum!' I say cheerily, cutting off the conversation before it turns into a full-scale diatribe about how no one makes a decent coffee these days yet they charge as though it were liquid gold.

Mum is always good for a shopping expedition. Not that we always agree on everything, but she has a good eye and is enthusiastic. And when she knows it's for a date, she won't be able to contain herself. She'll probably want to start looking at wedding gowns.

*

When I arrive at the café, Mum is already there, seated at her favourite table, her seniors' card in hand.

'You tell me what you want and I'll buy it with my seniors' card,' she says in a hushed voice, as if we're embarking on some sort of covert operation despite the fact that the entire place is overrun with seniors and their magical cards.

What's funny is that Mum doesn't think she's old nor does she behave like she is – except when it comes to seniors' discounts or cheap travel on public transport. She goes up to the counter and orders two flat whites and some banana bread, proudly showing her card as she pays and then sits back down.

'Do you know it only cost me two dollars fifty for my bus ticket and I can use it all day?'

'Yes, I know, Mum, that's great.'

It's not that Mum and Dad are hard up. In fact, it's quite the opposite; they're more than comfortable. But they both love a bargain. Dad is always entering competitions to win stuff and so far has managed tickets to the cricket in Melbourne, a television, a microwave and an overseas holiday. Whereas Mum just uses public transport. All the time. Even if she doesn't need to. As far as she's concerned, if you have to get older, you may as well get what you can out of it. And if she can save a couple of bucks by hopping on several buses around town and taking two hours longer to arrive somewhere she didn't really want to go in the first place, then she's going to give it a whirl.

'What's going on?' Mum asks suspiciously. 'You don't often ask for my assistance buying clothes. You always know exactly what you like. Not that I mind, it's lovely to see you.'

'I'm going out to dinner with Jake on Friday and I need a new outfit. I really like him and I have to look totally gorgeous, so I thought a second opinion might be helpful.'

'Oh, darling, you could wear a paper bag and look fabulous,' says Mum, supportive as always. 'You're absolutely beautiful and he'd be lucky to have you.'

I know Mum means well, but it will definitely take more than a paper bag to seal the deal with Jake.

We finish our coffees and make our way through the Westfield maze, eyes peeled for the perfect fall-in-love-with-me outfit. Unfortunately, nothing stands out. Even Mum agrees that the selection is far from enticing. It's always the way. When you want something specific, you can never find it. Yet if you're just randomly strolling through the shops on your way to work, not needing any new clothes, you see nothing but must-have items. But not today.

'Look at this.' Mum picks up a shift dress off a rack in David Jones. 'So badly made! And the price tag – three hundred and forty dollars! Unbelievable. You could make something far better than that.'

'I haven't sewn anything in ages. Not since, well, you know . . .' Not since that disastrous summer after college. I look a little closer at the dress in Mum's hand. It really is badly made. And boring. I wouldn't wear it if you paid me three hundred and forty dollars. I turn over the label, and to my surprise, I recognise the name of a woman who was in my year. Jainee Johns. Or JJ as she used to be called. I can't believe she has her own label, in a major department store. She was no more talented than me. Just a lot more confident in her abilities. She never doubted herself for a minute. In fact, she probably called David Jones in her calm, confident voice and insisted they take her pieces. Which they clearly had. That's why it happened for her and not me. But then I look at the elegant design on the label. Maybe Jainee took it step by step rather than naively renting a shop and expecting instant success. Maybe she thought things through a little more. Did her research and took her time. I guess slow and steady does win the race after all.

'You should get back into it. You could do better than anything we've seen today,' says Mum. 'I always loved your outfits back in high school – so creative and individual.'

Mum's right. When I was at school, I made all my own clothes. At fourteen, my grandmother's Baby Elna sewing machine had turned up at my bedroom door. Nana's eyes had deteriorated so badly, she finally gave up sewing and gave her machine to me. I wasn't too sure about the sewing machine at first, but I soon learnt its magic, spending many hours whipping up all manner of creations, courtesy of *Vogue* or *McCall* paper patterns. Most girls were shopping at Sportsgirl or Dotti while I was doing my own thing and loving it. Until I made an outfit for the Year 10 formal, which was an absolute disaster. Not the outfit – that was amazing. But a few girls, led by mean queen Tiffany Simpson, hadn't agreed.

Tall, blonde, with legs starting somewhere in her armpits, Tiffany Simpson had been top dog since the start of Year 7. Everyone looked to her for the latest trend. How to dress. What to think. Who was cool, and who wasn't. She was a total bitch and never liked me, but I didn't care. Clem and I kept out of her way, but my sewing creations became a source of constant entertainment for her and her razor-sharp tongue.

After inheriting my nana's sewing machine, I chose textiles as my elective and I loved it. My teacher, Miss Wilton, was fantastic. She was young, hip and inspiring, and encouraged me to really push myself and my creativity in all sorts of wacky directions. Then we had to create a final assessment piece and I decided to make something awesome to wear to the end-of-year formal. The only sorts of formal dresses I'd ever seen looked like fluoro taffeta pompoms. But mine was going to be different.

The end result was better than I could ever have imagined. It was a long maxi pantsuit in a stunning floaty fabric, with a sash around the waist, a plunging neckline and full flowing pant legs that looked like a skirt. It was classic in style, yet the black-and-white zigzagged fabric was so chic and contemporary. Back then, no one wore pantsuits, but I'd seen a '70s retro-style photo shoot while poring over fashion magazines and I was captivated. I chanced upon a great pair of yellow pumps at Vinnies that contrasted beautifully and my outfit was complete. But the very moment I walked into the hall I felt self-conscious under the critical gaze of Tiffany and her crew. Then half an hour later, I went to the toilet and my night was totally ruined.

'What is Lizzie wearing?' I overheard Tiffany scoff from the cubicle next to mine.

'No idea, does she think it's a fancy-dress party?' replied one of her followers.

'She never wears anything normal, so what'd you expect?' said another.

I sat frozen in the cubicle for ages, waiting for them to leave. And if that wasn't bad enough, I came out of the toilets to find my date – a boy I had a huge crush on – laughing with Tiffany Simpson, and I just knew they were talking about my outfit. I'd never felt so mortified in my life. Actually, falling off the wheelie bin the other night was pretty bad, but at least the whole of Year 10 hadn't been there to see me. This had felt like I was a piece of garlic in a garlic crusher, squeezed out in bits and then discarded because it wasn't actually needed in the recipe.

I ran back to the safety of the toilet cubicle and wept all down the front of my stupid pantsuit. Clem did her best to coax me out, but to no avail. Humiliated beyond repair, I wanted to leave. Eventually, I got Clem to call my mum, who arrived in a flash, didn't ask any questions (Clem probably gave her a run-down) and took me to McDonald's. One of those chocolate sundaes was a massive treat in those days, but that night, it did little to ease my devastation.

Of course, nothing happened between me and that guy – and about a week later he was going out with Tiffany, breaking both my heart and creative spirit in one fell swoop. And I've had little success in fixing either ever since. It was a shame. Not the guy – he turned out to be an idiot. But that outfit was probably the most original thing I've ever made. Mum always said that it should have been on a *Vogue* cover, but thanks to mean Tiffany, I momentarily lost faith in my ideas and ability.

Later on, after I'd finished my Arts degree, Mum was cleaning out the attic and found that pantsuit. All those years later, it was still spectacular. The Year 10 formal instantly flashed through my mind, but it all seemed so long ago at that point. I didn't even know where Tiffany Simpson was anymore, but I did hear through Clem (who knows everything about everyone) that she'd recently been fired from her job. Clearly, she was not the success everyone thought she'd be.

Seeing that outfit again had been like a revelation, though, and I'd known it was time to finally follow my dream and study fashion design. Except it was hard. And people looked at my work as critically as those bitches at school, which made me feel self-conscious. I felt that my ideas were never as exciting to other people as they were to me. Don't get me wrong, not everyone at college was as conservative and narrow-minded as the girls at high school. And, thinking back, most of them were only trying to push me further with constructive criticism. But somehow, my experience with Tiffany Simpson had had such a detrimental effect, I'd lost my courage to be daring. To follow my instincts. At school, Miss Wilton had thought I was a genius, but at college, my final year major works were received with only a lukewarm reception. Still,

I kept going, determined to make a name for myself. Determined to stand out. Except I was in too much of a hurry to do so, and didn't stop to think about what I was actually creating – and why I was creating it. I was driven by all the wrong motivations and as a result, nothing I made was original or different. After college, when my clothes-making venture failed dismally, I was thrown into a world of debt and self-doubt. I couldn't see my way out. I told Clem that I was over it, but that wasn't entirely true. I'd wanted so much for it to happen, but I just couldn't get there. It was easier to walk away. And lately, all my energy has been focused on selling cases of wine and chasing boys. Right now, especially considering my current predicament, I have little time for anything else.

In the end, Mum and I agree on a beautiful slinky top in a silvery-grey with skinny black jeans. My black patent-leather pumps at home will complete the picture. I look in the mirror, pleased with what I see. Casual. Sexy. And just a little bit rock-star. Perfect for Jake. He won't be able to keep his hands off me. Besides, in a couple of months I most certainly won't be wearing any skinny jeans. Or slinky tops. At least not in the size I'm trying on now.

'Darling, you look absolutely stunning. So stylish, and those jeans really suit your lovely long legs. I hope you have a great night.'

Mum gives me a hug.

'Thanks for your help, Mum.' I feel a little teary. It's been a while since we've had such a nice morning together. I should make more time for Mum. She's always there when I need her, and it can't be easy having a daughter like me. I haven't exactly been a huge success, what with my flailing career and lack of babies.

She can be pushy when it comes to how I should live my life, but I know that deep down, it's because she worries about me and wants me to be happy. I shouldn't be so impatient when she offers her ideas or advice. She always looks at the brighter side of my murky life, and has kept me going through the tough times. Times that occur more often than I like to admit.

What if I end up with a daughter like me? My God, I never thought of that. Will I be as supportive of her as Mum is of me? Will my daughter want to meet me at Westfield to go shopping for clothes? I hope I can be there for her when she needs me, like Mum is. I know that's what mothers do, but will I be able to tolerate my daughter when she's thirty, single and not particularly receptive to my advice?

I push my anxious thoughts to the depths of my brain. I'm doing that a lot lately. It's getting pretty crowded back there. I'd better be careful or it might burst, with my dilemmas splattering everywhere for all to see.

We say goodbye and I watch Mum scurry off in the direction of the bus stop. She probably has a few journeys mapped out for the day and doesn't want to get behind schedule. It's nearly two, so I need to go to work. Then I'd better make a list, there's a lot to prepare for the big night and everything has to be perfect. I have to say, I've never felt quite so positive about a guy before. And not just because I'm carrying his baby. My tummy flutters at the mere thought of him and since I can't think of anything else, it's like I've swallowed a butterfly farm. This is what it must be like to be in love. Really in love. Jake is definitely the one for me, and fingers crossed I can make his birthday so amazing that he realises I'm the one for him too.

9

After what must have been the weirdest week on record, Jake's birthday arrives. I drag myself out of bed early to organise everything before work, despite feeling like I'm going to hurl at any minute. I couldn't possibly bake a cake, since any food first thing in the morning smells disgusting, so yesterday I ordered one from the bakery down the road. It's a chocolate mud cake with 'Happy Birthday Jake' iced on it. I don't start work until eleven so I have time to pick it up and deliver it to the restaurant before my shift. I've planned everything perfectly.

I'm somewhat obsessed with birthdays. My own birthday usually turns into a week-long Lizzie-fest, full of lunches, breakfasts and dinner dates with anyone who's remotely interested.

But it's not just my birthday I love. Celebrating other people's birthdays comes a close second, and I want this one to be memorable – so memorable, in fact, that it makes Jake realise how lucky he is to have such a caring girlfriend, not to mention such an incredibly sexy and attractive one. But I guess he knows that already.

Jake isn't working today so I already texted him this morning, then called and left a message on his voicemail. He must have been in the shower. It was good to hear his voice, even if it was a recorded message, as he hasn't called or texted since I was at his place. Surprising considering our last encounter. And he's been caught up in manager meetings for the last few days, so I haven't seen him at work. The poor guy has been so busy, he probably hasn't had a chance to pick up the phone.

After dropping Jake's cake in at the restaurant, I arrive at the call centre feeling excited about the night ahead. I plonk my bag down at my workstation and Nathan wanders over, eyeing me suspiciously.

'You're dressed up today, Lizzie. What's going on?'

'Nothing. Can't a girl dress up for work?'

'Sure, but you look different.'

Nathan has this supersonic intuition that always seems to pick up on exactly whatever I'm trying to hide. Very annoying. He's like a male version of Clem.

'I'm no more dressed up than usual. I just bought this top recently and I wanted to wear it. Is that okay?'

'Sure, yeah, it's a great top – you going on a date?'

'No!' I say, flustered. Honestly, how does he get that from a new top? I must be as open as a display book in a public library. 'Well, yes, actually, but it's no one you know.'

'Is it Jake?'

'What? No! Not Jake, why would it be him? I barely know him. Why would you ask me that?'

Honestly, he has some sort of sixth, seventh, even eighth sense, and always homes in on the subjects about which I'm most vulnerable.

This is probably a situation where the less I say the better, but I'm in such a spin, I babble on nervously, so much so that if Nathan only suspected I'm going out with Jake, now he knows for sure.

'He's not my type anyway, and if he was, which he's so not, I would never date a supervisor. Jake! Ha! As if!'

'Are you guys logging on to your computers?' Steve interrupts our little tête-á-tête. 'Technically, the shift started fifteen minutes ago.'

'Sorry, Steve,' I say as sweetly as I can, glaring at Nathan.

'And, Lizzie, you know the policy about jeans,' says Steve. 'We'll leave it for now, but next time, I'll have to send you home. If someone from upstairs comes down and sees you dressed like that, it's me who gets into trouble.'

'Sorry, I forgot. Won't happen again.'

I certainly do know about their ridiculous policy on jeans. Because it's so important when you're talking to someone on the phone that you're dressed correctly! They might look down the phone, see a pair of jeans and think, *Oh my goodness, how can I possibly buy wine from that girl in those jeans, far too casual for a workplace.*

Anyway, today I couldn't care less. It's imperative I look as hot as humanly possible for my date. Everything is riding on tonight. Plus, I need to get as much wear out of these clothes as I can before I become a beach ball and can't wear them again for goodness knows how long. (When will I get my body back? Better google that.)

I try texting Jake again but there's no response until around lunchtime, when my phone finally dings back.

Friends are taking me out for lunch. See you later?

I text back immediately because I think I can do that by now, without looking desperate. *For sure! See you at 7 pm. Have fun xxx*

I can now also put kisses in a text message. It's such a relief to get to a more comfortable and familiar stage of a relationship.

I amble through the shift, not really concentrating on selling wine as my mind keeps drifting to the evening I'll be sharing with Jake. If tonight goes well, I will definitely tell him about the baby.

I call Jake around four to see how he's going. He picks up, but it's so noisy in the background, I can hardly hear him.

'Hi,' I say as loudly as I can get away with, when I'm supposed to be selling wine.

'Hello, who's this?'

'It's me!'

'Sorry?'

'Lizzie. It's Lizzie!'

'Oh right, hey, babe.'

'Where are you?'

'Still with friends. Having a blast.'

My heart sinks a little. I'm happy he's happy on his birthday, but I can't help feeling left out. I suggest I come and meet him, but apparently they're leaving soon.

'You still feel like dinner?' I say, trying to sound casual.

'Sure.'

'Great, see you there at seven. I'm really looking forward to –'

He hangs up before I can finish. A voice in my head, the one that sounds a bit like Clem and my mother rolled into one – the one I usually ignore except that lately it's been so vocal it's hard not to sit up and pay attention – is telling me I should go and meet him wherever he is, be introduced to his friends. If I'm his girlfriend, why wouldn't he want that? But I firmly tell the voice to be quiet, and that it doesn't know what it's talking about.

The rest of the shift drags like the last hour of a long-haul flight, but to my surprise I sell thirty-two cases of wine, an improvement on my last few shifts. Thank goodness. I was beginning to think I'd lost my touch. On the dot of seven, I log out of my computer and bolt out the door. For once the lift is there. A sign! The doors finally open on the ground floor and I sprint out of the foyer straight across the road to the restaurant.

Panting slightly, I arrive at 7.02 pm. No sign of Jake. I try to catch my breath. I shouldn't be running in my condition, but maybe once I have the father of my child sorted, I won't need to.

I choose a stool up at the bar rather than going straight to the table. I tell the waiter that I'm waiting for my boyfriend, which makes me smile on the inside. Butterflies jostle in my tummy at the thought of him walking in any minute looking devastatingly handsome, but that could just be hunger pains. Or the baby. Or both?

I order a glass of mineral water and scroll through my phone for a while before eventually checking the time.

7.40 pm.

Right, he's late. That's okay. Probably lots of traffic. The barman asks if I want another drink. I'm about to decline, but it would look strange sitting at a bar and not drinking, so I agree to another, even though it'll just speed up my need for the bathroom. I'll just sit on it. I won't even drink it.

8.05 pm.

I realise I'm starving, and it's making me nauseous. I see a big fat steak go by and it takes all my willpower not to jump up, grab it off the plate and rip straight into it.

The waiter shows me to my table, double-checking if I still need a setting for two.

'Yes, of course,' I fire back. Okay, I'm definitely feeling 'hangry'. I check my phone again. Nothing. Not even a text to say he's running late. Maybe he hasn't got his phone? Maybe he left it wherever he had lunch in his hurry to come and meet me? Or forgot to charge it and it's gone flat? Maybe his fingers are broken and he can't dial or even text . . .

I look at the door for the millionth time and a cute couple walks in. I sigh. I wish that was me, arriving with my boyfriend. They look so happy. He has his arm around her and he –

Wait. The couple turns to face me and I get the surprise of my life. The guy half of the equation is Mal! Clem's no-good ex-boyfriend, who she thinks wants to get back together with her. I have to tell Clem, but she won't believe me for a second. She'll think I'm making it up because I don't like Mal. But here he is, looking very much like one half of a happy couple – a new couple that's excited to be together. A couple that does not include Clem. I see him lean in and give his date a very gentle kiss on the lips.

Should I confront him? I don't want to make a scene, so I grab my phone and very subtly take a picture. At least I have evidence. Clem has to believe that. I then turn my back on them and try to blend into the decor.

The waiter asks in a loud voice if I'm ready to order. I shake my head and try to explain that my partner (sounds more definite than boyfriend) is running late.

'I can't hold the table much longer. It's a busy night,' he says haughtily. 'And I believe you have a cake in the coolroom?'

People are looking over, but luckily Mal is too enamoured of his lady friend to notice. I say firmly and very quietly to the waiter that I'm sure my life partner (again, sounds better) will be here any minute.

I watch the door like the future of the world depends on it, scared that Jake will arrive and not see me, then turn around and go back out. Surely he would look around before he left? Ask a waiter? What if he's been here the whole time and thinks I didn't turn up, so he left in a huff? Wouldn't he text me, though?

8.55 pm.

I'm gently asked to let the table go and move back to the bar, the cake discreetly placed at my side. The newly arrived diners wait patiently while the table is re-set, sympathetic smiles on their faces. They can obviously guess the whole story. Fabulous.

Now I'm not only starving, but my anxiety and longing have slowly given way to absolute fury. This doesn't feel like a good combo for a pregnant lady. How dare he be so late! How dare he not call! What's going on? Why am I sitting at a bar, alone and pregnant, minding a chocolate mud cake? Oh, that's right. Waiting for the father of my child to turn up. Yes, the one who's not here and who hasn't bothered to call.

I'm so angry now I can hardly think straight. My head feels woozy, but my heart is racing out of control and I can't get my breath. At least I'm actually sitting down, even if it's alone at a bar, otherwise I might have collapsed on the floor. Jake's behaviour might have been acceptable for the old Lizzie, the desperate-for-a-boyfriend Lizzie. But it's not anymore. Not for the all-new Lizzie, who wants more from a relationship than just casual fun. My eyes prickle and a tear runs down my cheek before I can stop it. I grab my phone to send him a text, which is difficult to manage because my jelly-like hands won't do as they're told.

Where are you?

I wait ten excruciating minutes. No response. I try again.

Where are you???

Three question marks should create a sense of urgency. But again, no response. I'm about to text for the third time when my phone finally, finally dings.

Sorry babe, went on to a party.

What? I can't believe what I'm reading. Is he mad? How could he have forgotten about dinner in only a couple of hours?

What about dinner?????

He responds quickly this time.

Sorry, got caught up. Wanna meet at yours?

Maybe it's the baby hormones, but something snaps inside my head. I can almost hear it crack like thunder as I furiously text back.

No!

It's all I can come up with. Not much. But I certainly don't want to see him right now. How dare he stand me up, and on his birthday? Lucky it's not *my* birthday or I'd be on my way over with the old school hockey stick that I keep behind my bedroom door for protection against burglars.

I clock Mal getting up out of his chair. Has he seen me? I definitely don't want him to know about my situation. Nor do I want him to know that I know he's cheating on Clem.

I stumble out of the bar as quickly as I can, clutching my cake, tears streaming down my face, and grab a taxi. There's one waiting. At least that's something.

'Hi there,' says a cheery female voice from the front seat. 'Where can I take you?'

I suddenly notice the red velvety surrounds, more like a late-night blues club than a Sydney cab. A gold lamé curtain is drawn back to reveal a glamorous female driver, maybe in her sixties. It's hard to tell exactly what her age is, with her bleached blonde hair cascading around a carefully made-up face of red lips and smoky black-rimmed eyes. She looks like she's just stepped off a red carpet or is off to the opera – and her taxi is equally impressive.

'So, where to, love?'

I'm about to tell her where I live when a loud and tragic sob tumbles out of my mouth. Even I'm surprised by its strength.

The sparkly-dressed driver looks at me with a concerned expression and hands over a box of tissues.

'Everything all right?'

'Yes thanks, fine!' I answer briskly, grabbing a tissue and wiping away my tears. 'Just. Fine!'

She looks even more concerned at this point. I don't blame her. Even I hear the wobbly edge in my voice.

'It's just . . . my boyfriend forgot our dinner date tonight.'

My driver raises her eyebrows without a word. She sees the cake box on my lap. I lift the lid and show her the cake complete with birthday message to emphasise the outrageousness of his behaviour.

'How about I take you home?'

I nod, crumbling into tears once more.

My taxi driver, whose name I discover is Cherie, has to be the nicest cabbie in the world and certainly the most upbeat and well dressed. And for a brief moment, she gets my mind off the disaster my life is becoming.

Turns out Cherie used to be a cabaret singer. Quite a famous one. Went by the name of Cherie L'Amour. Had a stellar career back in the day, made a few records and performed overseas. She finally retired from show business ten years ago and hasn't sung professionally since. She needed money, so started driving a cab.

'Not a bad job,' says Cherie brightly. 'Not as good as working on the stage, mind you. Nothing beats that. But showbiz is like a fickle lover. Sometimes it wants you and makes you feel great, then it rejects you and you're left with nothing. The minute you move on, it lures you back. But in the end, it didn't really want me back. Haven't sung properly in years. Sometimes I sing to my passengers. Some of them remember me from the good old days, even ask for my autograph. Tourists are the best, they really get into it and they always tip well.'

Cherie's tumultuous career path sounds like my love-life, only much more glamorous. But I'm sure she didn't expect to be belting out the odd number as she drove people to and from the airport. Just as I didn't think I'd be trying to find out why the father of my unborn child forgot to come on our first proper date.

'I'm pregnant,' I say out of nowhere. I don't know why I tell this to a complete stranger. I just feel like I need someone on my side, and for that they need to know the whole story.

'Really? And I'm guessing this guy is the father?'

I nod.

'No wonder you're acting so crazy, love.'

She gives me her card, saying if I ever need a cab to call her directly. My eyes are brimming with tears. Thank God Cherie picked me up. She's just what a girl needs when she's up the duff and has been stood up. I thank her and get out money to pay, which she refuses to take.

I let myself into my flat and my phone dings rather coyly.

Coffee tomorrow?

Is Jake out of his mind? Does he really think that we can meet for coffee after tonight? *Don't think so*, I reply.

He tries to call, but I hang up on him. Then I turn my phone off. And put it into a drawer, just in case I accidentally turn it back on in a moment of weakness. Which is not going to happen. I've never felt anything like this. Sure, I've been dumped once or twice – okay, quite a few times – but the place I'm in now feels totally new. Like a foreign country where nothing makes sense. Where I can't speak the language, I've run out of money and I don't know what to do. My world has been turned upside down and I just allowed it to happen.

I've never felt so angry and panicked in my entire life. Nor have I ever felt quite so hungry. Eyeing the box that I've just put on the table, I rip it open, grab handfuls of mud cake and stuff them into my mouth. One after the other, like I haven't eaten for days. It tastes fantastic for about two seconds, and then I feel completely nauseous. It's all too much. I feel sick, I feel fat and I feel unloved. I slump to the ground, chocolate all over my hands and face, and start to cry. Not just a silent weep, but a gut-wrenching howl from the pit of my stomach. My baby is probably trying to cover its little peanut ears to block out the noise.

I cry for everything. For my disastrous relationship, for all my disastrous relationships, for my non-existent career and for my unborn child, who is going to have an absent father and possibly the worst mother in the world! And the fattest, judging by the amount of cake I just inhaled.

I don't know what to do or think. When I finally pick myself off the floor, I have a long hot shower in an attempt to wash the failure out of my life, but despite my rigorous scrubbing, it lingers like a bad smell. Before now, I would have behaved very differently. I might have texted back, *Sure, let's have a coffee.* I might even have said, *Come over when you're finished at the party.* Or *I'll pick you up when you're ready. Will text when I'm outside.* I wouldn't have discussed the mishap for fear of causing trouble or being considered difficult. Or once again being dumped and all alone.

Is that really what I would have done? Do I really expect so little from the men I date? In the cold, hard light of this terrible evening, I can see that the answer is yes. It was like I lay on the ground, gave Jake some boots and said, 'Hey, walk all over me!' And gave no thought to how it made me feel.

And you know what?

It feels like shit.

I put on my pyjamas and climb into bed, wrapping my doona around me.

I have never really considered what I want from a relationship. Now, with the possibility of becoming a mother, I know I don't want a life with someone I can't trust. I don't care how hot Jake is, how sexy he is, how incredible his biceps are, particularly when wrapped around me, how his mouth crinkles up at the side when he's just about to . . . Lizzie! Stop it. No. I don't care what or who he is. He's not good enough, and I never want to see him again.

Except I will at work on Monday.

Damn!

10

I wake in the morning feeling groggy and sick to the stomach. I can barely open my eyes because of my state of pregnancy-induced exhaustion. Gently, I sit up and make my way to the bathroom, where I'm shocked by the grey reflection in the mirror. I look as bad as I feel. The thought of food makes me want to vomit, but I'm so starving I know I have to eat. I find an old packet of Sao crackers in the kitchen cupboard. They're a bit stale, but they do the trick. I sit in bed, gently sipping peppermint tea and nibbling a cracker, and slowly I start to feel a little more human.

I think back over the previous evening, reliving every painful moment. What do I do now? And what do I say to Clem? As well as the Jake catastrophe, the memory of Mal and his date elbows its way into my sleepy thoughts. That's a conversation I'm dreading but one I will have to have soon.

The ringing of my home phone makes me jump. That's probably Clem. I can't tell her about Mal over the phone. That news will have to wait. I take a deep breath and pick up.

'Did I wake you?'

Mum. Phew. 'No, I was already awake.'

'How'd it go last night?'

'Not so good.'

'Darling, what happened?'

'He got caught up, didn't make it.'

There's a pause while Mum takes this in.

'Are you sure you had a definite arrangement?' she asks, as tactfully as an elephant tiptoeing over eggshells. 'He was aware that he was supposed to be meeting you?'

'Of course. What are you saying? That I made it up?'

'Of course not, darling! But . . . occasionally, you do exaggerate a situation just a tad. Sometimes you think something is one thing when it's most definitely another. I'm just saying that if he knew about the date and never arrived, he's obviously not that keen.'

'Thanks, that makes me feel great.' I can always rely on Mum for a reality check.

'Sorry, but what do you want me to say? He's not good enough for you. You deserve more respect than that. He's definitely not The One. The One would turn up.'

Mum's absolutely right. Of course The One would turn up. It's something Clem would say. It's something any normal woman would say. But I don't seem to be normal because it's something I've never said. Until now, that is. I've always made excuses for bad boyfriend behaviour. One particular memory pops to the surface, making me cringe. This guy I was going out with came to pick me up for a date one night. It was raining so he texted from the car, saying I should just run out as he didn't want to get his suit wet. I didn't think anything of it at the time, but Clem was shocked.

'What's wrong with that?' I'd asked, genuinely surprised.

'He should have come to the door, *especially* if it was raining,' Clem said. 'And brought an umbrella to stop you from getting all wet.'

At the time, I thought Clem was being a little old-fashioned. Why should we both get wet? It was only a quick dash out to the street. But now I see that it would have been a kind and thoughtful thing to do. Especially as I actually got really wet. My hair went flat and I was uncomfortable all night.

Mum's right. I deserve more respect, and part of me wants to walk away from Jake with my head held high. But the other part reminds me that I have his baby inside, and I still don't know what to do about that.

'I have to go, sorry, Mum.' I'm well and truly over the conversation. And my life, for that matter.

'It was lovely to go shopping the other day, darling. Let's do it again soon.'

I hang up and make another herbal tea, unsure what to do next. Out of interest, I google Cherie and am amazed by what comes up. She really is famous! Or was. There are pictures of her singing to adoring crowds, hanging out with celebs, walking red carpets and generally looking fabulous. And last night she came to my rescue.

Last night.

Nausea swells in my tummy like a rising tide. Whether I tell Jake about the baby or not, he'll always be in my life. Or at least his baby will. Should I give him another chance? I swore last night I wouldn't, but now in the light of morning sickness, I realise it's not just about me anymore. I'm so angry about how he treated me, and if there was no baby, it would definitely be over. But there *is* a baby, and I need to start thinking about him or her and not just about myself.

As if on cue, my stomach lurches and I only just make it to the bathroom in time.

11

'Lizzie, you have to walk away.'

Clem rings straight after Mum to see how my night went, and she's furious. Almost ridiculously so. Probably because Mal hasn't called her since they last slept together, so she hates men altogether.

'He apologised,' I say. 'And just because we have one disastrous date doesn't mean he's a lost cause.' I don't know why I'm defending him, but Clem is taking it all so personally that I feel I need to be the voice of reason.

'That's exactly what it means!' shrieks Clem. 'If he can't turn up to a date, it shows exactly how he feels about you and your "relationship".'

I sigh. 'It's not that simple.'

'It's precisely that simple. You've given it a go. He's not up for it.'

'Clem –'

'When are you going to grow up and see that bad boys are not the answer? You're so desperate for a relationship, but you wouldn't know a decent guy if he got down on bended knee right in front of you and proposed. What's wrong with you? You're never going to be happy if you don't start expecting a certain standard of behaviour. If you believe people can treat you like that then they'll only ever treat you like that . . .'

Clem is on a tidal roll, like she's regurgitating every self-help book she's ever read while barely stopping to draw breath. She's never confronted me quite so forcefully, but I can see now that there's some truth in what she's saying. Jake's behaviour last night was unacceptable. I deserve someone who turns up for a date. But I can't go there right now, because of one very small, peanut-like reason.

'I'm pregnant!' I scream at the phone. Clem's volcanic babbling stops mid-sentence.

'What?'

'I'm up the duff. Jake's the father. He doesn't know yet but I'm hoping he'll take to the idea.'

'You're *what*?'

Clem's clearly having trouble understanding what I've said. In fact, it sounds like she's hyperventilating. I tell her to sit down and have a sip of water, maybe put her head between her legs and breathe into a paper bag.

'Sorry to blurt it out. There hasn't been a good time to tell you, what with Mal leaving you and everything –'

'Mal hasn't left me,' she snaps back, suddenly finding her breath. 'We're just working things out. Why wouldn't you tell me?'

'I just thought you had a lot to cope with –'

'I can't believe you'd think I wouldn't be happy for you!'

'It's not that. The thing is, I don't know how I feel about it. I don't know if I want a child and I don't know if I want one on my own.'

I feel a bit shocked putting this into words. It makes it feel very real, somehow. Clem would make it work if it happened to her, but I don't see how I can. I earn so little money. I have no savings, no career prospects, absolutely no future. I don't want to make life harder by bringing a child into the mix. And what about the child? It's going to take one look at its mother and new environment, roll its eyes and think, *Why me?* By the time the poor thing becomes a teenager, it will have no attitude left, as it would have used it all up as a newborn.

'Jake might want a baby,' Clem says hopefully.

'Sure.' I try to sound positive.

'You'd better tell him. He has a right to know. I'd want to know if I was him.'

I wish Clem were Jake. If I were in a relationship with Clem and had to tell her I was pregnant, she'd be thrilled for us and excited about our future. We'd be madly discussing names and whether our child would be going to a private or a public school. But I'm not. Instead I'm involved with Jake who doesn't even remember when we've arranged to meet up. As far as Jake is concerned, I'm simply someone he's sleeping with.

Still, Clem is right. I need to tell him.

'I just want him to recognise the connection we have before I tell him about the pregnancy. I don't want it to be about that.'

'But it will be about that,' says Clem, rational as always. 'You don't have the luxury of dating for the next five years. At some point he'll notice you get very fat, go through excruciating childbirth and have a crying baby under your arm.'

'I'm not entirely sure I want to keep it,' I say in a low voice. I haven't actually said that to anyone yet, not even myself. It throws me as much as it does Clem.

'What?'

'I know that's hard for you to hear, because I know how much you want to have a baby, but I can't see how I can possibly care for a child.'

'You could do it, I know you could.'

I shake my head. 'No, Clem, I couldn't. I mean, look at my life. I live in a tiny flat, I have no money and I work in a call centre with zero future prospects. I can't see how it would work. It wouldn't be fair to the child.'

'Have you told your mum?'

'No. No one knows, apart from Dr Mitch, Sue the Midwife and the man on reception at the hospital. Oh, and I told my taxi driver the other night, this really fantastic singer –'

'Lizzie, I'll help look after it!'

Tears swell in my eyes. I know Clem means this in the moment, but she works long hours and will no doubt be in a new relationship soon. She's not always going to be around. And I don't want to ask my parents to look after my baby while I eke out a measly income at WineCall. I know Mum and Dad would help as much as they could, but they have their own lives now with holidays and new interests. Mum loves her yoga and often goes on retreats and Dad has taken up photography. They've had their baby. And even thirty years later, they still have to look after her. I can't ask them to do it all over again.

Unless I can get Jake to fall desperately in love with me, and this possibility seems more remote by the minute, I'll be having a baby on my own. And that was never part of my grand plan. Maybe it's time for a new plan.

'You have loads of support,' Clem continues. 'Me, your family. You're better off without someone who can't even manage to get to his own birthday dinner. And if he doesn't appreciate what you have to offer, then he's not the person you want in your life.'

'I can't do it on my own.'

'Yes, you can, and you will.'

Suddenly I remember Missy's baby shower. It's today! Oh God! With all this drama going on I almost forgot. I haven't even asked Clem yet.

'Do you want to come to a baby shower this afternoon? I meant to mention it before.'

'Who for? Not you!'

'No! It's for Missy at work. You met her once when you came to the Christmas party.'

'Yes, I remember, bit of a school monitor?'

'The most organised person in the world, next to you. I think she's registered at David Jones for gifts even though she seems to have already bought every baby product on the market. Did you know they have a ludicrous contraption to warm up baby wipes so they're not too cold on your baby's bottom?'

'Unbelievable!' Clem pretends to be outraged, but I know, even over the phone, that she's thinking that a baby-wipe warmer is an ingenious idea and that she must add it to her own imaginary baby shopping list.

'You have to come with me. I can't face it alone – and I already asked Missy and she said that you're very welcome.'

Clem hesitates. I know she's tempted. She loves baby showers.

'Come on, Clem. You can drink champagne, eat cupcakes, you . . . well, I'm not sure what else you do at these things.'

'You support the mum-to-be, you wish her well, you shower her with gifts and tell her it's all going to be great even though you have no idea, and anyone who's had a child conveniently forgets all the bad bits.'

I told you Clem loves baby showers.

'So, you'll come?'

'Okay, if you really need me.'

'I really do,' I say fervently, because right now, Clem is my everything. I have absolutely no one else.

I arrange to pick Clem up before the baby shower and hang up feeling a little better. But then I realise I haven't told her about Mal and his date. I consider calling her straight back, but something stops me. Maybe I got it wrong? Maybe that girl is his sister, cousin, best friend from childhood? I think back to the gentle kiss across the table and the fact they couldn't keep their hands off each other. No, definitely not a relative. Yes, I'll have to tell Clem about Mal. But not right now. One piece of life-changing news is enough for one phone call.

12

I beep for the third time outside Clem's building. What's she doing? I'm just about to text when she comes running down the path.

'Hi, sorry I'm late. I was just finishing icing these.' Clem carefully places a large platter of beautiful pink and purple cupcakes on the back seat.

'Wow! They look great,' I say, regretting my bottle of vodka. Maybe I should have done a cheese platter or something.

Clem climbs into the front passenger seat and gives me a hug.

'You feeling okay?' she asks, before spying my party offering. 'Vodka? What are you thinking? It's a baby shower. No one drinks vodka at a baby shower, Lizzie – and *you* certainly shouldn't be drinking anything.'

'I know, but it was all I had. I wanted to get a really nice bottle of bubbly for Missy, for when she feels like celebrating, but I didn't get to the shops,' I say, a bit embarrassed. 'Anyway, what about all the single non-pregnant girls? I bet they'll appreciate a vodka and cranberry. They'll need it to get through the afternoon's festivities.'

*

We arrive at Missy's beautiful terrace and walk into the lounge room, which looks like a florist just threw up everywhere and makes me want to do the same. And not because of the foetus in my tummy. Flowers, funny-shaped balloons and enormous bows are strewn from one end of the room to the other.

A group of women are sitting down, drinking champagne and chatting. One of them looks up and I feel like I know her but can't think from where. She has beautiful olive skin and dead-straight hair, two qualities I would be tempted to give away my mother to have. She gives me a smile as I approach the group.

'Hi there. I'm Lizzie, have we met before?'

'I don't think so, I'm Rebecca, but everyone calls me Becca,' she says with a smile that reveals cute little dimples in her cheeks.

'You look familiar. Maybe through Missy?'

I know I've seen her somewhere. She has such a pretty face, so friendly and shiny . . . and slowly the rusty cogs in my pregnant brain start turning and then everything falls into place. She's the girl that Mal was out with the other night! As if this day wasn't hard enough already. I look at her. I look at Clem. My mission for the day, whether I accept it or not, is to keep the two of them apart.

Clem is just about to introduce herself when I butt in.

'Clem, let's get a drink and find out where we should put the food.'

'Look at those cupcakes,' says Missy, who has just walked up to greet us. 'Aren't they fabulous! Did you make them, Lizzie?'

'No, I did,' says Clem, pleased to have her handiwork admired. 'Hi, I'm Clem. We met at your work Christmas party.'

'Hi, Clem, good to see you again, and thanks for the cakes.'

I whisk Clem away before the equivalent of a natural disaster occurs. We take the platter to the kitchen and pop it on the food table, along with my bottle of vodka.

'Where shall we put the presents?' asks Clem, looking around. 'There's usually some sort of designated spot, until the big unwrapping.'

Present! Damn! Clem brings out a beautifully wrapped gift with a pretty card that says *Mums are the Best*. I only invited her this morning and somehow she's come up with award-winning cupcakes, a thoughtful gift and an appropriate card. I don't know how she does it.

'I forgot to buy a present.'

'Lizzie!'

'I've had a few other things on my mind,' I say in my defence. 'What did you get, anyway?'

'A set of three onesies.'

'Oh, great.' I pretend to know what those are, but Clem is not fooled.

'They're all-in-one outfits that newborn babies wear,' she says, slowly, like she's explaining something to a small child. 'You can never have enough of them.'

'I know what a onesie is, Clem,' I say, even though I'm grateful she has clarified this. I make a mental note to add that to my list of things to google.

Now I'm here, I wish I'd bought something. There was talk at work of all putting in to buy a gift together. I remember a collection envelope going around, but I had no change that day.

I look at Clem with my most hopeful eyes. She looks at me and rolls hers.

'You can go in with me,' she says with a sigh. 'Here's a pen, just pop your name on the card.'

We find the present table without much problem. You couldn't miss it, piled up with pink, frilly, wrapped gifts, almost as high as me. And I'm tall and wearing heels. Clem pops our present down among the parcels and it looks a little bit small. Still, I can't complain, seeing as I brought nothing but a bottle of vodka.

I study the overflowing table with interest. There seems to be a lot of things that you need for a baby. I poke around, trying to get some idea of what I should be buying myself, but everything is wrapped up in pastel-coloured paper with babies and flowers on it and tied in curly ribbon. There's one present that isn't wrapped, though. It just has a big sparkly pink bow on it. It looks like a carry bag of some sort. One of those novelty oversized cards is tucked inside, signed by everyone from work. Everyone except me, of course.

'That's a great nappy bag,' says Clem. 'It's the My Baby Deluxe, only just come out on the market. It has a place for everything: nappies, wipes, change of clothes, bottles. A cool section for food when baby starts solids.'

Clem is talking like a presenter on a morning show. I can't believe she knows so much about this stuff. Probably because she has two baby nieces who she adores so much, you'd think she'd given birth to them herself. She should be having Jake's baby, not me. But that would've been awkward.

The bag doesn't impress me, and it wouldn't have been cheap judging by how many people went in on it. It's certainly spacious with heaps of compartments inside. But it's bulky and cumbersome and the fabric is so folksy. It looks like something my grandmother would have kept her knitting in, not what a glamorous new mother should be toting about town. Why does everything have to be so old-fashioned and dull just because a woman is pregnant or has a baby? Why couldn't these presents be wrapped in fabulous contemporary wrapping paper with bold stripes or spots? Why do people suddenly have to use cutesy paper covered in bows, flowers and babies? And that nappy bag with its ugly rose pattern and inelegant shape! Don't even get me started. I'm glad my name isn't on that card now.

'Isn't it great?' Clem is still admiring the nappy bag.

'It's ugly.'

'Lizzie!'

'Well, it is! You won't see me carrying something like that. Honestly, don't people think that new mums are allowed to be chic or stylish?'

Clem loses patience with me and is about to head back to the lounge area, towards the very likely prospect of bumping into Becca, when I hear a voice that's far too deep for a ladies' baby shower.

I turn to see Nathan, clean-shaven and immaculately dressed in slim-fit jeans and a cool checked shirt. Every eye turns to look at him and not just because he's the only guy at the party.

'Didn't know you were into baby showers,' I say. 'Nice shirt by the way.'

'Thanks, it's new,' he says. 'And, no, I don't normally hang out at baby showers. Missy invited me, so I thought I'd drop by with a gift, but don't worry, I won't be interfering with any female tribal baby business.' He finds a spot on the teetering pile of presents to leave a neatly wrapped parcel.

'What did you get?' Even Nathan thought to get a gift.

'A cute mobile to hang from the ceiling,' he says. 'Apparently newborns love them.'

'How gorgeous,' says Clem, before she can stop herself.

I realise the distraction I need to keep Clem away from Becca is standing right in front of me, so I launch in. 'Nathan, this is my friend Clem. Clem, this is Nathan who I work with and who is our token male today.'

'Guys can go to baby showers too, Lizzie,' says Clem sternly.

'Thank you, Clem. Yes, we can,' says Nathan with a chuckle. 'Why should girls have all the fun?'

'You call this fun?' I say, looking around the overly pink and floral room dotted with women eating cake and talking about kids, breastfeeding and toilet training.

'I have to get going. Tell me all about it later. Nice to meet you, Clem.'

Nathan walks away, stopping to talk to a couple of people from work until he eventually makes his way out the door.

'He seems nice, Lizzie.'

'Gay.'

'Really? I didn't get that.'

'So gay, don't even think about it. I tried to kiss him once. He didn't kiss me back.'

'And that makes him gay?'

'Pretty much. Except it was confirmed by Missy. Who knows absolutely everything going on in the call centre.'

'Does she know about Jake?'

'No! No one knows about Jake.'

Desperate to change the subject and keep Clem out of the lounge room, I take her over to join a group of women who are happily discussing the births of their children as if it was the best day of their lives. Missy is there along with a handful of women from work. Just as I decide to go and get us some drinks, one of the women turns to Clem.

'Do you have any kids?'

Clem suddenly looks like she's about to cry, so I briefly explain that she's recently broken up with her boyfriend. Immediate warmth emanates from the group and begins weaving its supportive magic. Once Clem opens her mouth, there'll be no stopping her and no shortage of sympathetic ears.

'Sorry, I'm still a bit sad, it was only recent.'

Just like that, everyone descends with open arms.

'Oh, you poor thing. What happened?' says Missy, who loves a good relationship dissection as much as the next person. The next person happens to be another woman from work, with the same obligatory look of woe on her face.

I leave Clem to it. Becca is at a safe distance, talking on her phone, so I resume my search for drinks and, now that I think about it, one of Clem's delicious cupcakes would hit the spot too. Some plain old comfort eating is what we need to get us through the afternoon.

I walk back into the room to see Clem oversharing, surrounded by a crowd of women, most of whom I don't know, who are all giving her sisterly nods and subtle head shakes.

'We were living together and had just got back from our first couple holiday.'

'I can't believe that!'

'Where did you go?'

'Thailand.'

'That bastard!'

'Then the other night he came around late and we had sex, and now I haven't heard from him.'

Clem is clearly enjoying the attention and the opportunity to discuss Mal with a fresh audience. But then Becca wanders over to join the gang, looking intently at Clem and clearly piecing things together. Oh no. I cross the room as fast as I can, ready to intercept. Everything goes into slow motion as I jump over a toddler, push a pregnant woman out of the way and nearly knock Missy's mother into the mountain of presents.

'Clem, I have to talk to you!' My voice comes out louder than I mean it to over the gentle baby-shower hubbub.

Everyone stops talking and looks at me.

'What is it?' asks Clem.

'I just need your help with something outside.'

'Okay.' Clem steps towards me.

'Is his name Mal by any chance?' says a voice from the crowd.

Clem turns in surprise. 'Yes, do you know him?'

Becca looks uncomfortable. A couple of women from the group look at the ground.

'Um, yeah, we work together.'

'Clem, come with me. Sorry, everyone, we just have to write in our card for Missy.' I drag Clem away by the arm.

'But we've done that, Lizzie!' Clem protests as I pull her

towards the kitchen. 'Wait, I need to get back and see if Mal said anything to that Becca girl from his work.'

'They don't just work together.' This is not how I wanted this to happen, but I know I have to come clean now before the situation becomes completely embarrassing for Clem.

'What do you mean? Do you know her? I've never heard Mal mention a Becca before.'

'Last night when I was waiting for Jake and he didn't turn up . . . well, I saw Mal.'

'What? Where?'

'At Franco's, near work.' I take a deep breath. 'He was with that Becca.'

'They must have been having a drink after work. That's not a crime.'

'Clem, I saw them kiss.'

'Mal kisses everyone. He's very affectionate.'

'On the lips.'

This stops Clem. After a long pause she says, 'Are you sure?'

'They couldn't keep their hands off each other and, Clem, they seemed to be eating nachos.'

'What? That's our dish!'

'I'm sorry, Clem.'

'But the other night, we had sex!'

'I know. Guys do that.' I try to put my arm around Clem's shoulders but she brushes it away. She suddenly looks really, really angry.

'When exactly were you going to tell me?' she hisses. 'Why did I have to find out at a baby shower for a girl I don't even know, who happens to be friends with the girl who's apparently having nachos and kissing dates with Mal? How could you do that to me?'

Put like that, I have to agree, it looks bad. And it's all my fault. How did I manage to get it so wrong? Clem finding out by bumping into Becca at a party I forced her to attend is so much worse than me just telling her at a bad time.

'I'm so sorry, Clem. I was going to tell you but the time was never right. I wanted to let you down gently.' I try to cover my careless tracks but it sounds hollow, even to me. 'And I didn't want to say anything, just in case he was trying to get back with you.'

'I think we can safely say that he's not wanting to get back with me anytime soon. I can't believe you, Lizzie.'

'He might still want to,' I say. 'Maybe Becca's just a blip, a little mistake that's reminded him of how much he actually loves you?'

'I haven't heard from him since our late-night shag, so I don't think he's seen the error of his ways just yet.'

Clem is seething. Not yelling at me like she would over a silly disagreement, but quiet, cold and controlled. And it throws me into a panic. The situation was not supposed to unfold this way.

'I'm so, so sorry. This is awful. I should have told you sooner.'

'Yes, you should have. You should have told me immediately! You should have called or texted the minute you saw them! Or taken a photo and sent it to me. Put me out of my misery.'

I now feel absolutely terrible. I thought I was saving Clem the heartache by waiting for the right moment to fill her in, but now I've only succeeded in prolonging the pain, even magnifying it. I couldn't let her go through the ordeal privately; no, I had to make sure it was in front a gaggle of girls, one of whom is now going out with Mal. Well done, Lizzie!

'Yes, I should have done that. In fact, I did take a photo,' I say, suddenly remembering. 'But there was a lot going on, I guess . . .'

'There's always "a lot going on" with you,' says Clem, the intensity and volume of her anger rapidly building. 'Or at least you think there is. But you know what? There's never really anything going on. Unless you count stalking inappropriate guys who are absolutely not interested. You constantly ring me with your non-existent problems, usually when I'm at work, and expect me to talk it all through with you. You think you've got problems? I deal with angry, miserable people every single day. No one is happy when they see a lawyer, and I hardly ever give them the news they want to hear. It never stops. I've been exhausted for about a decade, and I never get a break. I have to account for every minute I work, so if I stop to counsel you, I have to make it up later. As it is, I regularly do fourteen-hour days. I desperately want to be considered for partnership, but that's not going to happen if you call me every five minutes with yet another drama, on top of all the other catastrophes I deal with on a daily basis.'

My heart starts racing as Clem continues to unleash a fury the likes of which I never thought her capable. Here I was assuming that Clem was more than happy to sort through the constant stream of dilemmas I seem to face, but never have I stopped to consider how stressful her life is. I never even ask how her day has been or think that, some days, she might need my support more than I need hers. She has always worked hard and she does long hours, but I thought she enjoyed it. And I always considered myself to be the one who balanced out her life, distracting her so she didn't get too stressed or overworked. Sounds like I've actually been adding to her stress and workload. Instead of being a welcome light at the end of her long working week tunnel, it seems I've been yet another annoying obstacle she has to get past on the way.

'Sorry, Clem,' I mumble. 'I won't call you at work anymore. I didn't realise –'

'What makes all this unbearable is that the one time I need you, the one time you can help me, like any friend would, you just don't. That's worse than Mal going out with that shiny-haired bitch. Who cares about some guy? If you can't rely on your best girlfriend to be there for you, no matter what, then who can you rely on? I guess we don't have the sort of friendship I thought we had.'

'Don't say that!' I say in a panic. 'We do! I was going to tell you. But what with the baby, and Jake, and the morning sickness, which is totally insane by the way, and the hunger! Oh my God! I constantly feel like I could eat not just a horse, but every entrant in the Melbourne Cup . . .'

My attempt to lighten the mood with humour falls into an uncomfortable silence. Clem is angrier than I've ever seen her. And it doesn't feel like she's quite finished.

'Honestly, you don't think about anyone but yourself. You and your stupid relationships with hopeless men. You don't even care enough to tell me when you see my boyfriend cheating on me with some tart in a bar, because you're so caught up in your own personal soap opera! As disastrous as your situation is with Jake, I still would have called you the minute I saw him with someone else.'

She has me there. Clem would have acted immediately. I can't believe I didn't.

'I have put up with you and your selfishness for years. I'm always there for you when yet another guy dumps you. And this is how you repay me?'

'I'm so sorry, Clem. I know, I'm such a bad friend.'

'That's an understatement.'

'I know I was wrong. I was just really concerned about how it might affect you.'

'Next time, let me be the judge of that. I'm a big girl. I don't need to be protected. From now on, keep out of my love-life – in fact, keep well away from me for a while. At least until I find a way to understand why you allowed me to be publicly humiliated.'

And with that, Clem turns her back on me and goes to find her bag. I hear her thanking Missy for the party and then she leaves without another word.

Standing in Missy's classic contemporary-style kitchen, I fight back tears. What have I done? How could I have treated my best friend like this? Clem's never been this mad at me before. Sure, we've yelled at each other over the years. Once, in Year 8, she wouldn't talk to me for a week because I hung out with Anna Johnson three lunchtimes in a row. But when Anna's group decided I wasn't cool enough for them, I went back to Clem. Eventually she forgave me and things went back to normal. But this is different. I can see that I've been treating Clem badly for years and now I completely failed her by not immediately telling her about Mal. And I don't think our friendship will recover. Maybe the incident with Anna Johnson was the start of a pattern in which I took advantage of our friendship, and today is the final straw? Clem's rage is so great that it's like it was me who went out to dinner with Mal. And fair enough. I was there, I saw him on a date and I didn't tell her. I'm having a baby, and I didn't tell her. I shouldn't have been so gutless, because now everything is ruined. I've pushed my friend away, and she's all I've got. All I had. And I have no idea how long it will take her to forgive me. If she ever does.

I grab a tissue from a box on the windowsill and blow my nose. All I know is that I need to get out of here as soon as possible. I creep back into the living room, delicately heave my handbag from underneath an extremely pregnant woman and scour the room for Missy to say goodbye. I can't see her anywhere, though, and am just about to make a dash for the door when Becca appears out of nowhere.

'I'm sorry, Lizzie, I didn't know that your friend was the girl Mal had told me about,' she says, running a manicured hand through her shiny hair. 'He said the relationship was over ages ago.'

'He had sex with her the other night, so understandably she wasn't so sure it was over,' I say flatly, wanting to make this smug girl squirm a bit, even though she may have been as oblivious as Clem of Mal's two-timing. She fumbles around her Louis Vuitton bag (fake, I'm pretty sure) for her phone and runs out to the courtyard.

Satisfied that at the very least I've sufficiently rocked the boat for Mal, I try to sneak out of this baby-shower nightmare, but Missy appears out of the crowd and corners me.

'We're just about to start the baby-shower games.'

My heart, already in the basement of my soul, sinks even lower. Tilda, Missy's sister, calls everyone over.

'Let's get this party started. I hope everyone has written a name suggestion and popped it in here,' she says, waving a box theatrically. 'We'll read those later.'

An excited murmur breaks out in the room, as if that will be something to really look forward to.

'First up, we're going to take turns acting out a birth,' she continues. 'The most convincing performance will earn a bottle of bubbly!'

I don't know about the others, but I can't think of anything I would like to do less. I've never even seen a birth. And right now the thought of it is terrifying. What if my pretend birth is nothing like a real one and everyone laughs at me? I won't want to go through with the real one when the time comes. I can't believe Missy would allow such a game.

'Come on, everyone,' says Missy hesitantly. 'It'll be fun.'

Somehow I don't think Missy knew this was on the cards. Everyone starts talking under their breath. One woman from work who I know has just had her third miscarriage starts to cry. Another one who's single says she has to go to the bathroom. And another woman remembers a sick grandmother in hospital, whom she has to go and visit.

'Anyone? Come on! Don't be shy.' Tilda tries to rev up the crowd, which is slowly retreating, like a Greek chorus, attempting to blend into the coastal Hamptons flavour that Missy has going on in her open-plan living/dining area, leaving me standing out in front.

'Lizzie? Great, you want a go?'

'Oh, no – I couldn't –'

'Come on!'

I feel I have no choice. There's a pleading look in Tilda's eyes as her first game suggestion is fast becoming a baby-shower faux pas. I breathe in and out, and assume what I imagine is a giving-birth position on the crisp sisal rug, which is far from comfortable.

Every woman is looking at me with rueful smiles and sympathetic eyes, glad they are not in my shoes. Or maybe because this isn't how you actually give birth.

'Why don't you start from, like, the really intense bit of labour,' suggests Tilda.

'Oh, okay,' I say brightly, as if I know all about it.

I close my eyes and begin.

'Ahhhhhhh . . .'

People start to giggle.

'Aaaaaaaahhhhhhhhhh . . . aaaaaahhhhhhhh.'

I sound like some sort of animal hollering in pain, which feels totally appropriate after my fight with Clem. I continue, slowly gaining confidence, building on the agonising cries and making them ever louder and more frightening. Then I introduce a bit of puffing, just like you see in television births.

The more I get into it, the better my performance becomes. I lift it up a notch until I'm screaming at the top of my lungs, and writhing on the floor. It feels great to have a good yell. I think I'm going to enjoy labour when it happens.

'Ahhhhh ooooh ooooh ooooooh!!!'

Then I start jumping around like a crazed monkey, making savage grunting noises. I jump onto an upholstered armchair, thinking I might leap into the crowd, like a rock star, but everyone edges quickly away. My ignorance about labour has given me licence to go wild with creativity and I have to say, it's invigorating. I'm getting out all my frustrations, all my worries.

'Ooh ooh aah aah AAAAAAAAAAHHHHHHHH!!!'

I'm about to push it up to yet another level when I realise no one's laughing anymore. In fact, no one's even looking at me.

Everyone has gone into a mad panic. I don't know what's happening, but Tilda is speaking urgently into her phone while Missy is leaning over the sofa, making a noise not too dissimilar to the one I was just doing.

Then it hits me. Missy's gone into actual labour. The baby isn't due just yet, so I'm hoping it wasn't my acting that brought it on. But no one really cares about that right now. Missy starts barking orders, more like the mother of a lazy teenager than a soon-to-be first-time mum.

'Has someone called the hospital? Where's my hospital bag? I haven't finished packing. Mum, where are you?'

No one seems sure what to do, especially as Missy has become a little scary.

'Mum! Pack the scented candles, my Norah Jones CD and the massage oil,' she yells. 'My tweezers, don't forget those! If I'm stuck in hospital without them for even an hour, I'll end up with a full beard. And grapes. Can someone get the grapes out of the freezer? And grab the bendy straws from the cupboard. And someone please call my doctor!'

'I'm on the phone to the hospital now. They're trying to find him,' says Tilda. 'Can someone else call a cab for me?'

'I will.' I remember Cherie's card in my purse. I might as well try her. That's something I can do. I find the card and quickly dial the number.

'Hello,' says a cheery voice.

'Cherie? Hi, it's Lizzie from the other week, you helped me out and . . .'

'Hello, love, how's it going? Broken up with that guy yet?'

'Actually, I have, but right now I'm at a baby shower and the guest of honour has gone into labour. Are you by any chance anywhere near Paddington?'

'Not far, darl, just dropping someone off. Be there in a jiff.'

I give her the address and hang up.

'Taxi's just around the corner,' I tell anyone who is interested.

'Did you say she was in labour?' asks Tilda, looking at me like I have no idea about babies, pregnancy and getting to hospital. Which is fair enough, considering my little performance. But if there is one thing I can do, it's call a taxi. I assure her that the driver knows the full story and I go out the front to wait for Cherie, who arrives just as I reach the gate. I wave madly at her and run in to tell Missy her ride is here.

Everyone inside has gone slightly mad now. Honestly, it's like the world is coming to a dramatic end. Tilda is on the phone trying to track down Missy's husband, Angus, who's on a flight back from Canberra. Someone is packing enough food parcels to solve the world's hunger problems, someone else is running around with a video camera trying to capture the moment, until Missy rips it out of the poor girl's hands and throws it on the ground. At least it hits the sisal rug, not the polished hardwood floors. I grab Missy and speak as firmly and calmly as I can.

'Missy, the taxi is here. Get your bag and come with me.'

No one notices us leave because they're all too busy freaking out. I take Missy out to the taxi, open the back door and help her in.

'Hello, sweetheart, how are you?' booms Cherie, who, today, is sporting a hot-pink taffeta dress and enormous false eyelashes. I'm glad to see her and not just because Missy needs a taxi.

'I'm okay, but you'd better go,' I say. 'You look fantastic, by the way!'

'Aren't you coming with me?' Missy asks as she nervously gives Cherie the once-over.

I wasn't planning on it, but I see the panic in Missy's eyes and no one else seems to be volunteering.

'Sure. Did you get hold of Angus?'

'Tilda's trying to call him now. Hopefully he'll meet us at the hospital.'

'Let's go, girls. Quick as a flash now,' says Cherie, taking charge and obviously enjoying the excitement. She's positively glowing. As for Missy, she has lost the glow she had last week. She's looking a bit pale and the contractions seem to be getting stronger. As Cherie pulls away from the kerb, Missy grabs her abdomen and groans.

'Ahhhhhhhhhhhh.'

'You okay?' I ask.

'No, I'm not okay,' she yells at me. 'How can I be okay when I feel like my insides are about to fall out?'

'Don't forget to breathe,' I say, trying to remember what people say at times like these.

'I'm breathing, okay? My breathing is not the problem here, it's the ginormous watermelon that's trying to come out of my VAGINA!'

'Is it a boy or a girl?' Cherie asks, trying to distract Missy from her agony and subsequent rage.

'Ahhhhhhhhhhhh AAAAAAA GIRL!!!'

The whole 'going into labour' thing is looking less attractive by the second. And the way this afternoon is going, I don't think I'll even need to read a book let alone go to the prenatal classes that Sue the Midwife mentioned. But right now, I don't really know how to help Missy. I hold her hand, hoping it's a comfort. Well, I'm holding her hand and she's clawing at mine with her beautifully manicured nails.

'Lizzie! I CAN'T DO THIS!'

'Yes, you can. You're doing really well,' I say.

'But it HURTS! It's not supposed to be like this. Contractions are supposed to be hours apart at first. I wanted to stay home for as long as possible. I left the linen cupboard all messy so I had something to do while I was labouring at home. Now when am I going to tidy it? IT'S NEVER GOING TO BE TIDY NOW!'

'It looks like the baby is in a hurry to see you,' says Cherie. 'Have you thought of a name?'

'A few, but I really like the name . . . ah . . . AAAAHHHHH HHH . . . MAYBE GRACIE-EEEEEEEE!'

Wow, that was only a couple of minutes since the last contraction! That can't be right. I look at Cherie's reflection in the rear-vision mirror and she puts her foot on the accelerator, overtaking the car in front with a bit of a swerve. Luckily, we arrive at the hospital before the baby makes an appearance. Cherie and I help Missy walk to reception. The woman takes one look at our odd group, one of whom is clearly about to give birth, and calls for a nurse.

'You're coming with me, aren't you, Lizzie?' Missy looks like a frightened animal staring into a car's headlights, and right now, I don't blame her. Who knows what's going to happen? Except a child being born, of course, but that alone seems positively terrifying.

'Yes, I'm right here. I've got your bag. Everything's going to be fine,' I tell her in a voice that sounds a lot more together than I feel. I can't possibly leave her now. Not until I know her husband has arrived. I try to give Cherie some money, but she tells me not to worry.

'Just let me know what happens,' she says, turning to the sliding doors. Once again, I'm amazed by the genuine kindness of someone who is practically a stranger.

With the nurse's assistance, we make our way to the delivery suite, which feels like an epic journey in itself, especially as any sort of movement is a challenge for Missy. Suddenly, a tall lanky figure in a white doctor's coat passes us in the corridor. He looks familiar. How do I know him? Of course. Dr Mitch!

'Hello!' I say, happy to see even a vaguely familiar face in the middle of a crisis.

'Oh . . . hi,' he says, obviously trying to place me. I guess there've been about a hundred of me since I was last here. Not that I expect to be special, but there couldn't have been that many girls who've had stalkery-type accidents followed by the discovery of a surprise pregnancy. But then again, maybe I'm just one of many trying to track down the love of their life, only to find out they're actually carrying his baby?

'Lizzie March,' I remind him. 'I came in the other day, when I cut my chin.' I point to my nearly healed chin.

'Oh, yes. You found out you're . . . is the baby okay?'

'My friend, Melissa, is about to have a baby. They're expecting us in the labour ward,' I say quickly, in case Missy gets the wrong idea. I look at Dr Mitch as if to say, 'Can you please not mention my condition as no one knows.' He must speak fluent eye language because he looks back at me as if to say, 'No problem.'

'Right, I'll come with you. How are you feeling, Melissa?'

He takes charge of the situation like the pro he is, which I have to say is extremely attractive. I can see why women have a thing about doctors. They have your life in the palm of their hand. Intoxicating.

'Really great,' says Missy sarcastically, clearly still annoyed that her labour is not following the correct schedule.

'The contractions were about five minutes apart on the way here, but we haven't had another one since we arrived,' I say, trying to sound like someone who is extremely knowledgeable about childbirth.

'That can happen. Sometimes labour goes away for a bit then comes back.'

Missy's labour must have heard what Dr Mitch said as an almighty roar comes out of her mouth. It doesn't even sound like Missy.

'I NEED TO PUSH! Is that okay? Am I supposed to be pushing now? It seems too soon, but I really . . . I'm pushing! I'M PUSHING . . . AAHHHHHHHH!!'

'I'll get a midwife,' he says calmly as we reach the birthing ward. 'Who's your obstetrician?'

Missy can't speak for a moment but then the contraction subsides. 'Dr Jonathan Koh,' she says in a hoarse whisper. 'My sister already called the hospital so he's probably on his way.'

'He might not get here in time,' says Dr Mitch.

'What? I need him here!' Missy is becoming angrier by the minute.

A nurse approaches and talks to Dr Mitch.

Missy looks at me strangely. 'Why did the doctor ask you about a baby? It's not like he knew we were coming in,' she asks suspiciously.

I knew it! Even during labour with super-painful five-minute contractions, Missy doesn't miss the slightest whiff of gossip. Two people could be whispering outside her bedroom window while she's fast asleep and she would somehow absorb what they were talking about.

'Don't worry about that now.'

'What did he mean? Come on, Lizzie, tell me. It will take my mind off things.'

I sigh. I guess everyone will know soon enough and it feels like an appropriate moment to share.

'I'm pregnant.'

The list of people who know is getting longer by the minute. Unfortunately, it doesn't include the one person who really needs to know.

'That's so great. We can have babies together,' screams Missy as if I'm her one and only true best friend. 'We'll go to playgroup, meet for coffee, go for walks to the park. This is going to be fantastic!'

I want to remind her that she's actually having her baby right now and mine won't arrive for another eight months or so, but thankfully Dr Mitch interrupts.

'Melissa, this is Annie, she's one of the midwives who'll take care of you today.'

'Hang on! Where's my doctor? Where's my husband? What's going on? THIS IS ALL WRONG!'

Missy sounds psychotic, but I guess Annie has seen it all before. She probably delivers thousands of babies every week.

'This is my first real birth,' chirps Annie.

'WHAT!' screams Missy, who looks like she is about to strangle the poor midwife. 'Where's my doctor? Where's Dr Koh? I have a birth plan. Lizzie, where's my birth plan?'

I don't know what she's talking about, but I try to placate her nonetheless. Maybe it's something in her bag.

'Yes, I've got it,' I say confidently. 'Do you want it now?'

'Keep hold of it and hand it to me when I ask. Or give it straight to Dr Koh when he arrives. Until then, guard it with YOUR LIFE!'

'Yes, okay, no worries, it's safe and sound,' I say, patting an imaginary pocket and wondering what I'll do when she wants me to produce it. Something else to google when I get home.

Suddenly people are everywhere. Angus finally rushes in, looking pale and panicked. He got the message as he got off the plane and apparently everyone in the long taxi queue agreed that his needs were the greatest, so he got the first cab. Dr Koh runs in, dressed in a dinner suit. He was getting ready to go to a wedding. Missy is screaming and crying alternately. Annie the midwife is cheerily helping Missy to kneel on all fours on the bed.

'How's that, Melissa?'

'Bloody painful! How do you think it is?'

I'm no longer needed. Angus thanks me for looking after Missy and turns back to his screaming and now also swearing wife. I've never once heard Missy blaspheme in the five years I've worked at WineCall, but she's certainly making up for it now.

I grab Annie as she goes past.

'I should probably wait outside, don't you think?'

'Aren't you the second support person?' Annie is starting to get a slightly startled look in her eyes. Probably not a good thing when you're a midwife.

'No. I just brought her in. I'm in the way. I should go.'

'Whatever you think Melissa would want,' she says, not quite as chirpily as before.

Missy has forgotten about me so I take the opportunity to creep out. Maybe we'll be better friends after today's adventure. I just hope she forgets the fact I'm pregnant.

I wander down the corridor, trying to find my way out. But it doesn't seem to matter where I turn, I can still hear Missy's agonising groans. I feel drained after the day's events – and totally starving. I didn't get the chance to eat so much as a cracker at the baby shower, let alone a pink cupcake. Now I feel like I could eat the contents of an entire bakery. I make a beeline for the café. I simply must eat before I faint. Lucky I'm in a hospital. Best place to faint, really. But a sandwich and a cup of tea is probably a better option.

I walk into the hospital café and check out what's on offer. I'm just tossing up between an apple danish and some fruit toast when a voice behind jolts me from my thoughts.

'Have a muffin. They're surprisingly good.'

Dr Mitch!

'Right, better follow doctor's orders,' I say, deciding on a raspberry and coconut muffin and a decaf latte. 'Can I get you one? It's the least I can do after all your help today. And the other day, when I came in.'

'It's kind of my job.'

'Still, you must need a coffee?'

'For sure, but I'll get mine. I'm getting a takeaway, I don't have long.'

I get my coffee and muffin and find a table. A minute later, Dr Mitch comes over with a takeaway cup in his hand.

'You hanging around to see how your friend goes?' he asks. 'She might appreciate it.'

'No, I'll head off after this. Her husband's there and I'm not a close friend. Just happened to be there at the time.'

'Lucky for her that you were. How are things going for you, anyway? How is the father-to-be coping?'

'He still doesn't know,' I blurt out. 'We're no longer together.'

Honestly, I have no filter. I barely know Dr Mitch and here I am sharing far too much personal and probably very boring information. Still, it's nice to talk to someone who knows what's going on.

'Sorry to hear that. You okay?'

'Yeah. Fine,' I say, trying to sound as if I believe it. 'Better, really. He wasn't that into me as it turns out, so I doubt if he'd have wanted my baby.'

'Maybe you should tell him, though. Some men are desperate for children. It's just the in-between stuff that stumps them. You never know, he might be over the moon.'

'Maybe,' I say doubtfully.

There's no way Jake would be over the moon. He's not one of those men. In fact, he's not a man at all. He's a child. And I already have one inside my tummy. I don't need another one hanging around on the outside.

'Do you want to take a seat?' I ask Dr Mitch, who's now hovering at my table while I stuff muffin into my mouth, like it's the first food I've seen in days. 'Sorry, just so hungry.'

'That's okay. You eat. I'll sit for just a sec.'

'Busy?'

'Always busy. Never stops.'

'Do you like being a doctor?' I ask, before I can stop myself. 'Sorry, that's a weird question.'

He sighs. 'Not so weird. Let me see . . . it feels good to help people and it can be really rewarding. But sometimes I wish I was doing something a bit more . . . I don't know . . . something else.' A dreamy look passes over Dr Mitch's face, and then like a fluffy cloud on a windy day, it's gone. 'What do you do?'

'I studied fashion design, but right now I sell wine over the phone in a call centre. I definitely wish I was doing something else.'

'Why aren't you designing clothes?'

I look at Dr Mitch and don't know what to say. I'm not sure why I'm not doing what I want to do. What happened to my dreams? What went wrong?

'I did try for a while, but I guess it just never really happened. It's a tough industry,' I say, picking up the last muffin crumbs on my plate and wishing I could eat it all over again.

'At least you gave it a go.'

I feel like I'm talking to an old friend, not some doctor I've met twice. It's no wonder he does what he does. One short conversation and I want to tell him everything. I want to say that I haven't given anything a proper go, that all I've done is left a trail of disaster from job to job, man to man. Now I'm pregnant to a guy who doesn't love me and I've been a bitch to my best friend, who's no longer talking to me. I want to tell him how I've made a mess of everything.

'I've made a mess of everything!' I wail. Tears pool in my eyes, threatening to leak out all over the table.

'Hey, don't say that,' says Dr Mitch. 'I don't know what's going on for you, but I know that can't be true.'

And that does it. Just a few words of kindness, and tears are sliding down my cheeks. I try to speak, but what comes out is engulfed by sobs.

'It's just that . . . I wanted to . . . but then Jake didn't even . . . turn up . . . then I didn't tell Clem . . . now she hates me . . . and . . . having a baby . . .'

Even I don't understand what's coming out of my mouth. But there's more than enough snot coming out of my nose to make up for it. I must look like something from a sci-fi horror film. Dr Mitch simply gets a serviette from the counter, hands it to me, and lets me ramble on for a few more minutes.

'You know what?' he says. 'Things may seem black at the moment, but it will all turn around. You deserve to be happy – and you will be. You have to believe that.'

Dr Mitch has finished his takeaway coffee and should probably be helping to save lives rather than witnessing my emotional breakdown. I dry my eyes and force myself together.

'Sorry,' I say with a heavy sigh. 'It's been a big few weeks. I haven't really dealt with anything yet, and my life is going from pretty bad to rock bottom.'

'Talk to him. Tell him about the baby. You might be surprised.'

'How would you feel, if it happened to you?'

'If you were having my baby, you mean? I'd certainly be surprised . . .'

I giggle, almost wishing that were the case. 'No, I mean, if your girlfriend told you she was pregnant. If you're straight, I mean, and had a girlfriend.'

Mitch laughs. 'Definitely straight. But no girlfriends at present, so I can't really comment. But I'd love to have kids one day, so I imagine I'd be thrilled.' He glances at his watch and then jumps to his feet, his long frame towering over me. 'Sorry, but I really have to go. Are you sure you'll be okay?'

'Yes, of course.' I force a smile.

'Nice to see you again, Lizzie. Look after yourself.' He pulls a card out of his pocket. 'Take this, and if you ever need to talk, give me a call.'

He turns and strides out with the purpose of someone who has important things to do. I can't believe Dr Mitch took the time to chat with me, when he obviously has no time at all. He's fast becoming my hero. Not in an I-want-to-have-sex-with-him way, which is surprising for me. He just seems kind and straightforward. He saves people every day and then, when he has a quick coffee break, he stops to help me too. Attractive. But for once in my life, I'm admiring from afar. He wasn't flirting with me anyway, simply comforting someone in need, like any doctor would. You don't meet men like that every day. At least, I don't.

I finish my coffee, saunter back out to the street and make my way to the bus stop, realising I'm alone for the first time since picking up Clem this morning. Normally I wouldn't mind, but for some reason, I feel so lonely. Who will take me to the hospital when the time comes? I don't think it will be Clem. Not now. Maybe Mum? She would do it, but that would mean telling her I'm pregnant. Another conversation I'm avoiding.

I pull out my phone and stare at the screen. I have to speak to Clem. Right now. But somehow I can't get my fingers to press Call. Mostly because I know she won't answer. And also because I don't know what I'd say. There's no excuse for my behaviour so why should Clem even take my call, let alone forgive me.

I push my anxieties away, which is a bit like trying to squash too many clothes into a tiny suitcase and finally getting it closed. I'll be just fine. I won't need anyone by my side. Funnily enough, one thing is clear. After today's experience, I know I definitely want this baby. Not that seeing Missy writhing in pain and screaming like an actress in a B-grade horror movie is what you'd call enticing. But there has to be more to life than just me. And what if this is my only chance? What if I didn't have this baby and never got another opportunity? That would be devastating. I've always wanted to be a mum one day. Maybe that day is today? I had a taste of something very real this afternoon, something meaningful (if absolutely terrifying), and I want to be part of it. Okay, so the timing is completely inconvenient, but nothing I've ever planned has ever worked out the way I wanted, so why not go with what life presents and see what happens? I've been so gutless with my career, my relationships and now my best friend – I've failed at everything. But that doesn't mean that will always be the case. And now there's something I can do, something amazing I can create. Maybe it's time to be brave, to close my eyes, take a leap and hope for the best . . .

I sit at the bus stop, lost in my epiphanic thoughts, when a car beeps at me, its driver waving wildly. Cherie!

'Hello there,' I say through the open passenger window.

'Hello, love, haven't had any takers around here. Seems that people at hospital are picked up by family and friends. Can I drop you home? You've had a bit of an ordeal.'

'Only if you let me pay.'

Cherie agrees and I climb in. It's a relief to be with another friendly person after the day's events. First Dr Mitch and now

Cherie. And her taxi with its glamorous plush interior is so inviting. We pull up outside my apartment building and before I know it, I'm asking Cherie into my very dirty flat for a cup of tea.

'Just a quick cuppa then I'd better get back to it,' she says without hesitation.

Cherie and I have only met a couple of times, but we chat easily for the next two hours, like old friends. I'm so thankful for the company, which I have to say is thoroughly entertaining. Cherie talks about her singing career and how much she loved performing. She has me in stitches with her stories of show life and all the famous people she met along the way. She also reveals personal snippets, how she was married twice, and is now single and childless. Eventually, as she got older and the work dried up, she started driving a taxi to get by and found she actually enjoyed it. Not surprisingly, she makes good money from her regular customers, especially when she belts out the odd number at traffic lights. She's known about town as the Singing Cabbie.

'Don't you miss the stage?'

'Yes and no. Like I told you, it's a bit of a toxic love–hate relationship. I was really lucky, got a lot of work and had a ball, but you can't do it forever and you still have to pay the bills.' Cherie pauses, looking off into the distance. 'But I'd love to sing on stage again. Maybe one day.'

'You should, I'd love to see you sing. I wish I had a talent like that.'

'I thought you were a designer? That sounds pretty good.'

'Well, I'm supposed to be, but it's never come to anything. At the moment all my energy has been going into selling wine and . . .'

'Being pregnant?'

'Well, yes. That, and trying to get the father of my child to show a little interest.'

'So you told him?'

'No. And now I don't think I will.'

'Do what feels right. Listen to your gut. You'll know how to handle it when the time comes.'

I look at Cherie and smile. At last, someone who's not telling me what I should and shouldn't do.

'I would have loved a child, but it never happened.' Cherie pauses. 'Actually, that's not entirely true. I fell pregnant when I was seventeen, just as my career was taking off. I hid it and kept working. Then I had the baby and gave it up for adoption. I was heading over to London for work so I couldn't keep it. I was too young. Too ambitious. That's what you did back then. I didn't even give her a name. In fact, I barely saw her before she was whisked away.'

'Oh, Cherie, that must have been awful.'

'I didn't think about it at the time. I couldn't afford to. I was so driven and hadn't even considered babies. I was still a child myself. It was a silly mistake that I dealt with. But lately I've been thinking of her as a human being who never knew her birth mother. I wonder who she is, where she is.'

'Would you ever try to find out?'

'I don't think I could. Not sure if there were even any records of the adoption. Besides, what would I say? Sorry, I didn't keep you because I wanted to be a star?'

'There are ways of tracking her down. And I'm sure she'd understand it wasn't as simple as that.'

'It's too late,' says Cherie resignedly. 'What would it achieve? What could I say if she asked why I left?'

I nod. I get it. We sip our tea in a comfortable silence. What if I was to do that? Would I spend my life wondering what happened to my baby? Or knowing where she was, but not being a part of her life? I don't think I could. I'd feel like I'd lost something. Maybe that's how Cherie feels now. It seems more and more that life is telling me to have this baby.

'Would you like another tea?' I ask as brightly as possible.

'No thanks, love, better get going. Thanks for the cuppa and the chat. Stay in touch, won't you? You've got my number.'

And with that she is gone, before I realise, once again, that I haven't given her money for the cab fare.

13

I finally call Clem on Monday morning but there's no answer. I'm so hesitant to interrupt her at work and so unsure of what to say that I don't leave a message. I try again later and once more my call goes to voicemail. This time I feel I should say something.

'Hi, it's me . . . Lizzie, that is, hi, I hope you're okay. Er . . . look, I'll call back.'

Hardly impressive. But it's impossible to say what I need to say on a voicemail message.

I pass by her flat on my way to work, but no one's home. It feels so strange. Usually not a day goes by without us having some sort of conversation. She's the one I always call to talk about my problems. But I know that's part of the problem. All I ever talk about is me and my disastrous life. What about Clem's life? I've never spent much time talking about her stuff, like Mal.

She always seems so together. Successful lawyer. Great job. Committed relationship. (Well, strike off the last part.) It's me who's always having some sort of crisis. But maybe there have been times when Clem really needed to talk. I feel sick to my stomach as I realise what a hopeless friend I've been lately. For a long time, in fact. Clem's always there for me. Like that time I nearly got arrested at that unruly speed-dating night. I don't know what I would have done without her.

The evening had started out so well. Promising even. We had five-minute sessions with each potential date, which weren't long, yet plenty long enough for me to hit it off with one particular guy. Little did I know another woman was equally determined to win his heart. I thought I was single-minded when it comes to finding love, but she was downright obsessive, and made it clear that I needed to stand aside. Which I had no intention of doing. What if he was The One? The angrier she got, the more fired up I became, until we were screaming at each other. The guy in question tried to calm us down, suggesting we all 'go out together', at which point she turned into the devil woman and pushed me into a table, breaking glasses and spilling red wine over another customer. The organisers of the event seemed to have disappeared and the venue owner called the police. Naturally, I called Clem, who promptly arrived and went into lawyer mode. She said something about the venue not having adequate fire exits and the whole thing went away.

And how do I repay her when she comes to me with her news of Mal leaving? I talk about Jake. Then I see Mal out with another woman and I don't get around to telling Clem. She's absolutely right: I would have wanted to know if the situation were reversed.

And as Clem said, she would have called me straightaway and shown me hard evidence. More than just taking a photo on her phone, she would have found a way to obtain the CCTV footage from the restaurant. She might even have confronted the guy in question, wanting answers there and then.

She was just so certain Mal was coming back that I didn't want to upset her. But she deserved the truth, and I should have given it to her, even if I'd known it would be hard for her to hear. I could have helped her avoid this whole humiliating mess and now I've only succeeded in making it worse and turning her away to boot.

Just when I really need her!

Lizzie, Lizzie, Lizzie, I chide myself. Back to me again! What about Clem? What does she want? A real friend, probably. Someone who puts aside their own needs to help her when she's going through a tough time. So simple, and yet I didn't provide that support. I'm going to have to sort this out.

I'm tempted to call work and say I have come down with a bug and can't stop vomiting. Which is sort of true, although I feel bad about calling my baby a bug. But I need the cash. If I'm having a baby on my own, I need to earn some money. I haven't spoken to Jake since Friday and I don't want to. He's rung a few times, and I haven't returned the calls. But I can't avoid him forever.

When I walk into the call centre, there's a big poster on the wall, which shows a giant stork with a pink ribbon around its neck saying, *It's a Girl!* Missy's baby obviously came out safely. I look at the poster. We've known it was a girl since the microsecond Missy could find out the sex. What is it with the storks? I can now say with all confidence, they have nothing to do with anything.

Frankie comes up and gives me a hug, which throws me a little. We're not that close, but it feels like ages since I've had a warm hug, so I just go with it.

'I hear you were a star on Saturday,' she says, smiling.

'I just called the taxi and went to the hospital, Missy did all the work,' I say humbly.

'Have you been to see her yet?'

'No. Should I, do you think? I don't want to interfere.'

'I'm popping in today with a pressie. Come with me. I'm sure she'd like to see you.'

'Okay, I might. Maybe I'll go out in my lunch break and buy a little something. What should I get?'

'I bought a little sunhat for the baby – you can never have enough of those. All my kids used to throw them out of the pram. I must have gone through hundreds.'

'Good idea.'

I'm having a baby and I have no idea what a suitable present might be for a new mum. Why isn't there some sort of manual for all of this? It would save a lot of confusion.

Unfortunately, Jake is working today. He keeps trying to catch my attention, but I totally ignore him. Eventually, he comes over to my workstation and tries to engage me in a conversation.

'Hi, Lizzie.'

I pretend a call has just dropped in.

'Good morning, this is WineCall. My name is Lizzie. How are you today . . . ? That's great to hear. Look, I'm just giving you a quick courtesy call to see how your wine supplies are going.'

'Can I talk to you after that call?' he asks softly.

I try to gesticulate that it's going to be a long call so I'm not sure when I might be free, but he still stands there waiting. I don't think mime is my forte.

'Oh yes, we have a number of premium reds. A lovely shiraz from McLaren Vale, which is heavily discounted today. Plus, if you take three cases you get two free cases of bubbly as a bonus.'

My pretend call is panning out to be a lucrative one. Even I start believing it's real. Jake waits patiently until somebody needs help with a cranky customer. Before he leaves, he leans in, grabs my pen and writes something on my wine list.

Can we talk at lunch?

Why is he suddenly so desperate to talk? He hasn't wanted to do much talking at all over the last month. I've moved on and now he wants to communicate. Well, I'm going to be strong. He has nothing to do with my life or my baby, and that's that.

No longer distracted by Jake and his exceptional biceps, I can concentrate and sell wine as the phone calls drop in. Indeed, I sell case after case, and before I know it, it's lunchtime. I can't see Jake anywhere, so I grab my bag and confidently head to the lift.

'Lizzie,' says a voice behind me.

'Yes?' I turn around without thinking and there he is. Damn. Where did he spring from?

'What are you doing over lunch? I need to go through your stats from the last couple of weeks.'

'I'm busy, actually.' Right, he just wants to tell me that I need to force more wine on people. Well, not today. He can't make me give up the break time I'm legally entitled to. Besides, I have to go and get Missy a present.

'Maybe at the end of the shift?' he persists.

Wow, my stats must be really bad. No one has ever wanted to discuss them so desperately before. At least I'm selling well today.

'I'm going to the hospital to see Missy after work. I've arranged to go with Frankie,' I say. Anything to get out of what will be an awkward conversation with Jake saying something along the lines of either, 'You're a great girl but . . .' or, 'Perhaps this isn't the job for you'. Nothing good could come out of any conversation with Jake right now so I'll do anything to avoid damaging my self-esteem any further. Lord knows I've heard every dumping technique in the book, but today I'm not in the mood.

The lift arrives, and I give Jake a half-wave as the doors close. I head to Westfield, not sure where to start. Missy got so many baby gifts, what could I get her that she doesn't already have? Something for herself, maybe? No one ever considers the mum-to-be. The focus is always on the baby. I find some delicious-smelling body balm in David Jones. It says that it's perfect for tired, overworked skin. Surely that's what a new mum needs.

I race back to work, arriving about a minute before my break ends, after buying not only the body balm for Missy but a couple of pots for myself. After all, I'm going to be a mum too, even though I keep forgetting. And the way I'm going, there won't be anyone to buy me a nice body cream, let alone offer support during labour.

I manage to avoid Jake for the rest of the day. He's hardly around because there's some supervisors' meeting upstairs, so I can relax. At the end of the shift, I walk over to Frankie's workstation where she's just finishing up a huge sale.

'That sounded impressive!'

'One of my regulars. I think he just likes talking to someone on the phone. And he loves wine so for him it's a win–win,' she says with a smile.

Frankie is so nice, people just can't say no, which is why she is one of the top sellers at WineCall. I'm not saying I'm not nice, but people just don't take to me the same way. Frankie has a personality that makes people feel like they've just made a fantastic new best friend.

'You're an inspiration, Frankie. You make life look so easy.'

'That's nice of you, Lizzie. Nothing is easy, but life's pretty good.'

'Is it? I'm not so sure right now.'

Frankie stops recording the sale on the already enormous list in front of her and looks up at me. 'What's wrong? It's not like you to be down.'

'Nothing,' I say, not wanting to go into the rather pathetic details of my personal life. 'Let's go and see Missy.'

'Okay. I've got the car so we can drive.'

Frankie battles the afternoon traffic and when we finally arrive, she drives us into the hospital car park.

'It's pretty expensive; I usually park on the street,' I say.

'What do you mean, *usually*?'

'If I visit someone or something like that,' I say quickly. 'The other day I had to take my mum for her mammogram.'

That was close. I face the front, my eyes glancing sideways to see if Frankie has bought my explanation. But I guess, seeing as Missy knows the truth, it won't be long before my secret is common knowledge.

Bleached Hair Man is on reception again so I look at the ground and let Frankie do the talking. Luckily, he doesn't recognise me, not that he would among the huge number of people going in and out of a hospital.

Missy's room is stuffed with flowers and balloons with Missy in the middle of it all, sitting up in bed, looking like her perky self.

'Hi! Thanks for coming. So glad to see you! Here she is! We haven't finalised the name yet. I still love Grace, although Angus is hoping for Olive after his grandmother, but it just makes me think of olive oil.'

Beside the bed, in a plastic crib, a little face pokes out of a bundle of blankets. Fast asleep. I'm hoping to feel something when I look at the baby. I stare intently for some time at the little prune-like face with eyes clenched shut. No, nothing. Disappointed, I give Missy my present.

'Lizzie, thanks so much for getting me to hospital,' says Missy as she rips open the body cream. 'You should have stayed for the birth, it was absolutely phenomenal! Thanks for this. Mmmm . . . smells nice, but I can't use that for a while. They say to avoid wearing any strong fragrances because it might turn the baby off and interfere with breastfeeding.'

Damn. Now I've got two pots of stuff I can't use. Well, I'll just use them up before the baby comes.

'How long was your labour?' asks Frankie.

'She arrived a couple of hours after we got here. Pretty quick for a first birth,' says Missy proudly.

'I'll say. My first took ten hours.'

What! Even two more hours of the agony Missy was enduring would be two hours too many as I far as I'm concerned! Just when I thought I was getting my head around things, here's a sign that maybe I'm not cut out for this whole childbirth scenario. I'd better find a few books and educate myself. I'm sure Missy has a million I can borrow. Hopefully there's some sort of crash course in 'baby-having' I can sign up for. In fact, didn't Sue the Midwife mention something like that? And there's the book she gave me, which is somewhere at home. Maybe I should actually read it.

'And how are you feeling, Lizzie?' Missy asks with a huge smile on her face.

'Oh me? Fine,' I say dismissively, trying to tell Missy with my eyes to not say anything in front of Frankie. But Missy doesn't seem to understand eye language or telepathic messaging as well as Dr Mitch does. Or Clem, for that matter; she and I just look at each other and know exactly what the other one is thinking. We used to, anyway. I have no idea what she's thinking about now.

'This will be you soon. Good to have had a practice run,' says Missy, looking at her newborn bundle.

'Oh yes, one day, I'm sure,' I say with a casual laugh. 'I just have to find Mr Right first.'

'But haven't you already found –'

'Looks like you need another vase,' I say, pointing at a nearby bunch of flowers. 'I'll go and find one.'

'I'll come with you,' says Frankie, following me out to the corridor.

'I'm pregnant,' I blurt out as we walk to the nurses' station to ask for a vase.

'I gathered,' says Frankie. 'Happy news?'

'Unexpected,' I say, trying to look like a radiant mum-to-be as the tears start to well once again.

'Hey, it's okay. Who's the father?'

'You don't know him,' I say quickly. 'But he doesn't know about the baby. Everything's gone wrong. It's all a huge mistake. I thought he was The One, but he's not.'

'Why haven't you told him?'

'I don't want him to feel obligated. Like he has to be in a relationship with me. I only want him in my life as a partner, otherwise I'll do it on my own.'

'He has a right to know,' says Frankie, sounding a lot like Dr Mitch. 'He might want to be a part of it all even if he doesn't want to be with you. He should know if he's having a baby. You'd be surprised how some guys react to news like this.'

I look at Frankie, who is wearing the coolest vintage frock I've ever seen with striped stockings and red high heels. She has the best husband in the world and probably never had to worry about anything like this.

'You wouldn't understand,' I say. 'Your life is perfect.'

'Nothing's perfect, Lizzie.'

'You're pretty close to it.'

'Don't be so sure. Mike had an affair once.'

I nearly walk into the wall.

'We got through it. Stronger than ever. It was pretty hard at the time, though.'

'What happened?'

'He was working on some show. Really long hours. Never home. Had to fly to Melbourne all the time. I'd been really stressed out with the kids. No sleep. We were fighting all the time. I felt like I was starting to disappear. Whenever he was working, I felt angry that he wasn't there and then when he eventually came home, I was even angrier. Instead of talking to him,

I pushed him away. He did the wrong thing. No doubt about it. But I was angry with myself for what I'd become. What I'd allowed my life to become. I guess I blamed him.' Frankie stops suddenly and looks at me. 'Sorry, you don't need to hear all this.'

'I don't mind, it's a relief to think about something other than me and my catastrophic life.'

'Just tell him and then deal with the consequences. If he doesn't want to know, then at least you've tried. If he does, well . . . having a baby is full on. There's nothing glamorous about it and the more help you have, the better.'

She's right. I just don't want to do it.

We find a vase and head back to Missy's room. Other people have arrived so we keep it short.

'Thanks for popping in. Great to see you.' Missy looks euphoric. 'I love you guys so much and, Lizzie, thanks for everything, I really appreciate it.'

We say goodbye to the gushing new mum and make our way to the car park. We don't discuss my situation again, nor does Frankie mention her previous problems. It's one of those conversations that comes along when you most need it – then goes into the vault, never to be discussed again.

Whether I like it or not, I have to tell Jake. He has a right to know.

Unfortunately.

Frankie drops me home and I feel like going straight to bed, even though it's still light. I want to speak to Clem. I even pick up the phone but then sadly put it down. She probably won't take my call anyway. Feeling a rush of emotion, I turn on my computer to write an email instead.

Hi Clem,

I know you don't want to talk to me right now and fair enough. I'm sorry for everything I've done. Or haven't done. You've every right to hate me. All I can say is I'm so sorry and I will never let you down again. You're my best friend and you're an incredible person. You're the person I want to be. I hang around you in the hope it rubs off. Obviously not enough of it has, yet. Please call me when you're ready to talk. I will be here.

Your not-so-good friend,

Dizzy Lizzie

I sign off with the name that Clem always called me at school, hoping to stir some happy memories to the surface and make her smile.

But all it does is make me cry.

14

'You look good, Lizzie. Have you put on weight?'

I look up with a start to see Nathan standing over my desk.

'No! I don't think so.'

Surely I can't be showing already? I've only been preggers for about five seconds. Well, seven weeks to be precise. Maybe because I'm just so damn constipated, I'm starting to puff up like a balloon. No one talks about that minor pregnancy symptom. Even Missy never mentioned it, and that's saying something.

Maybe it's what I'm wearing. I couldn't find anything suitable in my cupboard this morning. Everything made me feel fat or sick. Finally, I chose a loose-flowing kaftan-like dress, an impulse purchase on a Bali holiday I took with Clem. Everyone was wearing them, so of course I had to have one. As with most holiday clothes purchases, I wore it every day until we came home and haven't touched it since. But now it's ideal. Wearing it today makes me feel happy, like I'm on a summer holiday once again, and Clem and I are still the best of friends. The downside is that it reminds me that Clem and I are nothing like that now. Suddenly I want to take the dress off, but I can't. I'm at work and I have nothing else to wear. And I don't think underwear would fit their strict dress code.

'It's just your face, it's . . . I don't know, a bit fuller, or something,' says Nathan, who is now looking at me very intently.

'Maybe too many muffins,' I joke, hoping he is satisfied with that and wishing he wouldn't examine me quite so closely.

'No really, you look great,' he says, in a serious tone. 'I like the kaftan. Hey, I heard about your friend at the baby shower.'

'My friend?'

'Yeah, your friend. Clem. Did she really have no idea about her ex going out with that girl?'

'Ah, no . . .'

'But you did?'

'Er, not really. I just saw them out one night. I didn't know they were together.'

'But you didn't tell Clem?'

'No, I was going to –'

'But you didn't.'

'No.'

'Right.'

'What?'

'Nothing.'

I sigh. 'Yes, I know I did the wrong thing, it's all my fault. I should have told her straightaway, put her out of her misery and spared her any further heartbreak or public embarrassment.'

Nathan's silence speaks volumes. Honestly, some days it feels like I'm at odds with the whole world, and everyone in it.

'Can I get her number?' he asks.

'Whose?'

'Clem's.'

'Why?'

'I thought she might like to get a coffee.'

'Clem and you? Having coffee?'

'Yes, is that so strange?'

I guess it's not so strange, except Nathan is gay and Clem might get the wrong idea and end up heartbroken once again. But maybe Nathan just wants to be friends, and Clem could do with another one of those. Maybe he wants a lawyer. That must be it. I remember I have one of her business cards in my purse so I fish it out and give it to Nathan.

'She's really good, by the way.'

'What?'

'Lawyer. She's a really great lawyer.'

'Right, good to know.'

Nathan puts the card in his pocket and saunters back to his workstation. A call drops in, so my attention turns to selling wine. Another potential customer. I've been so focused at work this week and I'm selling well. Steve's really pleased with me. I've even been put on the list of big buyers. It makes all the difference as I'm only talking to customers who purchase huge amounts of premium wine on a regular basis. And with my head down and my attention firmly on selling the next case of expensive reds, I've hardly noticed Jake at all.

The best thing is that we get a commission for every case of wine we sell, so the more I sell, the more I earn. It's a relief to know there'll be a little more in my pay packet at the end of the week. I definitely need it, especially if I'm going to be a single mum. But what's going to happen when I have the baby? How will I afford to live? Who will help look after the baby when I go to work? There are so many things I haven't thought through, but as usual, I've stuck my head in the sand and am hoping it all sorts itself out. But nothing is getting sorted out at all. Life, it seems, doesn't let you off that easily.

The days pass by slowly. No Clem, no Jake. Not much of anything apart from an overwhelming feeling of having completely mucked up my life. Not that my life was ever really going to plan.

When I'm not at work, I spend most of my time sitting on the sofa, looking at the wall or watching episodes of *Friends*. I do the entire series. Mostly because it makes me feel like I have some friends and we all hang out together every day in one of our flats, or the local café.

I don't think I've ever felt so alone. My parents still don't know about my latest predicament. I desperately want to call them and come clean. They would know exactly what to do. Not that they'd be thrilled with the news, particularly Mum, although they'd stick by me and tell me that everything was going to be fine. But it feels like I'm always going back home with yet another disaster. I just can't do it to them again. And I'm too ashamed to explain why Clem and I are no longer friends.

While my sales have picked up at work, how long will it last? The job is incredibly boring and my ability to sell so inconsistent. Some weeks are great, while others I barely make enough to pay rent. Put that together with the fact that my child will have no responsible father-figure, and I have plenty to panic about, which I mostly do in the middle of the night. That is, when I'm not feeling totally overwhelmed by the fact that I know so little about having a baby. I don't even know what to buy. Even before her shower, Missy already had a house full of products. I know there are things a baby needs, I just lack Missy's enthusiasm. Why does society put so much pressure on women to buy stuff for their baby? It merely creates a sense of guilt, of not being able to adequately provide for your child. I already know I'm not going to be able to provide for my child in all the ways I want to. I don't need the world judging me, making me feel worse.

Physically and emotionally exhausted from late-night worrying, I decide to take this pregnancy by the horns. It's time I find out what's going on for me now, and what's going to happen in the next few months. My next free day I head straight to the library and take out every baby book I can find. I read each one cover to cover, and I have to say it's illuminating. Pregnancy is extraordinary, women are incredible and childbirth is absolutely mind-blowing! Apparently, right now, my baby is the size of a medium kalamata olive, not a peanut as I thought. Hands and feet are forming and the eyelids are starting to appear. Actually sounds a bit creepy, but miraculous all the same.

Apart from giving birth, I'm intrigued to read about what happens afterwards – day-to-day life with a baby, which all sounds pretty intense, what with the feeding, crying and nappy changing. And that's before you walk out the door! It seems when you do go out to the park or shopping centre, life gets even more complicated with all the things you need to take. But the thought of Missy's awful nappy bag fills me with dread. There's no way I'll be seen carrying around something so frightful. When my baby arrives, I will be sporting something fabulous. Something *trés chic* that looks nothing like an old lady's bag. I will be a girl-about-town who has embraced motherhood with the greatest of style. Plus, as a single mum, I need to look super hot if I have any hope of finding the real Mr Right.

Surely someone somewhere must have created a cool baby bag? I jump on the internet, determined to find out. And if it doesn't exist, I'll have to damn well make one.

My mother's voice cuts through my thoughts, reminding me how much she loved my high school creations. How my designs were as good as those we saw shopping the other day. She's right. I should get back into it, and maybe this is what I should make for starters. A bag. A nappy bag, to be precise. Could I do that? It's been so long, I've probably forgotten how to thread the machine, let alone design a pattern. I wish I could talk it through with Clem. She always loved my designs back at school, and would often ask me to whiz things up for her. I'd love to hear her opinion on a nappy bag. She's so into babies and their accessories, she'd know straightaway if my idea has legs.

However, thanks to my thoughtless, selfish behaviour, I don't have Clem. Still, I can't stop thinking about my idea, to the point where I become completely obsessed. At least it's a bag I'm fixated on, and not an inappropriate relationship.

Since my disastrous design venture after college, when I tried to create my own pieces and nobody bought them (except Clem), I haven't felt the slightest inclination to create anything. Quite frankly, I would never have bought any of them myself, they were so boring and unoriginal. And I don't think Clem ever wore them.

I don't know what I was thinking. Maybe I was trying to make what I thought people wanted rather than staying true to myself? These days, I never like what I see in shops, but I've been too busy to do anything about it.

Or a tiny bit lazy?

Okay, I've been lazy.

And scared, if I'm perfectly honest.

I try to sleep on my new idea but fail miserably, my mind jittery with inspiration. Maybe it does have legs, like my Year 10 formal pantsuit. I know, that didn't end well, but I really think this idea will work. I just know it. A fabulous nappy bag for the happening mum-about-town, ingenious!

I have the next day off but I leap out of bed early and grab some paper and start sketching before I've even made a cup of tea. The hours slip by while ideas crowd my head, forcing their way through all the worries and self-doubt.

I go back to the library, but this time I take out a pile of fashion magazines and pore over them. Then I go to the newsagent and do the same. I sit in a café in a busy strip of Potts Point with a hoard of magazines, a notebook and a coffee, and watch the glamorous passers-by. It doesn't take me long to know exactly how I want the bag to look, and the sorts of patterns and colours I want to use. I just have to come up with a prototype. And, because it's something I'll need pretty soon, I have to get on with it. If I don't, then I'll be stuck with a grandma bag. Nothing like a good incentive.

Next I visit a local park I've never noticed before. Filled with prams and babies, it's the perfect place to see nappy bags in action. I watch the mothers intently, noting what they have and how they carry it. I settle down on a bench, which no one is using because no one else in the park is actually sitting. All the mums are on the go, chasing runaway toddlers, wiping faces, pushing kids on swings, handing out snacks. It's not relaxing for mums at all. And I see why a big bag is essential. So much is needed. One little boy smears his Vegemite sandwich all down his top and tries to wash it with his water bottle, drenching himself completely. His mum produces a whole change of clothes out of her bag, like a magician pulling a rabbit from a hat. Another cute little girl, only just walking, sits in a muddy puddle. Her mother pulls more than a rabbit from her bag to sort that out.

Apart from wardrobes of clothes, I watch as mothers grab little plastic containers of neatly chopped fruit, sultanas, rice crackers and tiny triangle sandwiches. Plus water bottles, milk bottles, wipes, nappies, little rattle toys, sunhats and suncream. One mother even has a spare towel to wipe down the slide after her child tipped out all the water from his sipper cup. I'm sure if I wait long enough, someone will pull out a kitchen sink and do all the washing up. Or more importantly, a fully stocked bar to whip up a few much-needed cocktails.

Dazed by the scene at the park, I leave and make my way to a big baby shop that Missy is always talking about. It's so big it's called That Big Baby Shop. It's the go-to place for all your baby needs, apparently, so it's perfect for my research. It might even help me sort out what I should buy for my own baby.

I walk into what feels like another dimension, filled with all sorts of foreign products and gizmos, not to mention an abundance of frills and lace. It's so powerful. I'm not even here to do any serious shopping, but it's drawing me in like a magnet. Keep focused, Lizzie. Nappy bags. Where are they?

A shop assistant takes me over to an accessory section where there's a display wall featuring all sorts of bags. Just as she starts asking too many personal pregnancy questions, another woman with a huge belly approaches, inquiring about some complicated travel cot/bassinet/change table combo, and the assistant happily takes her off in another direction, leaving me in peace.

I check out the bags, one by one. I carefully study the different pockets, clasps and straps. Some of the designs are passable, but the fabrics are simply awful. You wouldn't catch me carrying any of them. I'd sooner pop everything in a plastic bag.

In my head, I hear a chorus of women led by Missy and Clem saying, 'Where would you put the water bottle? Where would you keep baby food nice and cool? Where would you put the baby wipes?' Yes, there are certain features a mum needs in a baby bag. But that doesn't mean she has to live without style or flair. And what about the non-baby items like makeup and your phone? Has anyone thought of those?

I choose the best one of the lot. It's bright red with large navy spots and has a wide adjustable strap and plenty of internal and external pockets. The fabric is too loud but the design is workable. Besides, if I buy it, then one less woman will have to carry it around. One more customer for me. I think about buying them all so no one has to go through the humiliation of using them, but that will destroy any hope of a profit margin. This one costs $150, which is more than I've spent on a single purchase since those ridiculous green stilettos. And look where they got me. But this is different. I need to study this bag, take it apart then make something one hundred times better.

Next, I drop into a fabulous fabric shop in Surry Hills, known for selling off-cuts at great prices. It's been ages since I bought fabric and can hardly contain my excitement as I joyfully sift through the bargain bins, which are overflowing with opportunity. Finally I choose a small selection (no need to go overboard yet) with quirky contemporary patterns in bright appealing colours. I also grab a packet of tracing paper to make up my own pattern and a few reels of different-coloured cotton.

The minute I'm home I get creative, for once not feeling at all self-conscious. I take the ugly store-bought nappy bag apart, unpicking all the stitches so I can see all the different pieces that woefully come together. I use it as a starting point but completely alter the style and shape. I imagine a more spacious design with a fairly wide base where the top conveniently opens out when placed on the ground. Chic, fabulous and deceptively roomy. I'll include a selection of handy internal compartments but none of those frightful protruding pockets on the outside. I want it to be sleek and stylish, not a bag that just says, 'Hey, I'm a mum!' I draw up my pattern pieces on the tracing paper. It takes a while to get it right. I play around with slightly different shapes, until I have a clear vision of what I want. Then I can't stop until it's out of my head and on the paper in front of me.

The next day, happy with my pattern, I push on and bring it to life (after calling in sick to work). The choice of fabrics is going to be what makes this bag different and quirky. So I pick out a mix of contrasting colours and patterns for both inside and out. I pin the pieces together, making tweaks along the way and carefully writing every adjustment in my notebook. I tack it all loosely together and, amazingly, the bag quickly takes shape in front of me.

By the next afternoon, after another top-selling shift, I'm ready to pull out Nana's old sewing machine and set to work. Surprisingly the machine still works like a dream and I feel like I'm fifteen and back in my old bedroom, in those days when sewing was exciting and full of endless possibilities.

By the end of the week I have a fairly good idea how the bag is going to work and the types of fabrics I want to use. I slave away all weekend and on Sunday morning my first bag is ready. And I'm thrilled. Granted it's still only a rough version but good enough to take out on the town to test it out. Well, just down to a café at Bondi Beach. If there are any mums who know what's what in the world of cutting-edge baby accessories, then these are the ones. If Bondi mums don't go for it, no one will.

I choose Rock Salt, a café where Clem and I started having coffee after doing a big walk. Well, we did a big walk once and then had coffee. After that, we just had coffee. I haven't been in ages, but now Rock Salt is the perfect spot to trial my bag.

When I arrive, I grab a seat in full view of the door and place my bag in a prominent position on the table. There's no point sitting in the corner, letting life pass me by. I order a decaf flat white, grab the paper and settle in for the morning. An hour later, no one has given me or my bag so much as a glance, so I order some toast.

Another hour passes and I get an organic muffin, another coffee and a few refills of tap water. But I'm running out of time. When the waitress brings over the bill (who brings a bill to your table in a café?) I realise it's time to go.

I pack up my things with a sigh, put the café's newspaper back and settle my bill, but I'm not ready to give up. I end up going back to Rock Salt the next day before my afternoon shift. And the next day. And the next. In fact, I keep going back every day before work until it gets to the point where the waitress has my decaf coffee and organic muffin waiting as I walk through the door. But still no one notices my bag.

So I take my bag to the streets instead, swinging it around so flamboyantly you'd have to be blindfolded not to notice. I take it to the supermarket, I take it on the train, I take it everywhere but still it doesn't draw so much as a sideways glance.

Finally, after a particularly vigorous morning of bag-swinging along the beachfront – where I'm almost bowled over by a pair of super-fit Bondi mums, jogging with the most space-aged streamlined prams I've ever seen (need to google that brand) – I'm ready to throw in the towel. Or rather throw the nappy bag into the bin. Those women are my perfect audience. If they don't notice my bag, then no one will.

Feeling exhausted, I decide I really do need a coffee, even if it's only decaf, and I treat myself to a little break at Rock Salt (where the waitress is fast becoming my new best friend).

Sitting at my favourite table, I get out my notebook to read over my notes. Where am I going wrong? Why isn't this working? I sigh heavily, feeling like I'm back at the markets trying to flog my latest uninteresting designs. Honestly, what did I think would happen? That someone would come up, tap me on the shoulder and say how much they love my bag? Life's not like that.

Coffee finished, I drag myself up to the counter to pay when, ironically, someone comes up and taps me on the shoulder.

'Excuse me?'

I turn to see a woman, absolutely stunning, about my age, who is strangely familiar. I can't think how I know her, but I'm sure I do.

'Yes?' I say warmly, in an attempt to hide the fact that I can't remember who on earth she is.

'Sorry to disturb you. I was just wondering where you got your tote?'

It hits me how I know her. Or know *of* her. Of course! She's an actress in a movie that came out last year. She used to be on a TV soap called *Timelines*. I watched it religiously while I was at uni. Did she really wonder where I got my bag? Or am I making that up?

She's probably waiting for me to say something, but I don't want to mention my bag, in case I misheard. She's so beautiful; it's no wonder she's in movies. I wonder if she's married with children? Maybe she's single with lots of lovers. How glamorous! But then I've been single, with not lots of lovers but one or two, and it's not so great. Hopefully, she's happily married.

I feel like I'm looking at her too intensely, so I look at the floor, which must confuse her even more. She starts to get impatient so I force myself to say something before things get really weird.

'This bag?' My voice comes out strangely high-pitched, more like that of a bleating goat than a cool designer.

'Yeah, I love it. Where'd you get it?'

She must have children and recognises the many benefits of my ultra-cool creation. I realise that I'm probably still looking at her a little strangely so I take a breath and force myself to get on with it.

'I made it. It's just something I'm developing. A work-in-progress.'

'Hey, that's awesome. If you ever make them to sell, call me.'

She hands me a card. Who knew actresses have cards these days? *Willow S*, it reads. That's right, no surname. Just a letter. How cool.

'It's actually a nappy bag . . .'

'A what?'

So she doesn't have children, but that's okay. Neither do I. Not yet, anyway.

'My original idea was to create a bag for mums to carry baby stuff around,' I say casually, trying to sound as if motherhood is another universe, distant from me. Which it sort of is at the moment. Probably not as distant as it is for Willow S, though. 'But I guess you could use it for anything really.'

'Oh yeah, right. Like an anything bag!' Willow pauses. 'Great colours. Good size. Really different. Let me know when I can buy one.'

She picks up her bag from a table nearby – soft brown leather and so totally divine, I can't imagine why she would want one of mine – kisses the café owner on both cheeks and glides out the door with her takeaway coffee in hand.

I can't believe what just happened. Someone likes my bag. Enough to want to buy one. And not just any old someone. A well-known and very stylish TV celebrity. Unbelievable! I carefully put the card in my wallet like it's a precious gemstone.

The universe is telling me that my idea might work. And for once, I'm not going to ignore it. Because right now, after everything that's happened, I need something to work out. And fast. And while making a bag for Sydney's latest It Girl is probably the last thing I thought I'd be doing this week, I couldn't be more thrilled. Like a little fleck of light in a dark tunnel, it might just lead to a way out.

15

Over the following week, I can think of nothing but bags. My first attempt is obviously working, but I need to develop it into something totally fabulous before I consider contacting Willow. I fine-tune my pattern and play around with all sorts of fabric combinations. I let my imagination run wild and do exactly what I want, with no one standing over me criticising my choices – and I have to say, it's totally liberating.

I no longer need to seek out new friends, television characters or otherwise. I may soon have one of my own, if all goes well. Maybe not as famous as Rachel, Monica or Phoebe, but a bit more real. And still on the telly from time to time.

I continue my shifts at WineCall to keep money coming in and surprisingly, I'm one of the top sellers for the week again. Bursting with ideas and excitement, I have a newfound energy that customers seem to find irresistible. Even when I tell a customer who is in two minds about a case that she probably shouldn't buy if she isn't one hundred per cent sold on the idea, she's so appreciative of my honest approach that she takes five.

I'm so focused on making bags or selling wine that there's barely a spare second to consider my complicated personal life. Even the morning sickness has eased up slightly, or maybe I'm just too busy to notice it. I hardly give Jake a second look and whenever he's out on the call-centre floor, coming my way, I sneak off to the ladies' toilet. It gets to the point where people must think I have some sort of bladder problem. Actually, I do need to go to the toilet quite often. From what I've read, it's a totally normal pregnancy thing, but it's also an excellent way to avoid a conversation with Jake.

At the end of yet another magnificent shift, during which I only threw up in the bathroom once (okay so it hasn't eased up that much) and sold an impressive total of ninety-eight cases of wine, I log off and bolt to the lift, desperate to get home and get on with Willow's order. However, just as I'm riffling through my bag for my Opal card at the station, Jake appears in front of me, giving me the fright of my life. I'm so rattled, I almost give birth on the spot. Before I can even say 'I don't want to talk to you right now', he gets straight to the point.

'Is it mine?'

'Sorry?' I try to look like I don't know what he's talking about, although there's only one thing he could possibly be talking about.

'The baby? Is it mine?'

Of course he knows. I'm actually surprised it's taken this long to filter through the call-centre gossip machine. There's not much I can do but come clean. Besides, whose baby is it going to be, anyway? What does he think I do, go around chasing every guy

I see, getting pregnant to each and every one? Well, I suppose there was a time when that would have been a fair assumption. Not the pregnant bit, but maybe the 'chasing every guy' bit.

'Of course it is!' I say hotly.

'When were you going to tell me?' Jake throws back with an equal amount of heat.

'Look, it's nothing you need to worry about. It's my problem and . . . who told you, anyway?'

Frankie, I bet. Or Missy. So much for the vault. Still, in some ways I'm relieved. He had to know sometime. It doesn't really matter how he found out. But he's caught me off guard. I had a speech all prepared and now I can't remember a word of it.

'Doesn't matter who told me. I just wish it had been you. Were you ever going to tell me?'

Surprisingly Jake is furious. Not about the baby, it seems to me, but about not knowing. Frankie and Dr Mitch were right. You don't know how a guy will react to such news. But it's not like he made it easy for me.

'I wanted to tell you, but you didn't even have the decency to turn up to our date. Why would I want a person like that in my child's life?'

'Like it or not, it's my child too, so I'll always be a part of his life.'

'I don't know the gender. It may not be a boy.'

Jake ignores my comment.

'I'm not walking away,' he says.

'You wouldn't be walking away – we're not even together. And I don't want you around out of guilt. My baby doesn't need a guilt father.'

'It's better than no father.'

I open my mouth to speak and stop. Jake is right. It *is* better than no father at all.

'Sorry, Jake.' I drop my head and look at my hands. 'Perhaps I should have told you, but I just don't want you to feel you have to stick around. I'll be fine, and you never know, there might be a stepfather one day.'

'But that person won't be the real father. There's a difference . . .'

Jake hesitates, looking a little flustered. Unusual. I've only ever seen him looking totally cool and in control and now he's completely weirding me out with this new, slightly vulnerable demeanour. I wish he'd just accept one of the many 'Get Out of Jail' cards I've offered and go away.

'I know that you're the one who has to actually have the kid, but I don't think I could sleep at night knowing I had a son or daughter out there who didn't know who I was.' He pauses as if struggling to find the words he wants to say. 'Look, my father walked out on us.'

'Oh, Jake! I'm so sorry.'

'It's okay. I was only a few months old so I don't remember. I never really knew him. And Mum remarried a few years later and she and Phil had my younger brother and sister. I've no complaints. Phil's great, I've always loved him. He's just not my real father.'

'Did you ever try to find your real father?'

'He turned up once. Out of nowhere. On my tenth birthday. He seemed nice enough, but there was no lightning bolt flash of recognition, or the rush of emotion I'd always hoped for.'

I don't say a word, mostly because I've never heard Jake speak so much, or so openly. Now he's started, he doesn't seem to want to stop.

'I know better than anyone that it's not always about a blood connection,' he says, putting a gentle hand on my stomach, on our baby. 'But I don't want my child going through life wondering who I am. And then finally meeting me and feeling nothing at all.'

I sigh inwardly. Of all the people to get impregnated by, I choose the one who was abandoned by his father. Not just a super-hot motorcycling man-about-town, after all. You never know what's going on for people behind the scenes.

'I'm sorry for not showing up to our date,' he says, with what seems like genuine remorse. 'I've never been very good at committing to anything or anyone, but maybe this can change me – a new leaf and all that.'

'Maybe,' I say, not feeling convinced. 'I just don't want you to be with me because you feel you have to. I'm a big girl, I can look after myself. I don't need your pity.'

'Look, sometimes you're a bit crazy and kind of full on, but I thought we were having fun. Why can't we just have a bit more and see where it goes? We're going to be in each other's lives now anyway. Why not enjoy it?'

I look at Jake, slightly confused. I hear words coming out of his mouth, the words I have been longing for him to say. And he's looking quite serious, almost misty, so he must mean it, mustn't he? But it's not quite the declaration of commitment I was hoping for. I want to believe this is what he intends, but something deep down in the pit of my growing tummy is warning me, like a neon sign flashing on and off. Should I listen to Jake or to my gut instinct? It's not much of a choice: Jake has been anything but reliable and my instincts have been way off since I thought going out with Jean Paul at uni was the best idea ever.

Jake is the father. And I can't deny that I'm still attracted to him. But can I trust him? This is not just hanging out with some guy. This is someone who will be in my baby's life forever, and therefore in mine. Next to deciding to keep my baby, this is one of the biggest decisions I've ever faced. And all I can think of is the awful feeling when Jake didn't turn up to dinner that night. How can I be with someone who does that? Who treated me like that? But maybe that wasn't all Jake's fault. I hadn't been entirely straight with him. We'd only been out a couple of times and he had no idea that he'd impregnated me and that I was planning a future for us together. Maybe if I'd been more honest, this would be a different situation.

Ever since Jean Paul, I've run away from anyone who really wants to get serious, always opting for bad boys who don't want to commit instead. Now a seemingly bad boy wants to commit, I owe it to myself – and my baby – to give him a chance. You never know, maybe Jake really is The One I've been looking for? Maybe I need to take a leap of faith and go against my unreliable instincts?

Jake is gazing at me as I churn through my dilemma, a look of concern on his handsome face that is making me weak at the knees. Am I prepared to give him a second chance? Things will certainly have to change. I will have new standards this time, one of which is that he must turn up for pre-arranged dates. I'm sure I should have a few more, but that's certainly a good place to start.

'Okay,' I say eventually, almost in a whisper.

'Okay, what?'

'Okay, we can maybe see how it goes.'

Jake pulls me towards him and kisses me, but I push him back. 'But stand me up again and the deal's off. Understand?'

'Sure, boss,' he says, standing to attention, a cheeky twinkle in his eye.

He pulls me towards him again. This time I melt into his arms and he kisses me like I've always wanted him to. But I don't feel any stomach backflips. Not even a flutter. Probably the pregnancy hormones are interfering with my sex hormones. Or that neon sign in my gut, still flashing its warning. Sure, there are probably millions of reasons why I should walk away. But I don't want to. I definitely want this. I want my baby, and I want Jake. Things will be different. I'll heed that flashing sign – I won't be a doormat anymore – but I know this is the right thing to do.

'So what happens next?' Jake asks.

'Well, you can start by massaging my feet every night and bringing me peppermint tea in bed every morning. If you manage that then maybe –'

'I meant with the baby, have you had a scan yet?'

'Oh, right.' I sigh, remembering that it's more about the baby now, rather than any of my needs. 'I'm supposed to go and have some blood tests, and I'm having my twelve-week scan in a few weeks. It's a big one, apparently. You get to see the baby and they check if everything is okay. Do you want to come?'

I didn't know I was going to ask Jake, but it pops out before I can stop myself. I figure by the time I'm asking the father of my unborn baby if he wants to come and see the first scan, it's probably time to dispense with trying to play hard to get.

'Do you want me to come?'

'Yes, I do.' And I mean it; I want Jake by my side when we get the first glimpse of our child.

'I'm so there, babe,' he says, his strong, sculpted arms around me.

'And in the meantime, how about I come and pick you up tonight and we celebrate?'

'Do you mind if we stay in? I'm exhausted.' If Jake really is The One, I have to start being completely honest.

'No problem. I'll cook you dinner. Don't worry about a thing. I'll pick up some groceries and come over around seven-ish. How's that?'

'Perfect.'

'Is there anything you can't eat? Aren't there things you are supposed to avoid? Soft cheeses or something like that?'

How come everyone in the world knows more about pregnancy than I do? Even my cool rockstar boyfriend. At least I've done some reading now so he won't think I've been negligent with our baby.

'Oh yeah, no soft cheeses.'

'Or shellfish . . . no prawns or lobster.'

'No, definitely not,' I say vehemently, trying to sound as if I would never eat such a thing in my state yet knowing that a week ago I would have jumped at the chance to eat lobster.

'See you then.' Jake kisses me on the cheek and walks back towards the call centre.

Life is odd. If that had happened two months ago I would have thought I'd died and gone to heaven. Now I finally have everything I've ever wanted within easy reach and I'm not sure how I feel about it. How I feel about Jake. I was definitely falling in love him before and I'm pretty sure I can do it again. So why am I having doubts? Maybe because something inside me doesn't quite believe what he's saying. Fair enough, it's not like he's proved himself to be reliable. Or perhaps it's because I've never heard anyone say things like that to me and actually mean them. Yes, that's probably it. I've never got this far in a relationship and I'm freaking out.

I'll give him the benefit of the doubt, just one more time. I've got nothing more to lose so surely there's everything to gain? Mind you, every time I say that, I seem to lose a little something more.

I lie down on my bed the minute I get home. Then I must fall asleep, because suddenly my phone wakes me and it's dark outside.

Have to stay late and do the lock-up tonight. Will 11 pm be too late to come by?

Jake. How could he forget he had to do the lock-up?

Yes, too late. See you at work tomorrow x

So no cooked dinner for me, but I don't feel like it now. I make some toast and a cup of herbal tea and climb under my doona. My phone beeps one last time.

Sweet dreams babe xxx

I lie in bed thinking about Jake, wondering if I've made the right decision, until I feel myself drifting back to sleep.

16

'Lizzie, you haven't even logged on.'

I look around from the lifeless screen of my computer to see Nathan, sitting behind me.

'Yeah, right, better get started,' I say, suddenly flustered. I just can't stop thinking about how this week has unfolded, with Jake jumping so eagerly aboard my baby train. It almost seems too good to be true. And it's certainly playing havoc with my wine sales.

Finally ready to start, I flick my eyes towards the supervisors' podium where Jake is taking command, firing out instructions left, right and centre, looking like a superhero. He glances over and gives me a sneaky grin. Completely gorgeous. The combination of him and me will result in one pretty cute baby. Not that I'm quite as good-looking as Jake, but he will more than make up for any shortfall.

'I bumped into Clem the other day.'

I swivel back to Nathan, my heart catapulting into my throat.

'Really? Where did you see her? What did she say? Did she ask after me?'

'Not really.'

'Oh.' Fair enough, I think to myself sadly. Why would she ask about me? I haven't tried to contact her again since my email. She never responded, but I wonder now if I should have kept trying.

'Did she remember you?' I ask.

'Yeah, we chatted.'

'Is she okay?'

'Yeah, pretty good. Busy.'

'Oh.' I feel so ashamed of my behaviour, I don't know what else to say. Luckily the calls start dropping in so our conversation ends there. But I can't get Clem off my mind.

Normally, I would have rung her immediately, to tell her that Jake finally knows about the baby and is into the idea. But I can't. No doubt she wouldn't even speak to me. Zoe is probably on high alert to block my calls no matter what. And anyway, I'm pretty sure I know what Clem would think about it all.

But I feel like I must talk to her and tell her how much she means to me. I've been a shocking friend and it's time to try again. Now the Jake situation has been sorted and I've cleared the cobwebs from one corridor of my confusing life, it's time to spring-clean another. Knowing there'll be no way around Zoe, I ring Clem's home number, which goes through to voicemail.

I listen to her happy recorded voice, which asks me to leave a message as though she really wants to hear from me. What will I say? Suddenly there's a beep and a silence to fill.

'Clem. Hi, it's me . . . Lizzie, that is . . . Sorry I haven't been in touch. Can we meet up for a coffee sometime? I really need to speak to you . . . I'm so sorry for everything. I would rather be telling you all this in person but you know how scared I am of Zoe . . . I guess I'll just say it now – you really are my best friend, I love you and miss you so much and I couldn't bear to lose you. I wouldn't blame you if you never wanted to see me again but I don't know what –'

Voicemail cuts out. Damn. Definitely more to say. I redial.

'Yeah, hi. Me again. Sorry, the machine didn't give me much time. I was just saying that I don't know what I'd do without you in my life. Our friendship means everything in the world to me and not being able to talk to you every day has been absolutely unbearable. I really –'

I'm cut off again. Damn. Stupid voicemail. I'm tempted to try one more time, but decide instead to go to her flat after work. She won't be able to ignore me on her intercom.

As soon as my shift finishes, I rush to the lift. Jake catches me just as the doors are opening.

'Get together later?'

I really want to, but right now Clem is my priority. I don't want to share all the sordid details with him, so I say I have to visit a friend and that I'll cook him dinner later. We arrange to meet at my place after he finishes work. Happy with that, he sneaks a quick kiss on my lips.

'Whoa, your boobs are getting big!'

I sigh. Everything seems to be getting big, and everyone feels free to tell me. It's early days and I'm showing already. What will I look like after about twenty weeks? Will I fit through doors? And forty weeks? The thought is horrifying.

By the time I leave work and catch a train to Edgecliff, it's nearly six-thirty. Clem probably won't be home but I walk around to her apartment building to give it a try anyway. I press her buzzer. No answer. I buzz a few people until I find someone who lets me into the building. I climb the two flights of stairs to Clem's floor and sit and wait. Forty-five minutes later, I leave a note, written on an old receipt in my lip pencil.

Hi, it's me. Call me. So sorry about everything. Miss you.

Except it looks a bit like 'Miss poo'. And I don't have a lip pencil sharpener on me. Not much of a white flag, but she'll get the message.

It's late now and I'm starving. There's nothing to eat at home and as I said I'd cook for Jake, I stop off at the local supermarket and pick up a mountain of vegies and some chicken to make a stir-fry. Surely the baby will appreciate that.

I text Jake on my way home but there's no reply.

Once home, I'm so hungry that even my kitchen table is starting to look delicious. In hindsight, probably a better option than the stir-fry. Without a wok or a recipe it turns into a sort of Asian stew. Too much oyster sauce. Too much everything. I don't know what has happened to Jake. It's nearly eight. Why hasn't he called to let me know where he is? I can't possibly wait a moment longer so I scoff it down. Then I feel sick. And exhausted. I try calling Jake again, but he doesn't answer. Maybe he's in a noisy bar and can't hear the phone. Eventually, I climb into bed, and even though I'm beyond tired, I can't settle.

I must slip off to sleep, though, because I suddenly wake up startled, feeling uncomfortable in my stomach. I toss and turn but can't get back to sleep. Maybe the chicken was off. I read something about having to be careful of undercooked meat during pregnancy. Maybe I didn't cook the chicken for long enough. It did look a bit strange, come to think of it. What if I've done something terrible to the baby?

I look at the clock. A quarter to two. Still no Jake. Unbelievable! Once again, he has let me down. Fuming, I plan exactly what I will say to him and this time I won't give in. He had his chance and he blew it. I furiously throw back my covers and get out of bed. I pad into the kitchen for a glass of water, when a sharp pain makes me double over. I stagger to the bathroom and sit on the toilet, where a gush of red screams at me. What? Oh, God. That doesn't seem right. What's happening?

I start to shake. I'm only ten weeks along; this can't be anything good. I call Jake immediately, my hands trembling so much I can hardly press the buttons. His phone rings out so I leave a message saying I'm worried about the baby and to give me a call.

Where is he? For the past week he has answered his phone every time I've called. I know it's never very far from his side. But I can't worry about it now. I have to deal with the baby, but I'm in such a panic, I don't know what to do. So I call the only person who will.

'Hello,' says a muffled voice.

'Clem, it's Lizzie.'

'What do you want? What time is it?'

'I'm bleeding. Quite a lot. It won't stop.'

Clem springs into action. I knew she'd have an instant plan.

'Call the hospital, and let them know you're coming in. Then call a cab. I'll meet you at Emergency.'

Thankful, I hang up. Right, ring the hospital, Lizzie. Another stab of pain stops me in my tracks. And another. It's like I've swallowed a knife that's trying to get out. As I breathe through it, a folder catches my eye. Thank God! All the information that Sue the Midwife gave me. I leaf through the brochures, find an emergency number for the maternity ward and dial it. I explain my situation to the person at reception who sounds a lot like Bleached Hair Man. He immediately puts me on hold and I find myself listening to Bette Midler singing 'Wind Beneath My Wings'. I wept my way through *Beaches* as a teenager and the effect is doubled right now. The tears start to roll down my cheeks until a calm female voice comes on the line.

'Yes, hello. How can I help?'

'My name's Lizzie March and I'm about ten weeks pregnant, but I've started bleeding quite heavily.' I try to keep it together, but my voice cracks.

'Right, try not to worry. Bleeding in early pregnancy can be quite common, but best you come in now and we'll check it out. Have you got someone to drive you? Husband, partner, friend?'

That opens the floodgates and I find myself sobbing. I want to explain that there is a partner, although I don't know where he is, but this woman doesn't need all the pathetic details. I pull myself together and explain that I'm about to call a taxi and a friend is meeting me at the hospital.

I hang up and try Jake again. No answer. What's going on? He should be here with me now, going to the hospital at two am. What about when the baby is on its way? Will he take my call then?

As panicked as I am, a small, clear-visioned part of me can see that he's not really part of my baby picture. Here I am, in my one-person flat, trying to get myself to Emergency. And not because I'm an independent woman who's trying to do it all – but because my so-called partner is not as responsible as he said he'd be. He couldn't even get himself over for dinner at my place, let alone answer my call in the middle of the night! He would hear his phone, and from past experience he would never have hesitated to take what would most probably have been a booty call. I am obviously not the priority to him I was hoping to be.

Besides Clem, there's another person I need to call. I grab my wallet and pull out a card.

'Hello?' Cherie doesn't even sound sleepy; she must be out working.

'It's Lizzie. Bit of an emergency.' My insides twist in a sudden cramp, heightening the urgency in my voice. 'I'm bleeding . . . please come and get me? I need to get to hospital.'

Cherie doesn't need any more explanation. 'Be there in five, love.'

I pull on my dressing gown and ugg boots, grab my handbag and close the door behind me. Just as I get to the street, Cherie pulls up.

'What's happening, love?'

'I think I'm losing my baby.'

'Don't fret, sweetheart. Let's get you to Emergency and see what's what. You never know.'

'I don't want to bleed all over your taxi.'

'Don't even think about it, love. I've got a towel in the back for exactly this sort of situation.'

I start to feel woozy. Cherie hands me the towel and helps me into her car and I sink thankfully into the cushy velvet seat. I ring Jake again, but now his phone is off. Dead battery? Must be.

As we drive to hospital, I fill Cherie in on the latest Jake update. If she thinks I'm an idiot for giving him another chance, she doesn't say so. She just listens and responds positively. Exactly what I need right now.

Despite the empty night streets the trip seems endless, but eventually we pull up outside Emergency. Cherie helps me out of the car and straight to the Emergency reception desk. The receptionist asks for my Medicare card while a nurse takes us through a frosted glass door to a little room and helps me up on the bed.

'How are you going?' she asks in a gentle voice.

'Not great,' I say, trying to smile.

She asks me all about the events of the night so far, as well as details of my pregnancy and health in general. She makes sure I'm comfortable and takes my blood pressure and temperature. It's nice to be momentarily distracted from my crampy tummy and impending bad news.

'Okay, the doctor will be with you shortly. Try not to worry,' she says kindly as she heads back out the glass door.

It's nice of her to say so, it's probably part of her job description, but it's much easier said than done. Cherie stays with me, for which I'm grateful, although she probably should be getting back to work.

'Don't be a goose, darl. I'm not leaving you now. Plenty of other cabbies around tonight looking for work.'

I sigh with relief. I couldn't bear waiting alone.

'Thanks. Really appreciate it.'

The nurse pops her head back around the door, asking if I'm up for a visitor. Just as I nod, Clem bursts in, a look of panic on her face. And for once, it's not about the germs she knows to live in hospitals. When I see her, the tears start running down my cheeks, like water from a leaking tap.

'Hey, Lizzie, it's okay, everything's going to be okay.' Clem immediately puts her arm around me and introduces herself to Cherie.

Of course, they've never met! As I sob into Clem's shoulder, I try to retell the story of the night when I first got into Cherie's cab, but the words are jumbled. Both women hush me and tell me not to worry. Two completely different friends, both here in my hour of desperation. No need for backstories right now.

'Hello there.' A friendly voice at the door interrupts our little group. 'What's up?'

'Dr Mitch!' I say, like we are long-lost friends. I am absurdly glad to see him. 'What are you doing here?'

'I work here, remember?'

It hadn't entered my head that Dr Mitch might be on duty, but now I'm completely thrilled. It's so nice to see a familiar face. We barely know each other, but there's something about traumatic experiences that bonds people, I think. And I seem to have been through a few lately. And mostly in the presence of Dr Mitch.

'Hi, I'm Clem, Lizzie's best friend. We met briefly the last time Lizzie was in Emergency.' Clem is looking flushed and is smiling far too much. What is going on? Clem hasn't spoken to me for the past two weeks and now, in a flash, she's back to being my best friend.

'And I'm Cherie.'

Dr Mitch looks at Cherie intently. 'Sorry, but do I know you? You look familiar.'

'I don't think so, love, but maybe I've dropped you somewhere in my taxi.'

'And sung a song along the way,' I add. 'Cherie was a famous singer – Cherie L'Amour.'

'Cherie L'Amour!' Mitch looks so excited he can hardly speak. 'I used to listen to your music all the time, growing up. My parents were huge fans. Still are. I think I've got one of your old vinyl records somewhere.'

'That's nice to hear,' says Cherie with a smile, then looks down at me. 'Looks like you're in good hands now, so I'll hotfoot it back to work.'

'If I find your album at home, would you sign it for me?' says Mitch, a star-struck look on his face.

'Been a while since anyone's asked for my autograph,' says Cherie. 'Still gives me a buzz. Just let me know and I'll swing by the hospital.'

Cherie gives Dr Mitch her card, squeezes my hand and says to let her know how I get on. Then she disappears out the door. Clem follows her out, in search of the toilets, saying she'll be right back.

Dr Mitch turns his attention to me. 'Now, tell me what's been going on with you.'

I fill him in on the bleeding and the cramps I've been having.

'Okay, let's have a look. I'll just pull this curtain around and examine you, if that's all right. We'll need to organise an emergency ultrasound but the X-ray department is flat out tonight, so we may have to wait.'

'Sorry about this,' I say, realising that Dr Mitch is going to have to get a little intimate with me, and not in a good way.

'No worries. It happens all the time,' he says cheerily.

Not much comfort.

'Am I losing the baby?'

'Hard to know yet. Maybe, maybe not.'

Dr Mitch slides smoothly into doctor mode, which eases the awkwardness. I'm sure he has to check out women's private parts all the time. Water off a doctor's back. A complete professional. I have nothing to be embarrassed about.

'Now try not to worry, I'm just going to get a nurse to help me for a sec,' Dr Mitch says after one quick peek.

'Why? What's wrong?' I reply, panic-stricken.

Why does he need help? Is my situation too much for one doctor to handle? Or maybe I have extraordinary bits and pieces down there, the likes of which he has never before seen?

'It's okay, there's still a fair bit of bleeding. We'll get you settled and I'll go and organise that ultrasound.'

With that he leaves. Clem pops her head around the curtain. 'How are you? Okay?'

I shrug my shoulders. The trouble is, I don't know. I can't help but think I'm losing my baby. A baby I wouldn't have chosen to have at this point in my life, if I'm completely honest. A baby whose father can't even take my call in my time of need. Or listen to my message and call me back. But now that there's a chance I'm losing that baby, I'm realising just how much I actually want it.

'You'll be right. I know someone who once had a bleed at ten weeks and everything was fine. It happens all the time,' says Clem, pulling out sanitiser and drenching her hands.

I don't say anything. Yes, it does happen all the time. Very normal. But for one in four women, it's not exactly fine. I don't know much about baby stuff, but that I do know.

'What about Jake?' asks Clem. 'Does he know about the baby?'

Of course! Clem knows nothing of the Jake development so I quickly fill her in, sticking to the basics: how excited he is, and how much he wants not only the baby, but me as well.

'That's great. So, where is he now?'

'Not sure. I couldn't get through to him and now his phone is off. I've left a message . . .'

Clem says nothing, but I know from her neutral expression and deafening silence that she's far from convinced. To be honest, after he didn't show up for dinner or answer my calls, not only is the neon warning light flashing brighter than ever but there's also an ear-piercing evacuation alarm going off. She's absolutely right to doubt Jake. I certainly am. But she didn't see the look in his eyes when he was telling me about his own father. Or see how much he wants to be in our baby's life. Until I know otherwise, I have to allow that there might be a good explanation for why he hasn't been in touch.

Before I can say this, Dr Mitch reappears with a nurse in tow, and Clem's cheeks turn pink around the edges. This is something that happens when she's nervous. She obviously finds him attractive. I file this information away so I can later persuade Clem to go on a date with him. Of course! Why didn't I think of that before? They'd be perfect for each other.

'Right, Lizzie, this is Jane. She's a nurse who will help me sort you out for now,' says Mitch in his gentle and reassuring voice. 'We're still waiting to see if we can get you an ultrasound. We may just have to wait until the clinic opens in the morning – whichever comes first. In the meantime, you'll be taken to the Emergency ward and monitored throughout the night.'

Clem excuses herself, and Dr Mitch examines me properly. The nurse takes all my vitals, puts a canula into my hand and helps clean me up. When Dr Mitch is satisfied that I'm as comfortable as I can be and that my blood pressure is normal, he leaves to go and check on some guy who put his hand through a window. He promises to pop in on me later.

Dr Mitch strides out of the room with the same sense of purpose he had when we bumped into each other at the hospital café. Clem wanders back in and I wonder if this is going to be weird. There's so much to say but I have no idea how to start. Besides, the nurse is still pottering around, so now is not the time.

'You okay to stay here tonight?' asks Clem, as if we only spoke yesterday over a couple of flat whites. 'Do you want me to stay with you?'

I look at my friend who has bags under her eyes. She'll be starting work early in the morning with another long day ahead of her. A lawyer's life is so exhausting and I can't deprive her of any more much-needed sleep. My problems and I have already taken up too much of Clem's time.

'Don't be silly. You go, I'll be fine. And Clem? Thanks so much for helping me.'

'Call me the minute you know anything. My phone will be right next to me all night, and I'll be back in the morning.'

Clem gives me a kiss. Then she leaves. Yes, a lot to say, but not right now.

My phone is sitting still and silent on the bedside table, taunting me, as if to say, 'Where is he when you need him?' I send an abrupt text saying that I'm in hospital, possibly losing our baby. Surely that will get a reply. But nothing.

'Are you warm enough?' Jane asks with a soft Irish lilt. She seems so lovely, I feel like crying. Nurses are wonderful. Who else would be so nice to a perfect stranger? I've never really liked the Irish accent, perhaps because the last time I heard one, it was from the mouth of a drunken backpacker, but now it sounds like heaven. I want to give her a hug and say we should have coffee one day, but then I don't really know her, and it might appear odd. Damn these stupid hormones.

'Are you okay, sweetheart?' she says.

'Not sure . . . tired, shocked.'

'Try not to think about it. We'll find out everything in the morning. Just get some sleep now, if you can. Do you want another blanket?'

I nod and she tucks another cotton hospital blanket around me. I can hardly keep my eyes open. Her singsong voice chatters away as I feel myself sinking into sleep, despite the fact that I don't want tomorrow to come, for fear of what I might find out.

17

I don't know what time it is, nor, in fact, where I am. I've left my uncomfortable hospital bed and am walking along a street, the warmth of the sun on my face. Did Clem take me home? What's going on?

I look down to see my hospital gown, still smeared with blood. But before I can work out why they didn't at least let me get dressed, a van drives past and a strangely familiar voice yells out, 'I LOVE YOU-OOO!'

I can't believe my ears. I look up and catch a quick glimpse of the driver. That was Jake, I'm sure of it. He's here and he loves me!

Except to my dismay, the van doesn't stop.

'Wait!' I scream. 'Wait for me! I might love you too!'

I bolt down the street at top speed. I don't even care that my feet are bare and my hospital gown, flapping madly in the wind, leaves little to anyone's imagination. All I know is that I have to catch up to that van. Jake reached out to me and I have to let him know that I know that he loves me. And to tell him that I love him too.

But the van keeps going so I keep running. Until finally, fraught and out of breath, I wave down a passing taxi, and jump in before the car even stops.

'Follow that van,' I yell. 'Please hurry! It's my possible future partner.'

My taxi driver, to my surprise, turns out to be Cherie dressed as Carmen Miranda, complete with elaborate fruit hat and thick Brazilian accent. She takes off like lightning, weaving in and out of traffic, keeping the van in our sights.

'Don't worry, darling! We won't let him get away!'

Finally, a red light. The van stops. We pull up behind it. I jump out and tap on the driver's tinted window. It lowers and I almost fall over backwards. It's not Jake at all, but Dr Mitch. Looking totally hot with no shirt covering what is definitely Jake's lean and tanned upper body. Everything moves in slow motion as he turns his head towards me, his chocolate mop of hair, longer now, flies out behind him, beads of sweat floating through the air. He looks at me with those crystal blue eyes and my insides ignite.

'Lizzie! You're here,' he says with a brilliant smile. 'I've been looking for you everywhere.'

Totally flustered, I can't seem to put words together, let alone make any sense. I was completely ready for Jake, but Dr Mitch? What's he doing here? And why am I tingling from head to foot?

'Lizzie, I love you,' he says as he reaches out to stroke my face, sending an electric shock through my skin.

I try to explain that we hardly know each other, and that we've only just met. He's also my doctor and surely that crosses some line? I can't deny the attraction at this moment, but I'm in love with someone else.

'Lizzie, I've loved you from the minute we first met.'

Now I know he's making fun of me. That was a highly embarrassing situation that involved falling on a sandstone path while trying to peer into a house that wasn't mine. He couldn't possibly have fallen for me then. And now, in my shapeless gown and with my hair all over my face, I can't look particularly attractive either.

'Oh, Lizzie, Lizzie, Lizzie!'

He just keeps repeating my name, which becomes frustrating, as I'm right here.

'Lizzie, Lizzie!'

I open my eyes with a jolt and Dr Mitch is standing in front of me, dressed in his doctor outfit, hair back to a toothbrush. Now it's my turn to blush. A ridiculous dream, yet strangely arousing. Which is odd in my current situation. I don't even find Dr Mitch that sexy. Why wasn't Jake driving the van, declaring his love for me? I swear I saw him drive past. But then it was Dr Mitch, and he was unafraid of displaying his true feelings. It was probably all about Jake, and Dr Mitch just happened to wander into the van because his real voice infiltrated my dream. Still, I feel awkward now just looking at him.

'How are you feeling?' Mitch asks in a normal doctor sort of voice.

'Okay,' I say, pushing the dream firmly out of my head. 'Although, I think I've been bleeding through the night.'

The reality of these words jolt me out of my dream.

Dr Mitch nods and says that a nurse will help clean me up, and then an orderly will take me to the clinic for an ultrasound.

His shift finishes soon, but he will check in on me before he leaves. I try to focus on what he's saying, but I can't stop thinking about me running after the van, thinking it was Jake. I thought he'd be with me now at hospital, but he's not. It seems I'm always chasing the wrong vans, so to speak, and now I'm totally exhausted.

'Is there someone who can be with you for the ultrasound? A support person?' Mitch asks, pulling my attention back to the real world.

'No one right now . . . maybe I could call Clem,' I say, not wanting to get into the whole 'Where's Jake' conversation again. 'She'll be here this morning, I think.'

'We'd better just get you checked out as soon as possible. If Clem arrives, I'll have her sent straight to the clinic.'

The orderly attempts a few jokes to keep the mood light as he wheels me off, but I can't bring myself to play along. I'm led through hallways, doors, into a lift and out again, which is like being in a never-ending rabbit warren, until we finally arrive at the clinic where I first met with Sue the Midwife. Except this time, as I look around the waiting room filled with round bellies and happy faces, I feel even more out of place. I'm wheeled in and parked in an alcove. A curtain is drawn around me for privacy. Then, after what seems like two hours but is probably only twenty minutes, my name is called and I'm pushed into a darkened room.

'Hiya,' says an upbeat voice. 'Sorry you had to wait. It's been a busy start to the morning.'

The sonographer, whose name I don't catch, is a little too happy for my liking. Maybe she's trying to keep my mind off the situation. But I can still hear pity in her voice and I can't bear it. I saw it in the eyes of the women waiting outside, too, and the nurse in Emergency.

'You okay?' she asks.

'Yep,' I say, even though I have no idea what I'm feeling. Probably because I feel nothing. No nausea, no discomfort, no hunger. I'm just numb and washed out. And very sad. 'I was hoping my friend would get here in time to be my support person.'

'Sorry, we may have to get started. There's a big queue out there and trust me, it's only going to get longer,' says the woman with a wry smile.

Since I haven't yet had a scan, I don't know what to expect. But nothing much shows on the screen. My sonographer is not sounding quite so chipper now as she explains what she's doing, but I try to keep an open mind. She then busies herself by pressing a lot of buttons on her machine. Finally, after what seems an interminable amount of time, it's over.

'Right, all done,' she says, obviously trying to sound as upbeat as before, but something in her voice gives her away. 'If you just wait here, a doctor will be in shortly to discuss the results.'

She leaves and ten minutes later, another woman arrives. She introduces herself and explains that she's the doctor on duty.

'I've lost the baby, haven't I?' I manage to say.

'Yes, I'm afraid so,' she says gently. 'I'm really sorry. These things happen. And it's best it happens sooner rather than later. The good thing about a natural miscarriage like yours is that your uterus is completely cleaned out, without the chance of infection, which can sometimes happen after having a curate – best way, really.'

I don't know how to respond, so I say nothing. Surely there's no good way to miscarry. I feel empty. Not only because there's physically nothing inside me, but also because I feel like I have nothing. I didn't want the baby initially, but now I do. I mean, *I did* want the baby. It feels as though I just lost my last chance of happiness.

I'm escorted back down to the Emergency ward by another orderly who knows better than to try to make jokes. A different nurse checks in on me and tells me that Dr Mitch will come by soon. I can't believe he's still here. Doesn't he ever go home?

'I want a baby,' I say before I can stop myself.

'Sorry?' The nurse stops what she's doing and looks up.

'Oh, just saying that I really wanted to have a baby.'

'And you will have one. You'll get over this and be pregnant before you know it. It's so common. One in four women miscarry.'

I know, I want to say. Maybe that statistic will reassure me one day, but it does nothing to ease the sadness right now.

Just then, Mum's head peeps around the door and I don't think I've ever felt happier to see her. Clem called her first thing this morning, she explains, and she rushed over straightaway.

'Mum! I lost my baby.' The tears start to tumble.

I hadn't even told my mother I was pregnant but she doesn't need the in-between story now. It doesn't matter anyway.

'Oh, darling, it's okay.' She puts her arms around me and kisses me gently on the cheek. 'It's disappointing, I know. Dad sends his love. He wanted to come, but he's volunteering for story time at the library this morning, and you know he doesn't like to let the kids down. Even though he can't seem to hold the book up and read at the same time. I don't think he read you one story when you were little and now he feels it's his duty to read to the masses. He's not so good with hospitals anyway. And Clem wanted to give you a little space so will call you later.'

Mum's chatter fills the silence. She gives me a hug and I cling to her, silent tears soaking into her David Lawrence blouse. The fact that she doesn't tell me how common miscarriage is makes me cry even more. In the end, I just let the misery wash through me. I cry because I don't seem to be able to get anything I want. Like true love or a successful career. I long stopped believing those things were possible. This latest failure underlines and highlights it all over again. But most of all, I cry for my lost little baby.

'Mum, I wanted this.'

'I know, darling, but it wasn't meant to be. There'll be another baby for you, I promise.'

'But what if that was my only chance, and I blew it?'

'Rubbish! Don't be ridiculous,' says my mother, suddenly snapping back to her usual brisk manner, which has no time for brooding on past events nor for negative, sentimental conversations. 'Nothing you did caused this to happen. It's just nature's way. Now come on, I think we can go.'

As if on cue, Dr Mitch appears at the door. 'Hello there,' he says. 'How are you?'

'Not so good.' I try to smile but can't. I feel mortified that Dr Mitch has seen me laid so bare, both physically and emotionally. More than any man. Even my pap tests are done by a female gynaecologist and she's so quick, I don't think she actually looks anymore.

'And the baby?' he says gently.

I shake my head miserably.

'I'm really sorry, Lizzie.'

My mother gives a peculiar sort of half-giggle, half-cough. I look at her, and she's positively blushing.

'Hi there, I'm Lizzie's mother, Annabelle. Nice to meet you,' she says, pushing past my bed and elbowing my chest in the process.

'Hi, I'm Dr Peters,' he says, politely shaking my mother's outstretched hand.

Tears start to run down my cheeks again. I try to focus on the fact that Dr Mitch's surname is Peters, wondering why I can never remember that – but it does little to distract me from the sorrow seeping into my skin.

'What about the baby's father?' asks Dr Mitch. 'Did you end up telling him you were pregnant?'

'I did. He was thrilled,' I say flatly. 'He really wanted to be part of its life and for us to be together.'

I see my mother's lips purse and I wait for her to ask where Jake is. A question I don't know how to answer. Luckily, at that moment, my phone rings. I look at the number. Jake. He must have sensed he was being discussed.

'That's him now. I might take it if that's okay.'

'Sure, I have to go. Please take care of yourself. And lovely to meet you, Annabelle.'

With that, Dr Mitch disappears. My mum follows him out, saying she'll get some takeaway coffees. I take a deep breath. I feel strangely reluctant to pick up; I am desperately hoping that there's a logical explanation for why I couldn't contact Jake on the night I miscarried our baby.

'Hello?'

'Hey, babe, what's going on? I'm outside your flat. You're not there. You okay?'

'Haven't you checked your messages? I'm still at hospital. I lost the baby.'

'What?'

'I started bleeding last night. I miscarried. I rang and rang then sent you some texts. Surely you saw them? Where were you?'

'Sorry, I didn't hear the phone and then it must have gone dead.' He sounds genuinely flustered. 'I recharged it this morning but haven't checked my messages yet. Just saw a bunch of missed calls?'

I feel tears welling up and I can't speak. Silence falls over us. Two people breathing into the phone, not really knowing each other well enough to know what to say. Is he sad? Happy? Relieved? Hard to tell.

'Sorry, babe.'

'Are you?' I can't help myself.

'Yes, I am. What's that supposed to mean?'

'Nothing.'

'Do you want me to pick you up?'

'It's okay, my mum's here.'

'I'll meet you at yours in about an hour, okay?'

'Sure.' I hang up the phone, feeling tired and fragile.

Mum walks back into the room. Probably heard the whole conversation. I wait for her opinion, but she tactfully refrains from offering it. Instead she takes charge, and for once it's a relief. I haven't got any clothes so I have to go home in my dressing gown. Mum collects my handbag, takes my arm and guides me to the door. It feels like the time I got sick on a school excursion.

Threw up on the bus on the way to some farm on the outskirts of Sydney. They couldn't turn around and take me back because of the tight schedule, what with milking the cows and collecting the eggs, so I had to suffer the fifty-minute drive, which seemed eternal. Particularly with the death stares everyone was shooting me because of the vomity smell in the bus. I think I just ate too many treats from my special excursion lunch, and coach travel never really agreed with me.

When we got there I was left on the vomity bus with a teacher, who was cranky that she'd picked the short straw. All I wanted was my mum. When she arrived to take me home, I burst into tears.

I think of that day right now because once again, in yet another of my darkest hours, Mum is there to take me home. It's probably just as well I'm not going to be a mum myself. I don't think I have what it takes.

18

Mum doesn't comment on my messy flat. It doesn't sound like much, but if you knew my mother, and were as hormonally unstable as I am right now, it would bring a tear to your eye too.

'You just sit here and I'll put the kettle on, make a cup of tea,' says Mum as she helps me to the sofa and heads to the kitchen.

Nothing has ever sounded quite so dreamy. I hear her fill the kettle and open and close cupboards. Five minutes later Mum comes out with two cups of tea on a tray I'd forgotten I owned and some shortbread biscuits I didn't even know I had.

'I just found some bickies. Thought you might feel like one,' she says.

'Thanks.' The tea and biscuits taste like heaven. So simple, so comforting. I wish life was that straightforward.

'Are you feeling all right?' asks my mother for the twenty-millionth time since the hospital. I try to be more patient than usual. She's obviously worried and has every right to be.

'Yes, Mum, just tired. Might have a sleep.'

'You don't have to go to work, do you?'

'No, definitely not,' I say, trying to recall my schedule. Right now, I can't even remember what day it is.

'And what about Jake? What did he say?'

'He's coming over soon. I don't know, he sounded sad.'

'You can always try again, when the time is right.'

'I will, one day. I know I want that, now. But I'm not sure it'll be with Jake.'

To my surprise, Mum looks relieved. 'Well, if you ask me, which I know you won't, it sounds like that Jake is completely wrong for you. You're better off on your own.'

I'm surprised to hear my mother say this because, when it comes to me, she has long had a 'give everyone a chance' attitude. She's lost hope over the years, and become desperate on my behalf. I don't know what to think, but Mum's right about one thing. I don't want to hear her tell me whether or not Jake is The One. That's for me to decide.

Knowing she's probably said enough for now, Mum gets up, tucks my fluffy white throw around my legs and kisses me on the cheek. It's a treat to be fussed over.

'Thanks, Mum. Sorry about all this.'

'Don't be silly, darling,' she says, taking the dirty teacups to the kitchen and continuing to talk as she fills the sink. 'You've had a terrible ordeal.'

Then Mum does what she does best in times of trauma. She gets busy and starts cleaning. She washes all the dirty dishes, tidies away all the mess and even gets out the vacuum cleaner. Normally it's something we do together. Not so much cleaning but rather cosmetic transformation, throwing things out, changing things around, rearranging my furniture. True, we usually find the original arrangement works best, but we have fun doing it. Today I don't think I can manage to stand, let alone clean, so I appreciate Mum helping out.

'What's all this?' Mum walks out from the bedroom, holding a pile of fabrics I'd bought to make bags. 'What beautiful colours! Are you sewing something?'

'Just an idea for a bag,' I say dismissively. 'Actually, a nappy bag. I thought I could use it for when I . . . anyway, there's no point now.'

'It's a great idea, darling! You should see some of the hideous nappy bags out there for mums. We had to buy one for Marcie from book club. Remember I told you her daughter's expecting? Anyway it was awful, but there wasn't a great deal of choice. You could make something divine. Could be lucrative.'

'Maybe. I've already had some interest so I'll see.'

'Why don't you just –'

'Please, Mum, I can't think about it now.' Mum's enthusiasm is too much for my fuzzy brain.

'Of course, darling. It's just you do sew beautifully and you always have such original ideas. You know I'm your biggest fan.'

It's true. Mum has always loved whatever I design. It was just the idea of a career in fashion that worried her.

'I need a sleep now. I'm so tired.'

Mum grabs her bag and my keys. 'I'll just pop out and get some groceries, milk, something to eat later. There's nothing in your fridge. Have a sleep now, I'll let myself in and leave the keys on the table.'

'Thanks, Mum. Call you later.'

The door closes and the silence wraps around me like my fluffy throw. I'm alone in the mess that has become my life. I wish Mum could tidy that up, like my flat. I have to sort things out, but I'm so exhausted from the night's events, closing my eyes is the only thing that's appealing. Just a little snooze. Then I'll definitely get on top of everything.

I wake with a start to find the afternoon sun filtering through the venetians. What time is it? I grab my phone but it's gone dead. I get myself up and go into the kitchen to look at the clock on the oven. Three-thirty? I've been asleep all day. What happened to Jake?

I plug my phone into the charger and turn it back on. Twelve texts! And seven voicemail messages! I've never had that many in a whole week, let alone a few hours. There was a time, in my twenties, when my phone ran so hot it would almost catch fire. Not lately, though. But then I remember why people are texting me, and my heart sinks like a rock tossed into a pond. That's right. I lost my baby. I feel like an empty milk carton that has been mistakenly slipped back into the fridge but has no purpose anymore.

As it happens, most of the texts are from Jake. He'd been waiting outside, but I didn't hear the buzzer and then my phone was dead when he tried to call. He sounds annoyed in his voice message. Good grief, what did he expect? But at least he tried. Clem called and texted, worried that she hadn't heard from me. Then she texted back to say that she spoke with Mum, so all was well, but to call her when I could. Cherie also left a message asking after me.

Work called to see where I was. I must have had a shift today after all. I call back to check and get put straight on to Steve. Apparently Jake told him I had stomach flu, which infuriates me no end. You'd think he might have explained things a little better, especially as there's no baby to keep secret now. He probably wants to forget it ever happened. I'm so angry, I can barely speak. Which is hard when I'm in the middle of a conversation with my work manager, who is asking a lot of flu-related questions. I firmly explain that I've been in hospital and I won't be at work for at least a week. Doctor's orders. I put the phone down with a bang. Stomach flu! Ha!

My phone rings back almost immediately.

'Hello,' I say, a little too aggressively.

'Lizzie? It's me.'

'Clem, sorry.'

'You okay?'

'Yeah, just a bit groggy. I've been asleep.'

'Thought so, I tried calling. Did you get my messages? I ended up calling your mum for a chat.'

The thought of Mum and Clem having one of their 'chats' usually makes me cross, as they generally discuss my many faults and wrong turns. But today, it's reassuring. Like there are people out there who love me and who are prepared to guide me through the chaos. From where I stand (or lie on the couch), I can't be cross. Especially with Clem who, despite the whole Mal disaster, is thinking of me and calling to see how I am.

'Sorry for not telling you about Becca straightaway,' I say quietly.

'I know you are. It's okay. I was angry. Probably angrier with Mal, and I took it out on you.' Clem pauses. 'I'm sorry about that fight. And I'm so sorry about the baby.'

'No, none of that was your fault. I've been a terrible friend. Absolutely awful. You're always there for me and where was I when you needed me? Worrying about my own ridiculous problems. I've been so selfish and it will never happen again. I've realised how much you mean to me, how much I need you in my life, and how I'd be nowhere without you. I honestly don't know why you've stuck by me over the years.'

'That's easy!' says Clem with a laugh. 'Because underneath it all, through thick and thin, we're best friends. I love hanging out with you, always have, I even love listening to your endless dramas. You're hilarious. Annoying sometimes, and self-centred, yes, but life is always more vibrant with you around. At school, you always stood by me. Don't you remember in Year 7, when those awful girls were teasing me about my new haircut? You told them to piss off, that they were boring conservative morons who "didn't know good hair if it jumped out in front of them".'

I'd forgotten that moment. Whenever I think of our friendship it's the highly embarrassing situations I managed to get myself into that I recall, situations from which Clem has always rescued me. But Clem's right: during our schooldays, it went both ways. We were there for each other, like a team. Clem has always been so capable and self-sufficient, I guess I forgot that she might need me too.

'I tried to email, even call, but when I didn't hear back, I assumed you never wanted to speak to me again. I wouldn't have blamed you. I even left a note on your doorstep last night. Did you get it?'

Clem sighs. 'Yes. I know you tried, but I wasn't ready to talk. I had to sort myself out and work has been insane. I didn't have the head space for any of it.'

Neither of us speaks.

'Are we okay, now?' I hold my breath and wait for what seems an eternity. Without Clem in my life, there is very little else. The thought is terrifying.

'Of course,' says Clem.

I sigh with a torrent of relief.

'Thank God! I've really missed you. I've even started sewing again and I really want to show you this great idea I have . . .' I stop, remembering again that I now have absolutely no use for my nappy bag.

'That's great, Lizzie. About time. What's your idea?'

'It's a . . . well, it was going to be this cool nappy bag, but I guess there's not much point . . .' I stop, feeling tears threatening and enthusiasm for my bags waning.

Clem jumps in. 'Sounds like an excellent idea. Can't wait to see what you've got in mind.'

It's so good to talk to Clem. So distracting. I want to tell her about Willow S, but she's not as into celebrities as me, and it might not mean much. Besides, I don't want this conversation, of all conversations, to be about me. Then I remember my plan to match Clem up with Dr Mitch. Surely a date with a charming doctor would make up for my recent behaviour!

'Hey, what about Dr Mitch?'

'What about him?'

I know that Clem is smiling on the other end of the phone. I can hear it in her voice.

'You should go out with him. He told me he's single and gave me his card when I saw him after Missy went to hospital. I actually started crying and he was really sweet. Oh, I know! We'll have coffee in the hospital café and just "bump into him". We can say we're visiting a friend. Or your aunt who's sick?'

'My aunt is not sick. She's holidaying in Vancouver right now with her second husband.'

'But Dr Mitch doesn't know that. You guys are made for each other, and you always said you wanted to go out with a doctor.'

'When I was fourteen,' Clem says snippily. 'Now I'm a lawyer, a doctor would be disastrous. We'd have to schedule in time to see each other and even then it would have to be "pencilled" into our diaries because our work would always get in the way.'

'Just give it a go. Have you gone out with anyone since Mal?'

'I'm not really wanting to . . .' Clem pauses. 'Okay, one coffee . . . and no stalking.'

'Of course not!' I assure her. 'But we could say that I left something behind at the hospital, my wallet or sunglasses, and we wait at reception for a while –'

'Lizzie!'

'Or what if you have an accident and go to Emergency! I'll just find out the nights he works so we don't go through it all for nothing. Not a really bad accident, just a cut hand, maybe a broken toe or . . .'

'Lizzie! I'm not having an accident on purpose.'

I see that Clem is going to be a little more traditional in her approach. But that doesn't mean I have to be. After all, it's not like I'd be stalking Dr Mitch so much as doing him a favour. 'Fine, nothing tricky. Just leave it to me. You don't have to worry about a thing!'

'The minute you say that, I start to worry.'

I promise Clem that I'll be so subtle even she won't detect

my matchmaking efforts. I hang up full of renewed energy. Fantastic! Another project. And one that's not about me. I think it will help.

I call Cherie, but it goes to voicemail. She must be working. I leave a brief message thanking her for everything she did last night and telling her how I lost the baby.

Now I'm at a loose end. No baby, no Jake, just me. It's not like I carried the baby for very long; it was just a brief moment in time. Yet such a momentous one. It's affected me more deeply than I ever thought possible. It was a part of me, and now that it's gone, I feel bereft, empty. Drained and useless. Like I failed as a mother before I even got a chance to try it.

I need to do something, focus on something, to help pull me out of this dark mood I keep sinking into. I'm tired, but I know I won't be able to sleep again. I try half-heartedly to read a book but I can't concentrate on it. Then I see my collection of fabrics, folded into neat piles by Mum.

My eyes prickle with heat and a tear rolls silently down my cheek. I have no use for a nappy bag anymore. I feel like throwing the lot in the bin, but instead I shove them in a cupboard to deal with later, closing the door firmly on the bright colours and fun patterns.

But Willow is interested in a bag. And Mum and Clem are right. There are others out there who deserve to be just as chic as famous TV actresses. Clem might need one soon if all goes well with Dr Mitch. Maybe I can make one for Missy, to replace that nasty floral one my work colleagues gave her? I didn't really give her a present unless you count the bottle of vodka and scented body balm, both of which were fairly thoughtless.

Maybe I should make the bags anyway. Maybe this is my chance to create something beautiful that people actually need.

I have a cup of tea while the idea floats indulgently around my head. I doodle, I make notes, I have a shower, but I can't let it go. Maybe Operation Cool Nappy Bag (as I'm now calling it) will be my new focus. Maybe it's exactly what I need to get my mind off recent events. But do I really want to design the latest must-have nappy bag to satisfy the super-cool Sydney mothers-to-be? That sounds like far too much pressure in my fragile state. And the thought of creating any accessory to do with babies makes me want to cry. Exhausted beyond any rational thought, I decide to call it a night. Maybe I'll start with one bag tomorrow. See how that goes and take it from there.

'Baby steps,' I murmur without thinking, my heart cracking ever so slightly, as I slowly drift off to sleep.

19

I am strong and will create my own path.
I deserve love and happiness.
Today will be a good day, because I've decided it will be.

The next morning I find some random mantras on the internet, write them out on pieces of paper and stick them on walls around my flat. But it doesn't matter how many times I repeat them, they don't sink in and my insides feel like an uninhabitable wasteland.

I do, however, feel a new sense of purpose. I decide it's time to really get stuck into the things I've been avoiding, to distract me if nothing else, so I roll up my sleeves and set to work. I pull endless piles of newspapers, bills and takeaway menus out of cupboards, recycling what I don't need, filing what I do. I scrub the kitchen to within an inch of its life, going over what Mum did yesterday. No stone left unturned. Even the microwave. Who knew that plate actually came out? Then I tackle the bathroom and realise that what I thought was a plumbing problem was simply the need for a thorough clean and sanitise.

By lunchtime, my flat is sparkling. I can't believe how disgusting I'd let it become. When was the last time I cleaned? Honestly, all this business with Jake has left my life in disarray.

I sink into my vacuumed sofa, now free of loose change, sultanas and toast crumbs, and heave an exhausted sigh. Despite my newfound enthusiasm and positivity, fatigue hits from out of nowhere. I guess I'm still recovering. I know I have to get on with the nappy bags, especially since one of the most glamorous stars in Sydney is eagerly awaiting my creation. But right now I need to rest.

Tomorrow I'll start afresh on Operation Cool Nappy Bag. I just have to. It's as if with all the cleaning, my eyes have been swept of dust and grime and I can finally see things more clearly. I have to make my bags whether I feel like it or not, because too often I walk away the minute something becomes difficult, telling myself the time isn't right or there's too much else going on. Not this time.

Once I contacted a designer who was looking for a personal assistant. She called back and left a message, asking me to return her call immediately. But I was caught up with an American university exchange student at the time and was thinking of heading off overseas, so I never called the designer back. Needless to say the American and I didn't work out, I never went overseas and the woman hired someone else – a girl I knew from design school, in fact. The two of them ended up going into business together.

I've always blamed others when things don't work out. The teachers at fashion school were complete idiots who had no idea. The guys I dated were all bastards who didn't know a good thing when it hunted them down and forced them to go out. Funny how I'm the common denominator in all those scenarios. Now I know: it's me who's been the problem – or at least part of the problem – and I've never acknowledged it. I've never taken responsibility for my role when things go wrong. And to top it off, I home in on the worst possible people and hand over all my power, like it's a cup of sugar they've asked to borrow. Except I don't just give them a cup, I give them the whole kilo packet. And never get it back. Who else would go out with a guy who doesn't show up to an arranged dinner date and who is nowhere to be found on the night when you're miscarrying his child? All alone on the couch, my face heats with shame.

Finding Mr Right became the single most important task in my life (thanks, Mum, and your book club). Well, not anymore. It's better to be alone than to hand the remote control of your life over to some guy who only uses it to tune in to crappy reality TV re-runs rather than quality drama. It's like I've been only half living my life, allowing my happiness to be dictated by other people's decisions. And not only that, I choose unsuitable people to make those decisions, leaving me miserable and dissatisfied.

So, that's it. Never again. The time has come to choose my own path and to focus on important things like my life, career and my fabulous bags. I've just been through what I can definitely call 'a significant moment' and it's changed everything. I can see that I've been sitting on the sideline and watching the game of life play out on the pitch, but have made very little effort to get up and give it a go. To be brave. To take risks that are worth taking and not those that involve climbing on wheelie bins to see into someone else's house. It seems the risks I've been shying away from are the ones that hold the promise of true happiness.

I jump off the couch with renewed energy. It's like I've just woken up from a ten-year sleep and don't want to waste another second. Sure I'm tired, but so what? Time to stop wallowing in navel-gazing. Time to get on with the rest of my life.

I set up the lounge room as my work studio, with my sewing machine on the dining room table (it's not like I ever eat there anyway), ironing board in the kitchen and furniture pushed back to create as much floor space as possible for cutting out. Then I get to work. I pick up where I left off, pre-miscarriage, sorting through the design ideas I had for Willow's bag, and I don't stop until I've pieced it all together.

The hours sneak by, and apart from receiving a few texts from Clem and a call from Mum, both checking in on me, I barely notice the world around me. When I finally check the time on the oven clock, it's three in the morning! I decide I'd better go to bed even though my head is still buzzing. I'm doubtful I'll be able to even close my eyes, but as soon as I sink under my doona, fatigue takes over and lures me into a surprisingly blissful sleep.

Within days my first proper bag is done and I'm thrilled! I was happy with the prototype, but this is even better. It just needs a finishing touch here and there, as well as a good iron. I put it to one side to focus on the next one. I'll give Willow a choice. More chance of securing the deal that way, I figure. Besides, with so many ideas flying around my head, I'm itching to go again. I'll stick to the same design, but just make a few variations in the detail. Maybe longer handles and a scalloped edge along the top. And a different mix of fabrics. I haven't felt so inspired for years. It's like rediscovering a natural high I'd forgotten was even possible.

I set to work, stopping for a quick lunch break, mostly because I'm so hungry I can barely see straight. Thanks to Mum's impressive grocery shop after she brought me home, there's still plenty in my cupboards. As I devour a plate of Swiss cheese, prosciutto and crackers, I suddenly remember my promise to organise a date for Clem. I'd completely forgotten! I can't let Clem down again so I make a cup of tea, grab a pen and paper and consider my options:

- Call Dr Mitch at the hospital and simply ask if he'd like to go out with Clem.
- 'Accidentally' bump into him outside the hospital as he's going to work – and then cleverly weave Clem into the conversation.
- Turn up at the hospital with a gift to say thanks for all his help during the miscarriage – and also explain how great Clem was that night, how lucky I was to have so much support, and how two such great people should maybe have a coffee together.

After careful consideration, I decide the last idea is the best. I don't know Dr Mitch well enough to talk over the phone. I barely know him at all, even though he now knows far too much about me. Waiting outside the hospital would require a sound knowledge of his work schedule and I don't have the time for that amount of research. (Plus Clem might consider it stalking, which I promised not to do.) But a present, perhaps a nice bottle of wine, to say thank you for all that he's done? Perfect.

I don't even know if he's on tonight but I'll take my chances. He seems to work most nights in Emergency, if my experience of seeing him there three times is any indication. And if he's not, I'll leave my present at reception. Hopefully he'll call me to say thanks. But do you say thanks for a thank-you present? Maybe not. Still, it's the best I can come up with, plus I can let him know how much I appreciated his assistance during my ordeal. Two birds, one stone.

I drag myself away from the sewing machine to buy a delicious pinot from the Adelaide Hills, hoping he likes pinot. Who doesn't like pinot? I know Clem does, so it will be a sign to see if they're suited. At about eight o'clock, I drive over to the hospital and, once again, park in the most expensive car park in the world. It will be worth the money if I find happiness for Clem.

I walk into Emergency and look around at the eclectic bunch of people sitting in the bleak waiting room. I feel I know this room intimately now, from the mottled blue lino on the floor to the stark fluorescent lights above. Nothing good about being in Emergency. At least this time, I'm here on another matter.

The woman on reception looks up as I approach the desk.

'Hi there, is Dr Mitch, I mean Dr er . . . Peters working tonight?'

'Dr Peters? Let me see,' she says, more to her computer screen than to me. 'Yes, he is. Is something wrong?'

'No, I just want to drop this off to him.' I put the wrapped-up bottle of wine on the counter. 'I was in the other night and he was so great. I wanted to thank him. Is he available?'

'You do realise this is an Emergency Department,' she says in a rehearsed-sounding voice, as if this happens all the time with Dr Mitch. No doubt it does. Women constantly falling at his feet, what with his saving their lives and being there in times of need. I'm not even attracted to him, yet he still somehow crept into my dream like a superhero, his incredible Jake-like muscles slick with sweat. Just the thought of that image sends my stomach into cartwheels.

But that wasn't real and Dr Mitch is so not my cup of tea. Mind you, I don't even know what my type of tea is anymore. I don't think there is a type for me. And if there was, I don't feel like any right now. Not even a little cup. I need to be alone to sort out my life, without any tea-like distractions.

'Yes, of course, I'll just leave it here.'

Damn! I'm not going to be able to see him. What was I thinking? He's probably dealing with some sort of life and death situation and here I am, wondering if he could spare a few moments so I can set him up with my best friend!

The woman softens, obviously sensing my disappointment. 'It's a nice gesture. I'll see if he's around. What's your name?'

I give her my details and take a seat. She picks up the phone and within ten minutes, Dr Mitch strides through the doors. He looks at me with his piercing blue eyes. My heart practically flips inside out and I feel like someone lit a packet of sparklers in my stomach. Unexpected. I try to be casual, relaxed, but it's hard when my insides are having some sort of street party. Suddenly every detail on his face becomes apparent, from the lock of unruly hair flopping across his forehead to his contagious grin that shines like a light bulb. Maybe it's because of that stupid hospital dream? Or the fact that he is actually very good-looking? Whatever it is, the doctor is having a surprising effect on me.

'Hello there. Everything okay?' Dr Mitch snaps me back to reality, probably wondering why I have such a bemused look on my face.

'Yes, all fine,' I say quickly. My overzealous heart is now thrashing out a whole gym routine. Which is annoying and more than a little distracting. Especially when I don't have long to achieve what I've come here to do.

'Hope I'm not stopping you from stitching someone up?'

'No, I'm going on a break.'

I hand him the wine. 'Just wanted to say how grateful I am for all your help the other night. In fact, all three times I've come in to Emergency.'

'Thanks. That's really nice. And a pinot! My favourite.' He seems genuinely touched by the gift. Maybe it doesn't happen that often after all. Maybe no one says thanks when a doctor comes to their rescue. And he likes pinot – a promising sign for Clem. Definitely meant to be.

'I'm just going to get a quick coffee,' he says. 'Do you want to come with me? I think the hospital café is about to close so if we hurry we might make it.'

Dr Mitch strides off without waiting for an answer. I break into a jog to keep up with his long-legged pace.

'I'm glad you dropped by, I need to ask you something.'

'Really?' I can feel my eyes widening. Maybe he does like Clem and wants to ask her out anyway? This is working out better than I hoped.

'Yes, I was wondering if you could give me Cherie's number.'

I didn't see that coming. Isn't Cherie a little old for him?

'I've found my parents' old record of hers and I really want to track her down so she can autograph the cover. She gave me her card, but, like an idiot, I left it in my pocket and it went through the wash. I couldn't believe it.'

I cast my mind back to the conversation between Mitch and Cherie the other night. I wasn't thinking very clearly, but I vaguely remember Mitch being totally in awe of her.

'Sure,' I say, pulling out my purse. 'Here's her card. I've got her number in my phone so you take it. She'd love to do that, I'm sure. I think she misses those good old days, even though she pretends it's all behind her.'

'Thanks, really appreciate it.'

We arrive at the café. Mitch orders a takeaway. He asks if I want one and for some reason I say yes, knowing full well I won't sleep if I have a coffee at this time of night. Still, I have to put myself out there for Clem. I'll just pretend to sip it.

We grab our coffees and head back to Emergency. Dr Mitch is chatting away, asking if I've seen any movies lately, which I haven't. So he starts telling me about a film he recently saw. It sounds really interesting and I wish we could just sit and talk for a while, but my window of opportunity is closing so I swiftly steer the conversation back on track.

'Thanks again for the other night. I really appreciate your help.'

'No problem. Thanks for the wine. Unnecessary, but thoughtful.'

Mitch gives me a cheeky grin that catches me unawares. His whole face lights up when he smiles and his eyes dazzle somewhat. As I force my gaze away, I notice his beautiful hands around his takeaway cup. Do all doctors have such lovely hands? Forget the hands, Lizzie, just keep going.

'If it wasn't for you and Clem, I don't know how I would have got through the whole ordeal.'

'Just doing my job.'

'So was Clem,' I say. 'Not that it's her job to help me out. Not that it's your job specifically, but you both are really just so . . .' I see Dr Mitch looking puzzled, wondering where this conversation is going. As am I.

'Okay, well . . .' Dr Mitch tries to move it along, while I clutch at it, like a limpet. I take a big breath and decide direct is best.

'Would you be interested in going out with Clem? Maybe a coffee or a drink?'

There's a look of surprise in Dr Mitch's eyes that I can't quite decipher. Is he interested? Is he embarrassed? Is he still single? Oh my God, he said he was, but what if he's met someone in the meantime?

'Sorry, are you single? I thought you were, but if you're not, that's so fine. I don't usually do this sort of thing, but you guys are so well suited. She's recently broken up with someone and I thought perhaps . . .'

'I'm single and it's fine.' Dr Mitch goes a little quiet. 'I'd better get back in there. Why don't I take down Clem's number? See how we go.'

I give him the number, which he writes on Cherie's card. We say goodbye and off he goes, pinot in hand, to save another life.

It's time someone tried to save *his* life, and maybe Clem is the girl to do it. Maybe they can save each other from their demanding, stressful jobs. They're such nice people. They both deserve to be saved and I'd be thrilled to be the one who makes it happen. It's an unexpected feeling, but for once I'm not concerned about my own crazy life. I've always cared about Clem but right now, the thought of helping her find love and happiness feels like the most rewarding thing I've done in a long time.

20

'Lizzie! Are you okay? What's wrong?'

Early the next morning I ring Clem on her mobile. I want to catch her before work so I don't annoy her with phone calls at the office. But all it does is make her worried that once again, something cataclysmic has happened in my life.

'Nothing. I'm fine,' I say. 'Just ringing because I spoke to Dr Mitch last night and I suggested you guys go on a date.'

'What? What did you say? I hope you didn't make me look desperate. Did you call him?'

'Not exactly.'

'Lizzie?'

'I went to the hospital –'

'You stalked him? What did I say about that? I specifically said no –'

'I didn't stalk him. I took him a gift to say thanks for helping me out. A bottle of wine. A pinot. I think he appreciated it. Then I discreetly introduced you into the conversation and one thing led to another.'

'How did he sound? Interested?'

'I think he is. It was a quick conversation. He didn't have much time. But he really likes pinot, so that's something you guys share.'

'I hate pinot.'

'No, you don't.'

'Yes, I do. Too unpredictable.'

'Not if it's a cool climate. What do you mean you hate pinot? I always thought you loved it.'

'No, you're the one who likes pinot.'

'Oh.' Whoops. 'Well, at least you know what to get if you ever buy him a drink.'

'Great,' says Clem sarcastically. 'But does he actually want to go out with me?'

It was a moment for one of my trusty, sympathetic white lies.

'Definitely. Very interested. I could see it in those dazzling blue eyes.' I cross my fingers as the words come out of my mouth. It's not exactly a lie. 'He took your number didn't he? So he must want to get in touch.'

'Okay,' says Clem hesitantly. 'Thanks . . . I think. I'll call you tonight.'

I hang up, feeling pleased with myself. They're both going to thank me later. Probably make a big deal about it at their wedding. There'll be some joke in their speeches about how I forced them to go out for a drink, and thank goodness I did, otherwise it may never have happened! I know that lately I haven't been the best of friends to Clem. In fact I've been so shocking, I'm still surprised she's agreed to continue our friendship. But I'm certainly making up for it now. Not only am I going to be the most incredible best friend in the history of all best friends, but I will also find her the most amazing boyfriend in the history of all boyfriends. The first task might take a little work but the second is definitely underway.

For the next few days, I barely leave the flat, apart from the occasional venture out for Thai takeaway or a latte from my local café. All I want to do is sew my nappy bags and it's making me so happy, I can think of nothing else.

I finish the second bag for Willow S and examine both of them critically as I do a final press with the iron. The fabrics are great and the design has worked well. They're good. Really good. Even if I say so myself. Not for the first time I wish I'd stayed true to my inner voice while at design school, not tried so hard to seek the teachers' approval; maybe then they would have had more admiration for my work. It's a similar story with all the guys I've dated. If I had focused more on what was right for me, rather than trying to please everyone else, I might not be where I am now.

But this time things feel different. I genuinely feel confident about my idea, a bit like how I originally felt about my Year 10 pantsuit. I'm not trying to shock or do things to simply break out of my conservative middle-class upbringing, as they always used to tell me at college. I'm not trying to be cool or edgy. I'm creating something honest that I feel is going to serve a purpose while being stylish at the same time. Plus, there's nothing like it out there on the baby market. Willow S loved my first attempt, so surely she will like these. And if she doesn't, someone else will.

It's late on Saturday night, and I'm just contemplating rewarding myself with my first glass of wine in weeks when a buzz at the door invades the safe little cocoon that my flat has become.

'Hello?' I say into the intercom.

'Hey, babe, it's me.'

My stomach falls down to my ankles. Jake! What's he doing here?

'Can I come up?'

Reluctantly, I let him in. I guess he wants to talk things through now there's no baby, and I suppose that's probably the right thing to do. Finish things off properly, like adults. I've tried to avoid this conversation mostly because I don't really want to see him after everything that happened. Hopefully I'll find him totally unattractive.

I open the door. And there he is. Still hot, can't deny it. Damn.

'Why didn't you ever call me back?' he says, getting straight to the point.

I sigh. Honestly, what does he want from me? Surely the situation is clear now. I've been through enough. Can't he just let the whole thing go?

'Look, Jake, we don't have to pretend anymore. You didn't want a relationship. You didn't really want a baby. This thing just happened, and it happened to happen with me. I don't think you would have ever chosen that situation. To be honest, I wouldn't have chosen for it to happen this way either.'

'Hey, Lizzie, can you stop talking for one minute?'

I stop talking.

'I just want to say how sorry I am. About everything.'

Okay, I didn't expect that.

Jake takes my hand in his. 'Can I come in?'

There's no way I'm letting him in.

'Where were you when I needed you?' I say, dropping his hand.

'I missed your calls and then my phone went dead. I promise. When I saw all your messages I called straightaway,' said Jake, his chocolatey eyes full of regret.

'But you never miss calls,' I say, not believing the words or the eyes. 'I was losing your baby. You'd literally just said how you wanted to be a part of it all. I call in the middle of the night – more than once – and you don't answer. Did it not occur to you that there might be something wrong, that I might have needed you?'

'I'm sorry. I should have made sure my phone was charged. This is all new to me. It won't happen again.'

Again? Is he for real? Can I possibly believe him? If he'd been with me that night, we might be together now, closer than ever. I would have loved him for being there, in my most vulnerable moment. But he wasn't there. He didn't turn up for dinner that night when he said he would, and he couldn't even take my calls. Now he's on my doorstep, wanting to come in (and we know what that means) and I know it's probably the worst thing I could do for myself.

Jake steps in closer, sneaks his hands around my waist and pulls me in so I'm pressed up against his rock-hard abs. And that's not all that's hard, let me tell you. Our lips are seconds away from each other. As wrong as this is, I feel myself slipping under his spell. It's hard to think clearly, mostly because all I can hear is Clem's voice in my head, pointing out all the reasons why this relationship will always be doomed. Then my mother, like some sort of backup singer, randomly chipping in.

'Go away!' I tell Clem crossly. My mother, I simply ignore.

'What?' says Jake, startled.

'Not you, it's just . . .' I can't be bothered explaining.

'Come on, Lizzie. Can't things go back to the way they were?'

'Why? So I can drive to your house late at night, at the drop of a hat, for a quick and unspectacular root?'

'No, I really . . . what do you mean, unspectacular?'

'Come on, we've never had a great situation.' I may as well start being completely honest now. 'Even that night when we first talked of the baby. You said you'd come over and cook me dinner, but you didn't. Why should I believe anything you say?'

'I had to stay back at work, I told you that. Come on, I thought we were having fun.'

'Sure, but the fun stopped when I was losing your baby.'

'But I've explained already . . . man, you're tough. Can we go inside? Please? I'm sick of standing on your doorstep.'

Actually, I've never been tough enough when it comes to men and relationships. I know I deserve better and I should, in fact, be a lot tougher with Jake, but right now, I just don't seem to have the willpower. Plus, I suddenly realise, a small part of me wants to be able to grieve for my baby with the one person who had shared it with me.

'Please don't make me beg.' Jake kisses me softly. And again. A little more passionately, his hands creeping somewhere down near my bottom. 'Sorry, I can't help myself, you're just so gorgeous.'

I pull away and look at him. His kisses don't cause a major explosion, but there was something. A small volcanic eruption, perhaps. Maybe you don't get the fireworks after you have chased someone relentlessly, slept with them a few times, been stood up by them and then carried and lost their baby.

Perhaps things have shifted. Maybe this is more real. He said he's never been into commitment and this would be a new leaf to turn over. Maybe it still can be, even without the baby. If he's willing to give things a proper try, then maybe I should too. Maybe this is another one of those moments to close my eyes and leap into the unknown.

'All right. But nothing's going to happen tonight, obviously.' I put a hand on my stomach and step back to let him in. 'And, you know, things have to be different. I'm not the same person I was before.'

Jake nods sombrely, then simply takes my hand and leads me into the bedroom. He helps me into bed and crawls in next to me, holding me, filling that empty corner of my heart, until I feel myself sliding off to sleep.

Suddenly, it's morning, after what has to be the most uneventful night I've ever spent with Jake. Nothing happened, of course, since it's still so soon after the miscarriage, but I slept like a log and wake up feeling fantastic.

Jake sees my eyes open. 'Hey, Lucy.'

Okay. Maybe not quite so fantastic.

'Sorry! Lizzie!' he says, mortified. 'I meant to say Lizzie. Just came out before I could stop it. I'm really bad with names. I'm surprised I remember my own.'

I don't believe him for a second but seeing him in my bed, smiling ruefully, mildly warms my feelings. And there's definitely something happening a little lower down. I'm in no state for action, but if I was, I wouldn't be letting him out of my bed in a hurry. He kisses me passionately and the mild volcanic eruption between my legs upgrades quickly to natural disaster status.

'I've got to go and supervise the Sunday shift,' he says, putting a soaking wet blanket on my private bushfire.

'Oh . . . maybe see you later?'

'A crazy week – but I'll call you. You're not coming back to work yet, are you?'

I'm reluctant to let Jake out of my sight. 'I was thinking of taking a few more days, but I'm feeling so much better –'

'I wouldn't if I were you. Your stats have been so great lately, you don't want them to drop because you go back to work too soon. You need to rest. Don't worry, I'll cover for you.'

'Yeah, maybe you're right.' The idea of a few more days at home with my bags is actually pretty appealing.

Jake quickly dresses, gives me a kiss and leaves. I lie in bed a bit longer, thinking about what's happened. I'm still not sure where it will go, but I'm going into it with my eyes open. And for now Jake is ticking all the boxes in the caring partner department.

When I wander out into the lounge room, I notice his sunglasses on my coffee table and my heart leaps so hard it hurts. Proof! That will satisfy Clem and her need for solid evidence. Jake probably left them on purpose. Something I would do. An excuse to see me again. Maybe he and I have more in common than the ability to conceive.

I don't go to work for another week and I don't see Jake, which is fine. He texts me most days to see how I am and say he's looking forward to seeing me on the weekend. I still doubt his words but then again, the sunglasses tell me he'll be back. Every time a doubt niggles in my head, I look at those cool aviators and calm down. He's left a little part of himself here to assure me this is something real.

Clem calls me regularly, as does my mum so I don't feel lonely. In fact, I use the time well, making another bag, again with a new combination of fabrics and slightly different detail. By Wednesday, it's time to stop procrastinating and take them out into the world. I find Willow's business card and with trembling fingers, dial the number, expecting to leave a message, but she picks up straightaway.

'Willow? It's Lizzie March here.'

'Who?'

I panic. Did I dream the whole thing up? I'm beginning to see why my mother is always on about my misunderstandings. But I'm fairly certain this one did happen so I persist.

'We met at Rock Salt. You said you liked my bag and gave me your card to let you know if I made any more, which I have, if you're still interested.'

My jumbly words are met with a silence that screeches in my ears. She doesn't remember and now I've rung a major TV and film star and made a complete fool of myself.

'Oh yeah, cool.'

My heart comes back down from my throat and my breathing resumes its normal pace.

'Do you want to meet back at Rock Salt, and check them out?'

'I'm working till late but why don't you pass by Lunar Bar tonight? I'm meeting friends for drinks around ten.'

I agree, trying to sound as if going to one of the hippest bars in Surry Hills is something I do all the time. I think I even say I am going to be 'in the area anyway'. I hang up. This is definitely a step forward and has nothing whatsoever to do with dating a guy.

I call Jake to see if he wants to have dinner, but he doesn't pick up so I leave a message asking him to call me. Probably at work so can't talk.

I try Clem to see if she wants to come out but she's already got plans.

'With Dr Mitch?' I ask hopefully.

She hesitates. 'Er, yes, that's right.'

'Why didn't you tell me he called?'

'I didn't want to say anything, he's more your friend.'

'Hardly,' I say. 'Just someone I met, who probably thinks I'm a complete idiot, which only makes you look even more like perfect girlfriend material. Which you are. Have a great time!'

I hang up, pleased that Clem and Mitch have arranged a date. I've no doubt it will all work out. At last I've done something for Clem that doesn't involve major embarrassment or illegal activities.

I manage to stay awake and get myself and my bags to Lunar Bar, but I can't see anyone who looks like my new best friend. I go to the toilets to touch up my lipstick. Looking in the mirror, I'm shocked to see a mark on the front of my top. What is that? Vegemite? Typical, just when I'm trying to give the impression of being an ultra-cool designer. I adjust my boho scarf to cover the stain, and am satisfied with the result.

I walk out and see Willow straightaway. You couldn't miss her. She's tall and striking with long blonde hair that looks like it should have its own agent, and is dressed in a red leather skirt, a Taylor Swift t-shirt and tan knee-high boots. I've never really been a fan of Taylor Swift but suddenly I must have that t-shirt, it looks so cool. Willow is talking to a couple of guys so I approach slowly, not wanting to interrupt or look like some crazy fan. She turns to go to the bar so I grab the opportunity to introduce myself.

'Hi, Willow?'

'Yeah?'

'It's me. Lizzie. The bag girl. From the café. We spoke earlier and you said to meet you here. So here I am!' I start to babble slightly, as is my habit when I'm out of my depth.

'Right, yeah, no worries. I'm just getting a drink. Want something?'

'Ah . . . no thanks, it's okay.'

'You sure? Let's have some sparkling.'

'Oh, okay.' Maybe we are new best friends.

I wait while she gets a bottle of prosecco and glasses and follow her to a table of extremely happening young hipsters.

'Sit down.' She hands me a glass. 'Cheers!'

'Cheers,' I say, feeling completely out of place.

Willow turns to the crowd.

'This is Lizzie, she makes great bags.'

I take this as my cue to get on with business.

'I have a choice of three – but if you don't like them, it's so fine.' I lay the bags out on the tabletop.

'Are you kidding?' Willow holds each one up in the air, displaying them to the group, like show-and-tell. 'They're awesome. I'll take them all. How much are you charging?'

She may as well have punched me in the nose. In spite of her enthusiasm, I hadn't expected that response, so I haven't thought about prices. I do a few hasty mental sums, taking into account my time, the cost of the fabric and the price of the bags I saw at

That Big Baby Shop. I decide to be confident and not undersell myself. I'll keep them for presents if they're too expensive for her.

'A hundred and twenty each.' I hold my breath, trying to look as if I do major transactions every day.

'Great.'

'Really?' My voice almost squeaks.

'Do you have any more?' asks a ridiculously gorgeous girl sitting next to Willow who has the whitest teeth I've ever seen.

'No, but I can take orders.'

'I'd love one,' she says with a smile that should be on a toothpaste commercial. Actually, she looks familiar, I think she *is* on a toothpaste commercial.

'It's really a nappy bag,' I say.

'A what?'

I'm so glad I wasn't the only one who doesn't know about nappy bags.

'It's just something for mums to carry stuff around,' says Willow. 'But I call it an "anything" bag.'

Anything Bag. That's what Willow called it back at Rock Salt. It's actually a great name. I wonder if she would let me use it? I hand the bags to Willow and she grabs an enormous electric-blue purse and gets out the exact money straightaway. I look at the cash in awe. It's more than I could ever make in a shift at WineCall. Admittedly it took me all week to make the bags but it was much more fun than selling wine. And I'm sure I'll get quicker at making them.

The conversation moves on from my bags to some cool indie film that's just come out. I seem to be part of the group. No one is wondering why the bag lady is still hanging around. By some sort of social osmosis, I've become part of the in-and-happening crowd.

I scan the room to see if anyone I know is there to appreciate my newly achieved status. Doesn't look like it. But as I refocus on my new friends' conversation, I notice a familiar shape at a table on the other side of the bar. Is that . . . ? No. Yes! It is! It's Jake! Hooray. This night is just getting better by the minute. He didn't tell me he was going to be out tonight. And he obviously didn't get my message. I could have met him here after I'd taken care of bag business.

I'm just about to get up and go over when I stop still. Who's he with? Is it someone from work? It looks a little more intimate than that, like a date, but surely that's not possible. I stare as hard as I can, an uncomfortable heat creeping through my veins. Jake is definitely sitting with a girl and the situation definitely looks cosy. She has her back to me so I can't see her face, but already I don't like the look of her.

I force myself to be rational. Maybe they're cousins, or old friends? Maybe they grew up together or lived in the same street and were always like brother and sister? There's only one way to find out.

I quickly text Jake. *Hey, where are you? Want to meet up?*

I see him pick up his phone and then put it down and continue his conversation. His date gets up and walks towards the toilets. Once she's gone, he grabs his phone and starts texting. My phone dings at me immediately. *Sorry, exhausted, going to bed early. Tomorrow night?*

White-hot anger bubbles in my stomach. Bastard! He just lied straight to my face, or rather straight to my phone. I am beyond furious. Not only with Jake, but also with myself. I actually let myself believe that he was for real this time. Why did I do that, when he's broken his word to me so many times? Well, never again. This is the last straw.

When the girl comes back from the toilets, she heads to the bar, giving me the opportunity to see her face, which I instantly recognise. She works at WineCall, but I don't know her very well as she only started recently and I haven't been around lately. But I do know she's really chatty. Everyone thinks she's lovely, but I don't understand what they see in her. All she does is talk, talk, talk. And not about much. Okay, she's pretty and bubbly, guys absolutely adore her, girls think she's really sweet and customers buy anything she offers. Plus, she seems to get all the shifts she wants and get out of the ones she doesn't, without so much as a stern word.

I suppose it's possible she and Jake are having a friendly drink after work. I do that with different people from time to time. Or I did. But come to think of it, if I did have a drink with someone after work, it was usually because I had an ulterior motive!

What can I do? Walk away? No, why should I? I have every right to know what's going on. After all, last week I was carrying Jake's child, and just the other day Jake convinced me to give our relationship another go. He owes me an explanation. I announce to my new friends that I need another drink, then I casually approach the bar and sidle up next to Chatty Girl.

'Hi!' I say, not wasting any time.

'Er, hi?' She looks at me with faint recognition, but can't quite place me.

'Lizzie March, I work at WineCall too.'

'Oh, right. Have we met? I'm Lucy. Are you here with people from work?'

'No, just some friends, you?' I raise my voice to get over the throng of the bar. What was her name? Did she say Lucy?

'Yes, well sort of. Just my boyfriend. He's over there. You know him? Jake Wheeler, he's one of the supervisors at work.'

I freeze. Boyfriend? Did I hear correctly? The word cuts into my brain like a rusty bread knife. We were having a baby and we never used that word. Now this girl is throwing it around like it's part of her everyday vocabulary. There must be some mistake. Have I time-warped or maybe woken up from some sort of hyper-sleep?

'Jake!' I say in a voice that sounds like we're best buddies. 'I know Jake well, but I didn't know he was seeing anyone new.'

'No one really knows, we've been quiet about it because of work and there's also his crazy ex.'

Crazy ex! That couldn't be me she's talking about? Maybe there's another ex-girlfriend hanging around. Jake is obviously living about three or four different lives. The anger in my gut is simmering away nicely now.

'Really? Who's that?' I can't help but push further.

'Yeah, this woman, I think she works at WineCall too. I don't know her, but she forced herself on Jake, got pregnant to him and wasn't even going to tell him. He was devastated when he found out, but then she lost the baby and that was even more upsetting. Poor guy, his father walked out on him as a baby, so it was all a bit of an emotional rollercoaster ride and we've had to take things slowly.'

I can't believe what I'm hearing. Jake – devastated? I look over to where he's sitting, drinking his beer, looking like he's just jumped off a Fashion Week runway. Completely handsome but a total shit.

'I heard she's really sweet,' I say, encouraging Lucy to do her chatty thing. 'I don't think the pregnancy was planned and apparently Jake let her down quite badly.'

'Did she say that?' Lucy laughs. 'Unbelievable! She trapped him into a relationship. She was stalking him, like, hanging around outside work every night and going to his gym and the supermarket, and there was this one time when she fell off a window, trying to see if he was home. He was walking up the street and saw it all happen.'

'I heard she really loved Jake,' I say in defence of myself. I can't believe Jake knew what had happened that night, and had told this girl about it. Humiliation hits like a sudden summer storm.

'Funny way of showing it. Do you know she completely forgot his birthday? That's when we first got together. He had a special birthday lunch, and she didn't even turn up. I happened to be at the same restaurant and ended up joining his friends. Had a great time and we've been together ever since.'

'Since his birthday!' I feel rage boiling up behind the shock. Apart from all the lies I'm hearing, I realise Jake's been two-timing us. As annoying as I find her, Lucy must be as deluded as me when it comes to men. I may have met my match.

'Yes, on and off. We broke up when he found out about the baby, but when that wasn't happening anymore, he broke up with her to be with me. Apparently she was devastated and didn't want to let go. But now we're back together and really happy. He doesn't want too many people at work to know. Might make things weird, especially as he's a supervisor. His ex isn't working there much, thank goodness. But he doesn't want people to think I'm getting any unfair advantages.'

'That's honourable of him,' I say. Now I know where he was

when I was in Cherie's taxi, heading to hospital. No wonder he didn't want me doing any shifts this week! He must have told Lucy he'd ended things with me, but in fact, he was hoping that he could keep me as his bit on the side. Just like Jean Paul all over again. I'm in total shock, but I don't say anything to Lucy. I don't like her one bit, but this whole thing is not her fault; she's been lied to and cheated on as well. But Jake isn't going to get away with it. Lucy! Oh my God! Jake called me Lucy when he came over. Slip of the slippery tongue. Her name was obviously more readily available in his microscopic brain.

With a monumental effort I try to conceal my anger, and ask if I can come over and say hi to Jake, as I haven't seen him for a while. We walk up to their table and Jake looks up with a smarmy smile that slowly melts away.

'Jakey darling, you remember Lizzie from work. We've just been chatting at the bar.'

'Yes, we have. Great to hear all about your new relationship, *Jakey.*'

Jake says nothing. What can you say when confronted by the two women you're currently seeing, one of whom has just miscarried your baby?

'Yes,' I continue, 'all the details, when it started, *how* it started. Sounds very romantic, like it's all meant to be.'

'Er, yeah, no . . . not really . . . it was, um,' Jake attempts to put words together, but fails miserably.

'Anyway, I have to go back to my table. I'm just here with a few friends. Do you know Willow S?'

'Willow S!' Lucy looks like she is about to wet her pants. 'I thought I saw her over there. Do you know her?'

'Yeah, we're friends from way back.'

I turn to go but stop, rummage through my bag and pull out Jake's sunglasses.

'By the way, Jake, I forgot to give you these,' I say casually. 'You left them at my house after staying over the other night. I've been carrying them around in my bag ever since, as I imagined we'd be seeing each other soon. Obviously not the case, so here you are.' I toss them with force at Jake and they hit him square in the nose, landing perfectly on their tiny, intimate table – couldn't have done it better if I'd placed them there myself. 'Have a great night.'

I go to turn and walk away, but stop when I see the look of confusion Lucy's face.

'Sorry for my undercover operation, but I had to find out what was going on,' I say directly to Lucy, ignoring Jake. 'He's a liar and a cheat, and has clearly been two-timing us since his birthday. You probably don't believe me now, but I just can't walk away without letting you know what an arsehole he is and how you're better off without him in your life.'

I smile kindly at Lucy and then walk away, wishing I could see Jake's face. I sit back down at my table. Well, not really my table. I look at Willow and her group of friends and wish I really was part of this group. So glamorous. People keep turning to stare, whispering to their friends, trying not to look impressed, but they so are. Some people ask for autographs, which Willow gives graciously. A couple of photographers are even hanging around. I guess that must happen to Willow on a regular basis. I sigh, feeling like I'd better get going.

'Hey, we might head out dancing soon,' Willow says in my direction. 'You up for it?'

Dancing with Willow S! I discreetly check over my shoulder, just to ensure she's actually talking to me. Then I look across the room and see Jake and Lucy in a fiery conversation. She might even be crying. Not so chatty now. I feel kinda bad for her, but it's much better that she knows the truth.

'I'd love to.'

I end up clubbing until three in the morning, something I haven't done since way before I was pregnant and obsessed with Jake. And Willow and her friends seem to have access to the most sought-after places in town. Wherever we go, doors miraculously open.

Willow and I dance all night and have an absolute ball. She is so my new best friend. Well, second-best after Clem, that is. We even choreograph a super-cool dance routine, which we do together up on a podium and manage to get the whole dance floor to join in, which is totally awesome. Until I get a bit overzealous with the arm movements and accidentally whack Willow in the face, knocking her to the ground.

'Shit! Sorry!'

Willow is clutching her cheek while her friends flock to her side. I can't believe I hit a famous person, just when we were getting on so well. I try to help Willow, offering to get some ice, but I'm shooed away by her entourage. Eventually she gets herself up and looks at me. I wait, unsure what's going to happen, when suddenly a smile creeps up on her blotchy red face and she bursts into laughter.

'Wow! You are strong, girlfriend!' she says.

And with those few words, I'm no longer that girl who hit Willow S square in the face, possibly bruising her in the middle of a tight filming schedule, but a tough girl you just don't want to mess with (especially on the dance floor).

Apart from that near disaster, it's the Best Night Ever! So great to be out with friends and not think about chasing a guy. The fact that I've only known my 'friends' for a few hours doesn't seem to matter. And since accidentally hitting Willow, I'm so part of the cool gang. Anyway, it's just the diversion I need. It feels like a brand-new chapter in my life. Things can only get better.

I mean, what else could possibly go wrong?

21

A knock on the door wakes me up with a jolt. What time is it? Out of habit, I look at the other side of my bed and sigh with relief. I'm alone. I was pretty drunk when I got in. Can't even remember getting into bed. Any other time, I would have been highly likely to discover a guest lying beside me.

The knock comes again. Louder this time. It wouldn't be Clem, she'd call. Not Jake. Maybe Mum, she can be pretty persistent. I grab my dressing gown, wondering how they even got buzzed into the building.

'Yes, hello? Who's there?' I call out.

'Police.'

'What?' I say, in what comes out as a high-pitched squawk.

'The police, we're looking for Elizabeth March. Is that you?'

'Yes, that's me. What's going on?' Police outside my door! What did I do last night?

'Can you please open the door? We need to ask a few questions.'

I open the door cautiously. Just because they say they're the police doesn't mean anything these days. A man and a woman, dressed in what seem to be legitimate police outfits, are standing outside my door.

'Can I help you?' I say suspiciously.

'Good morning, I'm Constable McGregor and this is Constable Thompson,' says the man, flashing a badge.

'Yes?'

'You're Elizabeth March?'

'Yes. Well, Lizzie actually –'

'Could you come down to the station to answer a few questions?'

'What? Why? What's going on? Has something happened? I haven't done anything wrong, have I?'

'Look, we just want to –'

'Okay, is this about Jake? Did he report me?'

The officers look at me blankly.

'It was only that one time and he was the father of my baby, not that I knew it then. But I lost the baby anyway. Not that night, but another night. Early miscarriage, very common, you know. But now Jake is probably angry at me because I –'

Unnecessary words are spewing out all over the two police officers. It's like I'm having some sort of speed therapy session. Which actually feels great.

'No, this concerns Willow Smith. We need to ask you some questions about your involvement with her,' says Thompson.

'Willow Smith?' I'm more shocked that her surname is Smith than by the fact I have police at my door, asking about my relationship with a beautiful and well-known actress.

'We'll explain everything down at the station.'

'Can I make a phone call?' I ask, thinking back to all those episodes of *Law & Order* I used to love watching. 'To my lawyer.'

'I don't think that's necessary, but you're certainly entitled,' says Thompson. 'Let's talk about it at the station. Did you want to get dressed?'

I look down at my fluffy pink dressing gown. Definitely need clothes.

'I'll just slip into something more comfortable,' I say, trying to make light of an odd situation, but I'm met with a stony silence. 'Won't be long.'

I throw on my jeans, t-shirt and trainers. No need for dressing up where I'm going. However, I grab my vintage leopard skin–patterned raincoat. Don't want to completely let myself go.

My street is bustling with people and, as I'm escorted to the police car, I feel eyes on me everywhere. I want to say to all the passers-by that I'm innocent, I've done nothing wrong, but I don't get the chance. And I don't know at this stage if I *am* innocent. What happened last night? I don't remember anything illegal like holding up a 7-Eleven, but maybe we did!

'Can you give me some idea of what is going on, please? I barely know Willow, I just sold her –'

'Please refrain from talking until we are at the station and can conduct a formal interview,' says Thompson.

When we arrive, I learn that Willow has been under suspicion for drug dealing. Apparently when I gave her the three bags in the bar last night, and she then handed me the cash, it looked like a drug deal.

'Did you sell drugs to Willow Smith?'

'No!'

'What was in the three bags?'

'Nothing.'

'Why did she give you money?'

'She bought them.'

'What? Drugs?'

'No! The bags. I made them. Willow bought them. End of story.'

No one seems to be listening to me. I ask if I can make my phone call. A call I'm dreading, but that I have no choice but to make. They grant me my call. I dial the number and take a deep breath.

'Clem? Don't freak out.'

'I hate it when you start a conversation like that.'

'So, I'm down at the police station.'

'What?' Clem is already freaking out. I knew she would.

'I've done nothing wrong but I've been brought in for questioning.'

'What?'

My eardrum is starting to suffer from Clem's reactions so I decide to get it all out in one go.

'You know I've been making those nappy bags I told you about? Well, that actress, Willow S – do you know her? Probably not – anyway, she saw my prototype one day and ordered one. In fact she bought three. I was seen handing the bags to her, in exchange for cash, and the police seem to think it was a drug transaction. Which of course it wasn't. I'm innocent, but I really need you.'

'Hang on, just back up a minute . . . you know Willow S?'

'Well, sort of, I was hanging out with her and her friends. She's an actress who was on –'

'*Timelines*! Yes, I know! I love her.' Clem is sounding a little hysterical. 'Hanging out with Willow S? Is this true? You know how you can sometimes misinterpret a situation.'

'Yes, it's true! But it was only because she wanted a nappy bag.'

'Is Willow S pregnant?'

'No!' Somehow, Clem is focusing on all the wrong issues. Here I am at the police station, practically going to jail, and all she is concerned about is how I know Willow and is she having a baby. Since when did Clem go in for TV gossip?

'Clem! Can you please come down here?' There's an edge to my voice that snaps her attention back to where it's needed.

Within minutes, Clem arrives and talks the talk. And gets results. There's no proof of any drugs, because there weren't any. I don't even do drugs, let alone deal them. She doesn't mention the fact that I did take half a trip during my time at design school. It cost me a fortune and all that happened was a temporary loss of fine motor skills.

Apparently, a journo with a grudge against Willow tipped off the police. She was questioned as well, but denied knowing me; she said I was just a designer she'd recently met, from whom she purchased three bags and that was it. When they asked her why she was partying with me all night, she said she'd felt sorry for me and didn't know how to ask me to leave.

I'm not sure how to process that piece of information. So much for my new second-best friend. I guess I'll only ever be a bag lady to her. Still, I'm finally allowed to go and that's more important than worrying about why some TV star doesn't want to be friends. Clem and I have a quick coffee before she goes back to work.

'Lizzie, how did you even meet Willow?' Clem asks when we finally sit down to a couple of very welcome flat whites.

I explain the whole story, starting from when Willow saw my bag at Rock Salt.

'I made three more and she bought them, and now all her friends want one too. Then somehow I got arrested.'

'Not arrested. Questioned. Very different. They had nothing to arrest you on because you're innocent. Willow was the one under suspicion of dealing drugs.'

'Unbelievable. Did you know her surname is Smith?'

'No wonder she uses a single letter, much more glamorous,' says Clem. 'Hey, you might make it into the papers with all this.'

'Really? I doubt it.' What on earth could be newsworthy about this simple misunderstanding?

Clem assures me they make stories out of absolutely nothing. She also makes me promise not to take calls from numbers I don't recognise, as journalists have a way of catching you unawares and twisting what you say to their own benefit. I know it's her job to be cautious but honestly, who am I? No one famous. Just someone making bags. There's no story in that. Not yet, anyway.

I sip my coffee, trying to digest the morning's events, when an image of Jake and chatty Lucy rudely pops into my head. I relay the night's events to Clem, who says nothing, quite loudly.

'I know. Believe me, this time, I know. He's no good. But he came over the other night and said he wanted to still see me, even without the baby. He wanted everything to go back to how it was.'

'I bet he did.'

'I thought he was genuine and I was willing to give him a final chance, but that's over now. Never again.'

'Good for you, Lizzie. I'm really glad. You are so much better off.'

Clem is right. I'm sick of even thinking about my disastrous love-life so my mind jumps ship to Clem's hopefully far more interesting one.

'Oh my God, how did you go last night with Dr Mitch? Was it the best night ever? Tell me everything! Goodness, was he with you this morning when I rang? You didn't tell him I was arrested, did you?'

'No, I didn't, because he wasn't with me this morning. Our date was fine, but nothing happened.'

'Honestly, Clem, you don't have to still do the five dates before sex thing, you're a grown woman; you can take a little bit of a chance. Break the rules every now and then.'

'Lizzie, I don't want to rush into anything after Mal.' She pauses, as if she's about to say something, but then changes her mind. 'Let's just leave it at that. He's a nice guy and I appreciate your efforts, but we'll see how it goes.'

It's crystal clear I'm not going to get any more information from Clem. She's like an expensive piece of Tupperware – nothing comes out. Must be a lawyer thing. But I will learn the truth eventually. I'm sure they'll be moving in together soon, wall-papering feature walls and planning their first holiday. Clem doesn't waste any time when she gets going.

We finish our coffees and Clem races off to work. I thank her once again for coming to my rescue. Every girl needs a lawyer friend like Clem. I hate to think where I'd be without her. Especially as my life has been such a slippery slope, much like the one Jack and Jill had to climb. It didn't do them any good, and now I understand why. Fingers crossed tomorrow goes a little better.

22

As it turns out tomorrow is worse than yesterday, from the minute I go out in search of a coffee. I pick up a paper from the corner store to see if there's anything in it about Willow and almost fall over backwards as the headline on the front page shouts at me, as if it has its own megaphone:

Celebrity Drug Deal Gone Wrong

There's an enormous and unflattering photograph of me. I don't think they could have made it any bigger. It's probably like any picture on the front of the paper, but from where I stand, it looks obscenely large. My hands shake as I fumble for coins to pay for what looks to be a confronting experience. I race out the door and stand in the street, reading the article, every awful word:

Local call-centre employee Lizzie March was seen with actress Willow Smith, who is assisting police with enquiries into drug dealing. The pair met in a popular inner-city venue, where a possible drug transaction was believed to have occurred. Police received an anonymous tip-off and both women were subsequently taken to Surry Hills Police Station for further questioning.

March is under suspicion of supplying drugs to a number of Sydney's celebrities. According to police, the single thirty-year-old ex-fashion designer may possibly be a crucial link to a bigger drug organisation in Asia.

March's manager at WineCall, Steve Jenkins, knew nothing of the allegations but commented on March's wine sales. 'For about a month she dropped to the lowest performer in WineCall's sales team,' he says.

I can't read anymore. I feel sick to my stomach. Sicker than when I was suffering morning sickness, even sicker than when I saw Jake in the bar with chatty Lucy. It's all horrible lies. And the whole of Sydney is reading it right now, thinking I'm a drug dealer! I've never felt so angry and yet so utterly powerless at the same time. The words are out there, in print, and there's nothing I can do about it. How dare Steve mention my sales? I sell wine! My stats have been great recently, up until the miscarriage. I was just momentarily caught up with a two-timing selfish prick who's made my life a complete misery. No one can sell wine properly under such circumstances. If WineCall hadn't employed Jake Wheeler, none of this would have happened.

To make matters worse, the photo they dug up is truly horrendous, taken on the night of the disastrous speed-dating event. How on earth did they find that? Must have been from the bar's security camera. The shot shows me fighting with that other woman over the guy we both liked (can't even remember his name). I appear to be pulling her hair but I know I never did that. She looks all sweet and pretty (which she wasn't) while I look like a desperate woman with a crazed glint in her eye. Unlucky shot. But lucky for the journalist who wrote this far-fetched piece of fiction. Just another misconstrued situation, creating an even more negative portrait of me.

I need caffeine. Now.

I run to my local café. The young girl behind the coffee machine, usually so friendly, looks at me strangely. Oh God, she's read the article. I try to look like someone with their life together, just on their way to a busy and fulfilling job, as opposed to a celebrity drug dealer caught in the act.

She's not convinced.

I sit down at a table at the back near a guy dressed in a suit, who's reading the paper. He looks up and does a double-take. He looks back down at the cover photo and then back to me with narrowed, suspicious eyes.

'That's not me!' I say to him with a nervous laugh. 'No, no, no, well, yes, okay, it is actually me, but it's all a mistake. Big mistake.'

The suit gets up without a word and heads to the door, leaving the paper on his table. I grab it, mostly so no one else in the café can read it. Maybe, if I get every paper from every café, then at least some people in the world won't think I'm a criminal. My phone rings.

'Oh, Lizzie, this is awful.' Clem has seen the paper and proceeds to read out bits over the phone, which I really don't need to hear. 'It says that you were recently taken to Emergency after a suspected drug overdose! And that shot from the speed-dating night is just terrible. I told you speed dating only leads to trouble.'

'Clem, why would someone write such lies about me?' I whisper.

'They haven't really lied about anything, Lizzie,' she says. 'Nothing is written as actual fact. It's all "suspected", "believed to be", "allegedly" . . . and that photo of you is very real . . . and you did go to Emergency recently.'

'Maybe Dr Mitch told them that. You have to find out. You're practically going out with the man.'

'Lizzie! I doubt that Dr Mitch –'

'They didn't have to say my age and that I'm a single. That's just mean. And how dare WineCall make a comment on my lack of selling!'

'But none of it's untrue, is it?'

She's right, but I don't want the world to see me this way, with all the worst bits of my pathetic private life on view for all to judge. What I want is to scream at the top of my voice, 'I'M NOT THAT PERSON!' Okay, I'm thirty and single and I work in a call centre, having not designed much in the way of cutting-edge fashion, but drugs? It's insulting.

'Can I write a response or go on the radio? Maybe I should sue for defamation?'

'You've watched too many American law dramas. You can't sue, it costs a fortune and you haven't really got a case. Okay, they were mean and they cherry-picked which information to give, but you can't sue someone for that. Plus, the more oxygen you give this, the longer it will continue. I've seen it all before and there's no way you can come out on top. Whatever you say will be misinterpreted and you don't want them to find out about Jake, the baby and all that – which they will, if you talk. My advice is to say nothing. At the moment they have nothing. If you give them nothing, then they'll still have nothing, and it will die down before you know it.'

I have to agree with my lawyer.

But it's infuriating.

People in the café are staring nervously over the tops of their newspapers now, so I pay for my coffee and leave. Honestly, why do people read such trashy journalism? It's only ten-thirty and I'm over this day already.

My phone runs hot for the next hour with journalists and radio stations wanting me to comment on Willow S and her drug habit. Why did she buy a baby bag? Is she pregnant? Why is she doing drugs if she's pregnant? Is she having a boy or a girl? Does she intend to breastfeed?

I even get a text message from the journalist who wrote the hideous article on me, asking if I'd be interested in a proper interview for a follow-up piece. I want to tell him where he could stick his interview and follow-up piece, but I can just see the next day's headlines: *Drug-addled unemployed designer lashes out at innocent journalist!* So I don't respond.

I don't respond to anything. I say 'no comment' to anyone who calls and to every stupid question I'm asked. Except my mother, who naturally rings me the minute she sees the article, wondering why I was dealing drugs when I could have asked her and Dad for a loan, or moved home if I was that hard up. I would have dealt drugs for real before that ever happened, but her concern is touching.

'It's all a misunderstanding,' I say when my mother finally pauses to take a breath. 'There were no drugs. I don't use them or sell them. I made some bags, I sold some bags. End of story.'

'What bags? Not the ones you were starting to make at home with all those lovely fabrics? The one I can see in this online photo of that Willow girl?'

'Yes. The nappy bag I was telling you about. Well, you can use it for anything. I'm calling it an Anything Bag.'

I'm definitely going with the name Willow came up with when she described it to her friends. It really is the perfect description.

There's a heavy silence as I wait for a lecture on how I'm mixed up with the wrong crowd, how I shouldn't talk to famous people as they are nothing but trouble, and how Willow looks like she needs a good wash and a decent haircut. I close my eyes and brace myself, determined to let it all pass over me like a cool breeze.

'How fabulous, darling! They're fantastic. I'm so glad you decided to make them in the end. You're so talented. I want one too. Do you still have those same fabrics I saw? Can I have a mix of those? You choose, darling, you have such great taste!'

'Of course,' I say, taken aback.

'So what happens now? Are you going to sell them elsewhere?'

'Not sure. I've had a few more orders from Willow's friends so I'll make those. Maybe I'll think about selling them at the markets.'

'Yes, yes, I'll help, I can make some little cakes to attract the crowds . . . and you should get Dad to do a promotional shot and then set up a website and sell them online. He's just got a new camera and it's really . . .'

Ever since my parents did a computer course they've realised everything happens online. They've finally caught up with technology and can't stop telling me how marvellous it all is.

'I don't want a huge production. It's just a project on the side.'

'On the side of what?'

'Can we not talk about it?'

'Come on, darling. This may be a wonderful opportunity. You've got so much to offer. It's time for everyone to see what I see. Take a leap of faith. Be brave. Who knows where this bag thing will lead?'

Mum's right. I have to give it a go, but deep down I'm scared. What if I fail again? What if, like when I was at design school, my ideas are 'not worth pursuing'? What if I start producing something that nobody wants and end up back in financial strife? It would be so humiliating. Thankfully, my mobile interrupts this train of thought. I say goodbye to Mum on the landline and grab the other call.

'Hello?'

'You're on TV! Quick!'

Clem is so excited, she can barely speak. I don't understand what she's talking about. I haven't gone on TV. She knows I was asked to make a comment on the news, but decided against it, on her advice. I try to work out what she's talking about but she just keeps saying, over and over, that I'm on TV. Is that what lawyers do? Don't listen, don't explain, just repeat themselves ceaselessly? No wonder no one likes them.

Slowly Clem puts words together to reveal that Willow S is being interviewed at this very moment on *The Lunch Break*, a mid-morning chat show that no one watches. Or at least, I thought no one watched it. Obviously, people do watch it and Clem is one of those people. Maybe that's why she stays up so late, too busy at work – she's been watching daytime chat shows on her phone. She demands I turn on the television immediately, which I do, and there is Willow S looking a million dollars in a gorgeous maxi dress with her fabulous hair and creamy skin and, on her lap, in plain view, is one of my bags. In fact, Sandy the plastic-looking presenter is asking her about it right now.

'And this is the bag that caused all that controversy?'

'It was a complete misunderstanding, Sandy. I literally bumped into this woman who makes gorgeous bags and I ordered one for myself. It's awesome, isn't it? I love it. It's supposed to be a nappy bag but I call it the Anything Bag.'

My heart skips a beat. Willow has said the name of my bag on TV!

'A nappy bag!' The presenter gives a tinkling laugh. 'It doesn't look like any nappy bag I ever had. But I wish I'd had one like that, it's simply divine. And what about the drug suspicions?'

'I don't do drugs. Never have. The police searched my house and car but, of course, found nothing. All I did was arrange to meet a local up-and-coming designer, so I could buy one of her bags. I ended up buying three. She handed me the bags and I gave her the money. That was it.'

'Well, I absolutely love that bag, it's fabulous,' gushes Sandy. 'Let's get a close-up for our viewers.'

The camera zooms in on my bag and I have to say it looks fantastic. I'm glad I took care with the topstitching because the shot is incredibly close.

'So, Willow S, a nappy bag?' says Sandy with a smile. 'Is there a little secret something you want to share with the viewers?'

'I'm definitely not pregnant,' Willow laughs. 'I didn't know it was a nappy bag. In fact, I'd never even heard of such a thing. But if I did have a baby, I would so want a super-cool bag like this. I'm not a mum and it's totally useful.'

'It's a sensational bag and that designer has a great career ahead of her – and certainly not in dealing drugs with an eye for style like that. What's her name again?'

I pinch myself. They're talking about me! And my bag!

'Lizzie March,' says Willow. 'Very talented lady and her bags are awesome.'

I almost faint. Willow is looking straight down the camera, right at me, like she is telling me to my face. I didn't like her so much when she completely dismissed me in all the newspaper reports (okay, I ended up reading quite a few) but she's not so bad. Giving me a plug like that. Maybe she felt bad about dragging me into such a scandal.

'I'll remember that name. Now, back to your exciting new show. When's it coming out and, more importantly, is there anything going on between you and your gorgeous co-star . . . ?'

'Did you hear what she said?' Clem screams down the phone.

'Yeah, that was nice,' I say, feeling a little dazed.

'Nice!' Clem almost spits out the word. 'Willow S is talking about you on the telly, saying you're talented. It's a universe away from nice, it's incredible!'

I open my mouth to respond, but no words come out. Must be in shock. Willow is still on the screen chatting about an upcoming project, a movie, shooting in Melbourne, followed by a trip to LA for a round of auditions. She's successful, charming and incredibly beautiful. But after dipping my toes into the world of celebrity where the media feels justified in saying and printing pretty much anything they like about you, whether it's the truth or not, I wouldn't want her life on a fulltime basis. Contributing to a celebrity's personal style is far more thrilling. If you'd said to me a couple of months ago that Willow S would be discussing my latest fashion creation on TV, I'd have suggested you have an immediate lie-down. Perhaps visit your nearest healthcare professional. But here she is, talking up my bags to the entire country. Clem's right, it is incredible.

It has been ages since I've even touched my sewing machine. That part of my life had all but drifted away, lost in the years of call centre drudgery. But now, it's back with a flurry and has landed a starring role in Willow S's famous life. If she likes my bag, then surely others will as well. Who knows what this will bring? Fame? Fortune? One thing's for sure, I'll be able to pay my rent on time. And for now, that really is incredible.

23

My phone hasn't been this busy on a Friday afternoon in years. Actually, it's never been this busy. And this time it's not the media, unless you count a publicist from a popular fashion magazine wanting to feature my bag in their 'Must have' column. The rest of the calls are from people ordering bags, which become more daunting than the calls from pushy journalists.

Clem calls to order a bag. She suggests it be big enough to carry her files home at night, or maybe include an internal section for her tablet or laptop, and I'm thrilled with the idea. Why shouldn't the working woman – mum or otherwise – have a great bag to carry documents and files as well as all the baby stuff? It's fast becoming not the Anything Bag, but the Everything Bag.

Missy wants one. My mother calls with seven orders from her book club. Apparently, most of them caught *The Lunch Break* and are desperate to have a bag like Willow S's. Now I know who else watches mindless morning chat shows – my mother's book-club friends, with their perfect offspring, who all have incredibly healthy relationships and can balance spectacularly successful careers with their super-advanced babies. At least Mum will finally have something impressive to say about me when they meet.

The orders keep coming. People I haven't spoken to in years track me down. Even a couple of girls from school, the ones who always made fun of my creations, call me to put in an order, which is hilarious as none of them would have given me the time of day back then – or even last week. Tiffany Simpson not only rings to make an order, but also apologises for how she treated me at the Year 10 formal!

My head spinning, I fish out an old notebook to write down all my orders and look over the ever-growing list in awe. How on earth am I going to be able to make them all?

The phone rings once again. Another customer, maybe?

'Hello?'

'Hi, Lizzie, it's Steve from work. How are you going? Feeling better?'

I explain that I'm on the mend, without going over the top because I know that there's only one reason for Steve to be calling me at home. He has shifts to fill, and my leave is almost up. However, his comments from the paper are still floating around like a bad smell.

'I heard that you're out and about and I figured you must be better,' he says casually. 'Do you think you could come in to cover a shift today? We've had three people call in sick.'

Stomach flu must be going around!

I look at my list of bag orders. I definitely need money to buy more fabric, and I'm going to have to pay rent soon. It's all very well getting orders, but I have to be able to fund the production. That three hundred and sixty from Willow is only going to scratch the surface. I don't want to be dragged into debt like I was after my last fashion design fiasco.

I have to say yes, but I'm not letting Steve off the hook that easily. 'Do you really want someone who "*dropped to the lowest performer in WineCall's sales team*"?'

'Oh yeah, sorry about that, Lizzie, I don't know who the press talked to here, but it wasn't me,' says Steve in a sheepish voice. 'See you at two?'

I can guess who would have passed on that information to the paper. Someone wanting revenge for being outed in front of his chatty girlfriend. I hang up and take myself off to the bathroom for a shower. I know I have to leave this job, but I can't afford to. Yet.

I regret agreeing to the shift the minute I arrive. Jake is working and waves at me like nothing's happened. I look straight through him. In my mind, he no longer exists. Now I know the full story, there's nothing left to say. I don't want to hear his pathetic excuses. And I certainly don't want to wave across the call centre.

Once the afternoon brief is over, I head to my workstation. I'm probably imagining it, but it feels like everyone's looking at me. Whenever I glance up, they quickly avert their eyes, and it's getting annoying. I go to the kitchen and make a cup of tea, bumping into Frankie on the way, who gives me one of her warm hugs.

'How are you?' she says.

'Yeah, um . . .'

'It's okay, everyone knows.'

'What?' I hiss, not so happy with the warm hug now. Great! So everyone knows that I was carrying Jake's baby and now I'm not. Fantastic.

'Don't worry, everyone's on your side. They know you don't do drugs.'

'Oh, that. I thought you meant about Jake and the baby.'

'Yeah, they know about that too. I think Missy got the word around pretty quickly, you know what she's like. But there's something else you should know. Jake and Lucy have become a bit of a thing.'

I roll my eyes. 'I know about that.'

'You know it's been on and off for a while?'

'Absolutely – and I'm fine with it,' I say, as confidently as I possibly can. 'He's a two-timing, lying bastard, who's actually not that great in bed. She's welcome to him as far as I'm concerned.'

'Good for you! And by the way, I want to order one of your bags.'

'Sure, I'll add you to the list.'

I get my tea and walk back to my workstation with my head so high, I almost hit one of the ceiling fans. I can't let people know how devastated I'm feeling right now. I don't want Jake, but I don't really want him to be happy with someone else. And so quickly. I sink into my seat, trying to be as invisible as possible, which is completely impossible in an open-plan call centre.

The shift starts, but I can't concentrate. Every time I catch someone's eye they give me a sympathetic smile or a reassuring nod as if to say, 'Go girl, you can do it!' Obviously, everyone knows all about my life, my relationship woes and my recent brush with the law. If only I could disappear into the dirty grey carpet.

In the break, people keep coming up and asking how I am. Do I want a coffee? Am I selling well today? I've spoken to more people in the call centre in the last fifteen minutes than I have in the entire five years I've worked here. Even Nathan doesn't tease me as much as he normally would. He does ask if he can score some drugs and I crossly tell him to go away, but at least he's being semi-normal and not treating me like I've got days to live.

As if the unwanted attention isn't bad enough, I can't actually sell anything. Not that I'm surprised. As everyone in the world now knows, my sales have been up and down. But normally, even on a bad day, I sell at least ten cases. Today, every customer I call simply doesn't need any wine.

Jake is up at the podium, announcing a change to the day's wine list, when Lucy breezes in, late for her shift. Everyone in the call centre stops and looks at her, then at me, then at Jake. The tension is as thick as honey stored in the fridge. Heads turn so fast, the entire sales team will surely give themselves whiplash. I ignore the sideways glances, but all I want to do is scream. Lucy approaches me with a condescending smile and a voice that should only be reserved for puppies or very small children with hearing problems.

'Hi, Lizzie, you okay? I hope we can put all this behind us. Jake and I have – and we really hope you can too. We don't want you to feel weird at work.'

I might have been about to crawl through the shift, but Lucy reaching out, eyes brimming with fake sympathy, tips me over the edge. All the emotions flooding my body join forces and morph into a mountainous tidal wave in my gut, washing over me with a power I've never before experienced.

'Weird?' I say in a voice that comes out louder than expected. 'Why should *I* feel weird?'

Lucy opens her mouth as if to answer my rhetorical question, but I don't give her the chance.

'I've never felt less weird in my entire life. In fact, for once I feel completely normal.'

Nothing is planned, but the words tumble out in perfect order, strong and authoritative. I'm angry, yet for once, totally in control. The room is hushed in an awkward silence, all ears standing to attention. Right now, I couldn't care less if the entire universe was listening. It's my one chance to set the record straight and I'm grabbing it with both hands.

'I just met a guy, got pregnant and decided to have the baby. That guy seemed really excited about having a baby and wanted to be completely involved. Except that on the night I miscarried, he wasn't with me, was he? He was with you. Then he doesn't even have the guts to come clean and break up with me, even though he's obviously been seeing you at the same time. If anyone's feeling weird right now, it should be Jake, the lying bastard. And you, for staying with him even after you found out about all this. He's an arsehole and you're a fool. And you're worried about *me* feeling weird?'

I turn to grab my bag and out of the corner of my eye I see Frankie, smiling proudly, and Nathan giving me a thumbs-up. Steve looks out of his office door, unsure how to deal with this situation. It probably wasn't covered in management training.

I turn back to Jake, who is now not so keen to attract my attention.

'I don't know what I saw in you, but thank God I've seen the real Jake before it was too late. And it's far from an attractive picture. Anyone who behaves like you is not worth the podium they're standing on.'

I turn to the crowd. 'Watch out, ladies! He may be all hot and incredibly handsome but underneath he's a total shit, who talks shit and treats women like shit. Don't let him or anyone get away with it. No one will ever treat me like that again. I deserve so much better, and so do you. And I'll find it – I'm just not going to find it here!'

I turn and march towards the door. Lizzie March by name, and now by nature. As I get to the call-centre door, I hear the faint sound of clapping. I turn to see Frankie quietly applauding me, smiling from ear to ear. Nathan joins her and in a second, the room is filled with loud cheering and woo-hooing.

The admiration of my audience hits me like a southerly change on a hot summer's day, and I want to bottle it so I can save it up for a time when life returns to normal and I need a confidence boost. This is my moment. I've never dared to say anything like this in public. Or even in private. And it's amazing. So much positive attention and approval! I should stand up for myself on a daily basis. I swear, if someone were to measure me right now, I would be at least a foot taller.

I hear Steve trying to calm everyone down, but I block out his voice, something I try to do at every briefing meeting but which today poses no challenge at all.

I open my eyes and drink in one last delicious gaze over the call centre that I won't ever work in again. My cheeks are aching but I just can't release the massive smile stretching across my face.

Slowly, I count to ten, making the most of every second. Then I turn and walk away, without looking back. I step into that battleship-grey lift for the very last time, the doors snap shut and my hands start to tremble. This is the start of a new me. A Lizzie who is strong, independent and empowered. A Lizzie who knows what she wants and will never again take crap from anyone.

I step out onto the street and I feel like I'm floating on air. God, I hated that job. Not that my alternative job is a stable option, but I can't stay in that sordid love triangle with everyone watching my every move or reaction. I don't know what I'm going to do in the short term. My bags are not going to support me yet, but something will work out. I'm going to make sure of it.

24

By the time I get off the train, my bubble of victory has deflated slightly. It's all very well proudly walking out of work, but now that I'm faced with the monumental task of setting up my bag business, I don't know where to start. Clem is still at work so I can't hang out with her. I see a random taxi go by and immediately think of Cherie. I never thanked her properly for coming to my rescue the night I miscarried. I've been so caught up with the dramas of the past week and I haven't needed to go anywhere by taxi since that trip to the hospital. I ring to see if she wants a coffee.

'Hello?'

'Cherie, it's Lizzie.'

'Hello there, love, how are you? Everything okay?' Cherie sounds concerned. 'I've been meaning to call. I got your message about the baby. Sorry to hear your news. And I saw all the hoo-ha in the papers. Those bastards. Just ignore it, sweetie.'

'I'm fine. It's been awful but it's all over now. Newspapers don't last long even though the internet is forever.'

'Either way, people forget pretty quickly. So what's happening?'

'I quit my job! Feel like a celebratory cuppa? I could meet you somewhere. Are you out and about? Or too busy working?'

'As a matter of fact, I'm not working today.'

'Where are you? Sounds noisy.'

'I'm . . . well, I'm . . . in a rehearsal . . . for a cabaret.'

I walk straight into the guy in front of me who looks at me and quickly puts his hand to his pocket as if I'm after his wallet. I smile with as much middle-class non-thief sophistication as I can, mouthing my apologies.

'Wow!' I squeal into the phone. 'I thought you said you'd never perform again, that you'd well and truly retired?'

Cherie explains. Apparently, things took a sharp detour when a producer asked if she'd consider doing a show in an old jazz club in Newtown, a venue that's gone through a revival and is fast becoming the latest place to be. The money on offer wasn't bad so after saying no a few times, she eventually agreed.

'That's fantastic, Cherie. When's the show?'

'It opens in a month's time and I'm booked for six Sundays. If it goes well, maybe longer. I'm a bit nervous, to tell you the truth. I haven't sung on stage for years. If it wasn't for Mitch, I don't think I'd have considered it.'

'Mitch?'

'Yeah, the doctor who looked after you that night.'

'My Mitch? I mean, not my Mitch, but the Mitch I know? Well, don't know at all to be honest . . .'

'Yeah, we met up so I could sign his copy of my album, and

we got chatting. Turns out he's one talented musician – piano and guitar. Played in a band during his university days. They were doing well, attracting a bit of attention. Could have made a name for himself, but he let it go to become a doctor. The band went on to become quite well known. He really misses it all now so he was keen to get together for a session. When I told him I was considering a comeback, he convinced me to do it and offered to rehearse with me. In fact, he's here right now.'

I try to imagine the tall, lanky Dr Mitch as a rock'n'roll star but can't quite see it. Still, Cherie must know what she's talking about. If she thinks he's talented, then he must be.

'Well, I'll be there!' I say, excited for Cherie. 'Text me the details. Have you got flyers yet? I'll organise lots of people.'

'Yeah, tell all your friends. I'll drop some flyers in your letterbox. I'd better go now, otherwise I'll have nothing to sing,' she says with a throaty chuckle. 'We'll catch up in the next few days. Have a cuppa and a chat. I'll fill you in on all the details.'

I know I shouldn't interrupt her at work, but as I walk home I call Clem anyway to see if she wants to meet this evening and celebrate my newly unemployed state. Thanks to some sort of miracle, Zoe is away from her desk and my call goes straight through, but to no end, as Clem is unavailable tonight.

'Are you going out with Dr Mitch again?'

Clem hesitates. 'Yeah, we might meet up for dinner.'

'I spoke to Cherie and he was there with her, playing guitar, helping her rehearse for a show. Did you know about that?'

'Um, I think he mentioned it,' says Clem.

'Do you want to go and see the show? Should be fun.'

'Definitely. But I'd better go now. There's a call I have to take that my life and stress levels are pretty much depending on.'

I leave Clem to it, happy to hear she's going out with Dr Mitch another time. That's good news. Or is it? Somewhere deep down, a tiny part of me feels on edge. Why is that? I should be happy for Clem. She deserves a nice-guy experience and I pretty much forced Mitch to ask her out. I'm probably feeling a bit left out, what with losing a boyfriend, a baby and a job all in a couple of weeks. Now my friend has possibly found the love of her life and I have no one.

I put my anxieties to one side as they have no place in the all-new, all-empowered Lizzie. Instead, I spend the weekend focusing on my bag orders. Happily, while cleaning out a drawer, I discover a second credit card that I never use. I applied for it so I could buy supplies for that clothing line I tried to establish after college. I bought fabric and other supplies, even paid for expensive publicity, all on that credit card. I had three other such credit cards, all of which had to be paid off and chopped up. I must have forgotten this one. Thankfully, now I can use it for fabric purchases and other sewing materials. But I'll be moderate as I don't want to get into the same financial strife as last time. Hopefully I'll be able to pay it off with the proceeds of my sales.

By Sunday afternoon, I'm exhausted and too restless to watch TV or read. I also have cabin fever and need to get out, but I have absolutely nowhere to go, and no one's available anyway. Even Clem is busy, apparently seeing Dr Mitch again. I can't believe how well it's going between them.

The time has definitely come to break out of my comfort zone and push back the boundaries of social constraints. Like an explorer discovering new lands, I'm determined to be brave and go where I've never dared venture before.

The movies. On my own.

I, Lizzie March, will go to the movies. On my own!

It doesn't sound like much when you say it out loud. Okay, it sounds a little pathetic. But it's something I never do. It's one of the reasons I like having a boyfriend. If a really great film comes out, and Clem's not available, I try to secure a date just so I can see it. A relationship was my prerequisite for going to the cinema. Completely absurd considering at one point I was planning to have a baby on my own – I'm sure that would have been more challenging than sitting in a darkened room, being entertained. I've just always been too scared of what people might think of me on my own, looking all lonely and single.

But things are different now. Everything is different. If I have to wait for a relationship to go to the cinema, I may never get to see another film. Yes, I'm single. But there's nothing wrong with that. I figure, why not give it a go?

I dress for no one in particular. I wear what I want to wear rather than what I hope will impress my date or any potential dates. Then I choose a movie that I want to see. Not something my date wants to see and I just agree to in an attempt to appear easygoing.

I'm excited about my night out alone. Why haven't I been doing this for years, rather than chasing wildly inappropriate men? It's such a simple alternative that never occurred to me.

However, as empowered as I am, I walk into the cinema feeling self-conscious. Still, no one knows yet that I'm here on my own. I could be waiting for a friend. I assume a confidence that I definitely do not feel. Funnily enough, no one looks twice. No one is staring and pointing at the sad single woman. I walk up to the counter where I buy a ticket from a girl who looks like she's about twelve years old.

'Just the one?'

'Er, yes . . . yes, please.' Why would she ask me that? What business is it of hers? I try to sound really happy and positive about it, but there is definitely a flicker of condescension in her eyes. Or is that just my imagination?

'It's just pretty full tonight so there are only a few single seats left. Not much choice.'

'Oh, anything is fine with me,' I say breezily, showing what an easy single customer I am, not like couples who all need to sit next to each other.

'Popcorn?' she asks as if the idea completely bores her.

'Oh yes, just a small, thanks.'

She grabs the biggest barrel of popcorn I've ever seen.

'Oh sorry, I just wanted a small one.'

'That is the small.'

'Oh, then what's that?' I point to a dainty cup in a display cabinet behind her.

'That's "the smallest". You asked for "small",' she says without even a trace of humour.

'I didn't realise that . . . I'll have the small-EST, thanks.'

People start huffing and puffing behind me and the twelve-year-old is far from impressed that she has to put the world's biggest small popcorn back, get the smaller one out and redo a calculation on the register. Honestly, you'd think I'd asked her to do my tax return.

I find the cinema showing my film and the girl was right, it's pretty much full.

I end up right down the front, which feels like I'm on a rollercoaster and strains my neck, but I've come this far, so I'm not turning back. I'm determined to conquer the single movie experience.

Once the movie starts, I forget that I'm alone. Seeing a movie is such a one-person experience anyway, it's not like you can talk. Although the couple behind me discuss every plot point in minute detail as though they're at a dinner party. Fortunately, someone else tells them to be quiet.

When the lights come up, I make my way out. It's a slow process as there are so many people chatting, laughing and dissecting the film. I look up and get such a surprise that I step on the heel of the person in front of me, an older woman who does a bit of a stagger, but thankfully doesn't fall over.

Standing near the exit is Dr Mitch. He's so tall you can't miss him. He and Clem must have come to the movies. What a coincidence. Maybe we can all go and grab some dinner or a drink? Or maybe they want to be alone. They might need their own space. I see Mitch turn back and smile at someone. I look in the direction he's looking and get another surprise, because the focus of his attention is definitely not Clem. I see a pretty girl with a bouncy blonde ponytail. That's weird. Clem told me they were going out tonight. I watch closely as Mitch says something to this girl and she laughs and then playfully punches him in the stomach. Wow! Pretty affectionate. They definitely know each other well. My blood starts to boil. It's Jake and Mal all over again! I text Clem to see what's going on.

Hey, are you with Dr Mitch?

I get a rapid response.

No, something came up.

Immediately, I know what's happened. Mitch has cancelled the date with Clem to go out with Ponytail. He made some pathetic excuse to Clem who is too embarrassed to tell me. Is it not enough that she was dumped and totally deceived by a complete cad and then publicly mortified at a baby shower thanks to her supposed best friend? Now it looks like her future fiancé is cheating on her behind her back!

I expected more from Dr Mitch and I certainly won't be keeping quiet about it this time. I will go straight over to Clem's house to tell her everything. But first, there's something that I have to do.

I hang back behind a group of people until Mitch and Ponytail have left the cinema. I fashion some sort of scarf out of my cardigan and wrap it around my head as a disguise. Then I follow them down the street. I know my stalking days are behind me, but this is different. This is my chance to help Clem, so surely that's worth a little light stalking? I decide it definitely is, while making a silent promise that it'll be the last time I follow someone who doesn't actually know I'm there.

I glide my way skilfully down the street, keeping them in sight up ahead but staying in the shadows. They seem pretty friendly and Ponytail laughs at just about everything Dr Mitch says. Then they stop at a bar and I hold back while they go in. I enter via a different door and spy them sitting down at a little round café-style table. Very intimate. Mitch says something to her and gets up and heads towards the nearby ATM, on the opposite side of the bar. I grab the opportunity to confront him head on.

'Where's Clem?'

'Lizzie, hi! How are you?' Dr Mitch is startled to see me. Guilty conscience. 'Where'd you pop out from? And what have you got wrapped around your head?'

Damn. I'd forgotten about my 'disguise'. I quickly pull the cardigan off, which proves difficult as a button gets caught in my hair. I untangle it with as much dignity as possible, while trying not to break my steely eye contact with Dr Mitch.

'Where's Clem, is more the point? Aren't you supposed to be going out with her tonight?'

'Um . . . no . . .'

'Don't you think Clem deserves better than this?'

People turn to see what's going on. Dr Mitch's eyes dart around the room like he's a goldfish trying to escape his bowl.

'She's already been cheated on and cruelly dumped by one arsehole,' I continue. 'I introduced her to you because I thought you might treat her with respect. But what do you do? You ditch her for a younger version with a bouncy ponytail!'

'No, Lizzie we –'

I throw my hand up to silence him. 'I'll tell Clem everything. I'm not making that mistake again. She deserves better. Better than you.'

'Lizzie, you're making a mistake right now.'

'Oh am I?' I say, far too loudly for a public place. 'This is unbelievable! Who do you think you are? Some sort of super doctor who does whatever he wants? Honestly, tell the truth. It's pretty clear to me. Movies, drink after. She's a bit young for you, don't you think?'

'She's my sister.'

'Oh, yes, of course!' I almost laugh out loud at this pathetic lie. 'Your sister, is it? I don't think you realise that I've heard every excuse in the book and that one isn't even original. So I suppose you and your "sister" are "really close" and "catch up at the movies on a regular basis"?' I exaggerate all the air quotes with my fingers.

'Yes, we do. We go to the movies about once a month. I haven't seen her for a while because she's been travelling overseas. She does aid work in South Sudan.'

'Of course she does. She's a saint!' I look over at the girl, who does look a bit like Dr Mitch, now that I think about it. 'What's her name then?'

'Clare.'

'Well, I shall call Clem to check this story out,' I say, slightly thrown but still not convinced. 'What did you say to Clem? I hope you were clear, she's really fragile at the moment.'

'She cancelled on me. Said something came up.'

He seems genuine, and his words reflect exactly what Clem texted to me, but I don't know what to believe.

'Look, do you mind if I get back to my sister? I have to work tonight, so I don't have long.'

'Okay. I don't know what's gone on between you and Clem, but you should try to sort things out. She's a great girl. You won't find better.'

'Thanks for the advice,' says Dr Mitch, now sounding a bit angry himself. 'But maybe you should get your facts right before confronting people while they're simply trying to withdraw money from the ATM.'

He grabs his money and receipt, turns and walks briskly back to his so-called sister.

Awkward.

I creep backwards and slink away, puzzled about the night's events. I consider calling Clem to make sure everything is all right, but it's late. I'll go over first thing in the morning. I will never again withhold information from Clem. She deserves to know the truth.

25

I jump out of bed at six-thirty am. Unusual but great! I have time to race over to Clem's and catch her before she goes to work. I need to tell her what I saw. And if she confirms that Dr Mitch doesn't have a sister called Clare, or lied about last night in any way, then I can find out which is his car in the hospital car park and slash his tyres. It's the least I can do for my best friend.

I get to Clem's by seven-fifteen, a miracle in itself, and the building door is open so I go straight up. I can't hear any noise in her flat, which is odd because normally Clem would be rushing out the door. Maybe she's gone to the office early. Or maybe she was working last night and is still there. Of course . . . that's why she cancelled on Dr Mitch. She had to pull one of her all-nighters. Or she tried to and, as usual, fell asleep at her desk in a sea of files. She has to stop working so hard, she'll end up with a heart attack or gallstones or something. Still, that might work well, as she could then accidentally on purpose bump into Dr Mitch at the hospital . . . Lizzie, stop.

I call her mobile and hear it ringing in the flat. Right, so she is home but isn't picking up. That's even stranger. I knock gently on the door. No answer. I try again, a little more confidently. Suddenly the door opens and there's Clem with a towel wrapped around her.

'Lizzie, what are you doing here? Sorry, did we plan a walk or something . . . ?'

'I have to talk to you, it's serious.'

'Really? Right now? Are you in trouble?'

'No, not me, this is about you. It's Dr Mitch. I don't think he's the nice guy we thought he was.'

'Oh, right. Look, now's not such a good time to get into all that,' Clem says, looking back towards her lounge room.

'He is so not for you, Clem, and I don't want you to make another mistake that will send you into a downward spiral. I may not have been a good friend to you recently and I know I should have told you about Mal and that stuck-up bitch Becca. Which is why I'm here to tell you that I saw Dr Mitch out last night with a girl with a bouncy ponytail.'

'His sister?'

'Well, so he says . . . hang on. You know about the movie date last night?'

'With his sister, Clare? Yes.'

'He told you about his sister?'

'Yes, she's been travelling so they haven't seen each –'

'Yes, yes, I know all that,' I snap back, feeling incredibly confused and increasingly embarrassed.

'Did you speak to him?'

'In a sense . . .'

'Lizzie, what did you say?'

'I sort of followed them and then I sort of abused Dr Mitch for dumping you to go out with someone else . . .'

'Lizzie!'

'Well, I didn't know!'

'Mitch and I are not going out. And last night *I* cancelled on *him*.'

I can't believe what I'm hearing. 'Why didn't you tell me?'

'Sorry, Lizzie, you seemed so happy about matching us up. We had a coffee and a chat but to be honest, I'm not particularly attracted to him. And I don't think he's that into me, either.'

'What do you mean you're not attracted to him? He's exactly your type, cute, smiley, blue eyes, kind of nerdy-looking.' I'm about to tell Clem she's being a bit fussy when I realise it's getting late and she's still on her doorstep in her towel. 'Aren't you supposed to be going to work?'

'Yes, yes, I'm running late.'

'So what did you do last night?'

Right on cue there's a sudden movement in the bedroom. My mouth drops open almost to the ground.

'Is there someone there?' I whisper. 'Are you entertaining?'

'Yes, but no one you know.'

Nathan strolls out of the bedroom in Clem's fluffy towelling bathrobe. I gave it to her for Christmas two years ago, thinking she needed a little luxury in her stressful life. Not so stressful right now, it seems.

'Sorry, I have to go to the bathroom, I couldn't hold on any longer,' Nathan says apologetically to Clem. 'Hi, Lizzie.'

He walks through to the bathroom and shuts the door behind him. My eyebrows are raised so high, I'm sure they've disappeared into my hair. I look at my friend's cheeks, which are definitely turning pink around the edges. Obviously, now is not the time to ask why she has a semi-naked gay man in her bathroom. Or maybe he's bisexual. Maybe he slept on the couch. No, Clem has a fresh and exuberant look about her that she never usually has before eleven am. It can only mean one thing. But with Nathan?

'I'll call you later, Clem.'

'Sounds good,' she says, pushing me out the door as best a woman can while trying to keep a towel around her private parts.

Right. So Clem and Dr Mitch are a no-go. That's the last time I try any matchmaking. It looks like Clem has managed very well without my help. Except for one little thing. Isn't Nathan gay? That's what Missy said and she's rarely wrong.

I'm fairly sure Nathan will be working today. He usually does the morning shift that starts at nine. I'm also fairly sure he will be running late.

When I get to the WineCall building, I loiter on the street, near the entrance, wearing my baseball cap and sunnies. I don't want anyone from work to see me, particularly Jake and Lucy. I see Nathan running up, sporting his usual preppy look, though a little more unironed than usual, like he had to get dressed and out of someone's flat very quickly. I move at top speed and stop him before he goes into the foyer. The last thing I want is to have to go upstairs to that call centre.

'Hello there.'

'Oh, Lizzie, hi, can't talk now, running really late.'

'That's because you spent the night with my best friend who is very much a woman!'

He gives me an odd look. 'I wanted to talk to you but I haven't had much time –'

'But have you had the time to tell Clem the truth? I don't want her heart broken once again.'

'What? What truth? It's only early days, but I don't intend to break her heart, I think she's fantastic.'

'You do realise she's female?'

'What's going on? Do I need to ask your permission to go out with your friend? We met at the baby shower and I got her number from you and things went from there,' says Nathan, looking puzzled. 'Can we talk later? I have to log on in about thirty seconds.'

Nathan is obviously not understanding what I'm talking about. Honestly, men! I see I'm going to have to spell it out for him.

'Have you told her you're gay?'

'What? Lizzie, I don't know what you're talking about. I'm not gay. Never have been. I like women. And I'm really attracted to Clem.'

'But I've never known you to have a girlfriend.'

'I haven't had many lately, and if I had, I wouldn't tell you, of all people. I keep my private life very private.'

'But Missy assured me you're gay.'

'She's wrong.'

'But you're so good with clothes.'

'I have three older sisters. They used to dress me up.'

'And relationship advice.'

'Again, three sisters.'

'And you love *Notting Hill*.'

'It's one of the best romantic comedies made, in my opinion. I'm a filmmaker, remember.'

He has an excuse for everything, but there's one thing he cannot deny.

'But that incentive dinner when I kissed you? You didn't kiss me back.'

'And that makes me gay?'

'No, but it's unusual.' I suddenly feel a bit silly.

'I know it's hard to believe, but I didn't want to sleep with you.'

'Oh,' I say, the wind completely knocked out of my sails. I'm not at all sure how to process this information. 'Didn't you find me even a little bit attractive?'

'To be honest, not really.'

'Wow.'

'You're great, but not really my type, and I didn't want to make things awkward at work by having some drunken one-night stand.'

I'm totally mortified. Not that I want to be with Nathan, especially as he and Clem are together, but I feel a little offended. Then again, it was probably a wise decision on Nathan's part. A one-night stand with me can lead to hospitalisation.

'Lizzie?' Nathan breaks my highly embarrassing train of thought.

'Right, sorry, I just heard that you were gay and I was worried about . . .'

'About your friend. That's okay. It's really sweet of you, but I can safely say that I only have sex with women and at the moment I'm only having sex with Clem. Safe sex,' he adds.

'I don't need any more detail, thanks very much,' I say, nipping in the bud what could potentially become an even more awkward and embarrassing conversation. 'You know she wants kids one day? A number of them, I think.'

Nathan quickly assures me that he too wants kids one day, but again it's only been a few weeks so they would maybe see how it goes. Then he bolts into the foyer and disappears up the lift.

How humiliating. Not only did someone just explain why they couldn't possibly sleep with me, but once again, through a stupid misunderstanding on my part, I've fallen flat on my face.

I heartily wish I could erase the last twenty-four hours, but as that's impossible, I must live with what I've done. Particularly as my conversation with Nathan tosses up thoughts of other guys I've gone out with. Nathan turned me down because he wasn't attracted to me and was decent enough not to take advantage of some overly enthusiastic woman throwing herself at him. And I was pretty pushy that night. Others I've targeted with my torpedo-like energy didn't show the same respect. Couldn't be bothered. Wanted the sex. What about Jake? Was he attracted to me? Did he actually like me? He said he did, but obviously not enough.

One thing is for sure. Being alone might once have been my worst-case scenario, but now, it's the best option ever. It's giving me the chance to really think about what I want, and what I deserve. I've done nothing but settle for all the wrong guys and it hasn't done me any good. If all I meet is Mr Completely Wrong, or even Mr Almost-But-Not-Quite-Right, then being alone is infinitely more attractive.

From now on when it comes to guys, I want absolutely everything. Or absolutely nothing.

Either is fine by me.

26

'I can't believe you stalked Mitch and abused him in front of his sister!'

Clem almost chokes on her champagne as I recall the finer details of my movie night. We're having a drink, mostly so Clem can fill me in on Nathan. Except somehow, we're talking about my misunderstanding with Mitch. Something which appears to be hilarious, to the point of near-vomiting.

'I didn't stalk him. I followed him for a very short distance. We happened to be seeing the same film. Big difference. Besides, I thought he was cheating on you and I didn't want to see you get hurt again.'

'That was lovely of you, Lizzie. But the poor guy! He'd done nothing wrong.'

'Can we change the subject?' My cheeks are heating up like a desert sun. 'Tell me about Nathan. Details, please.'

'He called not long after Missy's baby shower and asked me out. I didn't get a chance to tell you. One thing led to another and it's going really well,' Clem says with a coy smile, and it's her turn to blush. 'I told you he wasn't gay. I'm never wrong in that department.'

'That was Missy's fault,' I say, eyeing her closely. I don't think I've ever seen Clem look so happy and relaxed. Not for a decade at least. She looks fantastic. Whatever's been going on with Nathan is certainly doing her good!

'You seem different,' I say. 'Not your usual stressed-out self. Is Nathan The One, do you think?'

'I don't know about that. But I'm having a good time. Nathan's great. Fun, generous, kind and so sexy.' She pauses. 'He's made me realise that all I ever do is work. Or did. Being a lawyer doesn't allow for much personal life. I've been so focused on becoming a partner, there's been no space for anything else. Mal always said I worked too hard. I thought he just didn't understand because he hardly worked at all. Unless you counted surfing. But he probably got sick of competing with law for my attention.'

'Mal wasn't right for you,' I say quickly. 'He didn't deserve you. Besides, you're good at what you do. Why shouldn't you work hard and be successful?'

'No reason, except I started to forget who I was and what I liked to do. I feel like all I've done for years is work fourteen-hour days. I've had my head in some file or other since my twenties. I didn't know how to do anything else. I used to have interests. Hobbies. I used to have fun! I used to *be* fun!'

'You're still fun! You're just exhausted from over-achieving.'

'I think that's why I like being with Nathan. Who knows where it will go? I don't care. I've let go of all my expectations of being partner in a top-tier law firm, as well as a loving earth mother of three. I can't let those things define my happiness. What if none of that happens?'

Clem stops to take a breath and looks at me. Her eyes are shining, but I feel like crying. Here's my friend telling me how unhappy she's been and I never really noticed. I thought she loved work above all else. I expected a husband and children would eventually come along and slot right into her busy schedule. But life is messy and doesn't always go to plan. That's one thing I know for sure. Nothing happens the way you think it should happen. As soon as you accept that you have no control, then everything happens and more. Look at my bags. Once I stopped trying to hunt down the perfect man and make him fall in love with me, other parts of my life tumbled into place – just not in the way I ever imagined. I may not be living in Paris, designing the ultimate little black dress, but I'm creating amazing bags, and who knows where that will lead? But if I hadn't shifted my goalposts and gone with what really inspired me, none of it would have happened.

'Have you spoken to Mitch? Explained why you got it so wrong?'

I cringe inwardly. 'I don't think I can ever speak to him again.'

'You should. He's a really nice guy. Just not for me. But maybe for you?' Clem looks at me slyly.

I shake my head.

'Lizzie, you never consider the nice guys. You know that, don't you?'

'Rubbish! It's not that he's nice. He's just completely wrong for me.'

'When have you ever gone out with a decent guy?'

'What about Jean Paul?' I say indignantly, trying to think of other nice guys I've dated, but I can't. Not a single one.

'Jean Paul was a wanker and he cheated on you, remember?' says Clem firmly. 'As hard as that was, you should be glad you discovered the truth before it was too late.'

Clem was never a fan of Jean Paul. And fair enough. He turned out to be a lying bastard, but it was an exciting time and I was definitely in love. Still, deep down, I know he wasn't good enough.

'When we met up, Mitch asked lots of questions about you,' Clem continues, drawing my attention away from past embarrassments and back to more present ones. 'I kept changing the subject and somehow it always came back to you. I think it's *you* he's interested in.'

'Perhaps,' I say, my mind flashing back to how much he adored me in my hospital dream. But that was just a dream, wasn't it? My dreams have never been prophetic. 'He certainly won't be interested now that I've publicly accused him of cheating on a girlfriend he never had. Surely that's a deal-breaker. Besides, I've sworn off men forever.'

'Forever, Lizzie?' Clem knows me too well.

'Okay, maybe not forever. But for now. For quite a long time,' I say firmly. 'You've always said that I throw myself at guys, usually causing some sort of pain or property damage, and you're right. For now, no more dates, no more chasing guys. It only ever ends in disaster.'

'Only because you go for the most inappropriate guys you can find.'

'It's time to take an official break. Especially after recent events. It's time to focus on my one chance for a successful career and perhaps a bit of personal happiness. So no men. None. At. All!'

I pause, taken aback by my strong words. Now that I've vocalised it, it feels definite. No relationships. No distractions. Clem looks so shocked, you'd think I'd just announced I was taking up professional rhythmic gymnastics.

'Sure, Lizzie, good luck with that.'

I know Clem doesn't believe a word I say, and why would she? I've never shown restraint before. But I've never wanted to as much as I do now. I change the subject, knowing she'll never take my decision seriously.

'Tell me more about Nathan. I want to hear every single sexy detail.'

As Clem starts relaying all the cute and romantic things that Nathan does, my mind drifts back to Mitch. Was he asking about me because he really is interested? Maybe. But there's little chance of his interest now. I've completely outdone myself in the embarrassing department. In fact, if 'turning a guy off me' was a legitimate job, I'd be employee of the month. I make a quick mental list of the many reasons why Dr Mitch could never consider me as a potential girlfriend. Just for interest's sake.

- The only reason I learnt of my pregnancy was because I had an embarrassing accident while trying to break into the house of the father of my unborn child. And Dr Mitch was the one to point out I was pregnant.
- My so-called boyfriend was nowhere to be found when I miscarried our child. And when I got to hospital, again, it was Dr Mitch who had to deal with my disastrous situation.

- A newspaper told the world that I'm a suspected drug dealer.
- I forced Dr Mitch to ask my friend out on a date, and ultimately she wasn't interested.
- I publicly accused him of cheating on my friend (which he wasn't) while he was having a quiet catch-up with his sister.

I'm sure there's more, but that's enough for now. Enough to know that I'm the last person Dr Mitch would be asking out. *I* wouldn't even ask me out, and that's saying something. But I just can't bear the fact that someone out there has the wrong idea about me. Much like I felt after that newspaper article. I want to ring Dr Mitch and say, 'I'M NOT THAT PERSON!' Maybe not yell it at him, in capital letters. That probably wouldn't help. Besides, there's nothing between us, so what do I care if he thinks I'm the sort of person who rolls from one disaster to the next anyway?

The fact I'm even asking that question tells me there's more to my feelings than simply trying to clear my reputation. I've never really cared what anyone thought of my life choices, even Clem. Now, for some reason, it desperately matters what Dr Mitch thinks of me. But is it worth calling him and possibly embarrassing myself yet again? A sneaky little feeling deep down is telling me, actually scolding me, that he is most definitely worth it. But I just can't do it after everything that has happened. So, if he is everything I suspect, then I'll have to face up to the uncomfortable fact that I blew it. And now it's too late.

27

With Clem now happily coupled and me with no desire to be, I close life's dating doors and put my creative energies to good use. The next week, I discover a wholesale fabric outlet on the North Shore, a seamstress's wet dream filled with nothing but promise and excitement. I spend one whole day sourcing gorgeous fabrics while making a mental note to apply for an increase on the limit on my newly discovered credit card. I'm determined to complete every bag in my order book. Whatever it takes.

The next day, snuggled up to my Baby Elna, I lose myself in Operation Cool Nappy Bag (or rather Operation Cool Everything Bag), which is well and truly living up to its name. My bags look fantastic, with contrasting colours and patterns that somehow come together as if they were made for each other. What might be a disorganised mess in the wrong hands looks fluid, stunning and brave in mine. It proves to me that it pays to be confident with my ideas. Actually, with my life in general. This is a good start, and one that gives me nothing but pleasure.

Apart from trips to the ironing board and the lounge-room floor, and occasionally the bathroom, I don't leave my machine all day. I'm so hungry I can't think straight. All the food Mum bought me is gone, and I have no money for takeaways. I hunt through my ill-equipped pantry and come up with pasta mixed with olive oil and dried Herbs of Provence. It's surprisingly delicious but, as I haven't eaten for some time, I'm probably not the best judge.

I work through to the early hours of the morning, eating all the snacks I can squeeze out of my practically bare cupboards – 'snacks' being a loose term for sultanas, stale taco shells and an out-of-date tin of peaches – and fall into bed around five-thirty am. I only sleep for a couple of hours and wake up feeling like I'm hungover. At least, for once, I've over-indulged in a good way. I shower, get dressed and make a strong coffee. Only instant as I have no proper coffee left, but it does the trick.

I open my diary to work out a realistic schedule for making the rest of the bags in my order book when four little letters jump out at me, giving me a lightning-bolt start.

RENT.

I can't believe I forgot to pay my rent yesterday and I currently only have $85.54 in my account. I've made four bags, but goodness knows when I'll get the money for them.

I look in bewilderment at the ever-growing list of bag orders. How am I going to get them done? I need more fabric and a bigger space in which to work. My flat is starting to feel cramped, with piles of fabrics and loose cotton threads everywhere. I need to be able to lay the fabrics out so I can cut out more than one at a time, but I can't even afford my one-bedroom flat right now, let alone a work studio.

I call my landlord and tell him I've been sick, which is why I forgot to put the rent into the account. Even though I put on my best croaky voice, I have to spend forty minutes convincing him I'm not dealing drugs. Even then he sounds sceptical. I assure him the money will be in the account by tomorrow. Not really sure how I'm planning to do that, I just keep putting it out to the universe.

By three in the afternoon, I've made two more bags but my rent is still overdue. I have no options left so with a heavy heart, I pop on my jacket and walk out the door.

'Darling, what a surprise!' My mother sounds a little tiddly when she opens her front door. 'Dad and I are just having an afternoon *apéritif*, would you like one?'

This is a common occurrence for my parents ever since they took a trip to the south of France and learnt the word *apéritif*. Normally, it would be too early for me, but if there was ever a day when I needed an afternoon *apéritif*, then today is that day.

'Sounds lovely, thanks.'

I follow Mum out to the deck where Dad is trimming the ornamental grapevine.

'Liz! How are you, sweetheart?'

I haven't seen Dad for weeks, what with recent events and goings-on, and I almost tear up as he puts down his secateurs and gives me one of his big bear hugs.

'I'm okay.'

'Mum told me about the baby,' he says, still holding me. 'I'm so sorry, love.'

'Oh, thanks.' Tears fill my eyes and I blink them away. Dad and I never talk about anything too emotional so his simple affection and concern is touching. A little awkward, but I love him for letting me know he cares.

'How are you going, Dad?' I ask, pulling away.

'Me? Marvellous. Never better!'

One thing about my parents is that they're always upbeat. Even in the middle of a disaster. Sometimes it's an annoying habit, but today it's comforting. My mother comes back out with the most enormous glass of wine. Hardly what the French would call a *petit apéritif*, but I'm not complaining.

'Would you like to stay for dinner, sweetheart?' she asks.

'Sure.'

'Great, I'll pop another potato into the oven.' She turns to my dad. 'Top your wine up, darling?'

'Thank you, my love.'

My parents give each other a look undetectable to the untrained eye, but one I know well. Like they're sharing a private joke. I've never really appreciated their strong, stable relationship, and how much they love each other. Through the ups and downs of life, they're like an unbeatable team that wins the championship year after year. True love is rare. If you find it, you're lucky. If you don't, then why bother with anything less?

Their inspiring relationship aside, I know I have to talk to my parents about my finances, but I just can't seem to broach the subject. I'm always going nowhere and Mum and Dad are constantly picking up the pieces. When Clem isn't available, that is. And I'm not in the mood for hearing how everything will work out, that I will one day find love, career and financial success.

I know they just want to make me feel better, but today it will only make me feel worse because things never seem to get better. And to prove it, here I am, once again, asking for my parents' help.

'How's Jake?' Mum asks as she comes back from the kitchen, her tone in no way attempting to disguise her true feelings.

'We're not together, Mum. It's all over.'

'Sorry to hear that, darling. I know you were very keen on him, but, I have to say, I'm relieved. He didn't seem to be treating you very well.'

'He just wasn't right.'

'Onward and upward!' says Mum. 'There'll be someone just around the corner, probably someone you've already met.'

'I don't know, I don't think I'm cut out for a relationship. I'm better on my own for now. So I can focus on my bags.'

'What's happening with those bags, love?' asks Dad. 'I saw that actress on the telly with one. Your mother dragged me out of the shower to see. I thought someone had died.'

'To be honest, I'm drowning in orders and I don't know where to start or how to finance it. I'm using credit cards to buy fabric, but since I've left my job at the call centre, I've got no cash to live on.'

'Left your job? Was that a good idea?' asks my mother, desperately trying not to interfere even though that is exactly what she's doing.

'Mum, I couldn't stay there. I didn't want to be around Jake. Everyone knew what was going on and now he's seeing someone else at work. It was too humiliating.'

I'm close to tears. My mother says nothing. She just gives me a hug and looks at my father. This is a different look, one that consists of an entire telepathic conversation. Dad gives her a little nod and turns back to me.

'How much do you need?'

'Sorry, Dad, I just have to pay my rent.'

'No, how much do you need to set yourself up? Buy the fabric, maybe rent a studio. It can't be easy working in that little flat.'

'No. But I can't spend that sort of money now. I've only sold three bags. What if it all stops tomorrow? Remember the last time?'

Dad puts down his wineglass and goes inside. Five minutes later he's back.

'Here's something to help for now,' he says, pressing a folded cheque into my hand.

I look at it and gasp. More than enough to cover my rent for at least a few months.

'Sort yourself out. Find a way to make these bags pay.'

Dad never says much but when he speaks, I listen.

'I'll pay you back, Dad. I promise.'

'I know you will, Lilly-loo.'

Now the tears really start to well. It's so reassuring to be home. At this moment, I never want to leave. Perhaps I should move back in where I know I will be loved and cared for . . .

'Maybe you should try online dating?' says Mum, snapping me back to reality. 'Jenny from book club said that's how her daughter found her husband and they're deliriously happy. About to have baby number three.'

I will never move back home.

I stay for dinner, which is delicious, as always. Then I stay the night and sleep in my old room. Which looks nothing like my old room because the minute I moved out, my parents transformed it into a 'media room'. I think someone told them it's an 'essential feature for resale value'. They're not planning on selling, but they like to know that if they do, they'll get a good deal.

As I lie on the fold-out sofa with my eyes tightly closed, I can still see the dark purple feature wall I insisted on having when I was fourteen, my old wooden desk covered in stickers, and the posters of Johnny Depp and of course Kevin Bacon. I saw that '80s film *Footloose* umpteen times because, in my young eyes, he was the perfect boyfriend. No wonder I've never found Mr Right. Who could possibly live up to the standards of Kevin Bacon, who managed to bring dance and music back to a small country town full of weirdly conservative locals? Certainly not that guy I took to my Year 10 formal.

My eyes wander to the back of the door and see my favourite poster of all. This one is really here, having thankfully survived the 'media room' transition. It's a black and white photo of a young Coco Chanel. Once I started sewing, I replaced the teenage heartthrobs with pictures and postcards of Coco Chanel's many famous creations. Her exquisite suits, gowns, little black dresses. I'd never seen anything so stylish. And Yves Saint Laurent. I'll never forget the first time I saw a picture of his famous cocktail dress, from a collection based on the artwork of Piet Mondrian. I thought I'd gone to fashion heaven. All I wanted to do was make such a mark in the fashion world. But it never happened.

Still, maybe I have another chance. I may not be the next Coco Chanel, but perhaps this is an opportunity to finally create something truly original that people want to use. Something that inspires joy and makes people feel good about themselves. And if I could earn a bit of money in the process, even better.

I sleep like a teenager and wake up feeling like I've been at an exclusive spa retreat. I can pay my rent and the sense of relief is enormous. Over breakfast, Dad and I chat about the new shrubs they've planted in the front garden and the paving they want to add. He doesn't mention the money. Neither do I. There's nothing more to say.

Eventually, it's time to get back to my real life. It so happens that Mum is hosting her book club today so I need to get out of there as soon as humanly possible. Dad wants to come with me, away from the 'screamers' as he calls Mum's gaggle of girls. He insists that my tap washers need checking, but I assure him they're all in order.

I go home to find a pile of flyers for Cherie's cabaret in my letterbox. But before I even think about handing them out, I head straight to the bank, deposit Dad's cheque and pay my rent. I immediately call my landlord to say the money is in the account. He's a bit cranky, but when he realises I've paid for three months in advance, he calms down.

Now I know I have a roof over my head, it's time to get on with Operation Cool Everything Bag. I have to pay Mum and Dad back as soon as possible, unlike last time, which took years of selling wine to achieve. This venture is completely different. This one will work, I just know it. Sure, I've got everything to lose, but I've had enough failure and financial debt to last me a lifetime – and I'm over it!

From now on, success is the only option.

28

The weeks slip by and I throw myself into establishing my flourishing bag business. Not only the bags, but also the promotional side of things. I set up an Instagram account and upload photos of every bag I make, each one slightly different, with its own detail and fabric combination. Every day, I turn on my computer to see more followers and heaps of 'likes'. It's so exciting, especially when I get likes from people I don't even know. Three in London, one in Amsterdam and one in Berlin. When I get my first like from some woman in Paris, I know I'm truly on the road to fashion success. However, when Willow becomes a follower, it all goes through the roof. She posts heaps of pictures of herself carrying one of the three bags she bought, and she has 492,000 followers! Can't ask for better publicity than that. Particularly when the wardrobe department for her next film contacts me to see if they can use my bag in one of Willow's scenes!

I design a business card and have it printed. Bright red, in the shape of a handbag. It looks fantastic with *The Bag Lady – Designs by Lizzie* in hot-pink lettering on one side and all my details on the other.

I complete the bags I have on order, and deliver them to eagerly waiting customers. I'm blown away by their reactions, and best of all, the money starts trickling in.

'This is awesome, Lizzie!'

Frankie and I are having a coffee before her WineCall shift so I can hand over the bag she ordered. She's absolutely thrilled, which makes my day. If stylish, quirky Frankie is happy with the bag, it's more proof I'm doing something right.

She holds it up to examine the detail. 'I want to order a few as presents, but then I don't want everyone to have the same bag as me.'

'They're all a bit different,' I assure her. 'I don't want to mass-produce. I want everyone to feel special.'

'I'm so impressed. You've done a great job. It's no wonder everyone wants one. Let me pay you and then I'd better dash in to work.'

Frankie hands me the money and as I get out my wallet, I see Cherie's flyers, squashed in my bag. Frankie might be interested.

'There's a great cabaret in a couple of weeks,' I say, handing her a flyer. 'A singer I know called Cherie L'Amour. She was a bit of a star once and is doing a comeback show. I'm trying to get a few people together for opening night. It's pretty low-key, but should be fun. Maybe you and Mike might like to come?'

'Her name sounds familiar,' says Frankie as she skims the flyer. 'Looks good. Mike would love it, right up his alley.'

We say goodbye and I watch Frankie rush off to work, thankful I'm not heading in there to push wine on people for the next five hours. Then I hurry over to Missy's house to deliver her bag. What with all the sleeps and feeds, I've only been permitted a tiny sliver of time to visit. It all sounded so complicated, I'm surprised she could actually fit me into her day at all.

'Lizzie, I LOVE it. It's fabulous!' gushes Missy. 'You're so talented.'

Missy is looking far from *her* usual fabulous self, dressed in trackie pants and a top with a dirty mark on it. Her hair looks like a bird's nest and there are dark circles under her eyes. But she seems totally upbeat despite it all, and delighted with my bag.

'How much do I owe you?'

'Absolutely nothing!' I say firmly. 'I never got you a proper gift when you had Gracie, so I want you to have it. I'm just glad you like it. Besides, you can show all your friends. I'm taking orders.'

I give Missy a few of my dazzling new cards, and before I realise what's happening, she hands me Gracie and says, 'Here, have a cuddle. My arms are exhausted and I'm desperate to go to the toilet. Do you mind?'

Missy races down the hall as I shift the human bundle inadequately in my arms, trying to get into a comfortable position. Her little face with its rosebud mouth looks up at me and, surprisingly, my heart skips a beat. She really is a natural wonder. The time wasn't right for me, but could I possibly create something so perfect one day? Could I be a mum to such a divine creature?

Suddenly, a spray of yellowy goo flies out of the rosebud mouth, straight onto my shirt. Disgusting. Gracie seems quite content, but I'm too scared to move in case there's something wrong. Was that normal?

'Sorry about that.' Missy comes in to see me floundering with the baby and her mess. 'She's a bit of a chucker. Here, give her to me and use this to clean it up.'

Missy takes Gracie with a mother's total confidence and throws me a damp tea towel. Okay, so maybe I'm not quite ready for the whole baby thing, but fingers crossed, next time I will be.

'I'd better put her down for a sleep now.'

I take that as my cue. 'Right. Leave you to it.'

'Sorry, I know that was quick, but she had her first sleep much earlier than usual and now everything's thrown out. The minute you think you've found a routine, it all changes. So unpredictable, but you just have to go with it.'

Sounds a bit like life in general. I say goodbye and sneak out so Grace can have her sleep. Missy too, hopefully. She looks like she needs an afternoon snooze as much as her daughter. I reach the front door, but turn back.

'Oh, there's a fantastic cabaret coming up. A friend of mine is singing. Interested? Clem and Nathan are coming. Maybe Frankie.'

'Maybe,' she says in a hushed voice, gently rocking her daughter. 'I haven't been out since I had Gracie. It's a bit difficult, but I'll try.'

'You could always bring the baby to the bar?' I suggest, only to be met with a very stony silence. Okay, maybe not my best parenting moment, but I'm not a parent. I'm allowed to say things like that.

'See how you go, it's not for two weeks,' I say quickly, leaving a flyer on the marble-topped hall table as I let myself out.

I was never very fond of Missy at work but now, after everything, I can imagine us even being friends. Maybe motherhood has softened her. Or rather, missing out on motherhood has made me more generous. I was always so envious of her perfect life. She seemed to have it all. Which she does, and that's great. But I'll have it all soon too. Just a different 'all' to Missy's 'all', and that suits me just fine.

I head home and plan the next step in my bag-making journey. A market stall is not a bad idea: a great way to get my designs out there and make a bit of money. I'll need to make a lot of bags for it, though, so perhaps in a couple of months' time.

I need to check out which market would be best. Maybe Bondi, seeing as that's where my bag was discovered. Probably the right audience. I also need to put more effort into promoting my bags online. Not to mention coming up with some new looks and purchasing different fabrics. I'm deep in thought when my mobile ringing breaks my concentration. I don't recognise the number, but I answer it anyway. Probably another bag order.

'Am I speaking with Lizzie March?' booms a voice.

'Um, yes, you are.'

'My name is Dee Richards. I work for David Jones. How are you today?'

'Fine, thanks. How are you?' Why is this very direct and officious woman calling me? Am I in trouble? Did I leave something in David Jones? Have I got something on layby that I've forgotten about?

'I'm fantastic, thanks for asking. Now. Your bags. Love them. LOVE THEM. WANT them. NOW!'

'Sorry?'

Dee Richards talks in short sentences that don't really make sense. She powers on.

'Saw Willow S on TV. With your bag. Perfect combination. Great look. Women everywhere want it. We want it too. WANT IT NOW!'

'Oh, okay. So you'd like a bag? Sure, I'll just get your details, I've had quite a few orders but –'

'More than one, darling. Perhaps fifty to start, just in time for winter? Take it from there. Let's schedule a meeting to discuss the prospect further. Are you having them manufactured yet?'

'Ah, no. Not yet, I'm just making them in my flat on my nana's –'

Dee isn't interested in Nana's Baby Elna.

'Discuss all that tomorrow. Ten o'clock? Does that work for you? Level 6 of our city store. Do you drink coffee?'

'Um, yes.'

'Fabulous.'

She hangs up and I call Clem immediately, which is the second time (or the third?) that I've broken my promise not to interrupt her at work. Unbelievably, Zoe puts me straight through. Apparently she's a huge fan of Willow S and also wants a bag. What a girl has to do to make a legal secretary happy these days!

'Lizzie, I have to save the world, remember, and I can't do it if you keep calling me.'

'I know, Clem, but this is big news: David Jones wants to buy my bags!'

Clem shrieks. I pull the phone slightly away and can still hear her, as if she were sitting on my lap. Between her and Dee I'll have no eardrum to speak of. I tentatively bring the phone back again.

'Lizzie! I can't believe it. What happened?'

'This woman called me. A buyer from DJs. Out of the blue. Wants fifty.' I seem to have picked up Dee's short-sentence speak. It certainly helps to get information out more efficiently.

'Great! Now don't sign anything without letting me read it first. You don't want to lose ownership or creative control.'

Clem has started speaking that lawyer language that makes me fuzzy-headed, so I steer her back on track.

'Yes, of course, Ms Lawyer. Anyway, I'm meeting her tomorrow.'

'Exciting . . . but, Lizzie . . . maybe try to be . . .' Clem pauses.

'What?

'I don't know. This is possibly a great opportunity. Just try to be . . . normal, okay?'

I'm about to tell Clem that her comment is a little unkind when I stop myself. She's right. I need to be normal. The problem is, I always think I *am* being completely normal and that it's the other people in the world who are nuts. However, I accept that recent events would probably suggest otherwise.

'Don't worry. I'll be so normal, even you wouldn't recognise me.'

Clem sighs her heavy sigh, custom-designed for me.

'Good luck. Call me after.'

I hang up, feeling slightly like I'm having an out-of-body experience. It's not every day that a major department store is desperate for my designs. It's the sort of thing we used to talk about at design school. Something you would never think could happen. And certainly not to me. Only to people like Jainee Johns, whose unimpressive dress I saw at Westfield. But if JJ can do it, then why can't I?

If only those uppity teachers from design school could see me now. They might not be quite so dismissive of my talents.

*

A week later, it's definite and my head is spinning. David Jones really wants my bags, which means a market stall is out of the question now. After a fast-paced, walking-talking-coffee-drinking meeting with Dee Richards, I realise exactly how much work I'll have to do to get this order together. At this rate I'm going to have to look into manufacturing my bags sooner than I thought.

Sitting at the kitchen table with my morning coffee, trying to work how I'm going to go about it, I yawn and stretch. This is going to be an enormous task, but I have to find a way. I glance in my diary and notice that Cherie's cabaret is coming up. I should hand out more flyers, but I've run out, so I give Cherie a quick call.

'Sure, darl, I've got plenty here, but I'm stuck in the rehearsal. Why don't you come past and pick them up? I can try out a few songs on you.'

'Sure,' I say, thrilled. 'I don't want to intrude, but I'd love to hear some of your material.'

Cherie assures me it's fine and gives me the address of the studio in a converted warehouse in Darlinghurst. Within half an hour, I'm gently tapping on the door.

'Come in if you're pretty!' chuckles Cherie.

I poke my nose around, not really sure if that means I should go in or not. Then I step into the space and there's Cherie . . . with . . . is that . . . Dr Mitch? He looks up, casually strumming a guitar like he's done it all his life.

'Hi, Lizzie, how's it going?' he says, cool as a cucumber.

I almost don't recognise him. In fact, I think my jaw drops like a cartoon character's. When did Mitch go and get all handsome? Maybe it's the guitar or those lanky jean-clad legs or that shock of brown hair, sticking up on end in its toothbrush way. Maybe it's the whole package, but whatever it is, I can't take my eyes off him.

'Just in time,' says Cherie. 'You know Mitch, of course.'

I mutter something that sounds like 'Hello-I'm-good-how-are-you' but I'm totally thrown. I haven't spoken to Mitch since I publicly accused him of cheating on Clem.

Mitch smiles a polite smile, but says nothing. In fact, he looks nervous. But maybe he's worried I'm going to start yelling at him again.

Cherie gestures towards a nearby chair. 'We're just about to go through my latest number. Wanna hear?'

'Sure,' I say, taking a seat. Okay, so he looks the part, but can he play?

Thirty seconds later, I realise he can. And Cherie can sing. She's extraordinary and together they sound beautiful.

'That was fantastic,' I say when they've finished the song. 'Really great.'

'Not just a pretty face,' says Cherie.

'And I'm not just a doctor,' adds Mitch.

'I was talking about you, sweetheart,' says Cherie with a laugh.

They bounce off each other like a seasoned double act.

'You're both fabulous. I can't wait for the cabaret.' I look at Mitch. 'Are you playing for every show?'

'Hopefully for opening night, but not sure about the rest of the season. It'll depend on my shifts at work. But there's a host of fabulous musicians eager to accompany Cherie. I won't be missed.'

'Not true, Mitch! You're my favourite.'

Mitch gives me a comical look. 'She says that to all of us.'

Cherie heads to the door. 'Can you guys excuse me? Just going to pop out for a ciggie. Bad habit, I know, but there's something about performing. Goes with the territory. Don't do anything I wouldn't do. Which isn't much!'

Mitch and I are left in an uncomfortable silence. Okay, an excellent opportunity to apologise for my movie-night behaviour. I take a deep breath to speak, but Mitch cuts me off.

'So, how have you been? You look great.'

'Oh, thanks!' I say, slightly thrown by his interest, his lovely manner and the unexpected compliment.

'Still selling drugs?'

Okay, that wasn't so lovely.

'I don't sell drugs!'

'I know you don't,' he says with a twinkly smile. 'Cherie assured me it was all made up.'

Great. He needed some sort of assurance that I wasn't a criminal who ruined people's lives.

'That newspaper article was terrible. Are you okay?'

'Yes, I'm fine,' I say, not sure if he's actually concerned or still secretly worried that I'm caught up with the wrong crowd.

'Particularly that picture of you at some speed-dating night. How did they manufacture that?'

I feel my face blush a deep red. 'That was genuine. Just unlucky. And out of context.'

To be honest, I don't feel like sifting through my many inelegant past events. Especially with Dr Mitch. I wanted to apologise for the movie fiasco but now I can't bring myself to do it. It's too humiliating and by apologising, it becomes even more real. I just want to forget it ever happened and get out of here as soon as possible. I close my eyes, wishing to be somewhere else, but when I open them, I'm still in front of Dr Mitch, and there's an expectant look on his face.

'I'd better go,' I say tightly. 'Leave you to it.'

'Really? We might take a break soon, get something to eat,' he says tentatively. 'You could come. If you want?'

'No, thanks. Far too busy. David Jones is buying my bags.' I sound curt, but I can't help it. 'You know, the ones that were supposed to be filled with drugs.'

'Wow! That's great.' He seems genuinely impressed. 'Congratulations.'

I move towards the door. 'I'll say goodbye to Cherie on the way out. Maybe see you at the cabaret.'

'Lizzie,' Mitch stops me. 'Do you want to have a coffee or a drink sometime before that?'

A coffee? A drink? Is he asking me out? Surely not. Why would he want to see me again? The whole idea sends me into a panic.

'I don't have time, to be honest. I'm flat out with my new business. This week is booked up.'

Mitch's face falls ever so slightly. Or did I imagine it? I look down and make a hasty exit. I can't believe I just said no to a date! Impressive! There was a time when Clem would have been so proud of me. Lately, I'm not so sure. She seems to have thrown her rulebook out the window. Or simply renamed it *Having as Much Amazing Sex with Nathan as Humanly Possible*. But I've made my decision and I'm sticking to it. Absolutely no dating. Even if it possibly involves some incredibly sexy doctor/musician with mesmerising blue eyes and an approachable manner. It just doesn't fit into the new Lizzie March agenda.

God knows if it ever will.

29

The next week speeds by in a flurry of multi-coloured fabric scraps, zips, buttons and cotton reels. I only leave my sewing machine to hunt down more fabric and have the occasional meal, coffee or snatch of sleep. I haven't worked so hard in years. In fact, I've never worked so hard. Probably because I've never had such purpose. I wish I'd thought of making bags years ago. But it took getting pregnant to make me think outside my little box. Looking back, I can see that although the idea of having a baby sent me spinning way beyond my comfort zone, it was the jolt I needed to see everything in my life from a new perspective.

Sadly there will be no baby this time, but the pregnancy and miscarriage changed everything. It's as though I needed to go through that heartbreaking experience and feel something raw to shake me out of my rut and show me what really matters. Sure, I'd been through upsetting break-ups before, but those were nothing compared to how losing my baby made me feel. I know a part of that devastation will always be with me. But now I can see that, without that whole experience, I'd never have unlocked the creative potential of my teenage years and taken my bag-making plunge.

I'm so caught up in my work that the opening night of Cherie's cabaret arrives out of nowhere. After weeks of intense bag-making, it will be good to get out of the flat and be social. Clem and Nathan will be there. I haven't spoken to Clem this week, so it will be good to catch up. I smile to myself. Clem and Nathan. It's funny how normal those two names sound together in such a short space of time. Frankie said she and Mike would definitely come. Missy seemed to think it might just work, depending on the ten o'clock feed.

The night doesn't kick off until eight, but I want to get there early. I stop work in the afternoon to choose an outfit, settling on the black skinny jeans I bought for my date with Jake but haven't worn since, out of protest. So much has happened since then, they now feel like the perfect choice. I throw on a sexy black top to match and grab my favourite wrap. I stare at the mirror, pleased with the look. Simple and understated – so my latest bag creation can be the hit of the ensemble. Nothing like a bit of free publicity! I go to grab my black pumps when a shoebox that's poking out on the top shelf catches my eye. I open it tentatively.

The green satin stilettos! Those troublesome shoes that threw my life into utter chaos.

I stare at them longingly. Surely by now I'm strong enough to control their seductive powers? Anyone who says no to a drink with a handsome doctor is certainly able to wear green satin stilettos without getting pregnant! I put them on and feel instantly fabulous. Yes, now I'm definitely ready.

I walk into the bar and look around. With a scattering of small round tables, and plush red carpet and thick velvet curtains, the space has the moody, seductive feel of a 1940s jazz club. Perfect vibe for Cherie. In fact, it feels like a more spacious version of her taxi.

I bought a huge bunch of flowers on my way, as I remember Cherie once reminiscing about receiving flowers on opening nights. I wanted to do the same for her tonight, only now I'm not sure what to do with them. One of the bar staff asks if I want to send them backstage.

'That would be great,' I say, a little unsure, hoping the flowers will get to her safely. I would hate for Cherie to not see them. I want to wish her all the luck in the world for tonight.

I order a glass of wine, and just as I grab a table, I see Clem and Nathan arrive. I wave them over and then see Frankie walk in with a handsome older-looking man, who must be Mike. I've never met him before but I feel like I know a lot about him after my chats with Frankie. Missy runs in too, breathless and excited to be out. Apparently, Angus is in the car outside with the sleeping baby.

'It's so good to see you guys!' she says, a slightly manic look in her eye, like she's broken out of a maximum-security prison.

More people wander in and the bar starts to buzz with laughter and animated conversations. Such a mixed crowd, even a few celebrities and ex–rock stars. I feel so nervous I could vomit, and I'm not even singing. But Cherie probably isn't nervous at all. It's probably like riding a bike on a high trapeze. Once you're used to it, it's not so bad.

Three musicians take to the stage to warm up the crowd, not that it needs it. Then Cherie appears like a Hollywood diva in a full-length red sequined gown, feather boa and a fabulous bouffant hairdo, looking as comfortable as if she's catching up with friends over a cup of tea. She explains how she always wanted to be a star, which is why she now drives a cab. The audience laughs as she segues into her first number with ease. There's no doubt, Cherie L'Amour is back – and the crowd loves every moment.

Interval suddenly arrives and Cherie announces a short break, encouraging everyone to spend up big at the bar as the venue owner is not taking a cut of the door. Everyone laughs, only too happy to help out.

'Oh, Lizzie, isn't she fantastic!' says Clem, her eyes shining.

'She really is.' I knew Cherie would be good after what I'd heard at rehearsal, but I had no idea she'd be so sensational. And hilarious.

Clem, Nathan and I grab another drink and chat about the show so far. I catch up with Frankie and meet her husband, Mike. Then I see Missy madly pointing to her boobs and dashing out the door. Maybe Grace needs a feed. The lights eventually dim once more and Cherie returns to the stage to deliver the second half, which proves even more spectacular than the first. I'm enjoying myself so much, I lose track of time and before I know it, the show is drawing to a close. I haven't seen Mitch anywhere. He's obviously not playing tonight and I'm so relieved. I don't need him being all handsome and talented onstage, confusing me more than ever.

But then again, you'd think I'd know better by now than to speak so soon.

'For my final song, I'd like to invite a friend to join me up here,' says Cherie in her husky voice. 'Someone I've only known a short time. He's a doctor, but let me tell you, he knows his way around a guitar. If you got sick, he could fix you up, then serenade you at the same time. Come on out, Mitch. Everyone, this is Dr Mitch Peters. Big round of applause, please.'

I sigh. Mitch walks out onto the stage and, if I thought he looked hot at rehearsal, it's nothing compared to how he appears now, bathed in moody lighting, dressed in black jeans and a red t-shirt. He grins at the audience and my heart momentarily stops beating. Then it speeds up like my Baby Elna when I remember to oil it.

'This is a little song I wrote a few years ago and never performed,' says Cherie. 'Mitch encouraged me to bring it back to life.'

Dr Mitch starts to play and Cherie's deep, rich voice melts into the music. Ten seconds into the song and I'm seriously in love with both of them. Damn music and its manipulative powers! The song is beautiful, romantic, slightly folky, all about loss and sadness yet happiness in having once known true love. My skin is tingling with goosebumps. There are tears in Cherie's eyes and instinctively I know she wrote the song about her daughter.

Who knew Dr Mitch could look so comfortable on stage, as if he's been doing it for years? Maybe he has. It's not something you generally ask your doctor about in Emergency. Even the second or third time you happen to be there. I can't believe I'm now finding myself utterly attracted to him. God, I'm superficial. Like some sort of groupie back at high school, hoping the lead guitarist will notice me.

Clem elbows me in the stomach, which sort of hurts. 'How great is he?'

All I can do is nod because words are not coming to me right now. I've forgotten how cross I felt when I saw him the other day. I've forgotten everything except one simple fact: Dr Mitch is the most beautiful man I have ever laid my eyes on. And let's face it, I've laid my eyes on a few. And it's not just because he's playing the guitar like a professional, beautifully enhanced by effective lighting. Not even because he is incredibly good-looking. It's because every fleeting moment we've shared is going through my mind, like a movie playing in my head. And each one sends my heart into a spin. He made me smile, he made me laugh. Comforted me and made me feel good about myself. Am I completely mad? Why didn't I see that the nicest guy I've ever met was right under my very nose? I was so busy setting him up with Clem, and feeling so good about myself for doing it, that I missed the fact that *I* like him! Really like him. And now I've finally caught up, it's all far too late in the day.

Sitting at my table, I feel like I'm the only one in the room. I'm not sure if I'm even breathing. I hope I am, otherwise I'll be passing out in a moment. Lucky there's a doctor present.

The song ends and the crowd goes wild – as much as it can in its cool laidback inner-city way. Our table applauds madly. Cherie bows and then holds Mitch's hand and they bow together. I try to catch Mitch's eye, but he either can't see me past the stage lights, or chooses not to.

'Thanks, Mitch. Please give our doctor a round of applause before he goes off to save a few lives,' says Cherie.

The crowd laughs and claps enthusiastically as the very

handsome doctor, who has been my type all along and who, despite witnessing the many recent and disastrous events in my life, seemed to like me anyway, gets up, gives Cherie a kiss on the cheek and leaves the stage.

'What do you think of the doctor now?' Clem asks me with a smile.

I shrug with feigned indifference, but underneath, my heart feels like lead.

Cherie does one final encore number. I can hear it, but I don't really take it in. Dr Mitch may have left the stage but the image of him playing guitar is now well and truly imprinted in my brain. Cherie takes her last bow and the crowd is on its feet. She looks like a goddess! What is it about the stage that makes people look so utterly divine? Most disconcerting.

Fifteen minutes later, Cherie comes out to the bar to be met by excited friends and colleagues. She sees me and makes her way over.

'Cherie, you were terrific! What a fabulous show.'

'Thanks, my love, and thanks for those flowers. Very showbiz of you to send them backstage.'

My eyes scan the room.

'He got called in to work,' says Cherie.

So much for my feigned indifference. And he's probably not at work at all. Probably wanted to avoid me.

'Wasn't he great?' Cherie smiles.

'He was incredible. You both were. That song you sang with Mitch . . .' I lower my voice. 'Was that about your daughter?'

'Yep. How could you tell?'

'Just a feeling. It was beautiful.'

'Thanks, love. You know, getting back into singing and working towards this cabaret has brought up a lot of memories for me. Good ones, sad ones. I've been thinking about my little baby. She'd be a grown woman now.' Cherie pauses and takes a deep breath. 'I reckon it's time we met.'

'Really?' I say, surprised. I remember Cherie saying she'd never attempt to find her baby.

'Yep. I've decided to try. I've already started the process.'

'Oh, Cherie, that is such great news,' I say, giving her a hug. 'How amazing it would be to see your baby girl once again.'

'It'll take time. They didn't want us to track our kids down in those days, but apparently it's possible. Although she might not even want to meet me after all these years. Wouldn't blame her. Still, gotta give it a go.'

After going through the ordeal of a miscarriage, I can't imagine how Cherie must have felt back then. I was only pregnant for a couple of months, and that was bad enough. But going through a whole pregnancy at such a young age, giving birth and then thinking you'd lost your child forever? That must have been heart-breaking. I know now that if that were me, I'd grab the chance to find my child with both hands and feet and everything in between.

'I'm so happy for you. And I'll cross everything I have that it works out.'

'Thanks, love, we'll see how it goes.' Cherie pauses, a cheeky twinkle creeping into her eyes. 'So, Mitch? Bit of a catch, don't you think?'

I sigh. 'Yeah, but not for me, I'm afraid. I well and truly blew it there, after following him out of the movies and into a bar where I accused him of cheating on Clem, in front of his date.'

'Wasn't that his sister? I think he mentioned that.'

'Yes, his sister. So he said.'

'Yeah, that's Clare, lovely girl. Works for World Aid.'

Why is it that the first time it really is a guy's sister, I completely don't see it? Mitch has been nothing but a nice guy, and yet he was the one I chose not to believe? I guess I've fallen for that excuse too many times, and I picked the wrong moment to assert myself – and the wrong person to unload onto.

'I've humiliated myself in front of Dr Mitch too many times. I ended up in Emergency twice. After I brought Missy in, I saw him at the café and cried all over him. And don't forget that I was picked up for drug dealing, which was splashed across the media.'

'Only suspected drug dealing, love. Not charged.'

'You sound like Clem. Still, he must think I am some sort of crazed, stalkerish druggie loser who would be a terrible mother. Not great prospects in his eyes, I imagine.'

'That doesn't sound like the girl I picked up in my taxi that first time. The one who wasn't scared to go for what she wanted.'

'I'm not that person anymore. Thank goodness. It's better for me to be on my own. Better for everyone, really. I think every guy in the world will thank me for not being on the dating scene right now. Mitch included.'

At that point Cherie is called away and I leave her to enjoy her post-show moment in the sun, surrounded by adoring friends and punters. Within five minutes, she's entertaining a cluster of enraptured fans with a highly amusing story. Centre stage, where she belongs. I go back to my table, where Clem and Nathan are giggling about something or other, arms and legs entwined. Clem looks so happy. Missy is showing the many baby photos on her phone to anyone who crosses her path, while discussing split nipples and haemorrhoids. But she too looks happy. Despite the physical discomfort she must be experiencing.

Clem sees me and smiles. 'Wasn't Mitch a surprise? Talented *and* handsome.'

'Hey!' Nathan's ears prick up. 'Not that handsome!'

'Don't worry, baby!' Clem soothes her now boyfriend playfully. 'He's not nearly as hot as you, but maybe you could take up guitar . . . ?'

Nathan pretends to tackle her and Clem bursts into laughter. Honestly, could they be any cuter? It's starting to feel a little nauseating, particularly as I have never heard Clem call anyone 'baby' apart from an actual newborn. She recovers and turns her attention back to me.

'Do you like him, Lizzie?' Clem looks at me with those legal-eagle eyes that see all.

'No, of course not!' I say hotly. 'And to prove it, when I dropped by their rehearsal to pick up flyers the other day, he asked me out for a drink and I turned him down.'

'What?'

'I . . . turned him down.'

The minute I say those words, a rush of panic sends everything into a spin, like I'm Dorothy in a tornado, off to Oz. The bar, people and lights start to whirl past me, all distorted, like a nightmare merry-go-round that won't stop despite the screams of desperate children clinging to the animal rides. What's happening to me? Is this a panic attack? Or a heart attack? I can't breathe, so maybe it is. Maybe it's both! I try to find something to hold on to, to steady myself. I can see Clem looking at me strangely, but I can't speak. Then, just as suddenly, like a ball in a roulette wheel landing on the winning number, everything slides into place. It's like I've been driving through a storm, but have now come out the other side and can see with perfect clarity.

I. Turned. Him. Down!

I turned down lovely, good-looking, guitar-playing-doctor Mitch. He asked me out for a drink – and I said no. I look at Clem, who is waiting patiently for me to work through my mini crisis.

'Shouldn't have done that, should I?'

She gazes at me with one of her exasperated looks, and for once, it's not because of any inappropriate stalking.

'What should I do?'

'Go and tell him you made a mistake.'

'He's left for work.'

'So? Don't tell me I have to suggest that you chase a guy? Maybe follow him to his workplace and accidentally on purpose meet him outside? Or wait in the café until he has a break? Honestly, Lizzie, you of all people should know what to do here.'

I don't know what to say. Mostly because Clem is encouraging me. The one person who's usually so balanced and calm, who would normally strongly advise against stalking, is telling me to go on the chase. How the tables have turned now. But I simply don't agree with the strategy. Surely it will only result in another moment of pure humiliation?

'I'll think about it,' I say. 'Right now, I need another drink.'

'We're heading off for dinner soon,' says Clem. 'Want to come? There's this tiny little French restaurant nearby that's famous for mussels. It only seats a handful of people and you have to knock at the front door, as though it's someone's home. Nathan's been dying to take me there and he's just got some funding for his next short film, so we're celebrating!'

'No, that's okay.' The idea of an intimate restaurant with Clem and Nathan, and me tagging along, sounds like the worst possible option tonight. I don't think Nathan would be that thrilled either. 'Thanks for asking, but maybe I'll just go home.'

'So that's it? You're just going to give up?'

I look around the bar. Everyone looks so happy, which makes me feel worse. It's been a great night. I'm thrilled for Cherie, but I'm done.

'Yep, I'm going.'

'Really?' Clem looks disappointed. 'Don't do that. Stay for a bit and come out for dinner.'

'No, thanks. You guys have fun.'

Clem gives me a hug. 'You know where Mitch is. What have you got to lose? Not much by now, surely. And –' Clem takes me by the shoulders and looks straight into my eyes, '– if you're wrong, about Mitch, you have everything to gain.'

I can't argue with that, but something is still stopping me. Clem snuggles closer to Nathan, who puts his arms around her and plants a kiss on her lips.

I look around. Missy's gone. Probably had to get back to the baby and put her nipples through more torture. Frankie is ensconced in conversation with her husband up at the bar. She sees me and waves. I smile and head over.

'Clem tells me that performing doctor is a friend of yours. Pretty cute.'

I nod. Seems I can't escape Dr Mitch tonight. 'Not really a friend.'

She gives me an inquiring look. I shake my head. 'No, nothing like that.'

'You okay?'

'Yep,' I say, trying to sound as upbeat as possible. 'I'm going home now. Just wanted to say goodbye.'

'Oh, I've been meaning to tell you how much I love my bag,' says Frankie, holding up the one she ordered. 'Everyone's been admiring it. When you're famous, I'll be able to say we worked together.'

I wave to Clem and Nathan. Cherie is caught up with friends, laughter and bottles of champagne. She looks vibrant and happy, like she's right where she should be.

The cool evening air gives me a jolt as I step out onto the footpath. I pull my wrap around my shoulders and look for a cab. This is the moment I would usually call Cherie. Or she would somehow magically appear just when I need her. But not tonight.

I eventually hail one down and climb in.

'Where to?' asks a gruff voice from the driver's seat.

'St Michael's Hospital, thanks.'

Did I say that? Did I really tell the driver to go to the hospital where, as we speak, Dr Mitch is possibly attaching someone's leg by reconstructive microsurgery? Or even performing a quadruple bypass?

'Everything all right then?'

'Oh yes,' I say quickly. 'No emergency. All fine. Great, in fact.'

What seems like a second later, we're pulling up at the hospital. This is a scene that feels a little too familiar by now. I get out of the taxi, wondering how this will pan out. I haven't really thought the situation through. I just know I have to talk to Dr Mitch and tell him . . . tell him what? That I would love to have a drink after all? Well, why not? Short and sweet. And true. I run towards the entrance of the Emergency Department, surprisingly agile in my green satin stilettos, hair flying like a '50s movie star. I can almost hear the dramatic swell of the soundtrack in my head. This is the moment. This is *my* moment.

Except he's not working.

'Sorry?' I snap at the woman on the front desk, who looks strangely familiar. She smiles like she knows me. Not surprising. I've been in the ED so many times lately, the entire staff probably know who I am.

'Dr Peters isn't working tonight,' she repeats, a little too slowly for my liking.

'I think you might find he is,' I say.

'No, he's not.'

'Yes, he is.'

'No. He's. Not.' The woman is no longer smiling and clearly losing patience. I don't want to have an argument with her, but I don't understand. Even Cherie said that Mitch was off to the hospital at the end of the show. This woman is simply mistaken.

Unless he really isn't at work. Unless he was never going to work in the first place. I stand frozen to the spot as my mind churns through all the evidence. Maybe he needed an excuse to get away from the cabaret as soon as possible? Away from me? Or maybe he is, in fact, at work, and told this woman that if Lizzie March turns up, she should say he isn't here? Maybe he has pinned up the newspaper article behind the desk with a warning saying, *Watch out, danger about*. Whatever's going on, it's time for me to walk away from the ED and Dr Mitch, and not embarrass myself anymore.

'So sorry to disturb you,' I say as politely as possible. I turn to leave but suddenly stop. Maybe he was rostered on, but the ED was completely empty so they sent him home? I turn back to the desk.

'Could you tell me if he was supposed to be on tonight?' I ask hopefully.

'No, not until Monday.'

Right. So never working at all. Good to know.

Realising the woman has much more important tasks than shielding Dr Mitch from crazed admirers, I leave it there. Mortified, I jump in a taxi and go straight home, desperate to end this night once and for all. I'm surprised by how miserable I feel. Why would he say he's working when he isn't? Why couldn't he talk to me after the show? I have a million questions in my head and one answer to all of them. He doesn't want anything to do with me. In fact, he'll do anything to avoid me. Even lie about going to work.

I let myself into my flat, which now looks more like an illegal sweatshop than a home. It feels messy and suffocating. And even though it's crammed with fabric and half-made bags, it feels empty and cold. I take off my green satin stilettos and toss them in a corner. Obviously, they have no special powers after all.

I have no right to feel anything about Dr Mitch. There was never anything between us. I can't believe I went to the hospital. The old Lizzie would have barged in with a fake (or self-inflicted) injury, demanding to see Dr Mitch, only to be escorted out by security. Then the old Lizzie would have found out where

Dr Mitch lives and knocked on the door. Either that, or climbed on a wheelie bin to see into his house, injuring herself for real in the process and ending back at the ED. At least I've moved up a notch from those days.

Besides, everything is going well for me now. I don't need a man in my life, taking up precious time and head space and stopping me from embarking on my bag-designing journey. Even one as nice and considerate as Dr Mitch. If he's not The One, then no one is.

I'm beginning to see that maybe there's no such thing.

30

'He what?'

Clem calls me in her lunch break on Monday and I give a quick summary of my trip to the hospital after the cabaret. I wasn't going to tell anyone how the night ended up, but momentarily distracted by the fact that Clem is taking a lunch break, I divulge all. She never stops for lunch unless you call a quick sandwich over her computer a lunch break. And even then, she'd never make a personal call while she ate it. But here she is, taking a midday break. Possibly even outdoors.

'Are you out and about?' I ask suspiciously.

'I'm in that café down from our building. Felt like a change of scenery. Come and meet me.'

In no time at all, I'm sitting in front of Clem sipping a much-needed latte and perusing a delicious-looking menu. Having been up since five, working on my bags, I'm absolutely starving.

'I wonder why he lied about going to work,' says Clem. 'I'm so sorry I suggested you follow him. I don't know what I was thinking.'

'It's not your fault,' I say with a smile. 'It's exactly what I would have done a few months ago. The old Lizzie. Lizzie the stalker. But this is another sign that I'm not that woman anymore.'

'Good on you. Forget about him. You've got so many great things in your life now. Focus on your work. How are the bags going, anyway?'

We spend the next three-quarters of an hour discussing my future plans, until suddenly Clem goes quiet.

'I've got some news,' she says.

'What? Quickly, tell me!' She's getting married, having a baby, moving in with Nathan, buying a new sofa. Any one of those pieces of information could have been about to come out of Clem's mouth. I hold my breath.

'I've been made partner.'

'Oh my God!' I scream. 'Clem, that's fantastic. When did this happen? You didn't tell me!'

'I couldn't talk about it until it was announced at work. I can't actually believe it myself. I wanted partnership for so long, but lately I've been thinking, if it doesn't happen, it's not the end of the world. But it happened!'

'We have to celebrate. A drink tonight? With Nathan, of course.'

'Okay, I'll text you later. I'd better get back to work now.'

Clem heads back to the office and I return home to my bags after devouring an egg and bacon roll. An hour later she texts me with details for tonight.

Bar Four T Four. 7 pm. See you then.

Bar Four T Four opened up in Surry Hills about a year ago, but I still haven't been, despite many write-ups in the paper touting it as the 'hippest bar around'. Not feeling like mixing with a cutting-edge crowd tonight, I heartily wish we were meeting at our usual bar, near WineCall. But the minute I walk through the chic black timber double doors, I'm in love. It's like an ultra-cool vintage shop that just happens to serve food and alcohol. Comfy sofas, quirky lamps, retro pieces everywhere. All sorts of nooks and crannies to sit in and have a chat.

I can't see Clem so I grab a seat at the bar and order a glass of wine. I'm already about half an hour late and Clem is still not here, which is unlike her. But then, she's so relaxed about everything these days. Who knows when she'll turn up? It's a whole new Clem world that I'll have to get used to.

I'm checking out the room and its very hip crowd when suddenly I almost choke on my New Zealand sauvignon blanc. On the other side of the room, settled into one of the comfy shabby chic lounge suites, is Dr Mitch! What's he doing here? My heart almost jumps into my wineglass and I'm paralysed with panic. He'll think I'm following him for sure now.

The way I see it, there are only two options:

- Scull my wine and sneak out.
- Quickly acknowledge Dr Mitch and simply say I've had a drink with a friend and I'm now leaving, so he doesn't think, once again, that I'm a crazed stalker.

Not much to work with, but I'm leaning towards the first option. He already thinks I'm a crazed stalker, so he won't believe that I'm here by chance. It's too much of a coincidence. Maybe I'll wait for

Clem and then we can both see him together. But Clem is taking ages. I hope nothing has happened. I send her a quick text, asking if she's on her way, but get no response.

After a short and fiery internal conference, I decide to not sneak out, but rather attack this scenario head on. For once in my life, I'm not stalking a guy. I'm going to make sure that Mitch and everyone else in this ultra-fabulous bar knows that I, Lizzie March, am not a stalker. I am here for a drink!

I throw back my wine and walk as confidently as I can over to his lounge. He doesn't see me coming as he's studying the menu, looking totally relaxed in this environment, like he's meant to be here. Unlike me; I feel weird, awkward and not at all cool. Why wasn't I attracted to him at first? He's completely hot. I was so blinded by Jake and those pesky pregnancy hormones, I couldn't see what was going on only an arm's length away. But enough of that. It's too late now – I just want to leave things on a better note than last time, and then I can turn the page on this awkward chapter in my life. I take a deep breath and jump into what is most definitely going to be an embarrassing situation.

'Mitch! Hi! What are you doing here?' The words come out a little too enthusiastically and Mitch jumps up with a start, hitting his knee on the rustic French-provincial-style coffee table in front of the sofa.

'Lizzie!' He looks genuinely surprised to see me. I even see a flicker of light in his eyes as though he's pleased. Just a flash. Then it's gone. Maybe I imagined it. He gets up and gives me an awkward kiss, which catches me unawares. I'm so flustered I offer my lips rather than my cheek, which throws him and we sort of kiss somewhere in the middle, near my right nostril.

'I'm meeting Clem for a drink and I saw you sitting here all by yourself, which is fine, nothing wrong with that. I was too. Anyway, I'm here to meet Clem. Oh, I said that, didn't I?' Shut up, Lizzie.

'Right,' says Dr Mitch, in a way that sounds like he doesn't believe me at all. 'I'm supposed to be meeting Cherie. We haven't spoken since the cabaret. Said she had something important to discuss.'

'Oh, right. That's a coincidence. Clem was just made partner at her law firm and we're meeting to celebrate.'

Neither of us really knows what to do or say. How unlucky that both of us arranged to meet for drinks at the same place, at the same time – and neither of our dates is here. My mind slowly starts to sift through the facts. Mutual friends arrange to meet us here, separately, at the same time and at the same place – and then don't arrive. Have I been set up? I mean, have *we* been set up?

'I think we've been set up,' says Dr Mitch.

'I think so too,' I reply.

Suddenly my phone interrupts our very stilted conversation. A text from Clem. She couldn't have timed it better. Or worse, really.

Lizzie, sorry not coming, something came up. Try to have a good time anyway xx

Mitch's phone follows suit. He looks at the message and sighs. 'It's Cherie, she's not feeling well, bit of a cold, so she's not coming.'

An uncomfortable silence wraps around us despite the noisy surrounds. So what do I do now? Buy him a drink? Or call it a day? Maybe just go to the bathroom and regroup? Yes, good idea.

'Can you just excuse me for a minute?' I say.

I practically run to the ladies' room, bumping into couples having romantic drink dates at every turn. I call Clem immediately and demand an explanation.

'Lizzie, how's it going? Why are you ringing now? Speak later, you can thank me then.'

'I can't believe you did this to me!'

'What do you mean? I thought you'd be thrilled.'

'Well, I'm not. Nor is Dr Mitch.'

'But he's crazy about you. I just know he is.'

Clem is talking like I used to. Maybe she's more like me than I thought. But I'm totally over trying to convince anyone to go out with me. I know love is hard work. My mother tells me so every second day. But it shouldn't be this hard, surely. Even Mum would agree with me on this one.

'Look, maybe you should just leave me and my non-existent love-life alone. I've embarrassed myself too many times recently, and every one of those times has been in front of Dr Mitch. I don't need you to help me do it again.'

'Lizzie, I didn't mean to –'

'Sorry, Clem, I have to go. I'm hiding in the bathroom and these incredibly cool hipster girls are looking at me like I've just been beamed in from the upper North Shore. It's freaking me out. I'll call you back later.'

Poor Clem, it's not her fault I feel completely idiotic and out of place. I appreciate that she's trying to help me.

I make my way back to our sofa, where Mitch is sitting with two glasses of red in front of him.

'Drink?' Those blues eyes look up at me with a twinkle.

I hesitate, tempted but confused. Then I remember that he'd said he was working after the cabaret but wasn't. 'I don't think so. You've probably got enough to deal with at the moment.'

Dr Mitch looks at me like he doesn't understand subtext, so I try to spell it out for him.

'You know work, life . . . work?'

'What are you talking about?'

'You working, the other night after the cabaret,' I blurt out, before I can stop myself. 'I really wanted to talk to you, so I turned up at the hospital only to find that you were never rostered on. Which is fine, but I just don't understand why you would lie about it. Why not be upfront and say that you don't want to talk to me, or even see me?'

Mitch is still looking confused, but I'm so over men who cheat and lie and then expect me to believe them. I quickly turn and head to the door, before he can offer an explanation, which he probably doesn't have anyway.

I run out of the coolest bar in Sydney and onto the street, vowing never to return. There are no taxis so I try calling for one, but find myself on hold. This is like my life, I think. Constantly on hold. I never get to where I really want to be. I've been waiting there for what seems like an age when a tap on my shoulder gives me a start. I turn around to see Dr Mitch standing in front of me. Handsome but a little annoyed.

'I thought I was working, but when I got to the hospital, I realised I'd made a mistake with my schedule. I wasn't avoiding you. Far from it. But it was too late to go back to the cabaret.' His voice is calm but pointed.

I don't know what to say. I feel like a party balloon that's just had its air released. What is wrong with me? Honestly, I must be the worst person in existence. Once again, I got the wrong end of the story, and Mitch has done nothing wrong.

'I'm sorry, Mitch. I just thought . . . it was a misunderstanding.'

'You seem to have a few of those,' says Mitch crossly. 'Like accusing me of two-timing your friend.'

I focus on the pavement, not knowing what to say.

'And trying to match me up with your friend in the first place. Like you felt sorry for me. And she wasn't even interested. In fact, she's started seeing someone else. Then I read in the paper that you were a drug dealer and . . .'

'*Suspected* drug dealer. But actually not dealing anything except nappy bags. Very stylish ones, though.'

Mitch ignores this. 'I have no time for drugs. Not in my profession. I see what they do to lives every time I go to work.'

'I don't do drugs!' I say, a bit angry myself now. Dr Mitch may be all nice, saving lives with that brilliant smile and secret rockstar persona, but he's being a little harsh, what with his jumping to massive and incorrect conclusions. That's normally my job!

'I know that now. Your mum assured me it wasn't true.'

'Mum?'

'Yeah, we had a good chat. She popped into the hospital for some sort of check-up. Cholesterol, I think.'

Good one, Mum! It's no wonder I find myself stalking from time to time. It runs in the family.

'Okay,' I confess, 'there was half a trip one New Year's Eve but nothing really happened, I think I got ripped off. And once I shared a joint back at uni, but I was trying to impress this guy from my History tutorial. Then I threw up on his new trainers and that was pretty much it. And I'm sorry about the whole movie-night disaster. I behaved appallingly.'

Mitch chuckles, the cross look evaporating. 'It was pretty funny, in retrospect. Clare thought you were hilarious, which is a compliment, by the way.'

'I was only matching you up with Clem because I felt like I should help her out. I've been a pretty bad friend lately. And I'd made a mess of everything up until that point in my life so I thought I'd be better off helping others find happiness. I didn't mean to offend you. I guess I was only thinking about making myself feel better.'

It dawns on me that I never really wanted Clem to go out with Mitch. It was just to get me off the hook after the whole Mal scenario and, of course, I wanted Clem to be happy. But also, on some level, I thought there was no way this man could possibly like me after everything I'd done, after everything he'd been a witness to. I discounted him because I thought I'd never be in with a chance when I'd done nothing but act like the token kooky character from a bad teenage sitcom.

'Lizzie, I don't know what it is about you,' says Mitch. 'You're so . . . unpredictable, and . . . quite crazy . . .'

'In a good way?' I ask hopefully, but Dr Mitch continues as if I haven't spoken.

'. . . and completely chaotic. When you were in the ED, saying you'd been locked out of your boyfriend's house, I didn't believe you for a second. And when I told you about your pregnancy, I could see in your eyes that it was a shock and there may be no father on the scene.'

'Not my best moment,' I say, wondering where this is going.

Nowhere good, I'm pretty sure. 'Things like that don't normally happen to me.'

'But they do. That's the thing,' Mitch continues. 'Disastrous speed-dating nights, cinema stalking, drug-dealing suspicions, B-grade celebrity friends . . .'

'Can we not go over recent events? Seriously, I've been trying to tell you, I'm not that person,' I say, feeling like I'm at an interview where it's completely clear I'm not going to get the job. 'Hang on. B-grade! That's a little unfair –'

'But that day you broke down in the cafeteria at work, I don't know . . . you looked so desperate, I just wanted to put my arms around you and . . . but I couldn't, I hardly knew you, and you were pregnant to someone else.'

'Again, not my finest moment . . .'

'You were so incredibly strong through your miscarriage. I know how hard that must have been. Apart from being totally gorgeous and, as I say, a bit crazy, you're very brave. And look at what you've done with your bags. You're finally following your dream. I really admire that. I wish I could do that too . . .'

I open my mouth to make a joke about how he too could make bags if he really wanted, but suddenly stop short. Did I hear correctly? Did he just say I'm gorgeous? Not that it matters, of course. There are far more important things in life to think about . . . but did he actually use that word?

'Your life is so complicated,' continues Mitch. 'Very different from mine. Our paths were never going to cross in the real world, outside of random hospital meetings. But then I started rehearsing with Cherie and thought maybe you might be interested, despite chasing me down that day and accusing me of cheating on your friend. But even then you turned me down. So I get the message. You don't have to tell me again.'

Dr Mitch pauses. I say nothing as his enormous words settle in the evening air.

'Hang on. You think I'm gorgeous?'

'Yes, I do,' he says, and gives me a truly adorable quirky grin. 'Look, can we go back in and have the drinks I bought? I left them behind the bar.'

'But you also think I'm crazy,' I say.

'I like crazy. I need a bit more crazy in my life. You're like a fun disco ball that turns up at a boring party. Everything's brighter around you. If it wasn't for meeting you, I wouldn't have had the chance to play with Cherie. It's been ages since I got into my music and it's been great.'

My heart beats furiously. What's he saying? He thinks I'm gorgeous, but so what? Does he want to kiss me? Do I want him to? Maybe I should make the first move? Or is that too forward? It doesn't really fit into my 'no dating' policy, let alone playing a little harder to get.

There's a moment of silence as I sift through all my options.

'Can I interrupt those busy thoughts?' says Mitch as he moves closer and gives me the answer I'm looking for, pressing his lips to mine in a slow, sensual and magnificent kiss. Right there on the street. I can hear orchestral music sweeping around us, as every part of my body sits up and takes note. It's like an all-over experience, which only prompts me to wonder what anything more heated would offer. My legs feel weak, like I've just run a marathon. Thank goodness his arms are enveloping me, otherwise I might have fallen on the pavement.

'Forget the drinks,' I say quietly. And like magic, a taxi pulls up. We get in and I give my address. Neither of us speaks until we get to my flat.

I open my front door and switch on the light to reveal my very untidy lounge room, strewn with fabric scraps and half-finished bags. I turn back to Dr Mitch. Is this happening? Or did I misread the signs, or worse, completely invent them? Then I remember the kiss on the street. Best Kiss I've Ever Had. No, it's definitely real.

'Here we are. Sorry, it's a bit of a mess. Do you want tea? I can make a cup of English Breakfast, or I might have a herbal of some sort . . .' Why am I so nervous? Tea? What am I saying? The last thing on my mind is a cup of herbal tea.

Without a word, Mitch pulls me towards him, enclosing me in his arms, our bodies pressed together. He's not thinking of tea either. He quietens my babble with another kiss, gentle at first. Then another, more insistent. My body responds hungrily, with a rush of desire from somewhere deep down, a place I've just about forgotten – like a dormant volcano showing signs of life. I can't remember feeling so turned on by kissing. In fact, I can't remember feeling so turned on. Ever. Unable to wait another second, I drag Mitch to my bedroom, not that he needs persuading. But once there, he takes over, slowing things down to a deliciously indulgent pace, until I can bear it no longer.

We peel away each other's clothes piece by piece, and the more that's revealed, the more aroused I become. Everything about this man is like heaven, his smell, his hair, his arms, which are . . . oh my God, incredibly strong and defined. Like a rock climber, or a yoga teacher. I can't fault him. From where I stand (or lie),

Mitch is the most extraordinary specimen of the male species I've ever encountered at close range.

How have I been so blind? I suppose it was all hidden under his doctor's scrubs. I gasp as his smooth flawless skin sinks into mine. Every time he touches me, it's like another electric shock through my body and I melt like butter on freshly made toast.

By now, my previous lovers would be done, dusted and sound asleep, but Mitch is only just getting started. And he obviously paid great attention to any medical lecture involving the female body. With most guys, it's like they're struggling through an impossible maze, hitting dead ends at every turn. But Mitch confidently navigates his way through and safely out the other side. No compass necessary.

We hardly speak as our bodies take over, completely in tune and fuelled by unexpected passion. Now I understand what Clem's been talking about with all her amazing sex. It's been so long since anyone's made me feel this desirable. Actually, has anyone ever made me feel like that? Why didn't someone tell me I was only getting bar food when I could have been enjoying the entire degustation menu? I'm like a bear after a long winter's hibernation: awake with a voracious appetite and boundless energy. Just (hopefully) not quite so hairy.

Mitch pauses and looks at me.

'Condom?'

'Definitely.' I smile, and as I grab the box from my bedside table drawer, surreptitiously check the use-by date. Phew, all good!

Once we're sorted, my thoughts run away like water as Dr Mitch works his way down my body, exploring every inch of my flesh with kisses that make me dizzy. I don't know this man well yet, but I feel completely free and uninhibited, replying to his every move like I'm now fluent in a language I never knew I could speak. A language Dr Mitch speaks to perfection. Almost faint with desire, the volcano inside me is now dangerously active and just when it's about to erupt, our souls meet somewhere in the middle and pleasure melts through my veins like warm liquid honey.

I have definitely met my match.

Close to dawn, we drift into easy sleep, ensconced in our own secret world. I wake up a few hours later, knowing for once where I am, who I'm with and how I got there. In fact, I know exactly what happened in the minutest detail. And apart from being the best sex I've ever had, it was also safe as safe with absolutely no chance of landing me in Emergency with some random doctor explaining how I'm up the duff.

I smile to myself as I slowly breathe in and out, relishing one of those elusive moments when all is well in the world. It's not often you feel like all your stars have aligned, and you're in the exact place you should be – with just the right person. It's an overwhelming feeling of contentment. Here I am, waking up next to – I don't want to say my 'boyfriend', but surely it's on the cards? I don't think I'm deluded when I say there's a strong connection between us. Yes, I know, I've said that a few times before. Like every time I go out with someone. But this is different. I think about Mitch's openness, his honesty about what he's feeling, despite the many embarrassing things I've done in front of him. Then I relive our spectacular bedroom action, moment by moment. Yes. He certainly feels like someone who could possibly be The One.

*

If I was at the cinema watching my life play out on the big screen, this is when the movie would end. After a series of hilarious antics and misunderstandings, the girl gets the guy and they fall madly in love just as the credits start to roll . . .

'Earth to Lizzie.'

Mitch is propped up on his elbow, watching me intently while I marvel my way through recent events.

I grin. 'Sorry, I was lost in thought.'

'Good ones, I hope?'

'Definitely.'

I can't believe this is happening. For once I, Lizzie March, get a happy ending, and not just in the way you might think, although I definitely got that too. I drink in the moment like a Friday-night cocktail.

'Lizzie, before anything else happens, we need to talk.'

My heart drops the equivalent of two flights of stairs. I've heard those words many times now and any conversation that starts that way has never ended well. Not for me, anyway.

'Really? What's wrong?' I hold my breath, prepared for anything but sincerely hoping it's nothing.

'I've just accepted a post in a hospital in Paris for six months.'

I almost fall out of bed. Mostly because it's been a while since an excuse has surprised me. It's so original it must be true. But it's not the movie ending I was expecting.

'That sounds exciting . . .' I try to be positive for my now ex-boyfriend.

'Come!'

'Sorry?'

'Come!'

I look at him, slightly confused. 'Look, I know I got there a few times last night but I can't just do it at the drop of a hat –'

'No, Lizzie, I mean, why don't you come and visit me in Paris? Have you ever been?'

I look at Mitch lying against my white waffle continental pillows like some sort of angel. Did he just ask me to come to Paris? My dream destination? Did I hear correctly?

'Paris?'

'Yes.'

As wonderful as the invitation sounds, it throws me into a panic.

'But I can't come to Paris just like that.'

'Why not? Take a holiday. When was the last time you had one?'

I don't know what to say. Am I looking for an excuse? Sure, we just had a great night together, but I can't just drop everything and head to Gay Paree because some (incredibly good-looking) guy has asked me. That's what the old Lizzie would have done – the stalkerish, man-crazy Lizzie, the woman with zero self-esteem, who dropped everything at the first hint of romance and ended up absolutely nowhere. If Jake, or anyone else I had previously dated, had asked me to go to Paris, I would have gone in a heartbeat. Now here is someone who appears far worthier and I'm hesitating. Actually, I'm completely terrified. Because deep down somewhere in the basement of my heart, a place not often frequented, I feel that Mitch is the genuine article. A grown-up. A really nice one. Sexy. Smart. Funny. A doctor. And he's not playing hard to get. I'm at a loss trying to find anything wrong with him.

Except for the fact that I've finally got on top of my life and now have the chance to pursue my dreams. Everything is looking up. I'm overcoming my financial crisis. Once David Jones pays me for its order, I will be able to pay back my parents and inject capital into my business. The last thing I should do is throw it away on a ticket to Paris, even if it is to hang out with Mr Nice Guy.

'I can't. I'm sorry.' I caress his chest as I speak, as not only is it totally touchable but I don't want him to think I haven't loved every minute of our night together. 'My work, I've just got this massive order from David Jones. I finally have the possibility of a career path.'

'Finish up the orders. Make the bags for David Jones, and see how you feel.'

I sigh, thinking about the money I owe my parents. If I tell them I'm flitting off to Paris with some guy they don't even know, they'll not be very impressed. Well, Mum's met him, but still. My parents have always been there in my bleakest moments, offering support and positive words. The least I can do is pay them back their money in a timely fashion. And follow this bag venture through to see where it takes me. It's too good an opportunity to lose on a whim. But six months! That's ages. If lovely Mitch is in Paris for six months, he'll no doubt be devoured by a host of strong sultry French women with open minds and fabulous fashion sense.

'I'm not saying you should turn your life upside down,' Mitch continues, as if sensing my thoughts. 'Just suggesting you get on top of everything and come for a visit. A week. Shop around for great French fabrics. Find inspiration for new designs. Claim it all on tax. If it doesn't work out, go home and we never have to see each other again. And if it does, we get to spend time in Paris together, speak French, eat croissants, make love . . .'

'Yes!' I almost vomit out the word, surprising myself more than Mitch. I'd like to say it was the thought of making love in Paris, but he had me at 'croissants'. I love croissants. How could I say no?

Mitch smiles. 'Is that a *oui*?'

'Yes, it's a *oui*. But a tentative one. It's a maybe. When I'm ready. And only if you ask me on a date beforehand. A proper date. With dinner. And dessert. Maybe a cheese platter. I don't really know anything about you. I know you're a doctor who plays guitar, you like pinot and drink coffee. But I have no idea what your favourite food is. Favourite colour? Star sign? We're practically strangers.'

'Pizza. Blue. Libran.'

'Dog or cat?'

'Definitely dog.'

I smile. 'It's a start.'

He pulls me closer to him, under the covers. 'Finding out the rest is all part of the fun. So, how about dinner tomorrow night? I'll pick you up at seven.'

'Sounds perfect.'

'And if all goes well, you'll think about France?'

'See how it goes,' I say. 'See if we actually like each other.'

I can't believe I'm considering going to the other side of the world to meet someone I hardly know. But somehow it doesn't feel as bizarre as it sounds. For once in my life a (really nice) guy has spent the night in my bed and not only is he still there in the morning, alive and unharmed, but he's woken up wanting to take things straight to the next level. Well, he's jumping a few levels, going directly to 'holidaying overseas together'. Is that even a level? I've never got that far before. And I didn't even have to stalk him.

Well, not much, anyway.

Oh look, there was a minimal amount of stalking. But still, this has to be an all-time first.

He wraps me in his arms. We don't speak for a moment and the silence is comfortable. I cuddle up to him with my head on his chest, his heart beating in my ear. I wonder if he can feel my mine, which is pounding at a furious rate.

I break away to look at him. He opens those piercing Mediterranean eyes that I've been trying to ignore for so long and kisses me gently on the lips. Surely this is where the Lizzie March movie ends? No sunset, no romantic music and the leading actor is not the one I expected to secure the role. But he's better than I could ever have wished for. Academy Award material. And now he wants to meet me in France! Possibly he will come to his senses and realise that I'm not quite what the doctor ordered, but hopefully he'll be so blinded by the beauty and style of our surrounds, he might not notice.

Still, I think this guy has seen the best and worst of me. All right, mostly the worst, but isn't that a positive thing? He won't expect too much, and hopefully the very best of me is about to appear centre stage. I place a hand on my belly, where there's nothing growing inside. No baby this time, but new beginnings all the same: a potential boyfriend and a kick-started career. What more could I ask for?

'Can I interrupt that conversation in your head?' Dr Mitch pulls me even closer with a firmness that turns me on more than I thought possible. 'If we are off to live like Parisians, we'd better get in a bit more practice.'

I smile. 'I think I'm already pretty good, but I guess you could do with a little improvement!'

I giggle as Dr Mitch playfully tackles me under the doona.

Happiness bubbles up in me like spring water. In the last twenty-four hours I've experienced the best relationship of my entire life.

Anything more is the icing on my wedding cake.

Oops, did I really just say that? Not out loud, anyway.

Acknowledgements

No book gets published on its own, least of all this one, and I have so many people to thank for bringing *Loving Lizzie March* into the world.

A massive thanks to the entire team at Pan Macmillan, in particular my wonderful publisher, Claire Craig, thank you a million times for choosing my manuscript and working so hard to bring Lizzie to life. I don't think I will ever be able to thank you enough! Big thanks goes to my ever-positive editor Danielle Walker and to Brianne Collins and Jo Lyons for all doing such an amazing job and making my story so much better. Thanks so much to my publicist Candice Wyman and marketing executive Adrik Kemp for all your work, enthusiasm and enviable talents. And thanks to Christa Moffitt for creating such a gorgeous cover. As a debut writer, I could not have wished for a better publishing experience.

To my agent Michael Cybulski at New Authors Collective, thank you for taking me under your wing and deftly changing my path with your unwavering belief and positivity. Thanks also to NAC's editorial department, in particular Andrea Barton, for working so tirelessly and generously on Lizzie and adding so much to my manuscript.

Thanks to the absolutely awesome Valerie Khoo, CEO of the Australian Writers' Centre. I wouldn't be writing at all, if not for your inspiration, expertise and much-needed tough love. Thanks for your belief in this book and for introducing me to the very supportive AWC community. In particular, special thanks to Lisa Heidke for reading the first couple of chapters of Lizzie all those years ago and responding so enthusiastically. Thanks for agreeing to mentor my manuscript in its early (and incredibly loose) stage and for teaching me so much about writing a book – and thanks now for the on-going writerly support and much treasured friendship. Also thanks to Allison Tait for #writeabookwithal and advice along the way which helped me (finally) get to the finishing line.

To Alexandra Nahlous, huge thanks for your excellent editing early on that miraculously brought my manuscript together, and for putting up with my endless emails about what Lizzie should and shouldn't do. You went above and beyond an editor's duty and I will always be very grateful.

Thanks to my friends who have followed the rather slow progress of this book, there are too many to mention here by name but your ongoing interest was appreciated and always kept me on track. I'd particularly like to thank Sophie Gregg, Niki Owen, Rebecca Rocheford Davies, Pilar Mitchell and Alicia Ash who generously gave up their time to read my words and offer feedback. Special thanks to Diana Glenn, my go-to writing buddy, thanks for reading scenes when requested and finding the funny bits funny (also when requested). In fact, a huge thanks goes to both Diana and Gabriella Maselli, my excellent girlfriends and co-members of comedy trio *The Girls*. I realise that I may have pushed you into that project in my bossy (yet enthusiastic) way, but those days of writing and performing *The Girls* for stage, radio and finally TV are some of my best ever. I'll always be grateful for the laughter, the lifelong friendships and the inspiration that ultimately led to the creation of Lizzie March.

Thanks to Edel Murray and Deborah Murphy for going through all my hospital scenes. Thank you for your time, expertise and delightful responses.

Thanks to Cathie McGinn from the Australian College of Midwives for answering all my midwifery questions. Thanks to Ann Normoyle for sharing your knowledge on studying fashion design, and Jacqui Kemmis-Riggs for your insights into the world of fashion and manufacturing. Any hospital, midwife or fashion design errors are very much my own.

I would like to also thank my friends and colleagues from Romance Writers of Australia, in particular Penelope Janu and Lisa Ireland, for so much support and advice, as well as the many opportunities this fantastic organisation has provided.

To my wonderful parents Liz and Peter Hardy, thanks for absolutely everything throughout, not just the life of this book, but also the constant ups and downs of my many creative pursuits. Thanks for the endless support, the babysitting, the many bookshelves, and always being at the end of the phone with such positive and encouraging words. Thanks also to my brothers Sean and Simon and their families, who have been there for me through thick and thin and kept me on my writing path.

To my darling Maggie and Phoebe, big thanks for putting up with your mother tapping endlessly at her computer. Thanks for being my cheer squad and for making every day worthwhile.

And finally a huge thanks to Andrew, my very patient husband and partner in love, life and laughter – my biggest support, toughest critic and best friend. You and the girls are my world and without you, this book would not have happened.

MORE FICTION AVAILABLE FROM PAN MACMILLAN

Liane Moriarty
Nine Perfect Strangers

Can a health retreat really change your life forever?

From the no. 1 bestselling author of *The Husband's Secret* and *Big Little Lies.*

The retreat at health and wellness resort Tranquillum House promises total transformation. Nine stressed city dwellers are keen to drop their literal and mental baggage, and absorb the meditative ambience while enjoying their hot stone massages.

Watching over them is the resort's director, a woman on a mission to reinvigorate their tired bodies and minds.

These nine perfect strangers have no idea what is about to hit them.

With her wit, compassion, and uncanny understanding of human behaviour, Liane Moriarty explores the depth of connection that can be formed when people are thrown together in . . . unconventional circumstances.

'She is . . . both hugely popular yet subversive . . . *Nine Perfect Strangers* shows Moriarty still taking risks with fiction . . . weighty issues writ with humour and a light touch. The hammer is still in the handbag, ready to smash a glass window or two.' LUCY SUSSEX, *THE AUSTRALIAN*

'Welcome to Tranquillum House where those Perfect Strangers . . . have come to sort out their lives . . . This gives Moriarty the opportunity to do what she does best, write about the human condition and connections that bind us all, with wicked humour, empathy and compassion – and a little bit of danger thrown in.' FRANCES WHITING, *COURIER MAIL*

Holly Wainwright
I Give My Marriage a Year

How far would you go to save your marriage?

Lou and Josh have been together for 14 years. They share two kids, a mortgage, careers and plenty of history. Now, after a particularly fraught Christmas, Lou is ready to ask herself: is this marriage worth hanging on to?

Every month for a year, Lou sets a different test for their relationship – from daily sex to brutal honesty – to help her decide if she should stay or go. Secrets are exposed, old wounds reopened and a true-to-life suburban love story unfolds.

I Give My Marriage a Year paints a sharply accurate, often hilarious picture of a modern Australian marriage. Lou and Josh are a couple on the edge, and their efforts to bring their relationship back from the brink will resonate with anyone who has ever asked themselves: is this enough?

Whose side will you take? Who deserves a second chance? And will Josh and Lou stay together or split for good?

'The most insightful novel on marriage I've ever read. I can't stop thinking about it.' Mia Freedman

'Poignant, compelling and full of aha moments, this book will have you nodding, laughing and crying, and most of all, incredibly invested in the outcome.' Sally Hepworth